An Ordinary Life

Edmun

Published 2015 Ceatespace

An Ordinary Life (2nd Edition)

Edmund Gubbins

Copyright 2009 by Edmund Gubbins

Rombuli Saga
Book 1   The Teacher of the Rombuli
Book 2   The Return of the Exiles
Book 3   The Prisoner of Parison
Princess Daphne

Other books by the author:
Tales From The Sea
Running After Maria
A Ceremony of Innocence
Innocence Exploded
Brotherly Love
A Legacy from Mary

Text Books:
The Shipping Industry
Managing Transport Operations

Chapter 1

" I don't know what I am going to do," Jane Houseman remarked to her son looking round the dimly lit room. The walls were a uniform drab green with notice boards displaying posters. Around the edges the rows of leather chairs with small tables in the centre of the floor. Over all she noticed the smell of a mixture of disinfectant and hard soap.

Her face, even now attractive despite her sixty years, with wide, direct blue eyes, red generous lips and short swept back grey hair, was lined with sadness and stress. Hands, clasped in her lap, twisted and turned a handkerchief into which she had been crying. Her shoulders, usually so straight, were slumped, making her look shorter than her five feet four inches.

" The doctor said you will have to speak to him," Paul Houseman answered. His blue eyes gazed at her steadily, his broad shoulders filling out his jacket and his arm resting lightly round her shoulders. " You have been married for over thirty eight years, Mum. There has to be a great deal you can talk to him about."

The doctor Paul had mentioned, opened the door of the waiting room in which they were sitting and said, " Mrs. Houseman? You can go in now. We have made him as comfortable as possible. There are a lot of wires and tubes but they are necessary to keep him alive. Follow me."

Jane looked longingly at her son her eyes pleading with him to relieve her of this task, just as Jeremiah had done in the bible. Paul could only smile in reassurance and, with a shrug, nodded towards the door through which the woman doctor had vanished. Looking white and drawn, Jane stood up and smoothed down her skirt.

" I'll go with the doctor to see Tom now." Her voice was strained and melancholy with a slight touch of hysteria. " Will you wait here for Mary and Luke to arrive? They should have a familiar face in the waiting room. Let me know as soon as they arrive. You can all come in and speak to him then."

" You go on in Mum and stop worrying about me," Paul said, with another attempt at a smile. " I will be here when they arrive and will bring them in to see you straight away."

With one last despairing glance at her son, Jane resolutely followed the woman, or girl, as she appeared to her, down a short corridor and through a door that swung open on well oiled, silent hinges.

In the room, Tom Houseman lay on a bed, his eyes closed and tubes and wires connecting him to various machines. His breathing was coming in very heavy gasps and the machine noises mingled with his breathing to set up a symphony to the unconscious. Jane stood by the bed and looked at her husband for a while. His hair had got very grey, she thought. The rather long face she had loved when they first met had filled out over the years but was now lined and grey like his hair.

When offered by the doctor, she took a chair. Obediently, Jane sat at the side of his bed letting her thoughts drop like raindrops into the silence. After smiling encouragement, the doctor withdrew to the desk station in the centre of the room to consult with her other colleagues. Jane was left alone with her husband.

This was the moment Jane had dreaded ever since they had entered the hospital. As soon as the ambulance had drawn up at the door, Tom had been rushed away, leaving her to follow as best she could her heart racing with the fear that she would lose sight of his trolley. When they arrived at the ward, she had been left sitting in the waiting room alone. Seeing her husband laying like a stranded whale on a bed with wires and machines attached for the first time, she shuddered. It was something she had secretly thought about in the quiet of the night after a particular programme on television but such thoughts had soon passed. Deep down she, like millions of other wives, had hoped that it would never happen to them. How can we prepare ourselves for something like this? she asked herself once more repeating the phrase like broken record. There was no true answer.

    For what seemed to her like an age, with her mind searching for an answer to her fear, Jane sat holding Tom's hand. Every time she moved, she tried not to interfere with any of the wires or tubes trailing over the sides of the bed. She tried to pray but her mind was blank. Even God appeared to abandon her in her moment of need. There was nothing she could think of to say. Over the years, since they had married, neither of them had been at a loss for words when they were together. This was different. Always before there had been two of them. A chance remark by one, sparking a reply from the other. Often, their conversation would then wander around the things that were important or needed to be discussed but the only silences were those of deep companionship when there did not appear any need for words.

In the half light of the room, she noticed a stain on the wall. Nearby, Tom's name with those of the nurses on a board above his bed. Every few minutes a nurse silently approached the bed and took readings from the equipment, entering these on a pad at the foot of the bed. The measured, gasping breathing of Tom punctuated everything even at times drowning out the pinging of the machines.

" You are in good hands," Jane started to speak tentatively. She spoke more to break the silence and stop her concentrating on that heavy breathing, than with any topic in mind. " They arrived with the ambulance very quickly after you collapsed. God, you gave me a fright there. Walking round banging into furniture and then not being able to say anything coherent. The ambulance man and woman were very good. They told me you have had a stroke and it was vital they got you to the hospital quickly. The doctor tells me we will find out how bad you are over the next two days. Paul is in the waiting room. He came as soon as I phoned to tell him what had happened. I don't know how he did it but he was at the hospital almost as soon as we arrived. He is in the waiting room waiting for Mary and Luke to get here. They will be a while, I am afraid. It will take a couple of hours from London and I only phoned Mary an hour ago. Luke will take longer from Nottingham but he says he will be here as soon as possible. As soon as they arrive, I will bring them in to see you."

' What can I talk to him about?' she asked herself desperately, squeezing Tom's cold hand. There was no response, not a sign that he had heard a word. Jane rubbed her forehead, feeling the creases of worry marring the once smooth skin, and looked at his face, drawn and grey with pain, the eyes closed and his mouth a thin, tight line. The sight of him lying there helpless pushed her mind back to their first meeting when his face was young and he always appeared happy, animated and without a care in the world.

" I can still remember our first meeting, Tom. I know it seems like an age ago now. It was the year England won the World Cup," she said, once more squeezing his hand. " Actually, I suppose it wasn't our first meeting. Years before we met that night, you went to Pound Street

Congregational Church Sunday School at the same time as me. While we were at the church, I never mixed with you or your friends. My parents didn't approve of you or your friends. Besides you were two years older than me and that makes a great deal of difference at that age. Mum would not let me go to the youth club because there were girls and boys there who were not children of church members. Your mother and father were not being members of to the church even though you came to the Sunday school and Bible classes. Anyway, you must remember that night when we first met. It was at a party. Tony and Belinda's as far as I remember? They were moving from their flat shortly afterwards as I recall, which was why they had the party. You were there with a girl, what was her name? I can't remember now. I can remember that she was the one with the big breasts and the outrageous views. She put me in mind that Greer woman with her views on women's place in the universe and the environment. I must say, from my memory, you seemed to ignore her most of the evening. You had had a lot to drink by the time the party finished but sometime during the evening you smiled at me and we danced a little. I can't remember what we talked about but I do know that Eric, the man I was with, did not like you. I can't imagine why. Everybody else at the party seemed to like you."

It was like being adrift aboard a boat in a fog. The opaque mist swirled around his brain, stopping him seeing or concentrating on anything. Far, far away a voice droned on, sounding for all the world like an angry wasp at a window. He tried to grasp what it was saying but all he could do was drift in the fog, seeing nothing, feeling nothing and not being able to grasp what he heard.

Then suddenly the mist parted like the curtain rising in a theatre. He was in a room. Where could this be? It was not his room at home. After a time he remembered. It was the lounge of the flat where his friends Belinda and Tony had lived. That's right, they were throwing a party. It must have been nineteen sixty four or five. The time was not important.

Tom had come to the party with a girl called Amanda. He had met her at university in Nottingham while researching for his Ph D and working as a research assistant. She was studying for a degree. Shortly after meeting they had started to go about together. Tom had soon realised that Amanda was one of those intense girls who held strong beliefs about what was right and what was wrong, especially regarding those things she cared passionately about. Her hair was long, red and very thick, framing a round face with thin, severe lips. She looked out at the world through very large glasses and seldom smiled, though when she did, her face lit up like a beacon on a dark night. Her skirts were always shorter than those worn by most other girls, showing off her shapely legs and round bottom.

On the night of the party, Amanda had dressed herself in a top which hugged her huge breasts and made every man there look at her body twice before looking away. As they walked across the room to meet Belinda, it had been obvious to Tom that all the men in the room wished they could get their hands on those breasts. Actually, Tom had to admit, even though he always claimed to anybody who would listen that it was a woman's mind he most sought out, it had been her breasts which had attracted him to her at first. Later, they had found pleasure in their discussions or sometimes intense arguments on the subjects which she held passionate views.

" The world will be ruined if we go on like this," she had said to him on numerous occasions when they had sat in his flat sharing a bottle of red wine. He had to admit lying in that bed that she worried about the environment a long time before most other people had become concerned. " If we, as a human race, keep chopping down trees and burning so much of the oil, the next generation will have nothing. We have to act now and reduce our dependence on oil and protect the wild habitat."

When the mood took him, Tom used to get her mad by laughing at her pronouncements and her certainties. To Tom, there were plenty of trees on the planet and it appeared, from what he had read, boundless amounts of oil. What was important to him was how society treated the poor and the oppressed.

" If you start to stop people using up resources, all you will end up doing is make it easier for the rich to gain even more control over the poor or disadvantaged," Tom would remark seriously after she had finished bemoaning the rape of the planet, as she was also fond of calling resource exploitation by the rich countries " The poor need the fuel that both oil and trees provide. They need the land to grow their crops. You have to get your priorities right. If the rich would give up just a little of their wealth and share it with the poor, then maybe there would be a chance to look at environmental damage. You are too one dimensional."

After a discussion like this, Amanda would storm out and refuse to see him for a few days but, for some reason, she always returned ready to put up with his mocking of her views. Maybe it was because, though Tom might not agree with her view of the world and might think she was scare mongering, at least he would listen to what she had to say.

Oh, Amanda knew that she was not the most attractive of girls in Nottingham. She knew that across the university there were girls who oozed sex, were very attractive and could have picked up Tom if they had wished. In quiet moments when she took off her make up at night, she had to admit to herself that Tom put up with her ways as long as the sex was reasonable and regular.

Tom had known Tony Jarvis, the host of the party, from their days while pupils at the Porthampton Boy's Grammar School. From their first year at the school, they had been in the same class and become firm friends. After leaving school, they had met often, even though Tom had gone to Nottingham University to study management and Tony to London to study law. Hence, Tony's invite to Tom for the party for which Tom had travelled down from Nottingham. The reason or the excuse Belinda and Tony gave for having a party, was that they were leaving the flat to move to a new house a few weeks later.

At the party that night, Tom sat in the corner of the living room arguing with anybody who might come within range. The late August sun was shining through the open french doors and people had spread out into the garden with their drinks and conversation.

Somebody had made a remark about the need for Britain to get involved in Vietnam. Unsurprisingly, given his views, this had annoyed Tom.

" Why should we become involved?" he asked frowning. " Vietnam is a French responsibility and it is a civil war. We should let them sort it out for themselves."

" But what if the communists take over Vietnam?" Barbara, a friend of Belinda's who Tom had met a few times, asked. She was thin and severe with her hair drawn back in a bun and had a look continually on her face that seemed to say that she was better than most other people. If nothing else, that look was likely to make Tom take an instant dislike to her. " Won't that mean that all the other countries in the area will fall to communism? Is that what we want as a free nation?"

" It is not necessarily true that all the countries around will fall to communism," Tom stated confidently. " Even if there is a danger of that happening, I do not think we should get involved. If a communist government is what the people of Vietnam want, surely it is not our business to stop them."

Looking round the room, Tom caught the eye of a very striking girl dancing with a man called Eric. He only knew Eric by sight. From what Tom understood he had been a university friend of Tony's. Though she was not tall, her brown hair shone in the light, cut just to reach the collar of her blouse. Her tight shortish skirt was expensively cut and her legs were slim and encased in flesh coloured tights. It was her eyes which made Tom look at her for a moment longer than was strictly necessary. They were large, brown and mysterious. They drew him into their depths as though he was sinking below the surface of her mind. As she danced slowly with Eric, Tom suddenly remembered her name. Jane, that was it. Tom felt as though her sex appeal was showing to everybody at the party.

It had been with a great effort of will that Tom pulled his eyes away from Jane's, as though his gaze had been attached to hers for that moment by velcro. He went on discussing Vietnam and the proposal to end the death penalty with Barbara and a few other people. For some reason, his mind was not fully following the give and take of the argument. This was strange because Tom likes nothing more than pontificating to an audience.

Shortly after his eyes had locked with Jane's, Belinda came and took him away from his informal discussion group. She pulled him out into the crowd for a dance. They jigged up and down until the record played something slow and then Belinda pulled him close.

" This is nice," he remarked into her ear, squeezing her waist and grinding his lower body into her's. " We don't get a chance to do this very often."

She looked straight into his eyes for a moment before lowering her head against his shoulder.

" It is nice to feel you close like this," she said in a voice muffled by his body. " Are you back home now? If you are, maybe I will see more of you."

Tom smiled at the hint of a hidden question in her voice. On impulse, he did not attempt to answer what he took to be her suggestion. " No. I have some research to do at the University over the summer. In a few weeks I go back to Nottingham to submit my Ph D thesis and finish off my research report to the Research Council. They are trying to find more work for me to do at Nottingham but there is a post going at Porthampton University next summer and I have applied for that. The interviews are after Christmas. If I get the post, I will move back at Easter. Then you can see more of me."

" I hope you get the post," Belinda said squeezing his hand as they left the dance floor. " Tony would love for you to be back here. He is always on about how you would enhance his football team."

The evening continued in a like manner. Tom sitting in his corner engaging anybody in an argument who happened to talk to him, punctuated by short spells of dancing when Amanda or any other woman came to force him onto the dance floor. The one exception was Jane. Looking up one time, he saw that she was alone near the french doors, obviously getting some fresh air. As though attached to a string pulling him to her side, Tom got up from his chair and joined her by the door.

" It is rather warm in here, isn't it?" he remarked rather bizarrely.

She turned slowly and stood looking at him with those deep brown eyes which portended to pull him inwards into their hidden depths. " I thought I would get some fresh air for a moment. Eric has gone to the kitchen to get me a drink. You must be Tom, Tony's friend. Aren't you at Nottingham University?"

" Yes," Tom answered nervously wondering what other people had been telling her about him. The subtle fragrance of her scent also seemed to be pulling him towards her. He resisted the temptation to put his arm round her shoulder and kiss her. " How do you know? I don't think we have ever met."

" Oh that is easy," the woman replied, laughing his expression. " Don't look so threatened. I am Belinda's friend after all. We went to school together. My name is Jane, by the way. Belinda has often spoken to me about you especially after you have been out with her and Tony. I have met you before, you know. It was a long time ago and I doubt that you would remember me. I was in the Girls Brigade with Belinda when you were in Boys Brigade at Pound Street Church. We used to go on parades together. I must say you never paid any attention to me. You only ever had eyes for that Caroline but I heard she did not really like you."

" Its a bit cruel of you to bring that up but I suppose you are right," Tom answered with a smile. " If I remember rightly, she had all the boys after her at the time. Being honest with myself, I realise now I never stood a chance. The last I heard, she was married to somebody who works in the shipyard and has a couple of kids. After I left Porthampton to go to University, I lost touch with a lot of the people I knew, except Tony. For some reason my mother keeps her eye on the boys and girls I knew and tells me all about it when I come home. She goes regularly to Pound Street Church now though she did not in the past even though she sent my brother and me to the Sunday school. Have you cooled down sufficiently now? Shall we have a dance before Eric gets back and monopolises you again?"

They danced for a while, talking of inconsequential things. Tom could not work out whether she was interested in him or was just passing the time while Eric was fetching her a drink. It was all too soon to Tom but he caught sight of Eric standing by the french doors glowering at him. He looked rather big and hard to Tom.

Jane looked across at Eric, smiled at Tom and said. " I had better go. He can get rather nasty if he feels I am paying too much attention to another man."

" It was nice dancing with you, Jane," Tom said squeezing her hand and winking at Eric as he escorted Jane back to her boy friend. Eric's expression was hard. " If you can ever get away from him, it would be nice to go out for an evening drink in the country."

" Here you are Eric," Tom said cheerfully. " We were just having a dance while you were getting Jane a drink."

For just a moment Tom thought that Eric was going to hit him but in the end Eric grasped Jane's elbow and steered her outside. For the rest of the evening, it seemed to Tom that his eyes kept engaging Jane's. Whether she was dancing, always with Eric, or sitting talking to some of the other girls, their eyes seemed to meet. Eric's expression was thunderous every time he looked at Tom. With mischievous intent, Tom did not help Eric's mood by smiling sweetly every time their glances met.

When the party broke up, Belinda suggested to Tom and Amanda that they go out for a meal next time they were in

Porthampton. Amanda was non committal which surprised Tom.

The day after the party, Amanda and Tom had decided to split up. They had come to that decision mutually as they drove back to Nottingham from Porthampton. It had been an amicable parting, as far as lovers' partings go. Indeed, when they did arrive back in Nottingham, Amanda had stayed the night in Tom's flat before collecting the few things she had left there, leaving the next morning. They had made love that night with more passion than they had shown for a while, if Tom was honest with himself. One thing she had said before she left had hurt Tom's feelings. With admirable restraint, he had thought, he had not shown Amanda that she had scratched the usual cheerful veneer he showed to the outside world but deep down she had hurt him.

" You were using me, you know Tom," she had observed calmly, as they lay amongst the twisted bedclothes after fierce lovemaking. " While we have been together, you lent me a sympathetic ear but never really agreed with anything I said. As long as I gave you my body whenever you demanded it, you were quite content to let me go on about my fears for the world. If I am to be truly happy, I will have to find somebody of a like mind to make love to. I realised during the party, there is no future for us in this relationship. Don't ask me why but the thought suddenly came. The people there are a lot like you and you are very relaxed in their company."

Tom had smiled and remarked. " I do like you Amanda and our love making like tonight is sensational. One problem I have with you is the intensity of your belief that the world is going to the dogs unless we change our ways. It might well be going pear shaped in the future but what concerns me now is how are we to help those less fortunate than ourselves. We have a new Labour government in power, though with a small majority, and we have to hope that they will help the disadvantaged in society. At least they are talking about the white hot advance of technology. That is the way to provide jobs for all the workers. Against the problem of the poor and disadvantaged, the challenge of the environment and using finite resources will have to wait."

" You will see Tom," Amanda's expression was so grim, Tom had to make an effort not to laugh. " In our lifetime, the problem will get acute. Then you will remember what I said to you."

For the next three weeks Tom had no time for anything but the final draft of his thesis. As he wrote, modified, redid the calculations and slaved away long into the night, he began to hate the very subject of the likely affect of deregulation on the road haulage industry. During that time, his whole world revolved round his flat, the secretary who was typing up his findings and his supervisor who demanded changes. At last one bright September morning, it was finished. That day, Tom had sat at his desk in the researchers office looking at the pile of pages in front of him wondering where all the time and effort had gone. In the back of his mind a little voice seemed to mock him. What will you do with your time now? it seemed to ask. A very good question, he had thought.

Sighing, he had taken the typed pages to the main office to be bound. Two days later he had taken the finished work into his supervisor's office.

" Don't worry Tom," Ken, his supervisor, had laughed at the look of apprehension on Tom's face. " It will pass with flying colours. I know the external and his work. He will like what you have done. If I were you, I would take a couple of weeks off now. Go home, go abroad. Whatever but just forget work for these two weeks. When you come back, we can then think about the report to the research council and extending your contract, maybe."

So Tom found himself after months of intense hard work at a loose end. There was no Amanda. She had departed for pastures new. It was only when his work was finished and he was alone, Tom realised one of the factors of why he had accepted the break up with Amanda so calmly was that he had always listened to her concerns. Amanda had never really listened to what was troubling him. When they had been together, she had been too intent on speaking about her own fears and hopes rather than listening to what other peoples were saying. There again, Tom had told himself, it was partly my fault. At times of crisis I tend to draw into myself and try to solve the problem on my own. He had to admit, he was much better at trying to help other people than he was getting other people involved in his concerns.

" Maybe I should have tried to get Amanda involved in my worries more than I did," he told himself moodily as he sat drinking a beer on his own the night he had handed in his thesis. " Well its too late now. She must have found another willing listener."

Taking the advice of his supervisor, he went home the next day hoping for a relaxing couple of weeks. It did not turn out that way but what materialised did take his mind of the impending viva.

Two days after arriving home, he telephoned Belinda in the evening hoping she was at home. " Hello Belinda. It's Tom. I was wondering if you had the phone number of Jane Brookes, your friend from the party?"

" What have we here then?" Belinda laughed down the phone. " Are we trying to set up a date behind Amanda's back?"

Tom felt himself blushing and then getting angry. " It was a simple question," he barked down the phone. " Do you happen to have Jane's phone number or not?"

" She doesn't have a phone at home or she doesn't give anybody the number," Belinda replied just as brusquely. " I have her number at work. When I phone her there, we always pretend it is a business call. From what I gather, her office don't like her taking personal telephone calls while she is at work."

" Could you ask her to phone me at home then?" Tom asked.

" What can I expect in return Tom?" Belinda was laughing but Tom detected a serious edge to her question. " You will be forever in my power if I do that for you."

" What could you ever want from me more than you have now?" Tom asked lightly.

" Oh I would like to see far more of you than I ever have," Belinda answered obliquely. " You could come and see me more often. It is only when you happen to be in Porthampton with nothing better to do that I see you. Then it is usually with Tony. Thinking about what we were talking discussing before we got onto the subject of you and me, the best way to get to ask Jane out would be for you to meet her outside her office as if by accident. I don't say this to wriggle out of phoning her for you. She is funny about those things and might just say no instinctively to any idea of meeting you if I suggest it. She works for Addock, Addcock and Shirley. Their office is on the High Street just passed the Midland Bank on the left walking towards the docks. She usually leaves the office at one o'clock and walks up the High Street towards Marks and Spencer. If you wait outside, when she comes out, you could make it look like an accidental meeting."

" Belinda, how can I ever repay you if this works out?" Tom was laughing now. " I hope she is not meeting that Eric though. He looks a mean bugger if ever I have seen one."

" Oh didn't I mention it?" Belinda feigned innocence. " She had a blazing row with Eric that night after the party. Some thing about making eyes at other men. Jane told him that she never wanted to see him again. As to what you can do to thank me. Don't you worry, I will think of something in due time. Good luck."

After replacing the receiver, Tom sat back in his chair and thought about what Belinda had said. From the hints thrown out by Belinda and the lack of surprise at his request, Tom imagined that Jane would be happy to see him again. I am glad that Eric is no longer in the picture, he thought. He tried not to dwell on the look of pure hate Eric had thrown in his direction at Belinda's party. Her had to admit that he got some pleasure at the thought of being alone with Belinda, with her slim body, deep blue eyes and generous lips. However, he was wary of letting her lead him on if only for the sake of his friendship with Tony.

The next day just before one o'clock, Tom stood looking into the window of a jeweller's shop across the High Street from the offices of Addcock, Addcock and Shirley. Every time a girl came out of the office door, he got ready to cross the road only to stop as soon as he realised it was not Jane. At last just after one o'clock she came out of the door and turned left towards the shops.

Tom turned from his study of wristwatches in one of the windows and walked rapidly up the street. At a crossing some distance away, he waited and then crossed the street. Glancing up, he could see Jane walking in his direction and he started to stroll back down the street towards her. A few paces from meeting Jane, he pretended to veer round somebody and almost knocked Jane off her feet.

" I am sorry," he said holding her arm. " I dodged round that person and bumped into you. Are you all right?"

" I seem to be in one piece," Jane answered shaking off his hand from her arm. Then her eyes opened wide and she smiled. " Tom isn't it? We met a few weeks ago at Belinda's party. I thought you had to go back to Nottingham?"

" Jane!" Tom exclaimed in mock surprise. " Fancy meeting you like this. What are you doing here?"

" I work in an office down there," Jane answered waving vaguely in the direction of her office. " I'm on my lunch break and was going up town to do a bit of shopping. I might ask what you are doing here."

" I had some shopping to do. I am going to the Unicorn for a drink and some lunch," Tom answered. " Would you like to join me?"

Jane seemed to consider his request for a long time and then shrugged expansively. " Why not," she said, though it struck Tom that it was not an over enthusiastic agreement.

The Unicorn was one of those pubs used by office workers at lunchtime and for friends meeting before going on to some other place in the evenings. Thus there were two periods of intense activity surrounded by a few hours of relative calm. The bar proved to be crowded with drinkers, many of whom nodded vaguely to Tom. Somehow, as though the gods were looking out for his welfare, he found a couple of seats by a table near a window looking out over the river seen between transit sheds in the docks.

" How are things with you?" he asked shyly when he returned from the bar with their drinks and a sandwich to share.

" Steady," Jane replied with a faint smile " Did you get your thesis in on time?"

" I managed it somehow," Tom grimaced. " I had to sit up all the last night so that I could get the corrections to my secretary the next day."

" Can't you type?" Jane asked bluntly. " I would have thought it was a part of your duties."

" Can you?" Tom asked equally bluntly.

" No but I am not a secretary," Jane replied.

" You have made my point," Tom grinned.

They were sparing, saying what ever came into their heads. It was obvious even to Tom that Jane wanted to ask him about Amanda and his relationship with her and he wanted to know about Eric. Without knowing it, they were both trying to establish whether there was any need to prolong their relationship passed this lunchtime. And so they continued, talking about the things that did not really matter, hinting at wanting to talk about other things but afraid to express what they were really thinking in case they upset the other before they had established the ground rules. What struck both of them after a while was that they enjoyed sitting together. The chance to talk about them is together came by chance from Jane.

" How long are you going to be in Porthampton?" she asked placidly.

" About two weeks, " Tom answered. " I am not certain because there is no legal requirement for me to go back to the university at a certain time. I have enough holidays to last me for longer than two weeks if I want to stay any longer. Why don't we meet on Friday for a drink? I could pick you up at about seven thirty and we could go to some country pub for a quiet drink. Or we could go to the Guildhall for the Saturday dance or both. Sorry that seems like I am rushing things and it must depend on how Eric feels."

" You don't have to worry about Eric," Jane said in a quiet voice, her expression non readable. " Just after the party at Belinda's, we had a row. Well not just an argument. He threatened to bash me up if I did not stop making eyes at men like you as he put it. I told him I didn't want to see him any more, if that was how he was going to act. Even then, he tried to warn me that if he ever saw me with another man, he would teach the man a lesson. I must admit I was frightened by his temper and possessiveness but I have not seen him since. What about Amanda? It seems you must have left her in Nottingham to enable you to play the field down here."

" Yes it does look like that, doesn't it?" Tom laughed loudly. " Like you and Eric, Amanda and I are no longer going out with each other. It was not as dramatic as your split up with Eric. She came to the conclusion that there was no future in our relationship beyond the sex. As far as she could see, that was all I wanted from her. Anyway, that was how she put things to me. While we were going out together, I put up with her views on certain subjects but really all I was interested in was the sex. Actually, I think it was Belinda and Tony's party again which got to her. I knew a lot of people there from my life in Porthampton and talked to those all evening almost ignoring her."

" Was the sex good?" Jane asked with a grin.

" As a matter of fact it was," Tom answered frowning. " But we did talk about other things and went to the theatre together. There was more to our relationship than the sex. What does Eric do? He gave the impression that he had a great deal of money."

" I never early found out but I must admit he appeared to be very rich." Jane answered frowning in turn. " All he would ever say when I asked was that he wheels and deals. Enough of Eric. Pick me up at seven thirty then on Friday. I live in Smith Street off the main London Road at Parkhill. No six," Jane said finishing her drink. " I have to go. Some of us have to do a days work, you know."

Tom drove home from the town centre lost in thought. He admitted to himself that he had been attracted to Jane when he had met her at Tony's party. He could still see her leaning against the window frame looking out over the garden the setting sun casting a halo round her head. It is funny, he thought, I almost considered her superior to everybody else in the room while she was dancing with Eric. She was by far the best dressed and groomed woman there. Eric intrigued Tom. There was something about him, now Tom was thinking about it, which reminded Tom of something.

He was looking forward to meeting Jane alone on Friday night. Then, on Wednesday evening when he was sitting watching the television with his father, his mother told him there was a Jane on the phone.

" Hello," he said.

" Hello Tom," Jane sounded bright and happy on the phone. " No, it is nice to hear from you Jane. Just hello."

" I am overjoyed to hear your voice," Tom spoke sarcastically into the phone. " Sorry Jane but it is the apprehension that you are going to tell me that Friday is off."

" No nothing like that," Jane said hastily. " It does concern Friday night. I bumped into Belinda today and she suggested we have a meal at her place before going to the pub with her and Tony. I sort of said yes."

" Why the hell does Belinda always want to interfere with other people?" Tom almost shouted down the phone. " Sorry Jane but I was hoping we would be alone for the first time we went out together. I suppose we will have to agree. Is her cooking any better than it was?"

" I don't know," Jane giggled. " Whenever I have eaten there she has got fish and chips for us from the shop. Shall I tell her that it is OK with you that we meet at her flat?"

" Yes," Tom said. " Does that mean that you want me to pick you up from work?"

" No. Tony will give me a lift back to his flat. He works just down the road," Jane said quickly. " Belinda thought it would be easier if we met round at her place. We will get there about six."

" I'll see you at Belinda's about six then," Tom said.

To say that Tom was disappointed was an understatement. He had been looking forward with anticipation to there being just the two of them on Friday night. Why did I let Jane talk me into spending the evening with Belinda and Tony? he asked himself as he half watched the television after her call. It had always been thus, he reminded himself. You are always content to let things drift by, as long as you were not inconvenienced too much. He had to admit to himself, there was no real objection to his having a meal with Tony and Belinda and then going to the pub for a drink. It was just that for once he wanted to be on his own with Jane. This might not be great for us for Friday night but I will get other chances to be alone with her, he concluded.

He had realised early in his life that Belinda always got her way though somehow without upsetting too many people. It had been like that when they went to the Pound Street Congregational Church youth club at the same time. Belinda had been two years younger than Tom and he had been too involved in dreaming and trying to chase Caroline, the girl Jane had reminded him of at Belinda's party, to really notice Belinda.

Tom would always remember the day Caroline walked into his life. He had been playing table tennis at the church youth club when this vision in a floral dress, long blonde hair, breasts that a boy could make out under her clothes and shapely legs, had walked through the hall. She had lent against the stage in such a pose that said she knew she was attractive. From that moment, Tom had been smitten and he tried everything he could to get her to go out with him. Unfortunately, all of the boys at the youth club lusted after her and some were more rich and handsome than he was. Those things counted with a fourteen-year-old girl when she looked at a sixteen-year-old boy. In the two years he pursued her, he never managed to get a date with Caroline.

Belinda hung out with a different crowd than him and they were only on nodding terms. It is strange how even at a small church youth club there were factions which did not mix very much. Though he did not make much of it at the time, he did catch glimpses of Belinda watching him. When he had left home to go to Nottingham, she had been quite enthusiastic to get a kiss good-bye the last time he went to the youth club. One of the problems with any relationship they might had developed was that, like Jane's parents, Belinda's were pillars of the church and they looked at Tom with undisguised suspicion. Not only did Tom's parents not come to church but any disturbance to the prevailing social mores of the church seemed to involve Tom. Of course it was not snobbery, Tom always told himself. There could be no snobbery at the church, they were Christians after all. It did seem strange, to him at the time, that most opposition to anybody not pulled into the fabric of the church and coming to the youth club was led by Belinda's parents. Her father was a bank manager and her mother a research scientist at the university. They looked on Tom's father as a labourer even though he was a qualified electrician and was a charge hand in the dockyard.

It had been a shock to Tom when he had come home from University one weekend to find Tony with his arm round Belinda in the pub where the crowd of Tom's friends always met at for a drink. Later that evening, Tom found out they had met while Tony was home from London University and after graduating, he had moved back to Porthampton and they had started to see each other more often.

Then they had been married the year before Tom met Jane but Tom had been unable to be at the wedding because he had been in hospital nursing a broken ankle. His passion for football, which he shared with Tony, had caused him to miss the wedding. Not only that but much to his consternation at the last minute Tony had had to find another best man.

The day after Jane's phone call, Belinda phoned unexpectedly. " Hello Tom. How are you?"

" Hello Belinda. Quite well actually," Tom answered trying to sound pleased to hear her voice. All the time he wanted to tell her that he was mad that she had interfered but kept that thought to himself.

" I phoned to say sorry, actually," Belinda went on hurriedly. " When I heard that you had asked Jane out for a drink on Friday, I had this thought that it would have been nice if we went out as a foursome. Then Tony suggested if that were the case, it would be a good idea if he brought Jane back to our place after work and I cooked a meal for us all. I would like that."

" I will not call you an interfering old bat because you are neither old nor unattractive," Tom stated bluntly. " I must admit I was looking forward to having the evening alone with Jane. What time shall I come then?"

" That is up to you," Belinda said vaguely. " I will be leaving work at lunch time because I have to take the football team to another school on Saturday. Anytime in the afternoon. Tony suggested that if you can get here on the bus, he will drive to the pub and give you a lift home later in the night. Then you wouldn't have to worry about how much you are drinking. Jane is going to stay with us for the night anyway."

" It looks as though you have thought of everything," Tom growled straining not to sound too angry. " I think I can get a bus across town to your place though it's a long time since I travelled on a bus in Porthampton. I'll aim to be there in the middle of the afternoon then."

" That would be fine," Belinda answered with a hint of promise in her voice. " If you arrive then, we will have a chance to sit and chat together before I have to get the dinner. I don't think we have ever been just the two of us on our own and talked. Whenever we have been together there have always been people around. I will really look forward to being alone with you."

Tom replaced the receiver and sat for a long time looking out of the window across his parent's carefully tended garden. The borders were a riot of colour, the grass green and smooth and the patio clean with the welcoming chairs. From that conversation, Tom felt that there was a danger that Belinda was trying to take over his life. It left him wondering whether that was a good idea. Should he have refused to arrive early? With an effort of planning he could have timed his arrival to coincide with Jane and Tony getting there. He tried to ignore the hint of a hidden meaning behind her invitation. With a sigh of resignation, Tom picked up the newspaper and went to sit in the sunlight. As the scent of the flowers drifted around him, he tried to stop thinking about Belinda.

On the Friday afternoon, Tom boarded a bus on the main road at the end of the close where he lived and undertook the journey across town. He had travelled this route every school day for almost seven years. Looking out of the bus window, he soon came to the conclusion that not much had changed since he rode the bus to school. Most of the new building had been on the outskirts of the town.

Alighting from the bus in the centre of the town, he crossed the road and waited a few minutes for another bus which took him through the town centre to the suburb where Belinda and Tony rented their flat. Stepping off the bus, he walked along streets of tall terraced houses which years ago had been the town houses of the rich but were now, in the main, converted into flats. Coming to Belinda's house, he rang the bell and was admitted by Belinda.

The flat was on the ground floor of the house, the entrance to the side of a flight of stairs, which led away into the gloom of the upper floors and the other flats. Inside the front entrance was a small hall with doors leading off. To the right was the lounge, next one bedroom, the bathroom, the kitchen and to the left the other larger bedroom. In other words the usual layout of a two bed flat.

Belinda led Tom into the sitting room, smiling in welcome. She was almost as tall as Tom in her high heels, rather slim but with small round breasts. Her hair was blonde, straight and reached her shoulders. Tom noticed that her lips were deep red and rather full. The eyes were blue but to Tom they had always been rather hard as though Belinda passed strict judgements on the rest of the world. To Tom there was no mystery about Belinda. She was open and straightforward with everybody.

" What would you like to drink?" Belinda asked with a smile.

" Coffee," Tom answered smiling in return.

When she rejoined him carrying the coffee, Tom was sitting on the settee reading the paper.

" I am glad you have made yourself at home, Tom," Belinda remarked as she placed the coffee on a table in front of the settee. After sitting by his side, she said, " It is nice that you could come early. We have about an hour to sit here on our own and talk before I have to get the dinner started. What happened to Amanda?"

" We agreed that things were not working out," Tom answered equally bluntly. " She was reasonable company most of the time. The trouble was we did not have much in common. The night before we split, she accused me of only wanting her for the sex."

" Was that the only reason you went out with her?" Belinda asked with a faint smile.

" You know me better than that," Tom snapped back, hurt by the implied criticism.

" Well that's not strictly true, you know," Belinda frowned. " I know we went to the same church, the youth club and mixed whenever the Brigades did joint things but I did not know you. Jane asked me the other day what you were really like and I had to admit to her that I did not really know. I have always been with Tony when we have met since the youth club days. Before that you were always with another group at the youth club. Besides you were always chasing that Caroline even though she did all in her power to put you off. So you see I don't really know you that well."

" Your parents didn't give you much encouragement to get to know me did they?" Tom laughed bitterly. " I remember being upset once when your parents invited the boys and girls from the youth club who belonged to the church for a get together at your house. At the time, they made it quite plain I was not included. The only reason I could think of was that my parents did not attend the church and were working class. It's funny really, because my Mum started to go to Pound Street Church regularly after I left home. How do your Mum and Dad treat her now?"

" I have no idea. The last time I went to Pound Street Church was when Tony and I were married," Belinda answered truthfully. " I expect they think differently now that you have a degree and are studying for your Doctorate."

" What a Christian way to go about things," Tom said with a cheery grin and wide eyes. " The Reverend Williams used to push it down our throats as young people that we had to learn to get along together no matter what our background, social standing or colour. All the time you Mum and Dad were trying to have me banished from the youth club, the church and the rest because they were afraid I would contaminate the others with my bad manners and breeding. Anyway you never showed any interest in me at all."

" That's not true," Belinda burst out, her eyes big, her expression indignant. " I always tried to get into your group whenever there were group activities and to sit next to you on the coach if we went for a trip somewhere. You always seemed to manage to sit with somebody else or to get into the group with that Caroline. I know it was silly but at the time I used to cry with frustration. Then when you finally seemed to accept that Caroline was not going to have much to do with you, off you went to university leaving me here on my own."

" Its funny really," Tom answered with a laugh. " At sixteen I was desperate to get a girl but could only see Caroline.

Maybe, if I had only looked round, you would have been there ready and waiting. Such is life. We all grow older and wiser though. You went and met my best mate Tony and got married. I continued to drift through life with a number of different girls. Still, we remain friends. Indeed, we seem to be better friends now than we were when we were younger."

" I still have the same feelings for you as I had then," Belinda said in a soft voice. " One of the reasons I invited you and Jane for a meal tonight was so that I could see you again. Oh, when I am with Tony, I act as is expected of me. I saw this as an opportunity to get you on your own."

Tom understood that Belinda was giving him an invitation but he was not sure he wanted to take the opportunity. He had not long ago parted from Amanda and today was supposed to be about Jane. Looking along the settee at Belinda, Tom saw her moistening her lips. He noted the blue eyes, the blonde hair and the small round breasts. He had never really thought about making love to Belinda. Now, with her sitting this close thrusting her breasts in his direction, her short skirt showing most of her thigh, he felt his desire rising.

Reaching out, he took her hands in his and pulled her towards him. She moved without any resistance and they were soon kissing fiercely. Tom let his hand sink down over her body until it was on her breast.

Belinda was murmuring in her throat but she pulled Tom to his feet still kissing his lips. " Let us go into the spare bedroom, " she said.

They made love slowly and passionately in the spare bed knowing that this might be the only opportunity they would have. Belinda was more straightforward than Amanda with none of the experimentation that Tom and Amanda had practised. Afterwards they lay in each other's arms, satisfied but not overly exhausted. Tom suddenly thought of Jane and how in a few hours she would be sleeping in this bed. At least, he told himself, it is not Tony's.

Tom sat in the lounge reading the paper while Belinda prepared the meal. Every time Belinda came into the room, she made a point of kissing him. It was as though, he thought, after all this time of wanting to make love with me, she was now laying claim to a small part of my affection. Tom was rather confused by what had happened. That doesn't take much, he thought. Was Belinda serious about him or was she just fulfilling a wish and would now treat him as normal? She answered that by the way she kissed Tony when he came home with Jane. Tom took the hint. She was making plain to Tom that Tony was her man no matter what had happened that afternoon.

It was a very pleasant if surreal meal they had together. The evening at a pub was much the same. Jane chatted away to Tom while Belinda sat holding Tony's hand, talking as though nothing had happened that afternoon. When the pub shut, they went back to Tony's flat for a nightcap before Tony took Tom home. Before leaving, Tom had chance to ask Jane if she would come to a dance at the Town Hall with him the next day. She smiled hugely and agreed.

The dancing was wonderful. They sat and drank a little, not too much because Tom was driving. Danced to the band and to the disco with disc jockey which was starting to invade the dance halls especially in the intervals between the band music sets. After the dance, Tom took Jane to the Jack of Diamonds nightclub, where he was a member, for a meal and a late night drink. It was while he was there that he came face to face with an unfamiliar part of life. In some ways it set the tone for part of his future.

Jane and Tom had just finished their meal and were sitting back with a coffee, when somebody stood between where they were sitting and the dance floor. The first Tom realised somebody was standing by his chair was when a shadow fell across the table. Looking up, he was confronted with the broad shoulders of Eric. His expression was like thunder and his hands were squeezed into balls at his side. Behind him stood two other men flexing their muscles.

" Hello Jane," he said, never taking his eyes off Tom. " What are you doing here with this scum?"

Tom started to rise from his seat but Jane placed a restraining hand on his arm. " I am having a pleasant evening with Tom. We have been dancing and he brought me back here for a late meal. If all you can do is insult him, you had better leave us alone."

Eric laughed. " I could lift him up with my little finger, Jane."

Leaning forward with his fists on the table, Eric thrust his face close to Tom's. " If you value your looks and your health, I would leave now on your own. I will make sure Jane will get home all right."

Tom did not move nor take his eyes from those of Eric. " Is this like last time when you threatened her with violence,

Eric? I have always thought it is a sign of cowardice when a man threatens violence to a woman. I might look like a nine stone weakling but I am more dangerous than you think. I reckon the best thing you can do is leave us alone to carry on with our drinks."

Eric reached out and grasped the front of Tom's suit. He looked round suddenly at the sound of another voice.

" Are we having any trouble Tom?" A man dresses in a wide lapelled suit was standing behind Eric.

Tom grinned. " Hello Derek. No, I was going to handle it myself."

Derek looked Eric up and down. " Get your hands off my friend's clothes," Derek said in a flat voice. " When you have done that you will leave the club and never come back. Oh and take your friends with you."

Eric laughed. " Who says so?"

Derek looked round the nightclub. " Mr. Hunt over at that table says so. He is the owner and all those hard looking men coming this way will make sure his wishes are carried out. Oh by the way, your membership has just been cancelled."

Eric looked desperately round the nightclub and the men lining the edge of the dining area. Then he looked for his friends but they had left all ready. Letting go of Tom's coat, he turned on his heel and walked away from Tom's table.

Derek smiled at Jane and called after Eric. " Oh by the way, mush. If I ever hear that you are harassing Tom or his friend again, I will personally come after you."

Tom smiled in relief at his friend. " Hello Derek. Thanks for the help though I was holding my own there."

Derek laughed and shook his head. " Just like all those times I had to rescue you after school."

Tom turned to Jane. " Jane this is Derek, one of my oldest friends. Derek meet Jane."

Jane smiled faintly and regarded Derek warily. " Hello Derek."

Derek grinned. " Hello Jane. It is nice to met Tom's girlfriend. I will leave you to finish your drinks. I look forward to meeting you again."

Jane watched Derek return to the table with Mr. Hunt and his party. He was a big man, not fat but big. His body looked as though it was hard under the well cut suit and the broad shoulders spoke of great strength. His hair was swept back in what she could only describe as an Elvis Presley look and his face was fleshy with dark hard eyes. The look Derek had given her was full of confidence, as though he was telling her he could look after himself, and in a way challenging her to make sure she did not hurt Tom. That puzzled her. What was the bond between these men from seemingly different layers of society? she had asked herself.

The fog swirled around Tom. With a sigh, he sank back under the surface leaving the world behind.

Jane sat looking at her husband asking herself if there had been a little movement of his eyes but she could not be sure. She got up from her chair and stretched but soon resumed her seat and her talk.

Chapter 2

" I meant to tell you," Jane said as she stroked Tom's brow trying desperately to ignore the lack of a response.

In a sudden flash of memory, it came back to her that all she had to do when they were younger was stroke his brow like this and he would be asking her to take off her clothes. Now he lay there breathing heavily, surrounded by machines which bleeped into the gloom and showing no sign that he knew she was there.

" I bumped into Marlene last week." Jane went on as she collected her thoughts together. " She asked to be remembered to you. She was back in Porthampton on her own visiting her sisters. Derek does not get away from Marbella too often now. With his heart condition and the limp he still has from that time he was attacked, he finds getting on aircraft difficult. She invited us to their villa in Spain when we have time for a holiday. I think we should think about taking up their offer once you are fit again."

" Derek has been a good friend of yours over the years since I met him in that night club. He never stopped calling on you when he needed help in his business. That consultancy you did for him at times was very lucrative along with the post of non-executive director for his company. I never did really understand how you got to know him so well. He mixed with some dodgy people at times, not the type of people I'd have thought you or your family would have dealings with. I did think he appeared to go legitimate later in life. It was an eye opener that time in the nightclub when you were threatened by Eric. When we went to join Derek's friends at their table, I don't know whether I liked them at all. To tell you the truth I was rather scared. They all seemed so hard. They greeted you like one of their own so I supposed at the time that they were all right. I never did really find out much about your childhood apart from the fact that you grew up on the edge of that council estate. Your mum and dad had moved by the time we got married, to that bungalow out in Clapton Hill. I think your dad always wanted to live in a bungalow. I did get the impression from him that he had no time for Mr. Jones, Derek's father."

As though the droning voice had struck a cord the fog started to lift. Then Tom was back on the mean streets of the council estate near the house where he had grown up.

Tom had known Derek for as long as he could remember. They had started in the infants' school on the same day and become friends. Well, they had become part of the same gang which had walked to school and back together every day. For some reason, even in those early days, Derek had always asked Tom for advice about what was happening around him or help with his schoolwork. If there were anything Derek did not understand, he would ask Tom. In return, though this was never acknowledged consciously, Derek had protected Tom from any hint of bullying. Even when they were six years old, Derek was bigger than all the other boys and much tougher.

Tom did not know at the time, but found out much later, Derek had to be tough to get by in the place where he lived. In contrast to Tom, who lived with his mother, father and brother, Derek came from a family of eight children three boys and five girls. Derek was number four with two sisters and a brother older than him and three sisters and a brother younger. They lived in a small council house with three bedrooms. It was just round the corner from where Tom lived. The girls shared one bedroom, the boys the other and their parents in the third. There was hardly room in the girls bedroom for two bunk beds for the five girls let alone any hanging space for their clothes. Whenever Tom had visited Derek's house, there had seemed to him little room to move with children all over the place. There again if Tom was honest with himself, it was not often he had been to Derek's home. Derek much preferred to come to Tom's house. This was a detached three bed roomed house in a Close near the edge of the council estate. In those days, Derek would love to sit in the kitchen drinking orange squash and talking to Tom and his brother Edward.

On top of all this, Mr. Jones, Derek's father, drank too much and often beat his wife and children when he came home from the pub. Derek confided in Tom when they were about eight that when he grew bigger he was going to beat the living day lights out of his father. There was a hint and a rumour, that Tom did not understand at the time, that Mr. Jones interfered with his daughters. Nobody would confront him with this because Mr. Jones was the toughest man in the area and everybody was a little scared of him. On the other hand, nobody from the council estate went to the police with their problems. They dealt with them in their own way without involving outsiders. That was the unspoken rule of their neighbourhood. ' We sort our own problems out in our own way,' people from the estate used to say. ' Besides, if the police come snooping round here too much, it is surprising what they might turn up. It is best to keep the police out of our business'.

Two other boys from the estate used to sometimes visit Tom's house at the same time as Derek, Ray Downing and Joe Fox. Ray was a small, rat faced boy, always wearing patched and shabby clothes that had seen better days. They never provided enough warmth during the winter. Ray was always shivering when he arrived at Tom's house. Ray's mother lived on her own, his father having been killed in the war while serving in the merchant navy. As far as Tom could make out his ship had been sunk on a Malta convoy not long after Ray was born. He had an older sister and the family were always struggling to make ends meet.

Joe Fox was average height but thin and good at football. He dreamed of playing for Porthampton Town when he grew up.

When they came with Derek, Ray liked to play the piano. It must have been the only time in his life that he had been told that he could play the piano if he first went into the kitchen and washed his hands. Actually, Ray did not realise how privileged he was. The piano was in the front room which was only used by the family for important visitors or family get togethers. Mrs. Houseman went in the front room whenever she had the time to play the piano, filling the house with the sounds of Schubert and Chopin. Edward took lessons and was reasonably accomplished by the time he was sixteen but Tom had been, much to the disappointment of his mother, a complete failure at piano playing. Ray, on the other hand, actually got quite proficient after a while though largely self-taught with some help from Tom's mum. It was accepted that Ray's mum could not afford piano lessons. Actually Tom always suspected that Ray never told his mother because she would have snorted at such a decadent way of filling his time. All Ray's mother lived for was the time when Ray would be old enough to get a job and bring some money into the house. School was there to get through. Only an interval before the important things became possible like earning money. Indeed, from an early age Ray did things to earn money, helping out here, giving a hand there. It was always for cash.

It was soon apparent to Tom, once he was old enough to think of these things, that his friend Derek was going to be a criminal when he grew up. Even when they were at junior school, Derek would always be bringing the results of his shoplifting to share with Tom. Out of fear, Tom refused anything other than chocolate bars and biscuits. It was not any high principles about accepting the results of Derek's crimes that stopped Tom accepting the books, papers or gadgets but the thought of what his parents would say when he took them home. His mother was very proud of how she paid her way and was never in debt. Whether Derek went out of his way to get the sweets and chocolate for Tom or not, it seemed that Tom had a constant supply of these everyday. Half heartedly, Tom used to warn Derek that he would get caught one day and sent to borstal. Derek just laughed at such fears in such a way that was full of the bravado of there being no chance he would ever be caught.

They separated at age eleven, Tom passing the eleven plus and going to Porthampton Boys Grammar School, his three friends to the local secondary modern. Frequently they met after school and in the holidays though Tom had other friends like Tony from his school. Tom also played football for his school and did not play so many times with his friends. Later, Tom, Derek, Ray and Joe played together in the

Stablegreen Junior Sunday League team. Joe was always the best player and he went on to play for Porthampton Schoolboys much to the envy of his friends.

They were fourteen when one day Tom got off the bus near Derek's house after school and as he walked towards his home, Derek rushed out and joined him as though he had been looking out of the window for the bus to arrive.

Derek looked angry, though at the same time confused. " Can I come back to your house and talk to you?"

Tom smiled. " Of course you can. I expect Mum will be cooking the dinner ready for when Dad gets home from work but we can have a drink while I am waiting for my dinner."

They walked down the road side by side, talking about the football, how Derek was doing at school and whether Joe would make it as a professional footballer. For the first time while talking to Tom, Derek started on the subject of girls and how he had a date for the coming weekend. Tom was still at the age when girls did not figure much, especially as he very rarely met any. The secondary modern was co-educational while his school was just for boys. Though he had started to notice that girls were not only different but called forth feelings in him which he did not understand, he was still not fussed whether he was in their company or not. Most of the girls he knew were seen as friends not as something mysterious which had to be pursued. He had asked politely, always polite was Tom when he was not certain of something, why Derek wanted to go out with a girl. Derek had laughed and told him that he would soon learn.

They were sitting in the sitting room of Tom's house when Derek broached the subject he wanted to talk to Tom about.

" I don't know how to put this another way but I have found out that Martha is on the game," Derek stated bluntly. " What I wanted to ask you is what I should do about it?"

Tom sat staring at his friend. He had no idea what Derek was on about, no idea of what on the game meant. He was a fourteen year old boy who had never been confronted with such an expression. Not understanding what Derek was telling him, Tom instinctively knew there was no way he could give Derek advice. Tom's mind whirled through all the things he could think of which could apply to that simple phrase. Though his mind soared through all of his experience there was nothing which gave him any insight into what Derek was referring. In desperation he considered all the sports he knew but, having seen Martha with her knee length skirts, very high heels and thick makeup, he could not imagine a sport in which she would have been involved.

Choosing the coward's way out, Tom hedged for more time hoping that Derek would not discover his ignorance. " How can I help?" he asked frowning.

" All right," Derek smiled faintly, holding up his hand as though to prevent Tom digging a larger metaphorical hole. " I suppose you have led a more sheltered life than me. To put things bluntly, what would you do if your sister was a prostitute?"

Now, the word prostitute was something Tom had read in a few books and newspaper articles. He was still lamentably uneducated about the full circumstances surrounding its true import. His mind once more churned as he thought of Martha meeting all those men. He was still not too certain what they did after they met.

" I can't say because I don't have a sister," Tom remarked slowly, still reluctant to say that he did not really know what Derek was on about. " No, it is difficult for me to give you advice. I have no knowledge of her circumstances. Christ,

Derek, I have never met any prostitutes as far as I know. What had you in mind?"

With the seriousness of a fourteen year old who has come to a momentous decision, Derek said bluntly, " I thought I might go and beat up the person who forced her into it."

" Not so fast Derek," Tom said, now on more familiar ground. " For a start you will be dealing with grown men. I know you are big and tough but from what I read, these men will be the toughest in the neighbourhood. I don't think you should mess with them until you are much older. Anyway, the first thing you should do surely is try to find out from your sister why she became a prostitute. It seems to me you are assuming somebody forced her to do it. This might be the case but you have to find out first before you start threatening to beat up somebody."

" Somebody must have forced her into it," Derek stated stubbornly, his jaw set in a hard line. " But I will take your advice like I always do."

They let the subject drift away then and started to talk about other things. Soon Mrs. Houseman came in and ordered Tom to lay the table ready for his father arriving home and Derek left. They saw each other a few times after that, not so many as before. Derek had become interested in girls while Tom had to spend more time on school activities.

A couple of years later, Mrs. Houseman said to her son when he came home from the job he had started, helping in a shop after school. " I hear that Derek Jones has been arrested. I never did like that family. It appears he had an argument with his father and it resulted in a fight. He beat his father up pretty badly, so Mrs. Parker was telling me when I went to the shop this morning. Then he was caught last night taking some cigarettes from Pullins down the road. The police were called because his dad refused to have anything to do with it. They are a bad family what with that daughter on the game and the oldest son in prison. Look at their house. Always in a mess as though they have no pride in where they live. I must admit though that Derek has always been polite to me when he has come round here with you. I hope he can get things sorted out. At least you and Edward are safe from that sort of life."

After eating dinner with his mother and father, Edward was working late in a garage, Tom told them he was going out to find Derek if he could. From what his mother had told him, Tom was worried about his friend. Even though he had been friends with Derek since before they first went to school together, Tom had hardly ever been to Derek's home and there had not been many times when he had been invited inside. There had been an unspoken principle that Tom would not be welcomed in Derek's house and they had better meet some other place. That had invariably been in a place that was affectionately known as the park to the people living in the council estate. In reality it was a piece of waste ground the other side of the allotments from the council estate through which a steam meandered. There boys would play football or cricket depending on the weather and girls would play with their dolls. A few times the boys magnanimously agreed to play rounders with the girls. Later in life during the late evening, the older boys would meet girls there to begin the courting rituals or more which then were part of growing up.

Tom approached Derek's house with his heart beating too fast. He had always regarded this house as strange and had to admit was scared of Mr. Jones. After picking his way through the rubbish strewn front garden, he knocked on the once brown painted but now peeling front door with his fist as there was no knocker. After a great deal of shouting from inside the house, the door opened. Mr. Jones stood there towering above Tom dressed in a dirty vest and looking as though he had not shaved for a week. The nails on his hands, Tom noticed, were black and his trousers stained and unpressed. His hair was matted and could do with a comb and wash.

" Yeh," he growled glaring at Tom through his one half closed eye. The other was swollen and completely closed. " What do you want? Sent by your stuck up mother to gloat at me?"

Tom stood his ground though all he wanted to do was run away. " I came to see Derek," he said as calmly as he could. " Is he in?"

" How the bloody hell should I know?" Mr. Jones almost shouted raising his fist as though he was going to strike Tom. Although he wanted to resist, Tom could not prevent himself taking a step backwards. " He is no longer a son of mine or welcome in my house. Now get on your way before I kick you out." With that the door was so violently slammed shut, the windows rattled in their frames.

Tom had stood looking at the closed door for a while wondering what to do now. He was uncertain how to take the naked hostility of Derek's father and even more shocked to find that somebody so disliked his mother. Oh, he understood that she lived with certainty to a set of moral principles, convinced that she was right. At the same time she could be blunt, informing people that they had failed her notion of what was right or wrong. He also knew that though his father worked in the docks as an electrician, his mother's principles could be seen as middle class rather than working class. Some of her neighbours might believe that she had ideas above her station but they respected her for her mores none the less. He also realised that her ambition to get his brother and him to university was almost unique in the area in which they lived. Even the other people who lived in the five or six houses in the close near the council estate did not have those ambitions for their children.

As he turned to leave, uncertain as to what to do, a girl of about fourteen poked her head round the back gate which was hanging off its hinges. Not only did it lean drunkenly away from the path but bits were missing giving the top edge a ragged look.

" You looking for Derek, Tom?" she almost whispered as though fearful of being overheard.

Tom smiled at the girl noticing for the first time that she was now starting to develop a figure. Her hair was long but unfortunately a tangled mess like her father's. The thin dress showed plainly her small developing breasts because she was not wearing a bra underneath. If she would only have a bath and get dressed in some decent clothes, Tom thought suddenly, she could look quite attractive.

" Yes. Sheila," he answered quietly. " Do you know where he is?"

" He's down the park," she said before ducking back behind the half hinged gate.

" Thank you," Tom said to the empty garden.

Tom found Derek sitting on a bank overlooking the stream that flowed through the rough grassy area they grandly called the park. There were two girls with him. As Tom approached through the bushes bordering the flat area used for football, he noticed that Derek had his arm around one of the girls while the other sat a few feet away.

Derek looked up when he heard Tom's footsteps and grinned. " Tom! What are you doing here?"

" I was looking for you," Tom replied looking shyly at the girls as he sat down on a tuft of grass near Derek. " My mum told me about your troubles so I went to your house to see if you were in. Your dad seemed mad at you and slammed the door in my face. I don't think he likes me."

" Just like my bloody dad," Derek growled.

" Sheila told me you had come down here to be on your own," Tom continued with a smile. " I thought I might come and keep you company but it looks as though I need not have bothered."

Derek laughed loudly. " Don't look so grumpy Tom. It was good of you to think about me and I still need to talk to you. I did not come round your house because I thought your mum and dad might object to me after what happened."

Derek then turned to the girls. " Tom this is Mavis my girlfriend. Over there is Pat, Mavis' friend. I told you I had a girlfriend."

" Hello Tom." Mavis smiled. Her face was round with large lips, a small nose and big eyes. To Tom it was a fleshy face on the verge of being fat but not quite. Her hair was cut short and spiky. From what he could see of her body, her breasts were large for a sixteen year old and she was dressed in a shortish skirt, which showed, off her legs. You could not call her pretty by any stretching of the imagination.

" Hi Tom." Pat said in her best imitation of an American accent, which was all the rage among the young in England. Pat was small and slim, a summer dress with a flared skirt clinging to her upper body showing her small round breasts. Her hair was blond and curly, framing her face, which was like a young Brigette Bardot. Whether she actually worked at this look or it was natural, Tom could not tell. Her eyes were deep blue and smiling.

" Hello," Tom greeted them. " I am pleased to meet you."

Turning to Derek, he asked bluntly, " What happened?"

Derek's expression turned thundery. " I don't know what you have heard or who from."

Tom laughed. " My Mum told me when I got home from my summer job. As soon as I had eaten my dinner, I came looking for you."

Derek smiled back but then looked serious. " I had a fight with my dad. He told me not to interfere in a family matter and went to hit me. I hit him before he could get to me."

" Why did your dad threaten you?" Tom asked unable to keep the bewilderment out of his voice. His father had reprimanded him on many occasions but never threatened physical violence.

"Look Tom, you are very naive when it comes to what goes on in the wider world," Derek said with a grimace but with friendship in his voice. " No don't take offence, Tom. I am saying this as a friend. You live in a world where there is laughter and love. Your parents have tried to protect you from what happens out in the world outside your home. You and your brother both passed the eleven plus and went off to grammar school leaving this neighbourhood behind. Yes, I know you have kept friendly with me, Ray and Joe since going to school the other side of town but we do not see as much of each other as we used to when we went to the same school together. Lets face it, you live in a different world from the rest of us round here most of the time. Don't get me wrong. I am not jealous of you but in some ways proud that somebody living on the wrong side of the tracks, like they say in American movies, is making a success of their lives."

" Me, I have to live with a father who beats his wife senseless every Friday night when he comes home drunk from the pub. A father who uses a strap on his children whenever he thinks they have been what he regards as disobedient. For as long as I can remember, he spends a lot of his dole money when he is not working on beer. Not only that but he has his way with his daughters. Why do you think Martha left home when she was sixteen and became a prostitute? To get away from my dad and what he was doing to her younger sisters. She challenged him to stop and all he did was laugh and beat her up." Derek stopped speaking and stared off across the stream. Mavis was looking at him with concern while Pat showed no emotion.

" Why didn't you go to the police?" Tom asked innocently. He imagined that is what would happen in similar circumstances at his home or among his parent's friends.

Derek, and surprisingly to Tom, Pat laughed bitterly. It was Pat who answered. "Nobody goes to the police from where we come from. It is against the custom of the people living on our estate. Most people who live round where I live in the middle of that estate up there, hate the police. Well hate is too strong a word but they are suspicious of the police. They're scared that if they call the police in for a small matter, the police will use that as an excuse to look further at what is happening on the estate and its surrounding area. As far as I know there are a lot of rogues living on our estate. Oh, not everybody is bent but a lot of people living there are. With the poverty and all, what else are they supposed to do? Most of those who are not bent will stick up for the other people on the estate, trying to sort out their problems between themselves. That is the obstacle to anything being done about family violence. Just like Derek's, my dad used to beat us at the least little thing which upset him. We were lucky in that he did not try to interfere with my sister or me. He only stopped beating us last year when my uncle threatened to smash his head in if he did not show some regard for his family. Uncle Harry is even bigger and tougher than my dad. Dad has always worked so we have plenty of money to live on unlike some of the people. Did you know, I passed the eleven plus? My dad told me not to get ideas above my station. I would not go to grammar school because he could not afford to send me and, anyway, girls should leave school as soon as they were fifteen and go out to work to contribute to the household. It was not for girls to go to grammar school. One of these days, I will be free and then I will go to college to get an education."

Instinctively, Tom reached out and took her hand in his. " I am sorry. I did not know any of this. I always thought most people lived the way my family did."

Pat smiled shyly and squeezed Tom's hand in return. " Don't ever think that your life is wrong Tom. You seem a very happy person."

Derek raised his eyebrow. " You be careful Pat. I have known him all my life and he usually gets his way with things without ever seeming to make any effort. He gives the impression of drifting through life but most of the time he is in control and manipulating things unbeknown to most people. Don't look so innocent, Tom Houseman. I have had plenty of time to see how you treat your life."

" Tell me what happened," Tom demanded blushing slightly at the way they were talking about him.

" As I said my dad had sex with his daughters. When my mum tried to stop him, he beat her up. Why she stayed with him, I have no idea except for the children. A few weeks ago when I came in from work, Diane was pleading with dad not to make her go into the bedroom with him. I told him that if Diane did not want him to have sex with her, he ought to let her off. He flew into a rage. Actually, he was so angry, I thought for a moment he was going to have a seizure. Then he came across the room towards me with his fist raised. For the first time, I stood my ground and dodged his fist before hitting him as hard as I could. He went down in a heap but struggled back to his knees. I kicked him in the head and sent him sprawling again. I suddenly realised that I was stronger and quicker than him and could beat him any time I wanted. When he got to his feet with blood running down from a cut on his head, I stepped close and punched him as many times as I could. He was soon on his knees again. I told him to leave my mum and his daughters alone from now on or I would deal with him again. He was scared. It was the first time I had ever seen my father scared of anything. It made me feel good."

" I went out then and down to the shop to steal some fags. For some reason I was clumsy and was caught. The shop owner called the police and they took me to the magistrates' court the next day. The magistrate let me off with a caution but I now have a record and the police will be keeping an eye on me."

Tom shook his head. " If you go on like this you are going to end up in prison just like your brother. You have to be more careful or your life will be like that. In and out of prison with each sentence getting longer."

Derek frowned. " What can I do?"

Tom shrugged his shoulders. " Why ask me? I have no idea what happens in your world."

" I have always come to you for advice," Derek answered stubbornly.

Tom realised he was still holding Pat's hand. Indeed he was now sitting so close he could feel her body's warmth through his shirt. To hide his confusion, he let her hand go as though it was on fire and stood up, gazing across the stream at the houses he could see through the trees in the distance. He was trying to think of how he could help his friend. Tom realised he was out of his depth like an explorer in a place where he had never been before. He knew nothing of fathers beating their children or of husbands beating their wives. It was unimaginable in his family circles. Most of the people with whom he mixed seemed, on the surface, to be caring and loving. Maybe they weren't. Maybe underneath they were as turbulent and violent as Derek's and Pat's. It was something he had never experienced, something in truth he had never thought about. He could not recall a time when his father had threatened either him or Edward with a beating. That is not to say his father could not be a disciplinarian at times but he had stopped their privileges rather than hit them. Each and every time their father had explained why they were being disciplined and so they had learnt what was right and what was wrong. As for sex with a daughter, Tom could not begin to comprehend this. Indeed, he did not have any experience with sex in the ordinary way without thinking about a father and his daughters.

Turning to Derek, he said. " Look Derek I have no appreciation of violence at home so I cannot give you any advice on what to do about that. The only thing I can say is if you have managed to spare Sheila further humiliation, that is a good thing. What are you going to do now?"

Derek grinned. " When things have calmed down at home, I am going to collect my things. I have been staying over the last few days at Mavis's house. Her mum and dad are very good to me. Her brother has joined the merchant navy as a deck boy and they have a spare room."

" That's good," Tom replied. " Look Derek, as I say, if you go on like this you are going to end up in prison just like your brother. You must find a better way of getting a living. "

Derek looked serious. " Its all right for you to talk Tom Houseman. You passed the eleven plus and went to the grammar school. From what I hear you are going to take your A levels and go to university like your brother. He's off to Oxford next year I hear. Now I have no qualifications and very little influence. Even Ray's uncle has found him an apprenticeship in the shipyard. My dad could not help me at all and my uncles do not want to know. I am not going to go labouring for a pittance. I am going to make some money even if it is against the law. It is the only chance somebody like me has of ever being rich or having any status in their community."

Tom grinned. " You have been like that ever since I have known you. Even in infants school you were always looking for ways to cheat the system. Look, this might not help. I remember a film I saw with my father and Edward a couple of years ago. It was about somebody just like you though in the States at the turn of the century. He started out on a career of petty crime until he tangled with the law. What he did then was attach himself to the master criminal in the area. He made himself useful and slowly worked his way up the ladder until one day he became the master. If I were you I would find out who is the big chief in Porthampton and see if you can attach yourself to him. Now whether this is sound advice or not, I have no idea. I don't even know if there is a big chief criminal in Porthampton."

Derek grasped his friend's hand. " Thank you Tom. I will think about it and see what I can do."

Putting his arm round Mavis, he said, " Come on. Enough of this serious talk. We came down here to snog. Lets find a place where we can be out of sight."

After they had gone off into the bushes, Pat smiled mysteriously at Tom and said, " Well Tom, it looks like we are left on our own. If you have nothing better to do, lets find a place to get away from prying eyes and explore what boys and girls do when they are alone."

Tom, almost blushing, took her hand and led her to a place along the stream where a willow tree trailed its drooping branches over the water forming a little grassy sheltered bower. It was a spot he had discovered years ago and where he came sometimes to be alone and to think. The sound of the water was in their ears as they discovered what a teenage boy and girl wanted to find out about the opposite sex.

After that encounter in the park, Tom did not see much of Derek over the next few years. Derek moved out of the council estate and into a flat near the centre of town. Mrs. Houseman was left a legacy from a distant aunt and Tom's father and she decided to move to a bungalow the other side of the main road leading into Porthampton town centre from the where they lived. Tom's mother started to attend Poundstreet Church every Sunday while his father took up bowls at the local club. Edward passed his A-levels and went up to Oxford. Tom took his A-levels and obtained a place at Nottingham University. He did see Derek a few times when he was out and about in Porthampton when on holiday from university but always they were with other groups and did not have the time to talk other than a quick hello.

So it was that Tom was surprised when Derek loomed over his table that night in the Jack of Diamonds, the night he had been out with Jane for the first time on their own. After leaving Tom to continue with his coffee, Derek went to resume his seat at his table. Mr. Hunt lent across the table before he sat down and spoke to him. Straight away, Derek came back to Tom's table and smiled.

" Mr. Hunt would like you to join his party," Derek said in voice that did not brook any disagreement. Jane noticed Tom's eyes narrow and take on a defensive look. There was a noticeable pause for a short few seconds before Tom smiled.

There is something here which I am not aware of, Jane thought. She could not speculate further because a waiter appeared at her elbow and put her drink on a tray.

They joined Mr. Hunt's party at their table, a waiter placing two chairs either side of Mr. Hunt.

Mr. Hunt smiled at Jane. " Hello. I am Mr. Hunt and my company own this night club."

Jane smiled nervously back. " Jane Brookes. I am a friend of Tom's."

Turning to Tom, Mr. Hunt said. " Hello Tom. You are the one who advised Derek Jones to get involved with me, are you not? Derek has talked about you to me before this."

Tom looked warily at Mr. Hunt before replying choosing his words with care. " Well not exactly you Mr. Hunt but somebody like you. I had no real idea there was a person like you in Porthampton."

Mr. Hunt smiled but not with his eyes Tom noticed. Turning, he pointed to the others round the table in turn. " This is Tom Houseman, Derek's oldest friend. To your right is Big Bob and his girlfriend Mary. To the left Knuckles Ken and his wife Loiusa. Over there is Derek, as you know and Marlene his girlfriend. What line of business are you in Mr. Houseman?"

" Call me Tom, please Mr. Hunt," Tom replied. " I work as a research assistant at Nottingham University. In parallel I am studying for my Ph. D."

" What is the subject of your Doctorate, Tom?" Mr. Hunt asked seriously. " Don't look so surprised, young man. Not all of us round this table are as illiterate as you appear to assume. I know what a Ph. D. is and what it entails. Unlike most of this lot, I did go to university and graduated before I took up my line of work. Now what is the subject of your Ph. D.?"

" It looks as though the government is going to deregulate the road haulage industry." Tom replied. " I looked at what effect that will have on the industry in the future and how to assess the impact."

" And what effect will it have?" Mr. Hutton asked.

" There will be a rush to set up road haulage companies and start road haulage services. If I had the money, I would look at getting into the market," Tom said. " It is just the type of industry one could invest in and spread the risk of one's other businesses."

" One piece of advice young man," Mr Hunt barked but he was smiling. " If I was you, I would not give advice like that for free. Everything in this world has a price. Information more than anything else. If anybody asks for that sort of information again, you should tell them you will write them a report and charge them two days consultancy at least. I will be in touch with you if I want to get some more advice. Now Miss Brookes, would you do me the honour of dancing with me?"

Tom came back to Porthampton four weeks later to meet Jane and to help Tony and Belinda move from their flat to a new house not far from Tom's parents. When he arrived at his parents' bungalow, his mother told him that a Mr. Hunt had phoned requesting that Tom met him the next time he was in Porthampton. Well not requesting exactly more of an order, she had added. Tom was a trifle puzzled at the request because he could not think of any information he might have which would be of use to Mr. Hunt or help in his business. He telephoned the next morning before going to meet Jane and Belinda and a pleasant sounding girl arranged for him to meet Mr. Hunt at his office across the square from the Jack Of Diamonds nightclub.

Tom spent a very pleasant day with Jane helping Belinda and Tony to move. They had hired a van of which, somehow, Tom became the driver. Belinda and Jane were at the house taking deliveries of furniture, the carpets having been laid the day before. Tom and Tony spent the morning at the flat loading the van with boxes lovingly packed by Belinda the week before. They delivered this to the house on Clapton Hill before retiring to the pub for lunch. In the afternoon, Tom drove Tony to his parents' house where more of his and Belinda's stuff was being stored in the garage. At last all was delivered and the other three spent some time arranging the furniture and the beds while Tom took the van back to the hire company.

After as much was accomplished as possible, they went out for a meal and brought some drinks back to the house for a nightcap.

Belinda smiled warmly as she served drinks. " Thank you for your help, you two. At last I have a home of my own. It is getting late. Do you two want to spend the night here? We have the spare bed and it will not take long to find the sheets and make it up."

Tom was about to refuse but caught a look in Jane's eye which stopped him saying anything.

" That would be a good idea. It is after midnight and it would save Tom a drive home. I suppose we can borrow a toothbrush from you. Don't you think that is a good idea Tom?" Jane smiled a secret smile across the room to him.

Tom was surprised at the wistful glance Belinda threw in his direction but he smiled back at Jane. " I must admit the thought of a driving you home across town and then having to get back to my home is not very pleasant. I did tell my mother that I was not sure what was happening or how long I would be so they will not be expecting me. However, I will have to get up earlyish because I have an appointment with Mr. Hunt in the morning. Before I go to meet him, I will have to go home and change."

They sat up for a while drinking and talking about life, conscious of the fact that they did not have to work the next day. At last, Jane said she was tired and got up to go to bed. Tom followed ignoring the grin on Tony's face.

When they were alone together, Tom asked, " Why did you say yes when Belinda asked us to stay?"

Jane smiled. " Don't you want to go to bed with me? While you are in Porthampton you live at home with your parents like me. There is no way my mum and dad would countenance us sleeping together under their roof. I expect your mum and dad think the same. The only way we could ever sleep together all night would be if I come to visit you in Nottingham. The only problem with that is you have not invited me yet."

" Come off it Jane!" Tom protested intensely. " This is one of the few times I have seen you since we first went out together. I was going to suggest that you come up to stay with me in Nottingham if this weekend turned out OK. Besides I have no idea of your attitude to sex. For all I know you are one of those girls who think they should save themselves until they are married. If that is the case, you might have thought that an invitation to Nottingham would involve sleeping with me. In fact I have a camp bed in my flat which is used if I ever have visitors."

" You did not mention this when you phoned me those times," Jane replied smiling. " Enough of this. Lets go to bed."

They went to bed and made love for the first time. To Tom it was wonderful and he was lost to any other woman. To Jane it was a culmination of her dreams of the last three weeks.

In the morning Tom pushed Jane aside and went down to make a cup of coffee before going home to change.

Belinda was in the kitchen and she grinned at Tom.

" Did you sleep well," she asked mischievously as she filled the kettle and put it on to boil. " Cup of coffee?"

" It was a satisfying night and I feel relaxed now," Tom replied. Reaching out he pulled her close and kissed her. " Thanks for the offer of your bed."

" Don't mention it," Belinda's eyes were misty and she turned away quickly to make the coffee. Continuing in a small voice which Tom found hard to hear. " I only wish it could have been me."

Tom took the tray with coffee from Belinda and went this back upstairs to Jane. When he pushed open the door and entered the room, she was sitting up in bed, his sweater wrapped round her shoulders. She smiled broadly and as soon as the tray was on the bedside table, reached out and pulled Tom close for a kiss.

" I feel wonderful this morning. A pity you have to leave or we could lie in bed for the rest of the day," Jane gushed.

" Sorry Jane but I have to go," Tom kissed her back. " When you come to visit me in Nottingham in a few weeks, we can have a long lie in on the Saturday and Sunday."

"I will look forward to seeing you there," Jane replied. "What time tonight?"

"Seven thirty at your house. I will book a table at this restaurant I know out in the forest and we can sit and relax over a meal. See you then," Tom disengaged her arms, quickly drank his coffee and dressed.

Tom parked his car across the square from the Jack of Diamonds in the old district of Porthampton. The square was lined by a mixture of buildings from the small Tudor house next to an old church in one corner to the Georgian terrace on one side, the Victorian terrace on the other and the modern on the fourth where the old had been knocked down by the bombs during the war. In the middle of the Georgian terrace was the entrance to an office flanked by columns. A brass plate near the door announced discretely "Hunt Enterprises".

Tom pushed open the door and entered a large reception area which he surmised must have been the entrance hall of the house when it was privately occupied. Behind a large desk was a man dressed in a uniform who looked hard at Tom. Even to Tom's untutored eye, the man looked as though he would be an asset in a fight. By the bottom of a staircase sat another man in uniform pretending to read the paper. He also looked like he could hold his own in a brawl.

" Tom Houseman," Tom informed the man at the desk. He noticed out of the corner of his eye that the other man was no longer pretending to read the paper. " I have an appointment with Mr. Hunt at ten thirty."

The man looked Tom up and down before consulting a book on his desk. The other man came over and growled, " Do you mind if I frisk you?"

It was Tom's turn to look hard. " Yes I do mind. I came to see Mr. Hunt at his request. If that is how I am to be treated, he can go hang." With those words Tom turned on his heel and made for the door.

" Just a minute," the man behind the desk barked.

Tom turned back and faced the desk. " Are you going to keep me here by force? Next time I see Derek Jones I'll tell him how you treated me today. Besides I don't think Mr. Hunt will be best pleased if one of his perfectly innocent visitors, here at his request I might add, was assaulted such that the person drew the polices' attention to his office."

The man's expression softened and he looked nervously at Tom. The other man went back to his seat by the stairs. " Sorry sir but we have instructions from Mr. Hunt to make sure anybody we do not know is clean before we let them into the building."

" Do you do that with all his business visitors?" Tom asked innocently.

" No but we know his legitimate business people," the man replied. " We have never seen you before and you do not look like a business man."

" I will take that last as a complement," Tom grinned. " Now where can I find Mr. Hunt?"

" Up the stairs and to the left. There you will find his secretary's office. I will ring to tell her you are on the way." The man looked relieved.

As Tom reached the stairs, he turned to the man," What are you called?"

The man hesitated and then said, " Dave Oliver."

Smiling Tom remarked, " I will tell Derek how I was treated when I arrived here."

Whistling to himself, he climbed the stairs. Under the surface, he was thinking furiously. It was a question of whether he really ought to be associating with the sort of person who employed hard men to guard his office. It looked to all the world that Mr. Hunt was a dubious character, as Tom's mother would have put things. For

Derek's sake, he decided, he would see what Mr. Hunt had to say.

Tom had no more time to think more deeply because he came to the head of the stairs and turned left towards a door on the other side of the landing. He was aware of somebody watching him closely as he approached the door but he steeled himself not to look round. After knocking, he entered when a female voice bade him come in. A woman of about forty sat behind a desk in what could only be described as a medium sized office. She wore glasses and her hair was pulled severely back from her face in a bun. Dressed in a dark jacket with the collar of a white blouse over the lapels, Tom did notice that she had a full figure. Her smile however was welcoming, the first time since Tom had entered the building when he had felt he was wanted.

"Mr. Houseman?" she asked.

Tom smiled back. "Yes," he answered.

"I am Shirley, Mr Hunt's secretary. He told me to tell you he will be with you shortly. Have you had a coffee?"

"No. They didn't offer me one down stairs."

Shirley laughed as she went to a coffee machine in one corner. Tom noticed that she did have a full figure but her hips gyrated sexily. " It is very unlikely you will ever get a coffee from those bruisers down there in the reception. Take a seat and I will bring the coffee over to you."

About ten minutes later just as Tom was starting to wonder whether the wait was worth it, the buzzer on Shirley's desk went and she indicated for him into go through into Mr. Hunt's office.

The office was large, stretching across the whole width of the building. Overlooking the square was a large window though Tom noted this was covered with a thin lace curtain. From his observation a person could see out but not in. Mr. Hunt sat behind a large desk placed in one corner by the window, the desktop covered in leather. Three phones sat on the desk, one white, one red and one black. To the other side of the office were some easy chairs and a couple of settees. To Tom, the leather with which they were covered looked very expensive.

" Tom," Mr. Hunt greeted him getting up from his chair and coming round the desk to shake Tom's hand in a firm grip. " I am pleased you could come. How is your Ph. D coming along? Lets sit down over there and I will order a coffee or something stronger if you prefer."

Tom sat in one of the armchairs and as soon as Mr. Hunt had sat down, the door opened and Shirley came in carrying a tray with a percolator and some cups. She poured the coffee and, after asking Mr. Hunt if that would be all, left.

" I am waiting for my viva," Tom said. " My supervisor reckons it will pass."

" I am pleased to hear that," Mr. Hunter smiled once more but Tom noticed again not with his eyes. " I hear you had a bit of a run in with Dave Big Hands in the reception. I would be careful of him. He is reported to be the toughest man in Porthampton. I am sorry about that but we live in troubled times. There are other men trying to muscle in on my business and I have to take precautions."

" I accept that apology Mr. Hunt. I do not know what your business is specifically though I can guess. If Derek is working for you then I have a good idea that normal law abiding citizens would not like to know about what you do. I must admit though, you have managed to keep my friend out of prison for the last few years which is a bonus in itself. When we were sixteen I was convinced that he was going to end up in jail for much of his life. What is it you wanted to talk to me about?"

Mr. Hunt laughed out loud. " You are smart, Tom Houseman. Let us say that what I want you to do is legal and above board. You said when I met you in my nightclub that night that you thought there was money to be made out of investing in the road haulage industry if it is deregulated. I have a proposition to put to you. How long would it take you to put together a small report for me on the opportunities in the road haulage industry if it is deregulated??"

Tom stroked his chin. " I have all the relevant information. About three days I expect."

" I will pay you for four days at thirty pounds a day plus secretarial expenses." Mr. Hunter lent forward. " How does that sound?"

" Why?" Tom looked puzzled.

" I could say because you need the money but I won't." Mr. Hunter laughed. " What you told me the other week intrigued me. I have the money to invest and you say there is an opportunity. Anyway will you accept my offer?"

" You are very generous but yes I will accept your offer." Tom smiled and shook Mr. Hunter's hand. " It will be another month before I can deliver the paper to you. I have my Ph. D. viva in a couple of weeks so I will have to leave your paper until after that if that is all right with you."

" That is all right by me. I will expect the paper to be delivered to my secretary by the first of November." Mr. Hunter inclined his head. " Once it is delivered I will authorise the payment of your fee."

" I will have to declare my fee to the Inland Revenue," Tom observed. " I hope this is above board for you."

" This is one of my legitimate enterprises," Mr. Hunter replied smiling and spreading his hands on the desktop. " You go ahead and declare it. The fee will appear in the books of Hunt Enterprises as a legitimate payment. Any future advice I might ask you to give will go through the books no matter what the subject. Changing the subject. Why does your father not come to the remembrance day parade?"

Tom was taken by surprise by the change of subject and he felt his anger rising. " That is none of your business."

Tom was about to stand up but Mr. Hunt waved him back into his chair.

" It was meant as a civil question," Mr. Hunt stated bluntly. " I know your father was in the army during the war. He was a gunner in Italy and fought at Monti Casino very bravely from what I gather."

" How do you know this?" Tom asked equally bluntly.

" You are an intelligent man, Tom Houseman," Mr. Hunt's expression was bland. " In my line of business, do you think I would let anybody into my organisation without trying to find out something of their background? Why does your father not come to the Remembrance Day parade or to the Legion Club? "

" I don't really know," Tom observed choosing his word carefully. " All I do know is that when he came home, I was five years old and could not really remember him. To me, our family was my mum, my brother and I. All I had ever seen was a photo of my dad on the mantle piece. My mum used to sigh every time she cleaned it and tell me it was my father. When dad came home, I hid myself in the toilet and would not come out. He had to break the lock in the end to get me out. For years I never got on with my father and even now we are a bit distant to each other. I think part of the reason why he never goes near other service people was his resentment at missing his boys growing up. Then there was the work. He went away, fought in the war and watched his friends all die outside Monti Casino when his gun was blown up. He was in hospital for six months after the war and could not have any more children. When he finally got back, all the best jobs were taken up by those who had stayed behind. He was in and out of work for a while after the war until he found a job in the docks. Finally, I can still remember this although at the time I did not take too much notice of it. They sent his medals to him in a brown paper envelope with out even a thank you note. He threw them into the fire and swore that he would have nothing to do with them ever again. Mum fetched them out and keeps them hidden in her jewellery case."

Mr. Hunter was silent for quite a while after that. " I know how he felt," he said in a quiet voice. " That is one of the reasons why I ended up doing what I did. I was in the Royal Navy during the war. When it was all over, I took up this line of work because I was good at organising things. Getting back to my look into your background. I know you were recommended by Derek but even the most sophisticated of us can be fooled. Lets face it, Derek is not the most cultured or sophisticated of men. A very loyal and competent man but not cultured. Have you ever been to the opera?"

" Yes last week in London with my brother and his wife. Why?" Tom frowned.

" You see what I mean," Mr. Hunt laughed. " I could ask that question of Derek and he would not know what I was talking about. You and I could sit here and talk about more than the business and the football but I could not do that with most of those who work for me. I do that with the other pillar's of the community I associate with at the Lions and the Round Table. One other thing. I found out while looking into your background. I used to know your mother."

" When was that?" Tom felt his head spinning.

" Oh when we were children," Mr Hunt smiled wistfully. " Her father, Mr. Boyden owned the greengrocers in Clapton Road and my father owned the shoe shop just up the road by the post office. I was not called Hunt then. I was called Bernie Kowalski in those days. After the war I changed my name so that I would fit into this life better. Give her my regards when you see her."

" I will do that," Tom said getting to his feet. " I will have the report with your secretary in four weeks, Mr. Hunt."

They shook hands and Tom left the offices of Hunt Enterprises. Once back in his car, he sat for a while looking out of the window and not seeing anything. He was wrestling with what he could only describe as his conscience. Oh he knew that the money Mr. Hunt was willing to pay for what to him was not a great deal of work and even less any intellectual exercise was good value for what he had been asked to deliver. The money would help him live in that much better style than was usually the case for a university research assistant. It was what the money represented which prayed on his mind. He had no real knowledge of what Mr. Hunt and his men did. From the hints thrown out by Mr. Hunt and Derek, he could have a good guess. He wondered how many people had been hurt in some way, forced to do what they did not really want to do, swindled out of their hard earned money or hard armed into obeying Mr. Hunt so that he could get paid an inflated price for his services. If he took the job was he not taking part in Mr. Hunt's game? he asked himself. But, he replied to himself, if I am trying to help Mr. Hunt go legitimate, maybe he will not have to harm other people any more. With that thought, Tom started the car and drove home.

When he arrived home he told his mother of Mr. Hunt and she smiled at the memory. Yes she remembered Bernie.

Unlike most of her friends, he had been sent to the grammar school and gone on from there to university. After that she had lost touch with him.

For the rest of that year, Tom met Mr. Hunt one more time though he did write many reports for him and deliver these to his secretary in the offices by the old square without meeting the great man. It seemed that Derek was given the job of arranging with Tom for the reports on various topics. The pay was good and even though Tom's conscience did prick at times, he accepted the money gratefully.

Tom and Jane were invited to the wedding of Derek and Marlene at the Clapton Hill Parish Church and the Kings Hotel for the reception. During the reception, Tom and Jane were on the same table as Mr. Hunt and his wife. It was a pleasant meal and Tom was surprised at how cultured Mr. Hunt was. He talked to Jane about art, ballet and the opera. They swapped stories about the best and most awful concerts that had attended and what the coming season would bring. It was a world into which Tom could sink because no matter what else anybody might think about Nottingham, it was there that he had pursued his love of classical music and especially the opera. Though throughout their meal, dark thoughts did cross his mind of Mr. Hunt's organisation running scores of Madame Butterflies in the docks area of Porthampton. Once more he shut his mind to the deeper questions about Mr. Hunt and where he earnt his money, and indulged in the company of a very intelligent man.

He tried to hold onto the picture in his mind of Mr. Hunt at Derek's wedding but the fog came and engulfed him. Once more he let himself sink into the comforting arms of the night.

Chapter 3

The lights were dim, the breathing still loud and measured in the silence of the ward. The pinging noises coming from the machines echoed through her mind like the monotonous tone warning of dangers to come. Nurses and other medical staff noiselessly came and went. Each time they appeared, a doctor or a nurse would consult the machines, take Tom's pulse and write some numbers in the appropriate columns on the charts at the end of his bed. As they passed, they would then smile at Jane as though to give support before returning to the desk at the centre of the room to watch over the monitors connected to all the six beds in the room.

Jane, having lapsed into silence while a nurse was attending to Tom, struggled to start the one sided conversation with her husband once more. For a while she sat in silence unable to think of anything more to say. All evening as she waited fro Paul to relieve her, it had been like talking to herself while she sat alone by his bed. There had been a fleeting moments of hope when she had had a feeling that Tom was responding to her voice with small movements of his fingers. Was he aware that she was there sitting by his bed, praying that he would make some sign that he knew? she asked herself over and over again. Did he understand what she was saying to him? Was this all a waste of time?

Trying to suppress such thoughts, Jane sighed. The doctor had assured her this was the way she could help, by talking to Tom. There may not be much response, the doctor had warned her, but we know so little about the unconscious mind that talking will not harm him and will definitely help. Whether she believed the doctor or not, whether he was only giving her something to hang onto or by which to hope, Jane resolved to carry on.

" Do you remember the day we got married?" she began again, holding Tom's hand, her eyes fixed on his face as though willing him to acknowledge the sound of her voice. " You were so nervous that day. I could not understand why. For the short time I had known you, you did not appear to turn a hair while standing up at international conferences and talking to all those experts. I still cannot understand why you were nervous the day we got married. Did you think I would not turn up? There was little chance of that, you know. I had invested too much of my time in you all ready for me to have cold feet on my wedding day. Besides, I was so much in love with you. When I came to Nottingham on the train on Friday evenings, I was so excited every time the train came into the station. I often wondered to myself what I would do if you had not been at the station to meet me. I needn't of worried. Every time I came to Nottingham, you were there standing on the platform. Thinking about it now, your so called flat was so small but it was like a sanctuary to me. We could be alone there, just the two of us with nobody to tut tut at what we were doing. If we had stayed together at my home, there was no way we could have slept together. Parents did not condone that kind of behaviour in those days. It was not like we are now. Times have changed. Your mother and my mother would have a fit if it was suggested that Paul and his girlfriends slept together while they were at our house. It is accepted now and nobody really notices. It would have been anathema to our parent's generation. How times have changed."

" While I stayed with you in Nottingham, we could get up when we wanted and wander round without any clothes on and make love in the afternoon. There were not many of my friends who had that good fortune at the time. Most of them had to make do with making love in the back of a car or late at night when their parents were in bed. A few were lucky in that their parents went away sometimes and they could have the house to themselves. Even that was not easy because there were the brothers and sisters for most of us. You were lucky only being two children in your family. You had a bedroom to yourself. I had my three sisters all older than me and I had to share with Helen. By the time you came along, the others were already married and I did have a bedroom to myself. We laugh about it now but can you remember the time we made love in Ruth's house while we were baby sitting? I was petrified that John would wake up and wander into the lounge while we were on the settee."

" Our children are lucky. We recognised that they were grown up pretty early and if they invited a girl or boyfriend round, it was likely they were making love already. We made it plain that it was up to them. If they wanted to share a bed, we would not object. Funnily, Luke never had a girl in his bed. He always arranged for his girl friends to sleep with Mary in her bedroom when they came to stay. Now Paul was different. I cannot count the number of different girls he brought home with him."

" I always wondered why you agreed to act as your brother's agent in the seventy election when he was a candidate for Eastfield. I suppose you and Edward were always so close. You both went with your father to the football every other week. He never stood a chance there though. Even I knew that and I was not passionately interested in politics."

The mist and fog swirled about his head. He tried to break through, to grasp what the voice in his head was saying but each time he swam towards the light, the fog once more closed about his head. He knew the escape was there somewhere but he could not find it. Then once more the curtain parted and he could see.

Jane and Tom had agreed to get married shortly after going to Derek's wedding. Tom never knew whether it was auto suggestion from being at a wedding or whether they had just slipped into agreeing to marry as a natural progression of their relationship. After Christmas in nineteen sixty six, they had started to meet almost every weekend, either in Nottingham, preferred because Tom lived in a small flat, or in Porthampton. Later that spring, Tom had applied, and been successful in the interview, for a lecturing post at Porthampton University. Even though it was in the Business Department, the modules were to be transport management which suited Tom as a follow on from the subject of his Ph.D. He was to start in the August after finishing all his contracts and completing all his reports to various organisations and research councils on behalf of Nottingham University.

Lying in bed on a Sunday trying to put off the moment when Jane had to leave, Tom had asked her to marry him. After that every time they saw a film or play where the man got down on his knees, Jane reminded Tom that he it had not been like that with them. It was only then that they remembered they would have to tell Jane's parents. This, they realised was serious. Though their parents had tolerated Tom while he was Jane's boyfriend and only called at their house a few times and then not to stay for long, getting married was different. Jane's parents would have to invite Tom into their house more and he would become one of the family. Her sisters would have to be told. They felt he was not the same as them even though he had been to the same church before going away to Nottingham. Jane's parents remembered him as a bit of a rebel who was always in the thick of things whenever there was any trouble at the church. Her father could remember when the Reverend Williams had come to the Elders meeting and asked for the youth fellowship which met after the evening Sunday service to be disbanded. It appeared that Tom had brought a record of My Fair Lady to the fellowship and instead of studying the Scriptures they were all singing very loudly along with the record when the minister arrived after locking up the church. It would not have been so bad but they were singing, " With a Little Bit of Luck, we'll do no work". Well, that was so much against the Congregational ethic.

When they told them, reluctantly, because Jane was over twenty-one anyway, her parents agreed to go along with her marriage to Tom.

Once the marriage was agreed, they had found a house out in the Melbrooke area, the other side of the river dividing Porthampton from where Tony and Belinda lived. It was close to the university and on a direct bus route into the town centre through the parklands to the north of the town which suited them exactly.

The wedding went pleasantly even to the extent that the families seemed to get on well together. When he thought about it,

Tom realised that was down to Jane who treated everybody who was a friend of his as her friend, an attitude which she was to carry on through all of their married life.

Before they left for an almost unheard of, among their circle of friends, honeymoon in Spain, Edward had taken Tom aside. Tom was not sure he should let his brother interrupt his wedding reception but Edward insisted.

" I won't keep you long. Anyway Mum would kill me if she thought I was taking you away from your guests. When you get back from your honeymoon and are settled into your house, we must have a talk. There is something I have to ask you," Edward had smiled broadly when he said this.

Tom was intrigued but he forgot about the implications during the pleasures of his honeymoon.

When he arrived home and was settled into his new house, Tom phoned Edward to enquire as to what he had wanted to ask him.

" I am moving to Bishopstead soon," Edward had said. " I will keep a flat in London for those evenings when I have to work late but the family will be moving to Bishopstead. Freddy and Alexandria are excited about moving to a small village especially at the mention of riding horses. I am not so sure about Sarah. She is a big city girl really. I think she finally agreed because she has always wanted to live in the country. It's a vision she has of riding horses, village fetes and country pubs. She can continue with her job part time while the children are young. The company will send the work through to her there. As you know, her parents do have a holiday bungalow down in Widemouth in Cornwall so she has some idea of what it is like living outside the city. When we are established, you will have to bring Jane over for an evening drink."

" Why the sudden desire for the village life?" Tom asked bluntly knowing his brother was a great advocate of living in London. " You are always going on about how you like living near to London so that you can indulge in all that culture. Does having daughters make all that much difference to how you feel about your life?"

" No not really," Edward replied almost tentatively. " That is what I wanted to talk to you about. I will be adopted as the Labour Party Prospective candidate for the Eastfield constituency next week at a local party meeting in Eastfield Labour Club. That is what made us decide to move down there. I can commute to London and still have weekends and holidays in the constituency."

" How many votes do you honestly think you can garner from that constituency?" Tom was laughing. " They must have had to twist your arm to stand because nobody in their right mind would put up for Labour there."

" That is not quite the case," Edward answered seriously but there was doubt in his voice. " Besides, if one is to have a political future, one has to start some place or so I have been told. Most members of parliament had to run for the first time in a no hope constituency. As I was saying, it is not quite the case that this is a Labour desert. There is quite a bit of heavy industry in Eastfield itself which gives a solid Labour vote. I will have to try to build on that base."

" Well you have bought a house in the right place to do that," Tom chuckled. " Bishopstead is more conservative than Winchester and that is no exaggeration. You have as much chance of retaining your deposit as Father Christmas bringing you a present down the chimney this year. What did you want to ask me?"

" Well I would like you to act as my agent?" Edward asked.

" You have to be joking." Tom exploded with laughter. " I am the most academic of people with no organisational skills what so ever. Why do you think I married Jane? She is a genius at keeping track of everything. Maybe you should ask her to do it. On the other hand, that would not do you much good because she votes Liberal when she can."

" Please Tom, agree to be my agent," Edward pleaded.

" Before I agree, you will have to send me all the information on what this will entail," Tom replied. " Then I will have to get Jane to agree because once the election approaches, she will not see too much of me."

" We will make a good team!" Edward almost shouted with joy as though Tom had already agreed. " Once I have captured the nomination and that is really a foregone conclusion because I have the backing of many in the Eastfield constituency party, we will tell the regional officer that you are willing to be my agent. I think you will have to attend some training nights but that should not be too hard. Lets face it. The party will not be paying much attention to what is happening in this constituency either before the election or on the night. I have a feeling they will jump at the chance of you taking on the task as my agent."

" Wait a minute," Tom growled. " I thought you said that you were the prospective candidate all ready. When is the adoption meeting? Can I come along?"

" Next Wednesday at the Eastfield Labour Club," Edward informed Tom. " As a fully paid up member and my agent you will be allowed into the hall but not have a vote. Lets face things. The other candidates are left wing in the extreme so I have been told that I will walk the vote. Then we can call a meeting of the local party and set up an election committee if there are enough interested people. How does that sound?"

" I'll see you there at seven thirty next week, if Jane agrees," Tom answered.

It appeared to most people he had ever been aquatinted with during his life that Edward had always been interested in politics. He had confessed to Tom that his interest stemmed from a talk he had gone to, when he was only sixteen, given by the local Member of Parliament. The Member of Parliament had almost been in tears as he passionately talked about the closure of the local factory and what that would mean to the men employed there. Even though the fight had really been carried on by the trades unions, though even Edward had to admit in this case to little avail as the factory remained closed, it had been the MP's passionate plea for young people to get involved in politics that had inspired Edward. The idea of fighting for social justice was what motivated him. He had promptly gone out and joined the Young Socialists and the Labour Party. In contrast to his brother who appeared to favour the trades union movement rather than political parties. When Edward had married Sarah, it had taken a lot of persuading to get her to accept that he would spend some of his nights at Labour Party meetings. She wanted him to concentrate on his job as a stockbroker and earn a great deal of money so that they could move to a large house on the outskirts of London. The girls had come along and Edward slowly rose in the hierarchy of the company. Sarah and her family started to live a comfortable life. Their first row came on that day when Edward came back from a meeting and announced that he was putting himself forward for the candidates list for the next election.

Sarah was unhappy. She did not like the idea and made her views plain. She was settling into a pattern of life having left her job when she found she was pregnant before marrying Edward. Well, she had not exactly left her job. Advertising was a young industry and she had joined the firm of a friend of her father when she had left Oxford. It had been at Oxford that she had met Edward and, even though it was frowned on, taken him to her bed. It had been a complete shock when, despite taking the pill, she had become pregnant. Now she was unhappy that Edward who worked late most days in the City, arriving home after the girls were in bed, would be making life even more difficult by traipsing off to some small constituency to fight a seat which was not winnable. Besides, Sarah was honest enough to admit, the thought of having to mix with all those working class people put her off the idea. It was not that she was prejudiced, she told herself, but what would she be able to say to all those grubby people. They would have nothing in common. There would be silence at times as she strove to think of something to say.

When Edward announced that it was to be Eastfield where his name was put forward and that he had a great chance of winning the nomination, Sarah started to accept the idea. She finally agreed when Edward promised that they would move to a village called Bishopstead on the outskirts of Porthampton. From there he could commute to London and they would buy a flat in London so that if he worked late, he could stay the night. If Sarah wanted to visit London, she would have a place to stay over for as long as she liked. Besides, Edward assured her, the nearest private primary and junior schools have very good reputations.

Edward was obviously excited by the idea of fighting an election and that worried Tom. He thought he had a good idea of what made his brother tick. To Edward, it would be the excitement of fighting the election which would count, not the prospect of winning. Also his brother had a tendency to let other people take the strain, make all the awkward decisions and make the mistakes, while he stayed in the background until there was praise to hand out. Then Edward would step forward and bask in the adulation of success. Tom could see the next few years passing as he worked to secure a base of support only for his brother to swan down every so often and be the so called icing on the cake. Still, Tom thought, the chance of running an election campaign does not come along too often. I could treat it as an academic exercise.

After discussing the whole idea with Jane, he got her mocking agreement. All she asked was that he made an effort not to neglect his wife too much. Tom made a solemn promise even though deep down he knew it was going to be hard to keep.

Still rather ambivalent about his own motives, he found himself walking into the Eastfield Labour Club the following Wednesday evening. The man on the door looked at his party card and waved him into the club. A notice on the swing doors leading from the reception area told him that the adoption meeting was up the stairs in the meeting room.

An officious looking lady, dressed in a plain dress over her ample figure barred his way at the foot of the stairs. Her dress was buttoned up to her chin, her hair pulled severely back in a bun, no make up and big black rimmed glasses. Her arms were folded across her ample breasts and her whole attitude made clear that she would brook no arguments.

" Can I see your local party card?" she demanded her voice making plain she would not tolerate any nonsense, as she consulted a list. " I do not recognise you and you are not on my list."

Tom smiled. " I am not a local member," he answered truthfully. " I am a member of the Porthampton West Constituency, Melbrooke ward. I am Edward Houseman's brother and I came to see how he was doing."

The lady looked him up and down with a thin lipped frown. It looked for all the world that she thought he was trying to curry favour with her. By the way she stood, it was plain that he would not find her a push over. " The rules state quite plainly that only member of the constituency party are allowed in the meeting room. If you go to the bar, I will give you a call when the meeting is over. You can go up then."

Tom shrugged, understanding quickly he was not going to win an argument with this woman. " I will be in the bar."

It was silly and rather cowardly, he felt. It was obvious she was only obeying the rules and he did not want to usurp the little power she felt she had. Besides, he thought, if my brother is adopted, I might need her support in the future.

The bar was very quiet, a couple of men playing darts, a small group sitting talking and the steward. They all looked curiously in his direction when he walked in but soon resumed their activities. After taking his pint from the steward, Tom found a newspaper and sat in one corner to await the outcome of his brother's adoption meeting. Inside he raged at the petty official who had barred him from the meeting but on the surface he accepted the restrictions.

An hour latter the woman who had barred his entry into the meeting room came back into he bar. She looked around, located Tom and came across to speak to him.

" Mr. Houseman," she almost smiled this time, a smile which lit up her face, a characteristic which Tom had often noticed in big people. " The meeting is finished and your brother has been elected. You can go up now."

Tom nodded. " Thank you...."

" Doreen Michell," she replied.

" Thank you Doreen. I will go and find my brother."

When he arrived in the room where the meeting was taking place, he found about twenty people talking in groups among the rows of fold away wooden chairs. Edward was by the stage at the front of the room talking earnestly to two other men and a woman who Tom vaguely recognised. Seeing Tom, Edward waved him over. Tom made his way between the iron tubed framed and canvas chairs to join his brother.

" Come on in, Tom. You are late again I see," Edward grinned. " You never could meet me on time when we were boys."

" No, Edward, not late this time," Tom laughed. " I have been sitting in the bar having a drink waiting for the meeting to end. Doreen used her ample figure to bar my way. I suppose she was right. By the rules only local members have a right to be in a meeting to pick the prospective candidate."

" She is a formidable woman, Doreen Michell. I suppose it was the best for you to stay down stairs." Edward turned to the people with whom he had been talking. " Tom this is George Nesbitt and Caroline Hobbs. George and Caroline this is my brother Tom."

" Pleased to meet you," George Nesbitt, a small dapper man dressed in a sports jacket and trousers, said, holding out his hand. His neatly trimmed beard showed touches of grey and his handshake was firm. " I hear you have volunteered to act as Edward's agent?"

" Hello George," Tom said, shaking his hand in return. " Volunteered might not be accurate in some eyes but yes I have agreed to look into the possibility of me being his agent at the next general election."

" Good to have you on board," George replied.

" Hello Tom," Caroline Hobbs greeted him. She was a striking woman about the same age as Tom. Her full figure was just on the point of being chubby like Marilyn Munroe's and her brown hair was cut short to frame a round face with large violet eyes and generous lips. The lips were bowed in a welcoming smile and Tom remembered where he had seen her before. " It's been a long time since we last met."

" Hello Caroline." Tom smiled at the look on his brother's face. " I am surprised you remember me the way you were always brushing me off when we were teenagers. We must have a quiet drink sometime and reminisce about our innocent youth."

Edward grinned again. " It looks as though you two know each other. That's good. Caroline has agreed to act as secretary for the election committee. Its obvious you two will be seeing a great deal more of each other in the run up to the election, whenever that is. George has agreed to act as chairman of the committee and we have four volunteers from the floor as other members. Basil Weston, over there is to be the treasurer in charge of the money we raise. Obviously you will have to sign off the declaration of election expenses after the election so you will have to make sure the accounts are kept in the correct form. We are going to have a short meeting now and then work out how often we will need meetings after that."

The meeting was brief, only what could be termed a get to know session. The other members of the committee knew each other so in effect it was a get to know Edward and his brother. George Nesbitt was the political representative from the local branch of the Transport and General Workers Union. Caroline was introduced as the local party secretary and member of the Eastfield ward on the town council. Basil Weston, a local school teacher. Rodney Reed a shop worker. Doreen Michell making baskets in a factory. Howard Lomas, a boilermaker in the docks. Finally Brian Hopper, a fitter in the iron works.

" This is the committee to elect a Labour Member of Parliament for Eastfield, " Basil grandly stated, much to the amusement of Tom.

In fact, Tom was about to get his first taste of what the next few years would hold for him when he remarked truthfully, " There is no way in which we can win this constituency. We have to start from a position of honesty with ourselves. The best we can hope for is to increase the Labour vote over what it was at the last election."

" There is always a chance," Basil insisted gravely and Tom could almost see him striking a heroic pose on the barricades. " The people will come to their senses one day and see the error of their ways in voting Conservative. All we have to do is set out our socialist principles and they will come flocking."

" And pigs will bloody fly over this building," Tom stated flatly.

" Don't get my brother wrong, Basil," Edward interrupted quickly. " He speaks his mind bluntly no matter who he is talking to. He does not mean any offence. Of course we all support the Labour Party philosophy but he will state what he sees as the truth come what may. Let us face things squarely. If the Labour party thought there was any chance of an upset, they would have sent somebody far more experienced than me to fight this seat."

" I am sorry Basil if I have upset you." Tom smiled and shrugged his shoulders. " If I am to be the agent for my brother, I have to start with a realistic assessment of how we are going to make out in this seat. If we are going to be hard headed about our chances, we have to be honest with ourselves. That is where I was trying to start. Now, as agent, what I want from all of you is ideas of how we can get publicity for Edward over the next two or three years. First we have to make sure that every voter in the constituency recognises Edward as the Labour Party candidate. Then we will have to make sure they understand what message he is trying to get across to them. Collectively as a committee and with the support of any other volunteers, we have to convince as many working people as possible that what he is proposing is in line with the rest of the Labour Party and in their best interests. The second thing we have to do is decide where can we hold public meetings when the campaign proper starts. Once we have identified those factors, we can work out a strategy and allocate responsibilities to each of you and anybody else we think might help. In addition, we have to identify those willing to help in a passive way by stuffing envelopes and filling the halls for public meetings. Let us all go away and think about these things."

" Is there any other business?" George Nesbitt asked. As there was no response from the committee members, he concluded. " We will meet here then in a month to report back. Can you have the minutes posted to everybody by then, Caroline?"

" They will be out next week," Caroline sounded peeved by the unspoken suggestion that she would be tardy in getting the minutes ready. Looking round the table, she went on. " I have made an address book for you to all put your addresses in before you leave and telephone numbers if you have them. That way I can keep in touch.

" I declare the meeting of the election subcommittee closed," George collected up his papers and stood up.

They all adjourned to the bar and, once there, Tom found he was sitting next to Caroline after buying a round of drinks. She smiled when he took his seat though he was not sure whether a place had been saved for him by design or was an accident. Unless she had changed over the last ten years, he assumed it was not an accident.

Once they were all seated, she asked him what had happened since they went to the youth club together. Tom had to explain about University and how he had stayed after graduating to study for a Ph D and do some research. He then told her about Jane and how they had been married in the summer.

" Didn't that Belinda have the hots for you at the youth club?" Caroline had asked with a malicious grin.

" I didn't notice at the time, I must confess," Tom replied candidly, though he it did remind him how he had made love to Belinda the day he first went out with Jane. " There were other girls I was more interested in at the time. Funnily enough she met and married my best friend while I was at university. I was supposed to be the best man. I had my speech all ready and had put all the arrangements in place. I was even looking forward to chatting up the older bridesmaids. Then I broke my leg playing football and was in hospital at the time. They did send me some cake. Actually, I kept the speech but nobody has asked me to be a best man since. What about you?"

" When I was seventeen and working in Smiths, I met Melvin at a dance," she smiled at the memory. " He works in Briggs, the heavy engineering company here in Eastfield, as a turner. He wasn't very good at dancing but we laughed a great deal at his attempt after he asked me for a dance. We don't go out all that much to concerts though he did take me to see the Rolling Stones one year. He likes drinking, playing darts and fishing. He also works a lot of overtime when he can. We take our holidays in Butlins, which is nice. There that about sums up my life. What do you do for your holidays?"

" Jane and I had our honeymoon in Toremolenus in Spain," Tom answered truthfully. " I have been abroad most years with some of my friends from University. Also I have been to some foreign places giving academic papers to conferences."

" It sounds like a different world from the one I live," Caroline remarked wistfully her eyes having a distant look as though she was imagining he visiting all those foreign places.

Their conversation was interrupted by George asking about Nottingham where he had relations. Tom spent some time giving an account of living in the city and answering George's questions.

As he drove home through the light traffic and the slight drizzle, Tom mused to himself about Caroline. How did a vivacious, very pretty girl who all the boys chased after at the youth club turn into a woman who sits at home most evenings with her children waiting for her husband to come back from the pub? What is it in human nature that can change a person over the course of only a few years? Tom recalled the first time he had met Caroline.

He realised that at that time, she had stirred the first feelings of sexual attraction that he did not fully understand. Well he had not really met her. She had walked into the dusty church hall with a girl friend who now, try as he might, Tom could not picture. Tom was playing table tennis at the time and he could recall how he stopped playing to watch this girl walk through the hall. She had stopped by the stage to look around and see what was taking place. Her friend had made some remark and Caroline had laughed. She did not just laugh with her mouth but her laughter made her whole body move in an exciting way. Her blond hair was straight and cut such that it just reached the neckline of her dress. That dress was floral, flared at the skirt and with the hem just below the knees. The top was just low enough to give the suggestion of blossoming breasts that Tom had noticed for the first time in a girl. It was with regret that he resumed his game at the insistence of his friend.

For two years until she left when she was sixteen, as he knew now to go out with Melvin, Tom had, what could only be described as, hungered after her. As he realised now, it had been to no avail. Caroline had ignored all his attempts to get close. She did not exactly snub him, which at the time would probably have been kinder, just ignored him. No matter how he tried to manoeuvre himself close to her there always seemed to be other boys at her side. And so his first love had not been reciprocated. It could have left him scarred for life but university had proved a good rescuer and, besides it was not in Tom's nature to let set backs like that deter him.

After that first meeting of the election committee, Tom's life settled into a pattern over the next year. He had to learn about lecturing full time and the skill involved in keeping a group of eager minds interested in what he was saying for up to two hours at a time. It surprised him that he found the whole experience exciting especially mixing with the students. Jane joined in by getting him to invite his tutees round for supper and drinks one night, which seemed to cement a lasting relationship with the students. One of his new colleagues who had been lecturing for a good few years cynically remarked that the enthusiasm would soon wear off but Tom resolved to try to keep it up.

When called upon, he went to meetings of the election committee though not much was resolved because there was no hint of when the general election would be. All they could do was to arrange for

Edward to meet some of the important people in the Labour and trade union movement in Eastfield. George Nesbitt became invaluable in this because of his extensive contacts, introducing Edward and Tom to many local trade union and left wing activists. For a couple of weekends, Tom had to go to a conference to familiarise himself with the role of the election agent.

And so the time passed over his first year of marriage. Jane passed her finals and became a fully trained accountant. She got a job as a junior partner in Bowles and Martins, a large accountancy partnership in the town centre. Much to the surprise of both Tom's and her parents, no children ensued. They had been expecting grandchildren as soon as Jane and Tom had married. Jane had said she wanted to become established in her profession before there was an interruption to her career to have children and Tom agreed.

It was in the autumn of nineteen sixty eight that Tom had the first hint that it was not going to be plain sailing all the way to the election and beyond. He had been thinking that his help for his brother was straight forward when out of the blue problems arose.

George Nesbitt had arranged for Edward to talk to his union following a branch meeting one evening. The union met in a room above the Lord Nelson pub and when Tom and Edward arrived they were asked to sit in the bar while the business of the branch meeting was carried out. After an hour they were invited up to the meeting room. There were about twenty five people in the room including Tom noticed Caroline Hobbs.

After being introduced by George, Edward stood up and thanked the union members for allowing him to address them. " I want to talk to you about what the Labour government has achieved since it came to power in 1964. It had a hard time after all those long years of Tory miss rule. We cannot praise Harold Wilson's leadership enough. He has been a towering Prime Minister leading the country through troubled times. Did he not get us re-elected in nineteen sixty six with an increased majority? The Labour Government has instituted a series of measures that broadly reflect the changing social climate in Great Britain. These include the Sexual Offences Act that decriminalised homosexual practices above the age of consent. This was controversial but the government helped it to happen. In addition, there is the

Abortion Act, which legalised abortion under certain conditions and with which I have no quarrel."

"One problem we have had has been with the economy. Let us face things squarely. The pound had to be devalued in the end and maybe we should have devalued earlier but that is in the past. The government has had to take harsh decisions in the light of this like cutting some public spending. They have also suffered from rising unemployment. The government implemented a prices and incomes policy in an attempt to stop inflation growing out of hand. I say this now. I do not like the way things have progressed with the economy but circumstances often dictate what happens and the response that has to be put forward. Now things are starting to turn up and we can look forward to a period of faster growth and more public expenditure."

" I think we have to be careful of what we say and what we do in the run up to the next election. If we are not careful, we will let the Tories back into power again and we do not want that. There is a tendency in the Labour movement in hard times to fall back on old forms of expression that bear no resemblance to what is needed at those times. This was most clearly reflected at the last Labour Party conference. An organisation called Militant ran a headline in their newspaper after the conference saying that 'Almost three million votes were cast for an alternative socialist policy at the conference'. This was because a resolution was moved by Liverpool Borough Labour Party and seconded by Bristol North-East Constituency Labour Party calling for 'the taking into public ownership of the 300 monopolies, private banks, finance houses and insurance companies now dominating the economy, and producing a positive national plan anchored to socialist production'. This is a laudable aim but we have to work towards it step by step which is what this government is doing. I agree that the government has to work closely with the trades unions but together we will make all people in this country prosperous."

" Take education. I am a passionate believer that education holds the key to the emancipation of the working classes. All right you might say that my brother and I have been lucky in taking advantage of the grammar school system. My father as some of you might know is an electrician working in the docks. I think the system has to change. There are many of my friends who given the chance would have thrived in a better education system. With this aim, the government is pushing forward with the implementation of fully comprehensive schools in this country. All the old grammar schools will have to comply or go private. We are doing away with the eleven plus. What matters is that every school pupil has the right to attempt through education to reach their full potential. Every child with the ability should have the chance to go to university irrespective of their financial circumstances."

" With this in mind, I suggest that two issues characterise the ideal pursued by the pioneers of comprehensive education in the United Kingdom. First, there is the notion that for all children education should be accessible regardless of capacity or background. Second, there is the notion of that what is taught enhances the future lives of the pupils."

" What I would help you all to do is work with me to get the largest Labour vote that is possible in this constituency. Only if something catastrophic happens to the Tory candidate will I have a chance to win. Obviously we will pray that something does happen but I have entered this fight in a realistic frame of mind. I can see some of you looking rather bemused by my comments. I say again we have to be realistic about our chances. What we have to do is deliver a resounding Labour vote so that the government is re-elected and the Tories are shown that there are people in this constituency who do care about what happens to working people. Thank you all again for inviting me. I will take any questions if that is all right."

A short thin man with long hair sitting in the front row put his hand up. George, as chairman, introduced him as Mike Pearce, a member of the boilermakers union.

" Mr. Houseman, welcome to Eastfield from your usual position in the City of London," Mike Pearce started in a gravely voice with a distinct Geordie accent which sounded out of place among the southern accents of all the other people in the room. " As you might be able to tell I came here from Sunderland to work in the ship repair industry. What is your opinion on the governments proposals we all hear about on industrial relations?"

It was dropped like a bombshell into the silence of the hall, a question which only many years later Tom realised was the start of a break with his brother. Now it all seemed perfectly innocent.

"There are necessarily conflicts of interest in industry today as there have been for many years," Edward began tentatively. " Any objective of an industrial relations system should be to direct the forces producing conflict into forming some kind of consensus about what is required from industry. This can be done if the government, the trades unions and the employers get together and devise a system which minimises conflict. The proposed system gives the Employment Secretary powers to impose ballots on union members before a strike can be held. There would be a form of overall board which would have the right to impose settlements if there was no likelihood of an agreement. This will in my opinion strengthen the industrial relations system without doing away with the best aspects of the existing system of collective bargaining."

" Bollocks," Mike Pearce swore. " What you are saying is so much shit. It is making the ordinary working man a slave to the employers. The trouble with you is you are a social justice person rather than a socialist. We have to nationalise all the means of production, the places where all the money is made like the banks and not allow foreign money men to take away our currency. I fail to see how we can be represented in this constituency by a man like you. Brought up in the privileged background of a middle class family, sent to a grammar school and then onto Oxford, how can you know what the working class are thinking?"

Edward struggled to remain outwardly calm. " I must remind you that I was elected to be the prospective parliamentary candidate for the Eastfield constituency according to the rules. I gained a majority of votes more than all the other candidates put together. Now you might not have been at the nomination meeting for some reason or you might have been there and voted against my candidacy. I have no way of telling because I was not present, as the rules state, when the vote was taken. My background is working class. My father is an electrician who works in the docks in the same manner as you. We might have lived in a house owned by my father and mother but most of my friends when I was growing up lived on a council estate next door. I passed the eleven plus to get a place at the grammar school. I had to work hard to pass that exam in a school where not many of the pupils ever went to grammar school. While at the grammar school, my parents made great sacrifices to make sure I got through and obtained the best qualifications I could attain to. The same goes for my brother. Are you saying I should have ignored my intelligence and left school without qualifications? Is that how you want everybody to be? Where is the progress for the working class in that?"

Phil Houseman had swept Betty Martin off her feet when they met in the early days of the depression. He was handsome with swept back blond hair and danced almost as well as Fred Astaire or so she thought. He worked as an electrician in the docks and though times were hard, seemed to Betty to be well off. Though he had left school like many of his contemporaries at fourteen, he was intelligent and well read. He had definite opinions about the world and how it should be run. The main thing he had proclaimed to her on numerous occasions was fairness. Wealth has to be spread around. The workers do as much if not more than the bosses to accumulate the wealth, therefore they should have their fair share. He was a passionate trade union member and went to all the branch meetings. He was so thunderstruck when Edward came along that he worked all the hours he could in those hard times to provide a comfortable home.

Then came the war. He was called up and had to leave his pregnant wife behind. When he came back six months after the war had ended, he was a different man. No longer the fun loving, out going personality but withdrawn inside and seldom saying very much unless he had to. He was most upset that his youngest son who he had never seen appeared to take an instant dislike to him and ran away to hide when he finally came home. He kept his hurt buttoned up inside and went looking for jobs. It was hard and he resented the fact that while those who stayed behind had secure jobs after the war, those like him who had gone away to suffer the anguish and fear of war on the front line were seemingly passed over for work when they returned. Silently he searched for work never mentioning his suffering in the war, throwing his medals in the fire rather than wear them and touch his forelock to the bosses who were to him the only winners from the war. He would not go and stand near the war memorial with these other people on remembrance Sunday, content to spend the day in his garden shed tinkering. Not that he forgot his friends who had fallen as his comrades fought their way up the spine of Italy. He had been wounded at Monte Casino but all the rest of his gun crew had been killed. On arriving home he found out that one of his brothers had been killed on a convoy to Malta while another was in a camp in the Far East. His father had been killed in an air raid. He did not speak of the war and what had happened even to his family. Whenever he met his brother Brian who was scarred for life by the Japanese, they talked of work, football and politics but never of the war.

Most people who knew him thought he was very left wing, hated the bosses and wanted more money given to the ordinary working man. That was somewhat belied by the fact that he used the compensation money for his father's lost business along with some money of Betty's to buy a detached family house in a quiet street. When Tom was almost ten, they made up their differences. What happened was Phil came to watch his son play football for the school and ended up shouting and cheering like the other parents. On the way home for the first time Phil had put his arm round his son's shoulder and to Tom it was a wonderful thing. They had been quiet companions ever since.

It was also through his father that Tom had found his love for opera. I had always laughed at people who would listen to screeching women, he had told his son.

Then Phil had experienced the opera in Italy while he was recovering from his wounds after the battles had finished. Until I sat through a whole opera in Milan, he had told his son, I did not realise it was magic. When his father was doing jobs round the house, he used his wind up gramophone to play arias from the operas from his record collection. Though Betty frowned and Edward refused the invitation, Phil took Tom to see an opera by touring opera company in Porthampton when Tom was a teenager. From that night, Tom was lost. From the moment the lights went down and the orchestra started to play, Tom was hooked. He cried when Violetta left the country house and when she died. Ever since, Tom had gone to see the opera whenever he got the opportunity accompanied by his father if possible.

Mike Pearce had made one mistake and that was to attack Edward's father but he now compounded that further. " You would say that wouldn't you? I struggle every week to make ends meet while the bosses surround themselves with luxury. Why do they get all the rewards? It's not them who do any of the work. They sit in their offices and watch us get ground down by hard manual labour. These proposals are there to give the bosses even more power and to push the faces of the working man further into the mire."

Edward smiled. " We are not going to get any agreement on this. I do think you are wrong. There is a need for rules to govern relationships between the worker and the employer. That is what the government are trying to do so that everybody knows where they stand and industry is not constantly interrupted by strikes."

There were other questions from the floor which Edward was able to handle easily. Throughout the rest of the evening, Mike Pearce stared at Edward and did not clap at the end. With friends like that we will not need enemies, Tom thought as he left the room.

It was pouring down with rain outside and after saying good-bye to his brother, Tom found himself standing next to Caroline in the doorway to the pub ready to make a run for the car.

" How far away do you live?" Tom asked.

" Oh about half a mile down that way," she replied pointing off into the rain.

" Can I give you a lift home?" he asked uncertainly.

" That would be nice," Caroline answered smiling. " It will save me getting wet."

Caroline lived in a two storey block of flats just off the main road to Porthampton. It was one of those new blocks made up of concrete slabs, very functional and very nineteen sixties.

When they drew up outside, Caroline said," Will you come in for a coffee?"

Tom smiled wistfully but answered," I had better not disturb your husband and the children."

Caroline smiled shyly. " There is nobody at home. Melvin is not at home. He has been sent away to Liverpool to do a job for a few days. My sister took the children to stay the night at her house. So you see I am all on my own so you won't be disturbing anybody. Come on up and we can talk a bit over a cup of coffee. I would like that."

Tom hesitated. He could not make up his mind whether there was a hidden meaning in her words or not. Finally, mentally shrugging his shoulders, he got out of the car and followed her into her flat. It was a small flat, a bedroom on each side of the entrance corridor, the sitting room further into the flat, a bathroom on the left and the kitchen at the end. Tom did notice that there were bunk beds in one of the bedrooms and he took this to mean that this was the children's room.

Caroline waved him into the lounge and told him to sit while she made the coffee. The room was conventionally furnished with a settee, two armchairs, a sideboard, a dining table with fold down leaves with four chairs and a television in one corner near the gas fire. The carpet square showed a foot of polished floor round the edge of the room.

When she came back, they sat and talked quietly about how life had treated them since those days at the youth club. By prompting each other, they remembered people they both knew but had lost touch with. When they could they updated the news but the subject was soon exhausted because most of the people they had known had moved long time ago.

There was one thing Caroline did say which made Tom think. " Tom Houseman, no matter what you and your brother might say, you were never working class. No don't protest because I expect you know what I mean. Your parents made sure that the two of you were always striving to better yourselves. As far as I can recall, there was never any talk of either of you getting a working job. You were very well mannered and ate off china plates with linen table clothes. Your mother would have nothing to do with the man selling things on tick. No you were not working class. You might be left wing labour but you are not working class socialists."

Tom laughed. " You might be right, I suppose. Working class and middle class are not about money but about attitudes to the way life should be lived. My Dad was left wing labour but his politics were grounded in the trades union movement far more than in political parties. He wanted workers rights and a fairer share of the financial cake. He actually thought the same way as Mike Pearce about workers earning the wealth and therefore having a right to a bigger share but he was not so dogmatic about nationalisation."

Caroline smiled and moved to sit on his lap. She kissed him and he responded. They made love there in her lounge with the photos of Melvin and her children looking on. And so after twelve years, Tom finally made love to his first flame.

As he was leaving, he asked Caroline why she had not liked him when they were at the youth club together. She had laughed and told him that he had been too argumentative during those years. You were the only person I knew who could pick an argument in an empty room, was her last remark.

For the next eighteen months the time passed slowly as Tom divided his attention between his job, his wife and his brother. At times it was difficult when the various parts clashed but in the main he managed to keep matters stable and uncontentious. Now that Jane had qualified, they were reasonably well off in comparison to most of their friends though not as wealthy as Tom's brother. During this time, Tom's probation at the university ended and he was appointed to a permanent post with the grand title of Lecturer in Transport Management. As part of his contract, he was given the task of looking after the admissions process for recruiting students to the department a task which he found rather burdensome. It was having to make choices between prospective students which worried him. Often he would sit at his desk after rejecting a candidate thinking about the effect his decisions would have on those young peoples futures. Oh some were easy because they had not fulfilled the criteria but it was the marginal ones which concerned him. He could not be anything but strict because there was a definite limit imposed by the university administration on the number of students each department could recruit.

Thus time passed and finally Harold Wilson called the general election for the eighteenth of June nineteen seventy.

The decision of the Prime Minister to ask the electorate to pass judgement on the Government had not come as a surprise. For months before the announcement, Tom had been working on a strategy for his brother's campaign. To this end, he had organised the committee into policy areas surprising everybody by asking Mike Pearce to help him draw up the personal statement of Edward's which would go on the leaflet for distribution around the constituency. Caroline was to put together an itinerary of where they would make their efforts over the course of the campaign including the booking of rooms for set piece speeches. George was going to organise the canvassing. Doreen was given the task of getting together a team to stuff the leaflets and other information into envelopes. Howard and Brian were to get as many people as possible to put posters in their windows and organise the lifts for those who needed them to the polling stations on polling day. It was emphasised by Tom that any committee member could recruit from the ranks of the local party any other person who might help in the weeks leading up to polling day.

It surprised Tom, that he and Mike appeared to agree on what had to be done. Tom had reasoned that Mike would be a help in writing the personal statement and give Edward some ideas of what to include in his speeches because he was closer to the grass roots of the party. This was vitally important when Edward was out talking to his constituents or while out canvassing, even though they could come to a consensus it did not mean that they agreed on over all philosophy or on what the wanted from the party over the long term. At first they had some wonderful arguments about policy, but they finally agreed what was needed for this election.

" We have to emphasise the positives and down play the negatives," Tom had remarked rather grandly as they sat in the bar of the Labour Club the first time they had met to exchange ideas.

" That depends on what we mean by positive and negative," Mike had smiled for the first time since meeting Tom. To Tom, Mike had always given the appearance of being one of those very earnest fanatics who found life so serious that there was never any time to smile.

"Well that is why I ask you to help me," Tom smiled back. "I know we don't see eye to eye on a great many things this government has done or in your case not done. We do agree that there is a need for the government to be elected again."

"I'll go along with that," Mike grimaced and shook his head. "I might think that this government has not gone far enough in the redistribution of wealth and have let the rich get richer but I would hate to think what it will be like if we have a Conservative government. I'll tell you what. You emphasise the positives and I will outline what I think are the negatives. Then we can argue from a basis of how we think differently."

"There are some positive achievements to its credit." Tom started to list these by tapping his fingers on the table top. "The amount of money spent on education has been increased in real terms which should be to the benefit of our children. There has been an increase in comprehensive education ideas. We have let some people gain the freehold to their properties. We nationalised the steel industry in nineteen sixty seven and ended the casual labour system in the docks. The government has started to end discrimination in pay with the equal pay act. I know to my cost that the government introduced the breathalyser to cut down on drunken driving. I remember it well because we hired a mini bus to go for a drink that first weekend though since we have designated one person to drive and stay sober. Working people in trouble who can't afford legal fees can now benefit from legal aid. The social security system was reformed and earnings related unemployment benefit was introduced. Lastly we gave the vote to eighteen year olds. There that is a rundown of some of the achievements."

Mike grimaced. " There were a lot of hopes in ordinary working people when the Labour party was elected in nineteen sixty four. Many of my friends both in the party and outside thought there was going to be an era of redistribution of wealth in the next few years. We are the people who create the wealth after all. All the bosses do is sit on their fat arses and watch as we sweat and die for their profits. Surely, I thought, something will be done about the iniquity in society. Well, since then a great many labour voters have been disappointed. There have been factory closures and unemployment has risen to two and a half percent of the working population. Ordinary working people are once more bearing the brunt of the failure of the government to provide jobs. Not that the wealthy mind. They are still earning good money or abandoning the ship to go abroad. Even though they have been educated here by the taxes paid by working people, they do not want to give anything back. Prices have been rising, the government has been forced to cut the welfare system and introduce an incomes policy. All these measures hit the poor more than the rich because they live from day to day and cannot make plans which allow them not to pay taxes. There was the much publicised national plan which came to nothing. As you can see, the impression given by that list is that the government has failed to live up to expectations."

" What shall we tell him then?" Tom was trying to avoid an argument.

Mike grinned. " Look Tom I want a Labour government returned as much as you so we have to hope that during a new parliament they will pass much more radical policies. For now we have to emphasise the positives and play down the negatives, as you. say. We will have to give him something to warn people about the Tories and what will happen if they come to power. They will use the economy and prices as the main areas of policy on which they will fight the election. Heath is already talking about inflation with an increase of two percentage points in May. It is a good ploy to talk about a "shopping basket election". I think they are going to keep hammering on about the tribulations of the housewife in party political's and on the doorstep. We will have to counter that somehow."

" We have it on good authority according to the polls that Heath is not popular with the voters. How could anybody feel comfortable with anybody who has such an obvious false smile? There is also the Enoch question. He is an embarrassment to the Tories with his stirring up of racial hatred." Tom looked full of conviction.

His certainty about the advantage of the race card was shattered by Mike. " I would not be too quick to pick up the problem of Enoch Powell, Tom. There are a lot of working men out there who agree with him. They do think there are too many immigrants coming into this country and taking their jobs, they do feel that these people are different in both their colour and their culture. There are people I work with who feel that black people are inferior and should be treated as such. For them, Powell speaks about things in a way which other people in politics might think but are not allowed to say. I know his intolerance of immigration and his opposition to race relations legislation got him the sack from the shadow cabinet but as I say many working people believe what he says. They are worried that there will be race riots like they have in the States unless immigration is stopped and black people are sent back. I am on your side as far as this is concerned but we have to remember there are a great many working men who applaud Powell."

" What happens if the subject comes up on the doorstep?" Tom could not leave the subject alone.

" He will have to use the party line about valuable workers and workers rights to live peaceful lives," Mike answered.

They worked on Edward's personal statement for the rest of the night and had the copy to the publisher the next day. They agreed with Wilson's strategy of four years before when he had to win the support of the floating voter. As the campaign progressed they were buoyed up by the opinion polls which seemed to indicate that Labour was ahead. The Tories under Edward Heath attacked over the economy and the running of the country. They pointed out that the Labour government had had to devalue the pound in nineteen sixty seven and the laughable attempt by the drunken George Brown of implementing a National Plan. Edward Heath was a passionate European and he derided Wilson for getting the French to refuse our entry attempt into the European Economic Community. Edward had to fight these battles on the doorsteps and in his set speeches. Canvass returns from George seemed to indicate that despite the problems of the national campaign, Edward was holding his own in Eastfield.

Two days before the election, Tom walked into the constituency head quarters to find all was gloom and doom.

" What has happened?" he asked Mike who was sitting in a corner deep in conversation with Caroline.

Mike shook his head. " Why the bloody hell couldn't they have kept these figures until after the election?"

" What figures?" Tom felt his stomach muscles tighten as he waited for the obvious bad news.

" The balance of payments have gone thirty one million pounds into the red. This means that interest rates will have to rise. It is not good, especially when added to the unemployment figures." Caroline looked worried. " Its not helped by that idiot Callagan's warning that if things carry on like this we might have to impose a wage freeze. What the hell was he thinking about?"

" We can't do much about that," Tom tried to lift their gloom. " It is up to Roy Jenkins to counter any effect of the balance of payments on our living standards. He did a good job last week of planting in the voters minds that the Tories will have to put up VAT to twenty percent on many goods to pay for their income tax cuts. We still have to fight this seat. According to George we are increasing our share of the vote. We have one last rally in the school tomorrow night and then it is up to the voters. Come on. I want every one of you to get out there and make sure we have a good turn out of our supporters. That way the local press will report that our support is growing."

And so the campaigning came to an end as the polling stations closed. Tom's people who had been manning the polling stations drifted back to the campaign head quarters until they were all there. They sat around drinking coffee and waiting until they were due in the Town Hall for the count. The talk was of the national campaign and whether there had been a shift to the Tories. Everybody agreed that the campaign had been about the leaders and had had a truly national focus. They had all watched on television as Harold Wilson and Edward Heath had headed the morning press conferences. Like any loyal foot soldiers though they might have private misgivings about the campaign, they all agreed that Harold Wilson had won the personality battle acting like he did as the Prime Minister. Wilson had spent a great deal of time visiting party workers throughout the country making sure as much as possible that these visits were televised. He came across as an ordinary person in contrast to the stiffness of Heath and displayed a ready wit. Jeremy Thorpe was seen as a flamboyant prep school prefect and dismissed out of hand.

Tom instructed Edward to go back home while they watched the early part of the Eastfield count which he calculated would not start until midnight. With a grin, he arranged for Caroline, George and Mike to come with him to the Town Hall to watch the ballot boxes arrive and asked the others to come later so that they would have enough people on the ground to watch the count.

Not long afterwards, Tom stood on the balcony at the Town Hall looking down at the scene below. There were tables laid out in rows on the dusty floor as though ready for some Mad Hatter's Tea party with the returning officer scurrying around like some demented White Rabbit. In his mind Tom could almost hear the returning Officer muttering, ' We are late for a very important date.'. Other people milled around giving the impression to those watching that there was no organisation, no plan to tackle the counting. As though by some mystical signal, orderliness developed out of chaos. The people milling around suddenly formed ranks and took their seats along one side of the tables. In through the back boor to the room came the sealed black boxes and as the returning officer inspected each seal and the accompanying documents, excitement mounted. The black boxes, once cleared by the returning officer, were carried to the tables and the contents emptied onto the tabletop like so many large snowflakes.

Turning to Caroline, who was standing so close at his side he could detect the slight tremor of excitement in her thigh, he said. " Now it begins. Get them all posted strategically around the tables. Call me if there are any disputed papers."

Caroline grinned and kissed his cheek briefly. " Aye aye Captain!" She hurried away down the stairs.

Tom stood on the balcony but he did not see much of what was taking place on the floor below. He was thinking, looking through a mist at evidence of all the effort his team had made. It was all over. He had fulfilled his promise to his brother and managed to get them through the campaign without too many disasters. In a strange manner, he was happy. Oh, he knew they had lost the election so he should be sad and bemoan all the supposed wasted effort they had expended. He remembered a film he had seen once where soldiers were given the task of piling stones up into a hill and then dismantling the hill only to start once more. It had been a little like that when they had started on this journey. They had tried hard, some had pretended that they could succeed but in reality as in the charge of the light brigade they knew their efforts were doomed to failure from the start.

Tom could not help smiling. Ah, he thought, at this point I would ask my students what constituted failure. In the same way that philosophers down the ages had argued about the meaning of life, the answer was not easy to define. It depends on the standards set at the start, he could hear Mike Downs one of his students arguing. Success can only be measured by the objectives set in the beginning. That is trying to apply business principles to an election and it will not stand up. There is only one way to measure success in an election and that is if your candidate was elected. The whole point of the exercise is to gain power. Without power ones philosophy and ideas cannot be put into practice.

Given all of that, Tom could not help smiling. During the election campaign, he had welded together a significant fighting force from people so different in outlook as George Nesbitt and Mike Pearce. George a traditional working man with traditional Labour values and Mike sprung from the new militant brand of Labour intent on taking the wealth and power from the establishment. They had all worked together and the word on the street and from the polling stations was that they might have increased the Labour share of the vote.

Then Tom sighed as he realised that Edward's increased share of the vote might be the only bright beam in an otherwise rather gloomy night. Doreen Mitchell had pulled him aside at the club as he left for the Town Hall and informed him that by all measures like opinion polls and exit polls the Labour Government showed every sign of losing the election. Of course she could not be certain but that was the dreadful rumour.

His thought were interrupted by the arrival of Edward into the hall. For the rest of the count, Edward tried to appear buoyant in the face of Tory smirks but as the count progressed and news filtered through, it was obvious they had lost the election. Still, Tom told his brother after the count was finished, we increased our share of the vote.

When Tom arrived home the next morning as the sun was rising over the rooftops and the dew was settling on all the lawns, the house was in darkness. Making himself a coffee, he drank this as his mood darkened at what was being said on the television. Then with a sigh as though the whole world had gone wrong, he rinsed his cup and went to bed.

When he slid beneath the duvet trying not to disturb Jane he realised how tired he was. Jane however murmured and turned to kiss him.

" Hello Tom. I have waited for you to come home. Oh I am not complaining but I have such news. I went to the doctor today and he says I am pregnant."

As Tom remembered those moments, the dark came up once more and he was sinking and then there was nothing.

Chapter 4

As the night wore on and the shadows seemed to get darker, Jane thought she saw a movement in Tom's eyebrows as she stopped speaking. With an audible sigh, she rejected the very idea of a response from Tom as a quirk of the dim light or her over vivid imagination. Blinking, she asked herself if she was getting like a drowning woman clutching at straws. Yes, she thought, it is like drowning. There is nothing I can do but struggle on while all the time the steady beat of the machine and the lack of any sign that Tom was conscious closed over her in the same way as the sea must close over the head of a drowning woman.

She bowed her head and placed her hands on her temples. Without any other support, she almost shouted out loud at her God to help her. All those hymns she had sung with hope in her heart, up lifted by the words. All those prayers she had intoned to support other people. Now she needed help and there appeared to be nothing. But he does seem to be peaceful and I have this desire to help. How could she continue to sit like this at his bedside when there was no response? she asked herself over and over again as though the needle was stuck on one of those seventy five records on an old gramophone.

When she looked up, taking her hands from her head, nothing had changed. Still the measured breathing with the small gasp at the end as though he was struggling to say something to her. Still the various sounds coming from the machines attached to him with wires. Still the nurses came every few minutes and wrote things on the pad at the foot of the bed. There is no sense to this, she told herself again. The doctor had told her to talk to him. No matter what the response. It can only do some good. It must be like this when a comedian flops on stage. No reaction, just a one sided conversation with no reaction from the audience.

Give me a sign, just one small show of understanding. Just a sign that you are in there somewhere Tom. Laugh! Goddamit laugh like I have seen you when something has struck you as funny. Throw back your head and laugh. If not laugh then rant against the cruel world and all those unfortunate people as though the conscience of the world rested on your shoulders. Do this for me Tom so that I can see some point in this talking.

Jane could contain herself no longer. She swept to her feet and walked away from the bed but there was no window through which to see the outside world. The nurses at the ward station looked and smiled faintly. But it was not enough and something drew her back to the bed where the person she cared about more than anybody in the world lay for all she knew dying.

What can I talk about, Tom? she thought as she regained her chair. We are such ordinary people. We have never done anything to really stir the fabric of history. Nobody will write about us or compose ballads as they do in those fantasy novels you read. So what can I talk about?

" Isn't it amazing. Paul will be twenty eight this year. It only seems like yesterday when he was born."

There was light above him and the all encircling darkness was giving way before his eyes once more. He strove towards the light but he could not move. Could not rise up. It was frustrating because he was almost there. A noise was constantly buzzing in his ear as though a fly had been caught in his prison. Then buzzing slowed and he could hear words.

Suddenly, he was back in his home the evening after the election count. He sat half watching the television impatiently waiting for Jane to return from work. Before he had had a chance to talk to her about her news, Jane had kissed him that morning and left him sleeping and dozing. But she had said she was pregnant. He, Tom Houseman was to be a father.

All that day after he had showered to bring himself fully awake, a joy rang out in his head. It was as though a veil had been drawn back and the world had taken on a brighter, more vibrant hue. Pulling back the curtains of his bedroom after he had dressed, he found the sun shining from an unclouded sky and birds singing perched on the branches of the shrub in the front garden.

Like Julie Andrews standing on her mountainside, he wanted to burst into song. He wanted to tell the whole world. He wanted everybody in the world to know. He wanted to stand on the tallest hill and shout as loud as he could. Jane, his life, his love, was pregnant. He, Tom Houseman was going to be a father. But Jane, through his drowsiness that morning, had impressed on him that she wanted to hold this just between them until it was absolutely established that she was pregnant.

There was only one snag to his feelings. He could not sing. Well, he could not sing like Howard Keel or Julie Andrews. Tom still smarted at being the only boy excluded from the final year choir at the junior school when the school was visited by some Duchess or other. The headmistress had come into his class one morning when they were practising their song for the Duchess. Frowning, she demanded to know who was singing flat. Then dread of all dreads to a ten year old schoolboy, like a battleship at full steam, she had marched down the aisle between the desks and singled him out. Without asking his permission or saying a word, she had taken his arm and marched him out of the classroom and back to her study. We cannot have the Duchess' ears assaulted by your awful singing, she had stated flatly as he stood bemused before her desk. While the choir is practising you can help me, she told him firmly. Tom remembered how terrified he was to have to report to this fierce some woman's study whenever the choir was practising. Children are cruel and though he was small, he had had to fight many a boy to keep up his honour. Even with that memory ringing in his head, that day he had heard that Jane was pregnant, he sang. 'Oh what a beautiful morning' rang around the house at full volume while he worked.

That feeling of joy and the desire to burst into song at any moment, sustained him over the weeks following Jane's good news. It took all his will power for Tom to refrain from telling his friends and work colleagues about his baby. The subterfuge did not stop him from being happy. His friends must have known something was happening but diplomatically nobody said anything.

Even realising that the Labour Party had lost the election, did not stop his happiness. Oh, Tom knew it was sad but the joy of his future buoyed him up like a life raft to a drowning sailor. He tried desperately to put on a serious face at the post election meeting which Edward called to see what lessons could be learnt from their campaign.

George took the defeat as a personal insult as though somehow he had been tested and found wanting. Caroline blamed herself or more precisely people like her for not turning out in greater numbers. Mike blamed the government for being too right wing and not pushing a left wing enough agenda.

" How could we lose seventy seven seats in parliament?" Edward had asked looking as though the world had come to an end. " That Heath now has a majority of around thirty."

" Because we fought the wrong fight!" Mike burst in before Edward had a chance to continue. His hands were twisted into fists and he chopped the air as though looking for somebody to hit. " There was nothing in the campaign about taking over command of the heights of the economy, of massive tax rises on the rich and massive redistribution of wealth. That's why we lost. Our natural support deserted us. The left wing of the labour movement consistently warned that tinkering with the system, attempting to manage capitalism better than the party of the capitalists themselves would inevitably lead to a setback for Labour."

" That maybe so but there are other short term reasons I think." Tom smiled slightly at Mike but his mind still sang with the thought of him becoming a father. This was what was carrying him through the shock of a Tory government with Ted Heath of all people in charge.

" What are those?" Mike demanded, his voice suspicious, his eyes challenging Tom. " Don't give me any of that intellectual crap you sometimes spout but simple reasons. I think you use that academic lecturing higher tone just to intimidate people. During this parliament, our M Ps will have to raise issues concerning who owns and controls industry in this country. The victory of Ted Heath and the Tories will have to lead to an emphasis on the class battles in Britain. They have to be opposed by all the means at our disposal if they explore how to translate their anti working class promises into action."

" I am always straight forward with you Mike," Tom smiled slightly again. His happiness was even going to get him through this meeting without making the acid comments he was so capable of. What of your stupid left wing rubbish spouted by you as a mantra, like an old, experienced catholic priest during mass, without any conviction or understanding, Tom was going to retort but his joy stopped him. He had no desire to pick a fight with anybody let alone Mike. " Harold Wilson was forced to take time away from the campaign to help settle that strike in the newspaper industry. Christ, even you have to admit it did not help when we had no national newspapers for four days during the campaign. It played right into the hands of those saying that the trades unions have too much power and there is a need to curb the excesses of that power. Then the Tories made hay with the demand for twenty five percent pay rises. How the hell do you think that went down with little old ladies on tiny pensions through out the country?"

" They had good reasons for going on strike!" Mike emphasised his words by banging the table.

" They held the Labour government to ransom right in the middle of an election campaign," George put in. " I am a staunch trades unionist but even I can see the stupidity of that move. Now we have to put up with Heath and the arrogant Tories. Will they bring more equality?"

" I thought we were winning until right near the end," Caroline put in as though to change the subject and head off a brewing argument.

" It did look reasonable but then came the trade figures," Edward had countered, shaking his head. " The figures announced during the campaign showed a substantial deficit. That seemed to turn the tide. It gave the Tories a chance to get the campaign round to their ground. They pushed the idea that we would be unable to manage the economy and that there would be a second devaluation soon after the election if Labour was returned to power."

" The Tories were trying to undermine the pound so that they could claim that Labour could not be trusted with running the country," Mike banged the table with his fingers as though to emphasise every word.

" Well it worked didn't it?" Edward countered.

Tom sat back and thought of Jane sitting at home with the baby growing inside. What was it going to be like for his child? Would the Tory government help the rich and condemn the poor to hardship?

" Lets face it," Tom joined in after reluctantly bringing his mind back to the meeting. " The public was beginning to feel uneasy about the future of the economy under Labour after the balance of payments statistics came out. It was a Godsend for the Tories. To cap it all, there were the poor unemployment figures, released in the campaign's final week, which further reinforced the Tory message that a new Labour government would wreck the economy. When we look back now, it was obvious that we were going to lose. Still we have to learn the lessons so that we fight a good campaign next time."

" All I hope is that the party will be more militant and radical in standing up for our principles," Mike barked glowering at

Edward. " Let the little old ladies go hang if that means becoming selfish like the Tories. We have to stick up for our principles."

" The one bright spark in the whole sorry business was that we increased our share of the vote in the Eastfield constituency," Tom remarked, his voice proud. " All I can do is thank you all for your support and help. We will have to see what happens when the time for the next election comes round but I think I will have to leave you and help in Porthampton West. They have a Conservative Member of Parliament for the first time since the war. How they could let their majority go is beyond me. I now disband this election committee."

He walked out of the room and down the stairs with Caroline just as he had the day of the meeting when they had found it pouring with rain on arriving at the entrance to the building. Destiny must have played a role that day in what happened, he thought. There could be no other explanation for chance of the rain and her being on her own at home coinciding. If it had not been raining, there was no way I would have asked her if she needed a lift home. I might have fancied her as a teenager at the youth club but I am happily married now.

Reaching the foot of the stairs, Caroline turned towards the bar, smiling in welcome to Tom. Tom shook his head.

" I have to get home," he said, kissing her quickly." I don't know when I will see you again but it was fun working with you."

He turned quickly on his heel and left her standing there staring after him. As he drove home he wondered why he had not taken up Caroline's invitation for a drink. It was not as though Jane seemed to mind. Jane had never questioned him deeply about his election meetings, no matter what hour of the day or night he had returned home. She would ask him what had been decided or how the meeting had gone. Besides, she must think that Edward would let drop a hint that there was more to these meetings than appeared on the surface. What am I saying? Am I getting a conscience about what happened between Caroline and me that night of the union meeting?

He did not dwell on the subject for a long because his happiness took over once more and he hummed his tuneless songs as he drove. His happiness carried him along on a crest of a wave over the next few weeks. The colours of the flowers in the gardens at the height of that summer appeared more rich, more vibrant. The bird song in the mornings was sweeter. The blue of the sky was like the backdrop to a water colour painting. All about him seemed happiness. It could not last.

It abruptly came to an end one day a few weeks after the election.

Tom arrived home from work to find Jane sitting in a chair holding her stomach, her face white and drawn.

" Are you all right," he called dropping his briefcase and rushing to her side.

" I have this pain and I am bleeding," Jane gasped, almost unable to talk. " I have phoned the doctor and he is on his way."

" Is there anything I can do?" Fear had gripped Tom. It lay hard and immovable in the pit of his stomach. He tried not to show Jane by turning away and racing up the stairs to the airing cupboard. Grabbing some old towels, he rushed back to her side.

She smiled wanly at him but was convulsed by another wave of pain. All Tom could do was hold her hand while they waited for the doctor.

At the sound of the front door bell. Tom almost tripped over his feet in his anxiety to greet the doctor. Letting him in, Tom led the way to Jane.

" Can we help her upstairs to her bed?" the doctor asked and helped Tom with Jane. Tom laid towels on the bed and as gently as possible laid her on her back. He did not know what to do. As all men down the ages, he hovered in the background as the doctor examined his wife. He assured himself he was there to help but his ignorance of what was happening to her was appalling.

After he was finished and Jane was more comfortable, the doctor pulled Tom aside.

" There is no way I can put this gently but Mrs Houseman has had a miscarriage." he told Tom bluntly. " I am afraid there is no point in taking her to hospital because it too far gone to save the baby. I have given her something that will help her to sleep. You will have to go to the chemists tomorrow and get some pads which are highly absorbent. She will have to stay in bed until the bleeding stops in a couple of days. I will come back the day after tomorrow to examine her. Then she will have to go into hospital for a check up."

He caught Tom's arm in an iron grip. " This is not going to be easy for you. She will have a bout of depression after this. How bad it will be, I have no idea. You will have to try to be strong for the both of you."

It was bad. Tom never imagined things could be so bad. For a man who had drifted through life taking opportunities when they arose, keeping his head below the parapet when things turned nasty, living with Jane after the miscarriage he found hard. The trouble was Tom had no experience to draw on, nothing in his past could prepare him for Jane's depression. He soon decided all he could do was take one day at a time. If I get through today without shouting at her, maybe tomorrow will be better, he had to keep telling himself.

At first it was relatively easy. There were chores that had to be completed. Jane lent on Tom heavily and he responded. He took her to the hospital, waited in the corridor for the doctors to finish with her and then took her home.

All the time they were doing these things, she hardly spoke. It might have been better if she had cried. Even when it was decided she was fit to go back to work, she did not cry. She sank deep within herself and would not let anybody, even Tom, inside. As though her world had become a desert, she showed no emotion. She cooked, cleaned, went to work in the morning and came home at night.

What Tom found hard to take was how she shuddered whenever their bodies touched, even at night in bed. At first Tom tried to comfort her by cuddling her in his arms. It was the only way he knew to show that he loved her. Oh, he told her this over and over again but he never knew if what he said penetrated her mind. Whenever he put his arm round her, she pushed his arm away and moved aside. He soon gave up the effort. At night in the dark, they lay like two stranded fish on a beach, each enclosed in their own world. What Jane was thinking was closed to Tom. He lay at night in bed by her side wrestling with his dilemma. How was he to get through to her? With every rejection, the answer became more distant.

In desperation he took her for a week in Brixham in Devon, one of her favourite places. It did no good. She accepted the weeks holiday, dutifully walked with him along the cliffs and round the harbour. She did not smile or make any but the shortest of comments. It was as though nothing mattered to her.

After concentrated weeks of trying, Tom finally decided there was nothing he could do to help her. In desperation he had gone to visit the doctor. Let time be the healer, the doctor had advised. It's all right for you, Tom had bitterly thought as he left the surgery. You do not have to live with her.

With a heavy heart, Tom settled for the hope that time would become the fabled healer. At least the university term started and the students were back. He had his lectures to prepare and to deliver. Between lectures there were his tutees to look after. It all meant that he had somewhere to go each day which took him away from Jane. On the surface, to their friends and neighbours, they still lived a normal life. Jane left for work at the same time as Tom after preparing their lunch boxes. They arrived home at about the same time and Jane cooked their meal. They sat watching television or working at the dining room table. To outsiders, there appeared nothing wrong. Oh, they remarked, Jane seems a bit sad but that is only to be expected after what happened. She will soon pull through.

During those long weary months, it was the little things which bothered Tom. He found it hard to accept that Jane no longer wanted him to touch her or to kiss her properly. When they parted, she would dutifully raise her cheek for a kiss but there was no love nor passion in her inert gesture. At night she would turn her back on him and sleep as far on her side of the bed as possible. They never shared a bath like they did before the miscarriage. They existed in marriage in name only.

But Tom soon realised that despite what was happening with Jane, he still loved her. Loved her in the true sense of the word. Whenever they went out together, his eyes were searching the room for her. When she was out late with her friends or work colleagues, he was on tenterhooks until she arrived home. He still worried that something would happen.

In some of those quiet moments when he was alone waiting for her to return, he had to admit to himself that there was always the fear that she would not return home, would leave him permanently. But she always returned and he never told her of his fears.

One part of his life did help him to remain stable through the long days, weeks and months of Jane's depression. A student named Vicky Hart. She was, to his eyes, pretty and attractive. Shortish hair a deep golden colour framed a face with large blue eyes. Her cheekbones were high, her nose small and her mouth generous. Like many students of her age, her figure was trim and firm with well pronounced breasts. Those breasts were unintentionally, Tom came to the conclusion shortly after term started, thrust out at the world in the same way as the breasts of a figurehead on an old sailing ship. Secretly Tom desired after her. In many ways, his lusting after her, helped him to forget his sorrow at Jane's neglect whenever he and Vicky were together.

    He had met Vicky the year before when she had come to the department for the open day arranged for those prospective students given conditional offers for one of the courses. To Tom, she looked so young and fresh on the day of the visit, that he had noticed her even when confronted by a room full of fresh faced prospective students. When he was giving his presentation about the course, he had noticed that she had smiled whenever he had looked in her direction. Like the rest of the prospective students, soon as she had left that day, he had forgotten her. There were soon another group of prospective students to deal with, to give the selling pitch to, so that any individuals sank into the mass of faces hardly remembered.

    Tom was made conscious of her again later that year when Vicky had unexpectedly turned up in the department one day. It was after he returned to the departmental building from a research meeting, the summer term having finished, he had found her sitting in the foyer waiting for him.

" I hope I did not keep you waiting too long," he had said to her with a smile. " If you had phoned to say you were coming I would have been available for you when you arrived. Come on back to my office and I will make you a cup of coffee. You can then acquaint me with the reason for you coming to the university."

Inviting her back to his office, he had felt an attraction to her as he walked beside her through the building. Her body, he noticed was not covered by too many clothes and he had to force himself not to look too closely at her breasts.

Once back in his office with a coffee, she told him that she had called in to see him on the way from Torquay to Brighton to visit relatives. What she really wanted was the reassurance that she could defer her entry without this affecting her place on the degree. After Tom had found the deferred entry application form and she had sat in his office to fill this in, they had talked about her desire to visit Australia before settling down to her studies. Tom told her of his impressions of Australia especially Melbourne which he had visited a few times for conferences. When she left, Tom found his spirits were uplifted.

When he thought about it later, he told himself not to be such a fool. There were over twelve years difference in our ages and besides she will be a student of mine in a year's time. There has to be a trusting bond between a student and his or her tutor, he reminded himself. It would spell trouble for both of them if the tutor allowed any adolescent feeling of a student to affect that trust. In the concentration on the election he forgot all about Vicky Hart.

In the middle of his predicament with Jane, Vicky had returned to the university after what now would be known as a gap year. It was not part of Tom's responsibility to assign students to tutors but by some coincidence, along with five other first year students Vicky Hart was assigned to Tom. He would be the shoulder to cry on, the voice of encouragement or the nagging word if they let things slip during the next three or four years.

Leaving his concern for Jane behind for a while, on the first day of term, Tom met the new intake of students to outline the course, tell them all about the timetable and make sure all the students met their personal tutors. After telling them where each lecture would take place and listening while Bert Whitehead, course director, explain the tutor scheme, Tom led his new tutees on a tour of the building and the campus. As they walked around, he happened to ask Vicky how her year in Australia had gone. She had awarded him a beaming smile.

" I have some photos," she had said. " If you like I will bring them in sometime and show you what I got up to while I was there."

In normal times Tom would have balked at such a suggestion. He remembered only too well some student who was a passenger transport fanatic wanting to show how he had returned to the university from Newcastle by local bus services. The very memory of that time made Tom shudder. It turned out that the student had all the route maps, the bus numbers, the times and the types of buses on which he had travelled in a logbook of the trip. It had taken all of Tom's diplomatic skills to usher the student out of his office before Tom got really sarcastic.

" I would like to look at those and to hear how you got on in your travels." Tom could not comprehend what he was saying but Vicky's answering smile melted his objections.

Thus, started a relationship which unfolded as the term passed. Every week, at a time when they both had a spare period, Vicky would visit Tom in his office. His other tutees came intermittently, usually when they required help or reassurance but Vicky was faithful every week.

When he mentioned having his tutees round for supper and drinks, Jane made plain that she could not face such an ordeal. It hurt Tom because he had always felt relaxed and friendly when they invited his tutees back to his home every year. For those occasions, Jane had really been happy because it had given her a chance to meet Tom's students away from the pressure house of the university. With a sense of frustration, Tom arranged for his tutees from all three years to meet at a pub for a drink. It was not the same as when they came to his house but it had to do. At least all of his tutees met together for a social evening.

Things were just the same for the department dinner held each year before Christmas. As far as was necessary it was a formal occasion with the head of department giving a speech and a student replying. Jane agreed to go, as she had every year, though without any real eagerness. They were placed on a table with his first year tutees and some of the other first year students. Tom watched Jane through the meal but even when she caught his eye, she did not smile in her usual way. She talked politely to the students sitting close but never with the amusement she usually displayed when with them. Tom, whether by chance or some grand design, was seated next to Vicky Hart. He never did find out how much input she had had with the seating plan or whether it was chance. Throughout the meal, Vicky chatted away to those around, nonchalantly pulling Tom into the conversation if his attention wandered. If it had not been for Tom's concern for Jane, it would have been an agreeable meal.

After the speeches, the tables were pushed back to form a square round a dance floor and a disco was set up. Tom was just wondering about how Jane, in her present state, would cope with having to dance with Tom close, when one of his students came over and asked Jane to dance. She dutifully rose to her feet and followed him onto the dance floor.

" Here comes my chance," a voice in his ear whispered and he turned to find Vicky grinning at him and holding out her hand. They danced for a while before Tom thought he had better ask some of the other students. Tongues will start to wag, he had told her. Vicky pouted a little but assured him she understood. So the evening passed, pleasant enough in its way but at the end not pushing Jane any closer to a normal attitude to her life.

Before leaving to return home for Christmas, Vicky came to say good-bye to Tom. After discussing what was going to happen over the Christmas holidays, they stood looking into each other's eyes for a moment. As though drawn together, their lips met and they kissed properly for the first time.

" See you next term," Vicky said in a low voice full of promise as she left his office, her eyes large and round.

After she had left, Tom sat for a long time looking out of the window, not seeing the trees or the clouds, lost in thought. He was on the verge of doing something he might later regret. Vicky was very attractive and so full of life when they were together. As he sat musing on what was happening in his life that morning, he came to realise that Vicky had been pushing him all term in an attempt to get him to acknowledge his attraction for her. There and then he resolved to keep his distance. He acknowledged to himself that would not be easy especially when she had to come to his office for advice or a chat. All right, he had told himself, I will to try to keep our relationship at arms length even when we are together. Just an innocent amount of flirting when she comes to see me because there is no danger of anything happening when we are in my office. Too many opportunities for people to catch us out, he reasoned.

If I am to avoid any suspicion of mall practice, I will have to make sure we are never alone outside of the university, he had told himself. He was reassured when he thought that there were not many chances of their being alone together. In his office, the door was often open.

The problem he acknowledged was Jane. It was not her fault he hastened to tell himself. He missed their closeness, lying with their arms about each other and their love making. Ever since that first time at Belinda's after helping Tony to move house, there had never been such a wall between them. Jane did not show any signs that she wanted him to leave her but she moved away every time he came close. Even on those occasions in the past when one or the other did not want sex, they had been honest about it and spent the night cuddled together. Now there was a barrier and Tom had no idea how to break it down.

That was the trouble he was having in coming to terms with what Vicky symbolised. There was no barrier, other than Tom's sense of responsibility for Jane and to his work, between them. The trouble was, Tom needed some comfort from somebody. He longed for another person to show that they cared. The condition he found with Jane had made him vulnerable to anybody who showed an interest in his welfare. Confused but resolute, he resolved once more not to place himself in the situation where his relationship with Vicky would go further than mild flirting.

That Christmas was awful for him. They visited Jane's parents on Christmas Day for lunch before her sisters and their families joined them in the afternoon. Jane made no attempt to hide her sadness and it was obvious to all that her mother blamed Tom. Her sisters were puzzled but did not push for an explanation too hard. On Boxing Day, they went to Tom's parents along with Edward, Sarah and the girls. Once more Jane was lethargic and distant not even helping the girls with their presents and new toys like she had in the past. Tom's mother, always practical, cornered Jane in the kitchen and told her in no uncertain terms to snap out of it. When they returned home later, Jane was in floods of tears but, and this hurt Tom more than he cared to admit, would not let Tom comfort her.

It carried on in much the same fashion as winter turned into spring. There was nothing Tom tried that would bring Jane back to him, back to the way she was before her miscarriage. He knew it was her mechanism for coping with the shattering of her dreams but, to Tom, it seemed to be going on forever. As far as he could, within the restrictions of his work, Tom made sure he was there waiting for her when she came home from work and that he was always there at the weekends.

In many ways during this time, he neglected his work. Oh, he would tell you that he did not miss a lecture, marked the coursework and looked after the students. What he never acknowledged was that he did not add updated material to his notes or think of new, exciting ways to present his ideas to his students. If he had been an actor, people would have said he was going through the motions. What he did not do was write any papers for publication about his research or try to obtain more research funds.

Early in the year, he found he could no longer ignore his research completely. The Department of Transport ask him to present a paper at a weekend conference in the spring. He wanted to say no, so afraid was he at having to leave Jane on her own. Professionally, there was no way he could turn this invitation down. He had to spend time preparing his paper but he did this in the evenings while at home with Jane. Once his paper was accepted by the organisers, he received an invitation to bring two of his students with him for the weekend at no cost. This was a way to get the students interested in transport as a subject, the Department of Transport organiser informed him.

Wondering what to do, Tom showed Roger Moffat, the head of department, the letter.

" How am I going to choose amongst the students?" he asked the professor when they met. " It will be a good opportunity for them not only to listen to a number of experts but also to meet people."

Professor Moffat smiled. " Leave it with me. I will offer it to any of the students who are interested and then hold a ballot if there are more than two. If I do this it looks like the department is backing the idea rather than you as an individual. I will let you know who will be coming with you."

A week later Tom was called into Professor Moffat's office. Sitting waiting outside in the secretary's office were Ted Burgess, a final year student for whom Tom was supervising his dissertation and Vicky Hart.

" Go right in," Carol, the professor's secretary said. " Professor Moffat is waiting for you."

They trooped into the Professor's office and he waved them into chairs the other side of his desk.

" Tom, Vicky and Ted have won the ballot to go with you to the conference," he said with a smile. " I hope you find it worthwhile."

" We will and thank you for giving us this opportunity," Ted replied politely.

Vicky accompanied Tom back to his office after speaking to Professor Moffat. Ted went off to prepare a coursework or so he said.

" What does a conference like this entail?" Vicky gushed her eyes bright and full of excitement. " I have never been to a conference with all these distinguished speakers and delegates before."

" A lot of tedious old men and a few women talking to each other," Tom grimaced at the memory of too many conferences he had attended. " We will not learn much unless somebody new comes up with a fresh piece of research. To you it will all be new and exciting but even you will not learn all that much from the papers. Look out for all the polite back stabbing as researchers and academics try to put down their rivals in research areas. Listen to the subtle questioning as academics try to judge what path some other academic has taken and whether this will be a hindrance or an advantage for them. In its way it is as cut throat as politics but many would say much more polite. Academics say sorry as they put the boot in where as politicians secretly laugh at the miss fortune of their rivals. It can be great fun taking part. The main advantage of going to conferences is to meet other people in your line of work. I expect I will know a few people there and I will introduce you and Ted to them. You will have to store their names away in case in the future they might be able to help you."

The conference was held just before Easter. Tom drove to the venue with Ted sitting by his side and Vicky in the back of the car. The hotel where the conference was being held was set in its own grounds just outside Oxford. Once they had registered and had a coffee, they were instructed on how to find their rooms. To Tom's relief they had rooms on different floors and after making sure that Vicky and Ted were settled into rooms next to each other, Tom returned to his room to make sure he was familiar with his paper which he was presenting the next afternoon.

Vicky and Ted were already in the dining room when Tom came back downstairs. They had saved a place on their table for Tom and around the table were already seated five other people. Tom nodded to some of the others who he knew by sight or reputation. He introduced those he knew to Vicky and Ted. The few others on the table introduced themselves.

Soon the conversation turned to transport and the much needed government policy. Vicky sat entranced at the ebb and flow of argument and discussion, her eyes bright and her expression serious. If asked directly, she shyly joined in the discussion.

When the dinner was coming to an end and the coffee had been served, a thin aesthetic looking man in a well tailored suit attracted Tom's attention from across the table. " Doctor Houseman?"

" Yes," Tom responded with an answering grin.

" I am Professor Garton from Liverpool University," the man gave a watery smile back. " I admired your preliminary paper on the affect of flags of convenience on the British Merchant Fleet. A bit out of your subject area considering the basis of your Ph. D.?"

" I was speaking to the officer's union representative in Porthampton at a meeting last year. He was very pessimistic about the chances of the British Merchant Fleet surviving for more than a decade if the flags of convenience continue to capture a greater amount of the cargo on offer," Tom replied politely noting the hint of menace in Professor Garton's seemingly innocent words. " After speaking to him, I thought I would look into it and came up with that paper. I am planning to put in a research proposal to look at that area. I see your people have that big research grant to look at containerisation."

" Yes. I had to stand down as the chairman of the maritime panel while that was being discussed. It will employ at least four researchers for the next two years. Quite a coup for my group." The professor sounded proud but went on in a flat voice. " You might be better employed in sticking to road haulage regulation you know."

Tom frowned and then laughed. " If that is some kind of warning, Professor Garton, I will bear that in mind."

Before Professor Garton could reply, a tall man with glasses, a face like one of those Greek gods and broad shoulders, approached the table and clapped Tom on the back. " Tom you old fraud!" he exclaimed. " We haven't met for more than two years. How is that adorable wife of yours?"

" Douglas Stokes. He was a researcher at Nottingham at the same time as me. We were on the research committee together. Be careful of him. He will try it on with anything in a skirt. I must say he is rich and handsome, so rich he does not have to work," Tom said as an aside to Vicky.

" I heard that," Douglas smiled a huge smile. " You must introduce me to your lovely companion."

" Vicky Hart, Doctor Douglas Stokes," Tom noted that Douglas bent and kissed Vicky's hand. It was like a caress with all the hint of promise that entailed. I wish I could do that Tom thought noting the thrill evident in Vicky's eyes. " What are you doing here?"

" As you know I got a post in the Department of Industry when I left university," Tom noted Douglas was still lightly holding Vicky's hand as he said this. " Unlike you, I could not face the thought of a future trying to bash ideas into young people's heads. Well, to cut a long story short, they have sent me along to learn something about transport from you lot. I must introduce you to the minister later. Ah, the speeches are about to start. I had better get back to make sure my minister does not say anything controversial. See you both later."

Vicky watched him go and then turned to Tom with a shudder. " I know some women are bowled over by that sort of thing but it tends to leave me cold. He thinks so much of himself, he cannot see what effect he is having on the people around. Did you know him well at university?"

" Not really," Tom said. " We sat on the research committee together as I said and went out for a drink every so often. He was in a different department to mine. I must admit, he had all the best girls trailing in his wake whenever we met for a pint of an evening. Even as a research student, he drove a Jensen which was a bird pulling car if ever there was one. You be careful of him. He can charm a bird down from a tree that one. But I must admit, the times I went out with him were fun."

As the speech by the minister started, Tom realised how relieved he was at the comment by Vicky. Not that it really mattered how Vicky felt about Douglas, he told himself hastily. All his life he had been fazed by boys and then men like Douglas Stokes. They appeared so self confident all the time in most situations. Tom was always conscious of what he was trying to do and tended to read the unfavourable into any early response to him from other people. He had to admit that reacting that way to many people did not seem to affect his life. He had managed to attracted some women, to get to the level in his job he thought he was due and was relatively happy most of the time. Oh, the last nine months had been bad but he was hopeful that this phase would pass. The trouble with people like Douglas Stokes was that they seemed to get all the best that life could give and to grasp it with very little effort.

After the speech by the minister, Tom took Vicky and Ted for a drink in the bar introducing them to as many of the people he knew as possible. He settled into a corner with some of his friends, happy to see Vicky and Ted in deep conversations with other people. One thing which did disturb Tom was the covert speculative looks cast in his direction by Professor Garton. He shrugged to himself and forgot about it.

It was getting late when Tom said goodnight to his friends and looked round for Vicky and Ted. He suddenly realised he had not spoken or seen them for a good hour. The last he had seen of Vicky was in a group of men, smiling her lustrous smile and joining animatedly into the argument. She had looked very attractive to him but he was soon talking about transport to his friends and she went out of his mind. Ted had been in another group also talking but again there was no sign of him. I am not their keeper, Tom thought as he turned away to leave.

Now looking round the bar for her he had a stab of jealousy when he could not see her. Some of the men she had been talking to had also left and he could only assume that she had gone to bed. It was difficult for him to understand why he felt let down by not seeing her. It must be a craving to see her to her room like a protector, he sarcastically told himself. Almost blushing at the patent lie, he had to admit to himself that deep down what he was thinking was not exactly the truth. It was the thought that some other man had jumped in on his neglect and taken her to his bed which was affecting his feelings. Don't be silly, he told himself as he climbed the stairs. You are acting like a shy school boy who has been rebuffed by the girl on whom he had a crush. She most likely went to bed without saying goodnight because you were too busy talking and she did not want to interrupt.

He reached his room and after looking longingly in the direction of the lift, unlocked the door and went inside. It did not take him long to make a cup of coffee, undress and clean his teeth. He lay back on the bed, naked watching the television while he finished his coffee. Even though he was not paying much attention to what was on the screen, it was relaxing. He jumped with surprise when there was a soft knocking on his door.

Hastily he pulled on his underpants and went to find out who wanted to see him at this time of night. When he opened the door a little so that he could see into the corridor without exposing his nakedness, he found Vicky standing in the corridor.

" Hello Tom," she smiled. " I wanted to say goodnight and you were too busy talking when I left the bar. So I came down to see you now. I have been waiting for quite some time to make sure you were back."

" Goodnight then," Tom growled starting to shut the door.

"Can I come in and have a coffee with you?" she pleaded.

Tom grasped the notion that if he opened the door and let her into his room, he would cross over the invisible line he had tried to draw in the sands of his conscience. If she came into his room, there would be nothing to stop him trying to get Vicky into his bed. He may have been mistaken all those times she had been in his office but he had felt the vibrations, observed the invitation in her eyes but the likelihood of somebody coming into the office had always placed a screen as protection between them. Now there would be no barrier, no possibility of anybody catching them.

Like an alcoholic pondering the bottle, he hesitated. As though watching from outside his body, he felt rather than saw his hand push open the door. Just as in one of those dream sequences in a movie where the whole scene is shot blurred as though through a net curtain, he stood aside and let her into his room. He noticed she was carrying a bag but the significance of the bag did not register.

Smiling, Vicky placed the bag on the bed and took the kettle into the bathroom. Tom slumped into a chair and sat mesmerised as he listened to the water rushing into the kettle. It sounded like the gush of approaching catastrophe. He had to admit to himself that he did not know what to do. On the one hand, it might be a perfectly harmless encounter, a need to seek his company in an unfamiliar situation. On the other hand, it could be intentionally planned to compromise him. He did not have an answer. Mentally shrugging his shoulders, he decided to await developments. Of course, he conceded, he was flattered but at the same time, he thought of Jane sitting at home depressed and without his support and comfort.

Vicky came out of the bathroom and plugged in the kettle. She prepared two cups of coffee and Tom watched her in silence. When she had finished she placed the cups on a table and drew up the other chair alongside Tom.

Smiling dreamily over the top of her cup, Vicky remarked, " What an exciting day. I have met some of the most influential people engaged in both transport research and working in transport. Douglas even introduced me to the minister. Douglas hinted that I should go to bed with him but I made it quite plain that I had other plans for tonight. Did you meet the people you wanted?"

Tom smiled back in return. " Yes, I suppose it was a good evening. Though I did get the distinct impression that Professor Garton was not delighted at my starting to show inquisitiveness towards shipping as a research area. I think he believes shipping is his domain and other academics should only invade his territory with his authorisation. We will have to see what happens."

Vicky lent sideways and kissed him. Then Tom, as that day when Belinda had invited him into her flat before Jane and Tony come home from work, knew he was stepping over that imaginary line he had drawn in the sand if his life once again. Even by conjuring up an image of Jane sitting at home waiting for him, he could not resist Vicky's approaches. He was now fully aware that he was sitting there in his boxer shorts while she was fully dressed. Sighing, he returned her kisses.

Pushing him away, Vicky climbed to her feet. " Stay there for a minute," she whispered and disappeared into the bathroom with her bag.

When she emerged from the bathroom, she was dressed in a short nightie and nothing else. At the sight of her bare legs and the shape of her body through the cloth, Tom abandoned all attempts to resist. Rising to meet her, he gently put his hands on her shoulders and lifted her onto the bed.

They made love then like young people alone together for the first time. Through the night, every time Tom awoke, Vicky was urging him to make love again. From a situation of no love making, of tension between bodies sleeping in the same bed but not touching, he was suddenly introduced to unrestrained, abandoned sex.

Sometime around dawn after one last bout of love making, Vicky rose from his bed, kissed him and dressed in the light which was seeping through the curtains. Smiling dreamily, she went back to her room.

After she had gone, Tom lay alone in his bed breathing in the traces of her scent while thinking deeply about what had happened. He had not wanted to go this far, he pretended to himself. On deeper thought, he had to admit to himself that he had looked forward to their weekly meetings. No, more than looked forward to their meetings but awaited those times with breathless anticipation. Oh, yes and with rising desire. Vicky had roused in him the longing to make love to her from the first time he had seen her at that prospective student meeting.

Oh, he tried to excuse his conduct last night by partly blaming Jane. If she had not forgone sex, made him feel that he was not wanted, he would have easily been able to resist the temptations of Vicky Hart. That's too easy, he had to admit even too himself. He knew that he loved Jane and that should have been enough to sustain his resistance to Vicky's charms. The reaction was one of revulsion with himself at first but this soon passed in the realisation that he had enjoyed love making with Vicky. The way Vicky had treated him made Tom feel that he was wanted once more.

Later as he showered and dressed, he steeled himself to tell Vicky that pleasurable as their love making had been, there might not be many chances to repeat the performance in the future. Indeed there was no future in their relationship and she would have to understand this. For the first time in his life he was no longer drifting, letting things happen to him but trying to control events. If Vicky did not accept his decision, he had no idea what would happen. His heart beat faster and his brain ceased to function properly when this occurred to him. He could not imagine life without Jane even with the malfunctioning of their marriage as it was now.

Focusing on the presentation of his paper took up the rest of the day. It helped him to stop thinking about what had happened and the danger this brought for the future. To his relief, Vicky, though not exactly disregarding him, found plenty of other people to attract. She did sit very attentively listening to Tom while he read his paper and answered questions, but sat talking to Douglas before and after dinner. Tom found he had no time to think about Vicky because there were many people who wanted to discuss his thoughts as expressed in his paper. It spilled over into the bar that night and he had no time to think of Vicky or Ted.

Later that evening, when he finally extracted himself from the other delegates, he could not find Vicky. The last he had noticed was her talking to Douglas in the bar but he had had no time to say anything before being cornered by another academic. Sometimes he thought it was harder to fend off the questions and obliquely critical comments after presenting a paper than during the actual presentation. It was like being trapped by ones aunties at a family get together, knowing one had to be polite and answer their questions without giving too much away and not being too aggressive. If some other researcher worked in a similar field there was no such thing as friendship. One might be polite, buy a drink or two but always there was the tension of probing and defence of ones ideas. It was with relief that Tom finally left the bar and wished the few remaining people a polite goodnight.

Walking up the stairs to his room, he could not work out whether he was relieved or upset. Relieved that he might not have to deal with the temptation of Vicky that night. Upset that she had ignored him all evening to talk to that Douglas and did not seem to want a bedtime kiss. At that he had to grin. While he was getting ready to face the conference that morning, all he had wished was that his love making with Vicky had not happened. Now he was showing all the signs of classic jealousy, like an angry Othello, and Vicky was not even his wife.

When Tom arrived back to his room and opened the door, he found Vicky sitting up in bed naked and reading a book. The smile she gave him was radiant.

" How the hell did you get in here?" Tom demanded more sharply than he intended.

"Oh that's easy. I went to the desk and told them that you had asked me to fetch some papers from your room but had been too busy to give me the key," she shrugged making her breasts bounce invitingly. " I have always found with my smile, I can usually get my own way. Actually it was not too strange. They saw us arrive together and they know I am a student of yours, so they put two and two together and made five. All I did was come up here, put the door on the latch, grab some papers of yours and return the key. Then when the time was right, I came back here with my night things. Well not that I need any nightclothes after last night. Why Tom, aren't you pleased to see me?"

Once more, despite all his resolutions of the day, at the sight of her sitting in his bed calmly waiting for him to return, Tom was lost. It did not take much, he thought, as he sat on the edge of the bed and kissed her.

Pulling away and resisting the temptation to stroke her breasts, he shook his head. " Vicky, you are the most desirable woman I have ever met. Just looking at you makes me want to make love to you no matter how you got here. There is something I have to tell you though before this goes any further. What I say might sound old fashioned but I have to be honest with you. I don't know how it is but I still love my wife even though making love to you is such a wonderfully fulfilling adventure. When we leave here I have no idea when we will be able to make love again. I will go back to Jane and you will continue your studies. I will ponder the question of whether it is possible to love two people at the same time without coming to any firm conclusion. Do you understand what I am prattling on about?"

Vicky laughed, a laugh which made her breasts bounce up and down, and kissed Tom back. " Tom, my love, do not worry. I wanted to kiss you from the first time we met but you seemed to make it plain that though you liked me you wanted to keep your distance. It was hard work for me to manipulate you into a position where I could grab a kiss. God I tried but it was not until last Christmas and then only a quick peck. As for making love, that seemed a distant dream. Imagine my excitement when I had this chance to come away with you for the weekend? I knew that given the right circumstances I would be able to make you invite me back to your room for the night. God, I was even wrong in that. I had to come marching in here blatantly offering my body to you. I have no idea what I would have done if you had refused and pushed me out of the door. Gone back to my room and cried, I suppose. In the end, it was worth it."

She kissed him again. " No, Tom you have nothing to worry about from me. Even though I would love it to be different, I understand the situation. Tomorrow you will go back to the cold bed of Jane and make out this did not happen. I will return to my equally cold room at the university but will not forget. I will hold this memory like the glow of pleasure from a birthday present, to be brought out whenever I need cheering up. Besides, I know that your job would be in danger if anybody ever found out what we have been doing. I would not like to see you hurt or lose your job. I will not tell anybody. But we will have the memories of these two nights to hold onto and who knows? Maybe in the future we will have a chance to make love again sometime. Now come to bed before I rip your clothes off."

It was just as Vicky had said. Tom went home to Jane hopeful that a weekend's separation might have changed their attitude to each other. Nothing had changed. Jane was polite, cooked him a meal but showed no affection at all. That night, still feeling the glow of Vicky, Tom slept a few inches away from Jane conscious that every time he moved she cringed away from any touch. That night he dreamed of Vicky and her warmth. In the morning Jane remarked that his sleep had been disturbed and she hoped he was all right. He replied that he was still thinking about how his paper had gone down but would soon settle back into a calmer routine.

It all came to a head a few weeks after the conference. All the elements which most influenced the way he lived his life appeared to be questioned in the space of two days. Until the day dawned Tom had no inkling that things were going to change.

Jane and Tom had gone to an opera, Aida to be exact. When they got home, Tom still moved by the plight of the lovers entombed for their love and betrayal, was hurt when Jane took her cup of tea and went to bed leaving him to tidy the living room and drink his coffee on his own. He watched the television for a while and then went off to bed himself.

Jane lay in bed listening to the radio when he came into the room. When Tom got into their bed, Jane turned to him and smiled. She was naked under the bedclothes. Tom did not know what to do. He had been rebuffed so many times, his instinct was to turn away. He was glad he did not.

" I know it has been difficult the last few months," Jane whispered, " but will you put your arms around me. I have this overwhelming desire to make love tonight."

They made love that night, gently and tentatively at first as though handling a precious vase or delicate piece of blown glass. Like the man in the glass making factory who was conscious that wrong move would ruin the glass, they were scared of breaking their relationship. It turned out to be wonderful. They rediscovered together what they had been missing all those months. They rediscovered how much they loved each other and how they could rouse the other to heights of desire. They rediscovered how to end the night fulfilled. Wrapped in each other's arms, they slept the deep sleep of relaxed satisfaction like young babies after being fed.

The next morning Tom sang once more as he made breakfast. Hummed his way to work in the car and even smiled as he collected the exam papers ready for marking. He had as usual scheduled the next week at home to be bored as he marked the same mistakes over and over again in different papers. Oh, every so often there was an answer that excited him but in the main it was the same turgid answers.

Vicky came by his office as he was preparing to leave to go home for lunch and then a few days marking the exam papers. To Tom she looked a shade uneasy as though she wondered what would happen. Tom ignored his feelings, smiled and told her to sit down.

" How are you?" he asked cheerfully.

" Oh I am fine," she answered. " How are things with you?"

" Things are OK." Tom answered guardedly keeping to himself like some expressionless poker player hiding his hand, the change in his circumstances.

Vicky got up from her seat and made sure the door to his office was shut. She came round his desk and sat on the edge, her thigh only a foot away from his chest. Suddenly she bent forward and kissed him fiercely.

" I hope you don't mind, Tom," she said quickly, still with her fingers stroking his face. " I have a new boyfriend, you know Roger Pennington from the accounts degree. We have decided to rent a flat together next year. We have found a place down near the river and started to live in it now. He is away on his industrial placement at the moment so I only see him at weekends. I can take you there this morning and show you around."

Tom pulled her close and kissed her, his heart beating faster. He knew he should be sad, frustrated that his few times of sex with Vicky looked like they were coming to an end. He should have been consumed with jealousy in the same way that Figaro was when he thought that Suzzanna was going off with the Count, at the thought of Vicky sleeping with another man. Wait, he told himself. I have no idea who she sleeps with. We only see each other once a week for an hour in my office. Besides, Vicky living with another man lets me off the hook. Gives me the chance to quit worrying about our relationship affecting both my job and my marriage. All in all, it is the best thing that could have happened. As a bonus, I will still get to see her once a week.

As they were leaving together, Professor Marriot's secretary called him into her office.

" Could you come and see the Prof. at ten thirty tomorrow morning?" she asked smiling. " I have the appointment in my diary."

" What does he want to see me for?" Tom asked bluntly.

"Don't ask me," she replied grinning. "I am only the Professor Marriot's secretary and I do as I am told. See you at ten thirty in the morning."

It was not often that Professor Marriot called Tom into his office. His usual practice was to come to the office of one of his staff if he needed to talk to them. Because of this, Tom was in a speculative mood as he walked out of the building accompanied by Vicky. He quickly ran through all the reasons he could think of about why the Professor wanted to talk to him. His lecturing load? His lecturing style? Some complaint from a student or another member of staff? He soon came to the conclusion that it was not productive to try to anticipate what the Professor wanted to see him about. Dismissing the speculation from his thoughts, he started to concentrate on Vicky.

The flat proved to be part of a small two storey block with six flats on each floor. Vicky's flat was on the upper floor at the top of the stairs from the entrance. She flung open the door and showed him round. Not that there was much to see. Bathroom to the left inside the front door, bedroom ahead. Corridor to the right with second bedroom on the right, kitchen on the left and living room straight ahead. In the living room was a glass door leading onto a small balcony overlooking the park leading down to the river. There was very little furniture, two arm chairs, a small table and plenty of cardboard boxes in the sitting room. A mattress on the floor and a portable hanging rail in the bedroom but the kitchen was fitted with a cooker and a fridge.

" A bit sparse," Vicky grinned as she made him a mug of tea. " When Roger gets back this weekend, we will go looking for furniture. The second bedroom we will have as a study room with a desk and some bookshelves. Both of us are getting jobs for the summer in Porthampton so it won't take long for us to have this presentable. The main thing is its convenience. The bus to the university goes right passed the door. What do you think?"

Tom did not know what to say but muttered about it being just the thing. He did realise it was handy. Close to the university but far enough away so that they could avoid other students if they wanted to.

Vicky appeared to accept his comment because, after taking away his mug, she sat on his lap and kissed him. After a while, she took his hand and pulled him to his feet before leading him into the bedroom. They made love on the mattress on the floor ardent and vociferous, thinking this might be the last time.

Later in the afternoon, as he sat marking his exam papers surrounded by a feeling of agreeable sensual warmth, the phone rang. It was Mr. Hunt's secretary to advise him that Mr. Hunt was feeling neglected because he, Tom, had not been in touch for over eight months. Could Tom possibly find the time to make an appointment and come to the office to see Mr. Hunt? They agreed a time for a day the following week, another interruption to his marking, Tom sighed. He ignored the feeling he had that there was an implied threat in the way the secretary had delivered the request.

That evening as he was settling down to watch television cuddled up to Jane before going to bed and starting to try for another baby, his brother phoned.

" You have not been seen at any Labour Party meeting this last year," Edward stated bluntly. " There is a meeting I think you should come to in Eastfield on the plight of Upper Clyde Shipbuilders. I'll see you there in the bar before it starts."

No how are you and Jane, just I want you at this meeting. I will not be pressurised into being his agent again, Tom told himself.

Before Tom could go any further with his memories, the mist came up and he lost track of his thoughts. It was good to sink below the level of the liquid and float thoughtless for a while.

Chapter 5

Joan stood up once more, stretched her aching back muscles and walked around the ward. The whole situation she found herself in was reaching into her very soul. She was desperately trying to remain calm as the time slowly ticked away. As though this was going to go on forever, she felt trapped, unable to escape. To attempt to remain calm and sane, she had fixated since arriving at the hospital on what the doctor had told her to do. I have to maintain my belief in what I am doing will eventually bring Tom through his crisis, she told herself over and over again. If the doctors say to keep talking, I will keep talking. It is the only hope that I have left. That's all I have now. Hope and a desire to have Tom back with me how he used to be. Leaning back against the wall with her eyes shut, she could see him laughing at something Tony had said when they were with Tony and Belinda. I hope one of the children has contacted Belinda and told her what had happened.

It all appears so pointless from here looking over at the bed. He lies there breathing regularly and heavily with the machines pinging away in the dim light of the ward. At times, I think there is a little response from him to my voice. At those times my heart lifts only to feel let down when there is no tangible lifting of his consciousness. Am I deluding myself about his state? she asked herself again. Is he just a lump of flesh that will slowly die?

I don't know if I can carry on like this. I hope Mary and Luke get here soon, she thought as she resumed her seat and took Tom's hand in hers. I do not want to appear uncaring, Tom but I am finding sitting here talking to you an enormous strain. If Mary was here maybe she could take over so that I can go and get some fresh air. I have no idea how long I have been here but it feels like a lifetime.

With an audible sigh, she started to talk once more, her voice falling lonely and a little lost into the silent void which was her husband Tom.

" We have had some good times together you and I, Tom. There have been holidays abroad at first with the children but lately, much more frequently, on our own. There have been some good evenings with friends and with your students. One I particularly remember was when that Mr. Hunt invited you to the Bishopstead Country and Golf Club out near where

Edward lives. I felt really important that night. Oh, we had been to some formal dinners before, what with your Institute and all but that evening was the first time I had ever experienced a car with a uniformed chauffeur being sent to pick us up."

The mist swirled thickly around his mind and then slowly started to lighten as though the sun was rising high enough to burn away the moisture. As though from a long way off, Tom could hear a voice echoing but he could not hear the words. He strained to hear what was being said but it was fuzzy and indistinct like a conversation heard through the walls of a hotel room when the people next door were speaking quietly. It droned on but still Tom could not make out the words. He was so close to the surface. Any minute he would break through. Suddenly the mist cleared and he was sitting in an office. Opposite across an enormous desk was a man. He was a medium build with broad shoulders and a round head. His eyebrows were bushy and his hair was swept back in a nineteen twenties style. Professor Marriot, Tom suddenly thought and then realised that once more he was reliving the past as he fought to get back into the present. In a way, like somebody caught up in the rush of a crowd, he wanted to scream that this was not what he wanted to do but it would take too much energy and as though visiting the cinema, he settled back to watch.

" Ah Tom," the Professor was saying with a slight smile playing at the ends of his lips. " Glad you could find the opportunity to see me at this time of the year. I know there are so many other things for you to do."

" I only have four module exams to mark but your secretary told me it was important," Tom stated bluntly. It had better be important, he was thinking, or I might lose my temper with you and say things which would be best left unsaid.

" I won't keep you long," Professor Marriot still smiled but there was a faint trace of warning in his voice. " This last month, I have been looking into the research record of our Department for this academic year. As you know, I have to compile the annual report of our Department's activities to the Vice Chancellor. I must say, the figures tell me that, collectively, the Department did not have a very good year. The Departmental research income is down and the average number of publications from each of the lecturers has also fallen. Now, I had you marked out as one of our potential stars, until this year. If things had turned out better, I was on the brink of getting you to put in for promotion to Senior Lecturer when the next round of reviews take place in the autumn. What happened to your research this year?"

" I have been preoccupied with a lot of things this year," Tom replied looking belligerently in the Professor's direction. " The admissions work has increased and I have taken on a new module. This increases my lecturing load to twelve hours a week. There has been a vast increase in the number of student final year projects to set and supervise. I also have three research assistants to supervise which is more than anybody else in the Department including you."

" I am aware of all of that," Professor Marriot snapped back losing his outward appearance of calm control. " Contrary to what you may think, I do have my hand on the pulse of the Department. That is why I said you were regarded as a potential star. As far as I am aware, you have not published a single paper either under your own name or jointly with one of your research assistants during this academic year. You know the rules as well as I do. Every lecturer in the university has to publish at least two papers a year in recognised journals as part of their contract. That should not be difficult for you with your three research assistants. God, you don't even have to do the bulk of the writing, only check everything your research assistants write and add your name."

" I did present a paper at that Government sponsored conference at the invitation of the Ministry," Tom put in bluntly. " Besides, the research grants are coming to an end and we are finishing the final reports. Papers will come from that."

" But that is another thing which worries me," Professor Marriot smiled, a bit like Mr. Hunt, not with his eyes. " If your research contracts are coming to an end, you should have had new proposals in to replace them by now. You should have been helped by the researchers already here. Even if they do not want to stay and will write up their Ph. D's before leaving, they can be an invaluable help in writing proposals. I know two of them want to stay because they have asked me about permanent posts. Look Tom, do not let us argue or have bad vibrations about this. The deadline for submissions of research proposals to the research council is mid September. This gives you plenty of time to get some proposals together. While you are doing that, you can also write a couple of papers for publication. Oh, I have a proposal in the pipeline which might benefit from your input. We could send it in jointly."

" I'll try my best," Tom said keeping his facial expression blank.

As he walked away from Professor Marriot's office, Tom was seething. How dare the bugger impugn my motives, he raged. I have given my all to this department since I came, more than most of the others.

Once out in the fresh air however, he calmed down and his anger vanished like the mist in the early morning sun. If he was entirely honest with himself, he had to admit that he had been going through the motions this year. All right, he told himself, unconvincingly, he had had to contend with Jane and her depression but some people would accuse him of using that as an excuse to slack off. I will make a supreme effort to get out these proposals and these papers, he determined to himself.

When he arrived back at his office, he arranged to meet Jack, Diane and Momo, his research assistants, to discuss what papers they could produce quickly out of their research. They all promised to come up with the final drafts of papers they had been preparing all ready. Tom had to acknowledge that they all sounded relieved, as though they had been waiting for some time to be given the go ahead from Tom.

For the rest of that summer, he spent some of his time contacting people he knew in positions of influence or who had some knowledge which would help him formulate research proposals. He went to talk to his contacts at the seaman's union and in the shipping industry. Surprisingly, he found his brother helpful in gaining him access to people in the city especially at the Baltic Exchange. Slowly, the outline of what was needed took shape. Finally he contacted Douglas Stokes who arranged for him to visit the Department of Transport. All in all, he told the Professor Marriot when his proposal was ready, it was the best and most supported proposal he had ever submitted. The Professor agreed with him and they waited in anticipation for the approval. All together, after a great deal of work and co-operation from his research assistants, Tom submitted three proposals to different boards and had four papers accepted in various journals.

A good summers work, Tom thought as he struggled to regain consciousness through the fog which enveloped his mind as he lay in that hospital ward. His mind then drifted back to the start of the summer of seventy one once more.

He remembered going to Mr. Hunt's office the day after his reprimand from the Professor. The office building had not changed since the last time he had been there almost a year ago to deliver his last report to Mr. Hunt's secretary. Situated in the middle of the Georgian terrace one side of the square in front of the oldest church in Porthampton, was the entrance to a suit of offices flanked by columns. A brass plate near the door announced very discretely " Hunt Enterprises". With a feeling of apprehension he could not fathom, Tom once more pushed open the door and entered the large reception area. Behind the large desk was the same man dressed in a uniform. Again, Tom detected from the hard eyed look the man steadily cast in Tom's direction, that the receptionist was more than a security guard. Glancing round, Tom smiled at the other man in uniform sitting at the bottom of the stairs pretending to read the paper.

" Tom Houseman," Tom introduced himself. From the look the man gave Tom, the man behind the desk recognised him but did not move.

" Yes?" the man growled, his voice far from welcoming.

" How are you Bert? I have an appointment to see Mr. Hunt this morning," Tom kept smiling conscious that this man could easily get violent if he said the wrong thing.

Bert gave him a slight smile. " Mr. Hunt is expecting you. You know the way. Terry, Mr. Houseman has an appointment with Mr. Hunt."

Terry shifted his newspaper slightly so that he could get a good look at Tom. It was noticeable that Terry reluctantly did not try to stop Tom as he crossed the foyer and started to climb the stairs. Tom felt the hair on the back of his head tingle and his shoulder blades tense but he did not look back.

When he came to the head of the stairs, he remembered to turn left towards a door on the other side of the landing. Once more, he was aware of somebody watching him closely as he approached the door. He steeled himself not to turn round and look but surmised that the watcher was in the shadows to the right of the top of the stairs. Tom wondered whether the watcher had a gun but dismissed this as fanciful.

After knocking at a blue painted door, he entered when a familiar voice bade him come in. At least, thought Tom, Shirley's smile is welcoming as he greeted the woman sitting at a desk opposite the door. The glasses once more struck Tom as severe with plain black frames. They matched the look of stern efficiency emphasised by the way her hair was pulled severely back from her face in a bun. The dark jacket with the collar of a white blouse over the lapels, Tom did notice, could not hide her full figure. In a way, she was quite attractive.

As soon as Tom was standing inside her office, Shirley spoke into the intercom on her desk. Mr. Hunt's distorted voice answered and bade her to escort Tom into his office next door. Shirley got up from her desk with a dazzling smile and opened the door to Mr. Hunt's office for Tom.

When he turned after closing the door, he found Mr. Hunt was sitting behind the large desk in one corner of the office by the window, the three phones, one white, one red and one black were arranged in exactly the same way as the last time Tom had called on Mr. Hunt.

" Good morning, Tom," Mr. Hunt greeted him, though he did not smile and his voice had a hard edge to it. " It has been quite a while."

" Good morning Mr. Hunt," Tom smiled and shrugged. " I have to admit it has been a while since I was here but I have had a bad time of it lately."

" Too busy to come and report to me?" Mr. Hunt said softly.

" You didn't ask me to do anything for you so I assumed you did not require my services," Tom answered blandly.

" I do not usually have to ask people to do things for me more than once especially those who I employ," Mr. Hunt was not smiling now and his voice had taken on a hard tone. " They usually are so friendly, they do it with out a second reminder."

" Are you threatening me, Mr. Hunt?" Tom asked.

" No not threatening you but just reminding you of your obligations." Mr. Hunt's eyes bored into those of Tom. Tom did not look away but stared straight back.

" Mr. Hunt, let us get things straight before this goes any farther," Tom voice was now hard and resolute. " I know you have a great many dodgy characters working for you and you can apply what Derek would call muscle when it is needed. I grew up next to the council estate across the river where Derek lived, so I am not completely innocent. I have a good idea what goes on in the world. Let us be honest and open with each other. I do not see myself as one of your employees. Far from it. I am an academic and was engaged by you on an ad hoc basis to supply you with reports on investment opportunities, if requested specifically by you. You have not requested any reports from me for the last year. Like anybody who asks me to prepare reports for them, if they are not satisfied I am not asked again. If that is how you feel, say so and I will leave now. There will be no hard feelings because this happens all the time."

Tom started to stand but Mr. Hunt barked. " Sit down before I get somebody in here to make you stay."

Tom laughed loudly. " Is that your usual reaction to anybody who tries to go against your wishes? It won't wash with me. I must repeat what I said just now. I am not one of your hired hands. I am an academic who agreed to do some work for you for which you have paid me. Now if you want to threaten me, that is your affair not mine. It would look really good for you and your organisation if I turned up at the casualty department of Porthampton Hospital all beat up. People might not notice if a thug turns up in the gutter now and again but there are too many people out there who know me. The police would be sure to investigate. You think I am credulous but, as I said, I have some idea of what goes on under your leadership. I have no doubt you could have me killed if you desired but I think you are going to be sensible about things."

Suddenly Mr. Hunt laughed and said in a mild voice, " Good for you Tom Houseman. It is ages since anybody has spoken to me like that. Sit down and I will tell you why I asked you here."

Tom resumed his seat and looked inquisitively at Mr. Hunt.

" It is really your fault, Tom," Mr. Hunt began, his brow furrowed into a frown. " You have advised me to invest in certain areas of the economy. I must say your advice has been very shrewd and I might say extremely helpful. The only thing is that all of this is still attached to me and my other activities. I have been thinking and talking to Rob Mercer, my accountant, and Malcolm Warne, my lawyer. They agree with me that the legitimate side of my enterprises should be formed into a limited company. We have looked into it and have found the right structure with me as Chairman and managing Director, Rob as finance Director, Malcolm as Legal Director and Derek Jones as Security Director. We will appoint a personnel Director and an operations Director. Rob reckons that we need a couple of non executive Directors with no vested interest either through operational duties or from my other activities. He suggested one and I suggested you. What do you think?"

Tom sat looking at Mr. Hunt for a long time while his mind raced. It was all too sudden. Oh, he was thrilled at being asked and he thought of what a difference the money would make especially if Jane had a baby next year. On the other hand, he was concerned that he was being drawn more and more into the murky side of Mr. Hunt's business dealings. He did not want to take part in any criminal activities but would be flattered to become a non executive director of Hunt Enterprises Limited.

" I am sorry Mr. Hunt," Tom replied carefully. " You will have to give me time to think this over. It is flattering to be wanted by you though I will have to convince myself that this is an authentic business. Plus, I will have to get the agreement of the university before signing anything. They have regulations about academic staff taking on outside interests."

" Of course you can have time to think it over," Mr. Hunt smiled. " I didn't for a moment assume that you would agree to my suggestion straight away. From what Derek has told me about you, you will go home and talk my proposal over with Jane. Look, I will have a contract drawn up and we can then discuss it seriously after you have thought about it. I'll tell you what. The main players in this are having a dinner at the Bishopstead Country and Golf Club in a month's time at the end of June. It might be a good idea if you came along with Jane and met the others. We will have the contract ready with all the details and can negotiate an agreement that night or you can say no. How about that?"

" I will agree to that," Tom answered.

" Good. It will be suits for dinner not dinner jackets. I will send a car round to pick you two up at seven thirty. Then you can drink as much as you like. The car will be available to take you home as soon as you require it." Mr. Hunt rose from his chair and offered Tom his hand. Tom shook his hand and left the office.

As he walked out of Hunt Enterprises office building into the brightness of a warm summer's day, Tom was felt disquiet at where Mr Hunt's offer might lead. He should have been happy but he was frowning. His mind should have been singing with joy because it was not every day that he was offered the chance to double his earnings. Mr Hunt had just offered him the chance to break into the business world. Still, uncertainty as to what he should do nagged at the back of his mind. Was he, by accepting Mr. Hunt's offer, helping to legitimise Mr. Hunt's shady activities? It was as though he could hear the echoing voice of his father talking about somebody on the council estate next door. " How many people's lives have been blighted by the uncaring actions of that man?" Phil Houseman had said on hearing about some villain. On the other hand, Tom assured himself rather weakly, what Mr. Hunt had proposed was nothing to do with his criminal activities. If he was to form a limited company for his legitimate activities, he would have to go through the legal process and prove that his proposed business was above board. Tom resolved to ignore the nagging doubts and put these to the back of his mind.

When she arrived home from work and they were sitting down to dinner, Tom told Jane what had happened when he went to see Mr Hunt. Unlike Tom, Jane appeared on the surface to accept Mr. Hunt's proposal as above board and encouraged Tom to agree. In addition she made it quite plain that she would do anything to fulfil an invitation to the Bishopstead Country and Golf Club.

" Gosh Tom, do you live in your own small world and pay no attention to what is going on around you?" Jane exploded when Tom appeared to shrug his shoulders at the invitation to the Country Club. " The Bishopstead Country and Golf Club is the most exclusive venue in the county if not in the country. Anybody who is anybody in local society is a member. It costs a fortune to join and even more to continue to be a member. Only the very rich join. People do not apply for membership. From what I hear at work, you can only become a member on the recommendation of other members. They invite you to join, you do not apply. Every time I have driven passed those closed, wrought iron gates, I have wondered what was on the other side. Now I am going to see. Tom, I must go shopping this weekend and get a new outfit. Your suit needs a clean. Maybe if you become a non executive director of Hunt Enterprises Limited, you will be invited to become a member."

" Don't get too excited my dear," Tom tried to calm her excitement with candid words. " Even if we were invited to become members, we could not afford the fees. Just enjoy your one night as a guest and keep the memories hidden away in your mind to dream about later."

The car arrived to take them to the club at precisely seven thirty as promised in Mr. Hunt's office almost a month before. It was a Mercedes with leather seats and a uniformed chauffeur. Jane talked excitedly all the way to the club while Tom sat in silence answering in monosyllables. He was still wrestling with the dichotomy of on the one hand being thrilled at being asked to be a non executive director for a limited company whilst on the other having a conscience about accepting money which might be tainted with crime. He was intelligent and, even though he drifted through life letting circumstances pull him along, deep down he felt it was wrong to get involved with Mr. Hunt in any way. On the other hand the police or the authorities had never arrested Mr. Hunt or, as far as Tom could tell, accused him of anything.

Again Tom had to admit to himself that he had no proof of any criminal activities by Mr. Hunt. All Tom had as evidence was the association of Derek and the hints from some of the people surrounding Mr. Hunt. Then there was the entrance to Hunt Enterprises building. All right, Tom had told himself many times most companies have a reception desk in the entrance hall. Some had security guards but these were usually retired men or low skilled people. They did not look like the thugs employed by Mr. Hunt.

I am not myself doing anything wrong, Tom told himself. Hunt Enterprises Limited will be a legitimate company with proper shareholders and registered at Companies House. It will have to produce accounts each year and a company report.

The car turned off the road, after driving through the village of Bishopstead passed the five bed roomed mansion of his brother, onto the drive of the Country Club. Ahead was a large house with paladin columns guarding the central section and wings on either side. To the left of the drive behind a row of popular trees was one of the fairways of a golf course. Behind the house Tom could see what he took to be a stable yard.

The car drew up by the steps leading up to the front door and a uniformed man jumped forward and opened the car door.

The chauffeur turned and said, " When you are ready to leave Dr Houseman, ask for your car to be brought round to the front of the house. I will be waiting for you."

The uniformed man led them up the steps and through the front door, bowing as a man in a morning suit stepped forward. with a raised eyebrow.

" Mr. and Mrs. Houseman as guests of Mr. Hunt," Tom said in as firm and confident voice as he could summon above his nervousness. He was always nervous when confronted with a situation with which he was not familiar but he made great efforts to appear calm and in control. On the whole he had always managed to appear in control to most people though his intimate friends had an idea from the tightness of his shoulders and the clip accent he adopted that he was tight and nervous.

The man in the morning suit bowed and said," Follow me and I will take you to Mr. Hunt's group."

They followed the man along an oak panelled corridor to a room over looking a formal garden at the rear of the house. The room was large and oak panelled like the corridor. On the walls were mounted a series of paintings whether of any real value Tom could not tell. There were green leather settees and chairs dotted round the room in squares that provided intimate space while still being part of the rest of the room. Several groups of people were sitting talking. The morning suited man led Tom and Jane across the room towards a group of people sitting round a low table. Mr. Hunt looked up and almost smiled.

" Thank you Perkins," he said to the man. " Tom, Jane! Come and join us. There is some room over there for you Tom while Jane can sit next to my wife, Vivien. Vivien, this is Tom Houseman and his wife Jane."

Vivien Hunt looked at Tom and Jane with wide apart blue eyes. Her face was slightly lined and her hair showed grey streaks but she was still a strikingly good looking woman. Her expensive dressed showed off her full figure and she waved slightly with a well manicured hand.

" Pleased to meet you Tom and Jane," she greeted them in a very cultured voice. " Come and sit down next to me Jane. We can talk of things other than business which is what these men are bound to talk about."

" Tom meet Rob Mercer, my accountant, and Malcolm Warne, my lawyer," Mr Hunt introduced the other men. " Sitting next to Rob is his wife Elsie. Beside Malcolm is his wife Cynthia. You know Derek Jones and his wife Marlene. You entertained me at their wedding."

Tom took his seat beside Elsie and ordered a gin and tonic when the waiter came to take his order.

Rob Mercer was a thin man, aged in his mid forties. He had that intense look of somebody who thought life was serious. His hair was receding, leaving a rather intellectually looking high forehead above a long thin nose. Tom noticed that the fingers of his hand resting on the arm of his chair were long with well tended nails. He was dressed in an impeccably cut dark suit with a cream shirt and sober tie. He smiled a thin serious smile at Tom.

Elsie was small, no taller than five feet from what Tom could see of her. Her light coloured dress showed off her trim figure. She peered short sightedly out at the world through large glasses perched on a small nose in the centre of a round almost chubby face. Tom was later to learn that she was a doctor in the local hospital.

Malcolm Warne was fat with a double chin, creased face, small eyes and thinning hair. Though his suit was well cut, it looked crumpled and uncared for on his broadly spread shoulders. Through the open jacket Tom could see what could only be described as a beer belly on which rested the end of his brightly coloured tie. It was difficult to tell what age he was but Tom guessed at around forty.

His wife was also over weight, filling the suit she wore to almost bursting point.

Her hair was cut straight framing a flabby face and puffed eyes. She was slightly drunk all ready. She did not work for a living but in between looking after her four children did charity work like meals on wheels.

The other thing which struck Tom as he looked around was the change in Derek. It must have been two years since they had last met but Derek looked fit and well clothed. He looked every inch the successful business man rather than the thug with a thin veneer of respectability. All Tom could think was that Mr. Hunt must have been giving him advice on how to look and sound in this sort of company.

They talked of what was happening in the world, of the looming crisis in the shipbuilding industry, the rise of militant trades unions and the abysmal record of this government. At one time they got into a deep discussion of Europe and the European Economic Community. Even though he had strong opinions on all these subjects, Tom remained for the most part silent.

When they had finished eating and were sipping Brandies, Mr. Hunt sat back in his chair and addressed the gathering. To the amusement of Tom who thought this practice was only known from Jane Austin novels, the ladies retired to the coffee lounge for their after dinner drinks. " There is a purpose to this dinner other than spending an agreeable evening in such agreeable company. I am proposing to form Hunt Enterprises, which is owned wholly by me, into a limited company. To this end, I will split up the various activities in Hunt Enterprises into divisions each headed by a director with a seat on the Holding company board. In the future we might separate off each division as a separate company. You people round this table are to be the Holding Company Board along with the directors of the divisions. Greg Norton has agreed to be one non executive director. Rob is to be the Finance Director, Malcolm the Legal Director and Company Secretary, Derek, Security Director and I will be the Chairman and Managing Director. The other non executive director I propose to be Tom Houseman but he has not agreed to my suggestion yet. I think he will accept the offer when we discuss it privately after dinner. All the legal papers and formalities have been accomplished and the company is ready to roll next week."

He paused and looked round the table. " There is an initial share capital of one thousand shares. This, I have divided in this way. I will retain five hundred and fifty shares giving me overall control. Malcolm and Rob will each get one hundred and fifty shares. Derek will get one hundred and the two non executive directors will get twenty five shares each. The profits after the first six months as calculated by Rob are expected to be close to one hundred thousand pounds. This will be distributed as is required according to the share holding. Those profits are expected to double over the whole year. Any questions?"

There were no questions. Mr. Hunt held all the cards. Everybody sitting around the table knew they were dependent on Mr. Hunt and his money for their own prosperity. They all had a part to play in keeping Mr. Hunt out of the clutches of rivals and the authorities but he was in control.

Later, he took Tom aside. " Well Tom?" was all he asked.

Tom hesitated but then smiled. " I suppose you get your way in most things, Mr. Hunt. I have been thinking about things for a long time. I know Jane would think I am being stupid if I turned down the offer you are making. I will accept though you have to realise that I will be a proper non executive director and will hold the board to account. If I think you are doing anything illegal as far as the company is concerned, I will tell you straight out."

Mr. Hunt chuckled and held out his hand. " Good for you Tom. Welcome aboard our enterprise. As I have with all new members of my team, I will arrange for you to become a member of this country club which includes the golf course. You will have to submit to the statutory number of lessons from the professional as the price to pay but once you are a full member, we will have to have a round of golf together. Don't laugh but Derek is a member. He is quite good at golf now playing off fifteen. I will see you at the first Board meeting next week. My secretary will post out the papers to you. Now let us go back to the others and have a few drinks and a laugh. We have been far too serious tonight."

When they arrived home, Tom explained to Jane what had happened while she was out of the room with the other wives. On hearing that Tom was to become a member of the club, Jane became excited. She could not wait to arrange for Belinda and Tony to accompany them to the country club for a meal.

" We are going to be well off with that amount of money coming in," she remarked, as they got ready for bed.

"I have been thinking about the money and what we should do," Tom told her as he sat on the bed to take off his shoes. " The way I see things, I think we should put half of the money as it comes in into some investments. That will give us a hedge against what might happen in the future. What do you think?"

Jane shook her head and then smiled. " There I was thinking of playing the rich lady for a while and you have to become all practical. Who can we go to for advice?"

" If you don't like the idea, tell me," Tom insisted. " What I was thinking is we have no idea how long this will last. I earn three thousand a year from the university and you earn nearly two thousand. To my Mum and Dad that is riches beyond their dreams. Even that is small beer compared to Edward. If what Mr. Hunt says is true, I will earn another nine thousand a year in fees and dividends. All together that makes fourteen thousand before tax. If we invest seven thousand a year, that will leave a great deal of money to live on. Besides, after it has been invested we will start to earn dividends on that money. I think I will ask Edward for advice. I am meeting him next week for that Labour party gathering to discuss the fate of the Upper Clyde Shipbuilders. I can ask him then."

Jane sighed, showing her disappointment. " I guess you are right," she admitted.

When Tom parked his car outside the Labour Club in Eastfield later that summer and walked through the front door, he thought how distinctly shabby it was in contrast to the opulent surroundings of the Bishopstead Country Club. It was not that the building was neglected but it was made shabby by constant use and infrequent decorating. The linoleum on the floor in the entrance hall was worn in places, the security counter chipped and scarred, the paint had once been red but had now faded to a dull purple and the glass panels in the door leading to the bar were miss matched.

The doorman looked up from the magazine he was reading and asked to see Tom's party card. With out a word, he inspected the card and handed it back to Tom, waving vaguely in the direction of the stairs to the function room.

Tom was back on familiar territory. All those months before the election he had spent so many nights here. He even found it amusing when he spotted the formidable figure of Doreen Mitchell at the bottom of the stairs barring the way to the function room. This time, however, she grinned as he approached.

"Tom Houseman," she exclaimed. "It is good to see you again. You haven't been in here since the election. How are you?"

"Hello Doreen," Tom grinned back and kissed her on the cheek, much to her delight. "How have you been? I am afraid I was tied up with family matters and struggled to find the time to get here."

Doreen looked serious. "I heard about Jane, your wife, and what happened. I am sorry. Oh, I haven't told anybody else. I wasn't certain whether you wanted everybody to know. I got to know because I overheard Edward telling Caroline when she was asking after you back along in the autumn. He told her not to tell anybody. I can understand Jane not wanting it broadcast all over the place. My friend Mabel was like that when it happened to her. She thought she was to blame somehow and nothing I could say would persuade her otherwise. We just had to support her and let her find her own way through. Caroline is up there now and she will be glad to see you."

"Thank you for your concern," Tom smiled sadly. "I think Jane has got over the shock now. She seems to be back on an even keel. We are planning to have another go as soon as possible. Will you be up later? If so, I'll see you up there."

When Tom had climbed the stairs and entered the function room with its stage at one end and rows of chairs taking up the floor, he found Edward and about twenty five other people standing talking in groups, obviously waiting for the speech to start. As he came through the door, Caroline waved from near the stage where she was talking to George Nesbitt and another man whom Tom did not recognise. Leaving the two men, Caroline walked over to greet Tom. Her full figure just on the point of being chubby, shown off by a tight dress, was just as desirable to Tom as it had been when they were teenagers.

" Hello Tom," she greeted him with a smile and a kiss on the lips. " It seems a long time since we last met. How is Jane, your wife? Edward told me about what happened. Has she recovered yet? I have friends who took almost a year until they started to get over their feelings of blame."

" Hello Caroline," Tom smiled in return. " It is nice to see you again. It must be almost a year since we had that meeting to analyse the election campaign. Jane appears to be fully recovered, thank you. How have you been keeping?"

" Oh, very steady," she replied ambiguously. " Melvin still works long hours and goes to the pub most nights. Susan is at secondary school now which makes me feel old. My sister is looking after them again tonight because Melvin is working some overtime. We could do with the money. I must say that Melvin does stay in most times when I have a Labour Party meeting. He is not really political though he does take an interest in the Upper Clyde Shipbuilders dispute and would have been here tonight if it had not been for his work. He reckons we all need to learn lessons from what is happening there."

" We shall find out tonight what has been happening and how we can help," Tom stated vaguely. " I have to admit, I have been rather tied up this last year and have not kept up with political events. My local party has been trying to get me to go along to their meetings but I have not got round to it yet. I know it is vital because Porthampton West has a Conservative Member of Parliament for the first time since the war. I'll see you in the bar afterwards. It looks like things are about to start."

All the people in the room took their seats and George Nesbitt took his place on the stage to introduce the speaker.

The man started quietly, his Scot's accent in sharp contrast to the way most of the other people in the room pronounced their words. As though to emphasise the seriousness of what he was about to say, he was dressed in a sober dark suit with a white shirt. His red tie was held in place with a gold tie pin. In his lapel was the badge pin of his union. He was not tall and rather slimly built.

At first Tom had difficulty in making out what he was saying and even turned to Edward for illumination. His brother shrugged his shoulders to indicate that he was struggling too. By concentrating hard, the message became plain and soon Tom was able to understand the deep Glaswegian accent.

" I will have to start at the beginning because there maybe people here who are not familiar with our situation," the man started a bit hesitantly.

' We all have to start at the beginning,' Tom thought scornfully but was ashamed of the thought as soon as he articulated it. It is all very well for you when you spend a great deal of your life trying to put abstract ideas into simple language to sneer at another person trying to do the same, the shaming thought burst into his mind.

" The election victory of the Conservatives under that idiot Heath has resulted in the renewal of class battles in Britain. I agree with what Jack Jones said after the election when he told us that it will be like the times of the General Strike if they proceed to legislate their reactionary promises into action. I know some reactionary people will argue that those promises were in the Conservative manifesto. As I argued at the time, if Wilson and Castle try to get In Place of Strife onto the statute book, given half a chance the Conservatives will try to complete the job if they ever get to power. They have done this with their Industrial Relations Bill and Act. This is all relevant to our case. After Labour lost the election last year, the Tories began to talk about the problems of industry and competitiveness. They talked about abandoning what they called industrial 'lame ducks'."

" I have to admit, I did not really understand what they were on about. To me, it is one of the government's jobs to support British Industry so that there is employment for the majority of the workers. It has become plain that what they were on about was not supporting any industry which was not profitable no matter what the social consequences. In February, what they meant was made completely obvious and for something that we had worked hard to sustain. Davies, Secretary for Trade and Industry, is the one who thought up this industrial strategy. What could you expect from a manager from industry? Anyway, as you know, he announced that Yarrows would be taken from the Upper Clyde Shipbuilders and returned to the private sector. Upper Clyde Shipbuilders had been formed by the Labour Government from the five Clyde yards namely John Brown, Charles Connell, Fairfield, Alexander Stephen, and Yarrows. The Labour Government had invested £20 million to help modernise the yards and this was having an effect. However, the management of yards claimed they were still losing money. When announcing that Yarrows would be placed back in private hands, the Minister indicated that no more public money would be made available to Upper Clyde Shipbuilders. Upper Clyde Shipbuilders had made no request for further money but the Minister's statement brought about a rush of creditors' claims and Upper Clyde Shipbuilders were refused further credit from the banks and financial institutions."

" This month the company has run out of cash. Give the chairman his due, he came to the trades union committee and told us what was required. About six million pounds is all. He told us he would ask the government for the money. The only alternative to government help was to place the company in administration. We warned the government through the papers in Scotland and the TUC that the collapse of Upper Clyde Shipbuilders would have an economic, political and social cost far greater than the sums of money needed to keep the yards going. The government refused support."

" The result has been a movement from the workers to arrange a work in at the yards as opposed to a strike. It is felt by the workers that an all out strike would help the government to close the yards quicker. We have a slogan. " The right to work; Not a yard will close; Not a man down the road!"

" The government is uncompromising. There are at least fifteen thousand jobs at risk, eight and a half thousand in the yards and six and a half thousand in suppliers. On top of this are the families of the workers and the shops, pubs and clubs they support. It will be a disaster for the area. The workers at the yards refuse to accept redundancy. We have decided to fulfil all the outstanding orders on the books. We will get paid by the liquidator out of what resources UCS had left. The aim is to rescue all the threatened jobs and demand the right to work."

" Jimmy Reid has called for the nationalisation of the yards as the only guarantee against massive redundancies. Many in the Labour movement have called for the nationalisation of the whole of the British Shipbuilding industry as a vital industry for jobs, skills and the areas in which these yards are situated. Swan Hunter's, which lost £10 million last year, Cammell Laird's, Harland and Wolf, indeed the whole industry is completely unviable on a capitalist basis."

" It is not our fault that the yards are falling behind the rest of the world. We have worked our socks off. It is the lack of investment in the yards which has caused the problem. Only the government can put in place the investment to make the yards competitive and retain our jobs. Thank you all for listening."

George Nesbitt thanked the speaker and called for questions. Tom thought that most of the questions and statements made by the people in the room were sycophantic not about how the problems of the shipyards could be solved. There was an assumption that the tax payer should fork out money to keep these industries alive. There was no hint that the workers should make any contribution what so ever.

Afterwards, Caroline, Edward and Tom walked down to the bar together. Edward brought the drinks and they found a table at which to sit. Mike Pearce suddenly appeared and asked if they minded if he joined them.

" I am sorry Mike, but I did not see you at the meeting," Tom grinned in greeting. " How are things with you?"

" I was late and sat at the back," Mike replied. " I have moved you know. I now live on the Thatcham Estate over near the docks. I am a member of the Porthampton West Constituency like you are Tom. I was asking after you when I went to the first meeting but they said they had not seen you since the election. How have you been keeping?"

" I have been busy," Tom replied vaguely.

" What did you think of the talk tonight, Caroline?" Mike asked her bluntly.

" Well," Cartoline seemed to hesitate. " I have a great deal of sympathy for the workers in the yards and for their families. We have to find a way of protecting jobs so that the yards are viable."

" That means nationalisation," Mike put in fiercely. " If the Tories and their system cannot guarantee the minimum requirement of a worker, the right to a job, then they and their system must be scrapped and a Labour government, based on taking over the 350 major monopolies, must be brought to power. We should nationalise the yards without compensation. Then we can put in money to make them viable so that they can continue to build ships."

" There is a problem," Edward remarked calmly. " What if nobody wants to buy the ships the yards produce?"

" The government will have to make the British Merchant Navy companies buy British built ships instead of foreign built ships," Mike was adamant. " That way there will be a constant stream of ships coming off the slipways and the workers jobs will be protected."

" If the ships are more expensive to build, what happens when the British companies have to charge higher freight rates than their competitors?" Edward asked.

" There is a case to make for having legislation which makes British companies send exports in British ships," Mike said. " If it costs money to subsidise the British fleet, that money can be found from taxes on the rich. As a manufacturing country, we cannot afford to let the skills and expertise fade away. If we could only truly politicise the working class so that all became active, they would take over the unions and make them do what the true working class want the unions to do. That is push for a socialist society. From a position of strength in the unions, ordinary people could then move into the ward and Constituency Labour Parties. I reckon the only way to save the Labour Party from the disaster of another election defeat is to start putting in place a Marxist agenda. There is a newspaper called Militant which argues this."

" That is not the way," Tom put in softly. " We have to create wealth. My brand of socialism has always been about how we use the wealth to create equality rather than the state running everything. Like you Mike, I fail to see how anybody can justify earning one hundred times more than the ordinary worker but we have to create wealth before we can embark on a socialist agenda. The rich and more fortunate in society have to be convinced that taxes are a way of encouraging the poor and disadvantaged to better themselves."

"In order to create wealth for the whole of society we have to encourage people to take risks and keep a great proportion of their wealth," Edward shrugged eloquently. " What is most important, as Tom said, is how we then use the wealth created. There has to be an element of redistribution within the system but more important is that everyone has access to a good health service no matter how rich they are. In addition, the education system should be funded so that every child has a chance to fulfil their potential."

" You would say that, Edward Houseman," Mike almost shouted. " You have wealth and a high standard of living. You never have to think about where the next penny is coming from. Your wife never has to make choices between whether to feed all the family small portions or whether to go without herself so that her husband and children will get enough. There is a lot of poverty out there which the world does not see. All poor people are not slovenly. Some struggle to put on the best outward appearance they can to the world. It is these people we have to help and letting the stinking rich keep more of their earnings is not going to help these people."

"Will it help the poor people of this country if we tax all the rich people to such an extent that they take their wealth and talent abroad and do not pay any taxes at all?" Edward put to Mike bluntly. " People with wealth spend their money here which helps with employment. We have to stay true to our Labour Party principles while finding a way which allows people to make money while helping those at the bottom of the heap."

" Rubbish!" Mike shot back equally bluntly. " The wealth of this country is made by those who work with their skilled hands. Could your average managing director make something from a block of metal? Could they stand the heat of the shop floor? Militant newspapers says that we should do away with the management classes as they stand and run our factories by workers councils."

It was the first time that Tom had heard the word Militant and the newspaper. He thought at the time that he would have to get hold of some copies to find out what it had to say. It was something that he thought was important but he was to come to see that the seeds of trouble in the future were being sown that night in Eastfield.

They decided to call it a day at that point. Tom asked Edward if he could have a word. When they were on their own, he asked Edward about setting up an investment account explaining where the money was coming from. Edward smiled and said he would be only too glad to manage Tom's fund for free. He would set up a bank account into which Tom could transfer any extra cash from which he would extract the money for the investments.

" I am good at that," Edward said matter of factly. " Given a little good economic news and I will double your money in a few years. I'll tell you what. We will create Houseman Investments and I will match your contribution with the same amount from me. I will have the documents drawn up with you owning fifty percent same as me. You will give me authority to invest as I see fit. Agreed?"

Tom grinned and nodded.

Edward frowned. " Who is behind Hunt Enterprises? I have never heard of the firm."

" A Mr. Hunt who is a friend of one of my friends," Tom told him.

" I will enquire around the City about this Mr. Hunt. See you soon," Edward grinned as he left.

Summer passed into autumn and the leaves turned brown and started to fall. For

Tom, the time was one of contentment. Very few things disturbed the tranquillity of his life and he was able to drift along letting the currents of living carry him along like so much driftwood.

One thing that did annoy him was when his research proposal about flags of convenience was turned down. He had been so convinced by the tightness of the submission, the support from both sides of industry and the government that it came as a shock to open the letter to find his submission had been refused. He went to see Professor Marriot about the refusal but got very little support and encouragement.

" Houseman, dear boy, you win some and you lose some," The professor remarked with a slight smile. " You have been awarded the research grants on your other three proposals starting next month and we have been awarded our joint funds. That will look really good in the Department's submission next year and brilliant on your C.V. We must get the contracts drawn up for your research assistants as soon as possible. I will get my secretary to get the legal people to draw up their contracts."

" I am disappointed, no mystified," Tom said trying not to show how angry he was. " That was the best supported proposal

I have ever written and it should have been a shoo in for a grant. Don't you think I ought to make inquiries about why it was turned down? Should I submit it again?"

" Look Houseman," the Professor was not smiling anymore. " As I have said some proposals get through, others fail. If I were you I would let the matter drop and accept that somebody did not like what you were proposing and move on. Lets make a success of what we have and put your rejection down to experience."

Tom was not convinced that this was the right response and he telephoned Douglas Stokes at the Ministry to find out if he knew anything.

" The Research Council committees are completely independent from the Government," he replied to Tom's question. " The Chairman of your Research Council is a Professor Garton from Liverpool. You were sitting with him at that conference we were both at. I'll try to find out why your proposal was refused over and above what you have been told. By the way, how is that delightful Vicky who was with you at that conference?"

" Steady, Douglas, steady," Tom had to laugh. " She has a boyfriend from the university rugby team. A back row giant and tough as they come. I'll tell her you asked after her next time she calls at my office. I'll give you her phone number if that is any help."

Before he could get too upset about his research proposal, Jane announced that she was pregnant again. Tom wanted to run out and shout it from the roof tops but Jane stopped him. In the light of what had happened before, she proposed caution.

" Let us tell everybody when we are sure that this time it is going to be OK," she had said.

That did not stop Tom trying to wrap Jane in cotton wool, to always insist that she take things easy and to look worried constantly when she tried to do too much.

They did have a moment of tension during that autumn which had nothing to do with their baby. In October, the House of Commons voted to accept the terms for joining the European Common Market. Joan was very hard in her wish for Britain to remain as an independent country outside of the EEC system. She put her arguments that Britain had never been a true part of the European scene very forcefully and passionately whenever anybody would listen. She had always argued her corner in any discussion but this was the first time Tom had heard her voice throb with a messianic fervour on any subject. The main problem for them both was that Tom did not agree with her on any level. He felt that joining the EEC would cement Britain into Europe, bring much needed economic benefits and help maintain peace in Europe. Tom had always had a horror of having to go through what his parents had been through. Thoughts of war in Europe sent shivers of apprehension through his body. He was well aware of what war could do to families and countries, from what had happened when he was a toddler. Some people did tell him that he was lucky that his father had come home. He had known quite a few people in his school and living near his home who had lost fathers or brothers or uncles. There was special bitterness in some parts of Porthampton that the British Merchant Navy had never got the recognition for the sacrifices that were endured during the war. Its all those bloody stuck up types from the Royal Navy that gets all the praise and medals, he had often over heard older people saying.

What was even more strange was that, despite his involvement, his wife had been very equivocal about Labour Party and Harold Wilson. It took a certain courage to face many of her friends after aligning herself alongside the Labour Party.

Tom supported the idea and for once was on the side of Ted Heath. They waited with baited breath for the vote in February 1972, to affirm the Accession Treaty which Ted Heath had signed in January. The second reading was passed by a majority of only eight and Joan was pleased to hear that there had been a minor brawl in the Houses of Parliament. To her the angry exchanges in the Houses of Parliament were the last defence of British values.

" Well Tom," she had bitterly stated after the debate was over. " You have your way now. Lets hope you do not come to regret it."

When they celebrated new year in 1972, Tom was lost in contemplation of the birth of his baby. It was due in early March and Jane had to tell everybody because it had begun to show. The New Year celebrations were hardly over when industrial trouble erupted and plunged Tom into gloom. The government had been having troubles over the last year because of rising unemployment and attempts to impose wage controls. The resistance to the government policy had started to come from sources outside the Labour Party's traditional base. Tom had come across this as more and more local Labour party meetings had become dominated by these very left wing people. They said they were sticking up for the shop floor and had to push both the trades unions and the Labour Party to the left. They kept bringing up the names of the Liaison Committee for the Defence of Trades Unions and of Militant. At the time Tom was certain it was only so much hot air and that come any election and the ordinary members of the party would accept the party's authority. Looking back from his hospital bed, he understood too well that he, like many others in the Labour Party at the time, were swept along and ignored the threat until it was too late. Besides, the Lecturing Union was in dispute with the Universities on exactly the same issues of comparison between the bosses and the salaried staff.

For Tom, doubts about what was happening started when on the ninth of January the miners went on strike. Although he had much sympathy for the miners, it was the way the strike was portrayed in the papers and by the strikers which made Tom fear for the safety of Jane and his baby. In the event the strike lasted for seven weeks and there was mass picketing of the steel works, major ports, power stations and coal depots. In fear Tom watch as a state of emergency was declared much to the glee of some of the left wing members of his local Labour party like Mike Pearce. To cap it all, to economise on electricity, Edward Heath's government had to reduce the working week to three days. Tom started to have visions of Jane's baby being delivered by candle light as though they lived in some developing country.

Everybody agreed that the turning point of the strike was the battle between picketing miners and the police at a coke depot in Birmingham. Local trades unionists and striking miners marched on the Saltley picket line to close the depot down.

Deep down Tom knew this was not good for the country but his sympathies still lay with the striking miners. When the result of the strike was to increase miner's wages so that they became the highest earners in Britain, Edward told Tom that he was convinced that this would all end in tears. Inflation will rise and we will all suffer in the end, he remarked one day when he had brought his wife over to see Jane.

In March, Paul arrived and politics were forgotten for a while. It was the greatest thing that had ever happened in Tom's life. He had spent the day trying to help, trying to get Jane to relax and ignoring her curses at the pains. When the midwife held up the baby and he uttered his first cry, Tom was in a daze. Jane cuddled the baby, smiled at Tom and all was right with the world.

When Paul was placed in his arms, Tom could only say. " Welcome into the world, Paul. I hope you have as great a life as I have had so far. What is in store for you nobody knows but remember, your mother and father will be here to help you."

One thing he remembered lying in that hospital bed struggling to regain his senses. The next round of research proposals had been submitted but with three individual contracts and one part contract, he had not submitted anything. When the results were announced he was surprised to find that Professor Garton's group had been awarded a contract too look at the effect of Flags of Convenience on the British fleet. When he read the synopsis of the award, he became angry. It was virtually the same as the proposal he had submitted and been turned down six months before.

He made an appointment with Professor Marriott and stormed into his office at the appointed time.

Flinging the research awards onto the Professor's desk, he angrily asked trying not to shout, " What an I do about this?

That award is virtually the same as the one I had turned down last time!"

The Professor smiled. " I can understand your feelings Tom but there is nothing you can do. Your proposal was not accepted and now another on similar lines has been."

Tom stared at the Professor. " Even if the Chairman of the Board was Professor Garton and it is his group that have been awarded this contract."

The Professor replied calmly. " There is a saying among my contemporaries. All is fair in love, war and academic circles. Tom, I know it looks as though you have been stitched up but you will have a hard time proving it. These boards are run by academics and any appeal will go to other academics, all experts in their fields. They will all be of the same club, Oxford or Cambridge graduates and a lowly lecturer like you will not stand a chance. They will close ranks on you and your reputation will suffer. Obviously I want you to stay here in this department but if you ever decide to move on, remember it is those same people who will be on any panel looking into your appointment. If they feel you are an iconoclast who rocks the boat, your chances of getting a job elsewhere are small. Next round of promotions, I will get you to put your name forward for a Senior Lecturer's post and support your application. Don't rock the boat."

Tom's eyes were hard. " As you know full well, Professor Marriot, I am basically an honest person. I thought when I started that academics were basically honest and supported each other. They might argue at conferences, disagree violently in journals but they never stole off each other. Now I know differently. Garton is no better than a common gangster protecting his position with threats and cheating. I will find a way to get even with him somehow."

With that he had stormed out of the Professor's office.

He was still fuming that evening when he met Mr. Hunt and the other Hunt Enterprises board members for dinner.

After a while Mr. Hunt lent over the table and said quietly," Why so gloomy, Tom?"

Tom told him what had happened. " I feel so helpless."

Mr. Hunt had smiled. " Do you want me to help? There is somebody I know who could warn the Professor off by giving him a beating or smashing up his house. If that is too violent for you, I will get somebody to dig the dirt. You could then get this published somewhere and ruin the Professor. Don't look so sceptical. Everybody, even a supposed saint like you has dirt in their background they would not like their friends and family to find out about. Give the word and I will send Derek to Liverpool to contact this man."

For the first time that night, Tom smiled. " Is that your answer to every problem, Mr. Hunt? Thanks for the offer but I will find a more legitimate way to get even with him."

Lying in his hospital bed, Tom tried to concentrate but his thoughts slipped away and the grey fog overwhelmed him once more.

Chapter 6

Jane fell silent as she sat once more and watched her husband lying unmoving on the bed. Just for a moment, fleetingly like a shadow passing across a curtained window, she had thought she detected recognition of her voice. In the dim light of the ward, she could not be sure especially now as she stared intently at her husbands face. The hope that had flared moments before died like a fire burning low late at nigh when not replenished. Silently to herself, she wondered how long she would be able to keep this talking going. Sitting by his bedside and letting her voice drop into the outwardly empty void of his mind was beginning to wear her patience away. All she was able to do was sit staring at Tom, or what passed for Tom, hoping and praying that there would be some change in his situation. It had become emotionally draining sitting thinking about what to say and trying not to wonder whether her words were having the desired effect.

There was a soft knock at the door and her son Paul came in.

" Mary and Luke are here in the waiting room," he said with a slight smile. " I thought you might want to talk to them before they came into see Dad. I'll stay here until you get back. Take this chance to get something to eat and a drink before you return."

Jane smiled although she was close to tears. " Thank you Paul. Try to keep talking to your father like the doctor advised us. I don't know what difference it makes but we have to try."

After his mother had left, Paul sat looking at his father for a while, at a loss for something to say. Before now when with his dad, he had never had trouble finding something to talk about. There was politics, books and, of course, sport whenever they were together. For as long as he could remember, his father had encouraged him to defend his own point of view even it was out of step with Tom's. Then something came to him and he began to speak, his voice dropping into the empty space left by his father's non response.

" Do you remember Dad when Porthampton Town got into the cup semi final and you went with Granddad?" he began tentatively. " I was only six at the time but extremely jealous. It was just before then that you and Granddad had promised to take me to my first match and I thought you would take me to the cup. I didn't realise about getting tickets or anything. It took you quite a while to get back in my good books after that. In a way it was good because Granddad died shortly after."

The fog was swirling through his mind, grey twisting and turning, the light more firmly established. Tom struggled towards the light trying to focus on the sound. It was a voice, a different voice, deeper, louder, echoing through the deep canyons of the desert of his mind.

Suddenly he was walking towards Villa Park and his Dad and Edward were by his side. All around were people dressed in red and white, waving scarves and singing. The excitement was so tangible as though he could reach out and touch it. To him it must have been visible in the air like mist obscuring the surroundings. The entire crowd were concentrating on that one thing, the match with sense sadness, it reminded Tom of something else. It was the last time he went to a football match with his father.

All those years of going to football matches together, generating all that excitement, all that joy and sorrow shared collectively. It had been a different world, that walking to the match. At first they had gone by bus, then by car. It had not been continuous for Tom and Edward. They had at times missed games when they played football as youths and then they had gone away to university. But whenever they could, Edward and Tom would go with their father to stand and sway and sing on the terraces of Porthampton Town.

His mind drifted. Images of football matches he had watched with his father were mixed with images of matches he had played both for the school, for the university and for the local team.

Then the fog cleared and he was sitting in the bar of the Bishopstead Country and Golf Club with his brother after a round of golf. Tom was puffing contentedly on a big cigar.

" Well Tom," Edward was saying. " Will that be your last?"

" I should think so now that we have two boys and a girl," Tom grinned. " I suppose Sarah is drooling over Mary at this minute. It was good of her to suggest that we played golf while she visited Jane and Mary and looked after the boys. I will have to look into having the same as you had done. How has it been?"

" After they did the vasectomy, it was as though a horse had kicked me in the balls for a few days," Edward said laughing. " I was black and blue and had difficulty sitting down. The sex life has been great once I got over the pain though. Sarah was relieved at not having to take the pill any more especially after all those stories in the papers about the side effects. If I were you I would talk it over with Jane before you decide though. Women get very sensitive about these things. I'll phone when I get home with the name of the surgeon who did me."

" Thanks," Tom replied dryly. " I will talk it over with Jane when I get a chance. There is no real rush."

" I hear you have been promoted to Senior Lecturer," Edward remarked.

" Who told you?"

" I met Douglas Stokes at a conference about private investment in transport the other week," Edward laughed at Tom's reaction. " You are quite famous in government circles, I gather. He said to send his regards the next time I met you. Bloody confident bastard isn't he?"

Tom smiled. " Coming from you, my brother, that must be a compliment. Yes they did promote me after the Professor made sure I put in for it."

" What? You have to put in for promotion to who?"

" Oh, it has to go before a university board. The Head of Department can support you but you have to make out the case yourself. There are strict rules about what criteria are used. It is to get round the problem of favouritism."

" Does it work?" Edward was amused." I have never known any system which could not be, shall we say, worked around."

Tom frowned. " I suppose everything can be worked around, as you put it. I haven't really thought about it too much. All I did was abide by the rules. Obviously, if a head of department wanted a certain lecturer to get promoted, he could have word in the ear of the members of the committee or write a bad report for another candidate. All in all, though, the process is as fair as can be arranged. There is an appeals procedure to the university council and visitor if somebody is not satisfied. Anyway, I am not so sure promotion is such a good idea. I am in charge of admissions and now they have given me the transport group to administer. I know it only has me and two lecturers along with a few research assistants but it adds to the time away from research and looking after the students."

" On another topic," Edward grinned. " Our investment partnership. We have both put in twenty five thousand pounds each so far making fifty thousand pounds in all. By judicious investments, I have managed to expand this to one hundred and fifty thousand."

Tom interrupted. " That sounds an big increase over five years. I trust you are not engaged in anything illegal."

Edward spread his hands and looked hurt. " Tom it would be more than my job is worth to take part in anything illegal. I have to declare the trust to my employers and it is vetted as part of the business. We even have to pay fees to the bank because the work is done in their time and through their investment arm. There is nothing illegal in what I do. The large returns are because of my knowledge of the markets and the resources of the bank. Don't you worry about the investments. You will have to trust me."

" Why does the phrase you will have to trust me ring alarm bells in my mind?" Tom shook his head.

" Look Tom I trust you though I am still concerned to find out more about your Mr. Hunt," Edward replied. " As far as I can find out all the companies you sure involved with are legitimate, file their audited accounts and the shareholders are registered at companies house."

" I suppose we will have to trust each other on that, won't we?" Tom countered.

They left things hanging in the air between them and went on to talk of other topics about old school friends and the chances of Porthampton Town ever getting out of the second division. They parted still on good terms though with a suspicion that each was not telling the other the whole story.

Tom was summoned to the Head of Department's office just before the exam boards were due to meet soon after his talk with Edward. It was not surprising because Professor Marriott liked to see all his group leaders before the external examiner arrived. When the secretary opened the door for Tom, he found Professor Marriott sitting behind his large desk studying a sheaf of papers. He vacantly waved Tom into a chair the other side of the desk, never taking his eyes off the papers.

" Have you seen these, Tom?" he asked brusquely thrusting the papers in Tom's direction. " They are the exam results of the second year."

" Yes. I have had a brief look at them. I have been busy preparing the paper with Josh, my research assistant. He is flying out to San Francisco tomorrow to present it in a couple of days. I was making sure he was up to speed with the likely questions. I would have liked to go with him but the department could not afford to send both of us. I was going to study the exam results tonight when I get home," Tom answered honestly.

" Josh will be OK," the Professor dismissed Tom's anxiety with a shrug. " We all have to start somewhere. It will be good experience for him to stand up in front of all those delegates at an international conference, put over his ideas and answer questions. What concerns me more at this time is that there is something that does not add up in these results. Have a look at the marks for Moira Oliver especially."

Tom looked down the column of results arranged on the papers that the Professor had given him, until he came to Moira Oliver's. They were near the bottom of the list just above the one's who had missed exams or course work for some reason. At first Tom could not see anything out of the ordinary until he realised in one subject she had scored a high mark while all the others were low. Averaging just above fifty overall, he realised this had been obtained with a remarkable sixty nine in one module.

" She must have found that module interesting and exceptionally taught," Tom looked up at the Professor with a raised eyebrow.

Professor Marriott shook his head. " Tom you are sounding naive and I know you are not stupid. Even you have to admit that there is a strong whiff of collusion here. Who lectures on that module?"

" Pauline Watts. She came from Leeds after her Doctorate and a few years researching. She is very good at her job and all the students give good reports in their assessments," Tom replied. " I can't believe that she would fiddle with Moira's marks or anybody's marks for that matter. What you are hinting at is very grave and if it came out could ruin her and Moira."

" We'll have to leave it until the exam board next week but I think we should keep an eye on things."

Tom was puzzled when he left Professor Marriott's office. He had never known the Professor as Head of Department single out any lecturer and student over exam marking. He might have queried a whole modules results, hinting that the marks overall might be too high or low. This was different and Tom was concerned. If the Professor was worried with all of his experience, Tom had to take the hints seriously. If there had been some kind of collusion between a lecturer and a student, and it could be proven, the only result would be the lecturer losing his or her job and the student being dismissed from the course.

After he got back to his office, he sat at his desk thinking about Pauline Watts. She had been by far the most able candidate when Department had drawn up the short list of candidates for the post of Lecturer in Transport Policy. Tom had been invited to sit on the interview panel and had seen at first hand her performance. There was no doubt in his mind that her interview enhanced her position as the most able candidate on the short list. It was no surprise when the panel voted to appoint her to the post.

"The start of your empire, " Professor Marriott had joked as they walked back to the Department after the interviews. Indeed he might have been right because Reg Brand had joined soon afterwards as a transport economist. Now there was a transport group in the department, maybe only three lecturers and six researchers but it was a start.

Pauline Watts, Tom thought, as he sat staring out of the window at the students walking between buildings or standing in groups chatting. She was rather serious like many academics, wore dark plain trouser suits with white blouses and had her hair cut short. It was strange, though he had never really taken too much notice of that, but among the many women he knew, academics, students and friends she was one of the few who did not wear makeup.

What was the Professor accusing her of? Tom asked himself again. Favouring one of the students, he answered his own question. Why?

The question hung in the air like a riddle from the Hobbit but for him there was no answer. Well there was but Tom did not understand the direction this idea was taking him. If what the Professor suspected was true, why had Pauline allowed this to happen? Out of friendship? Well, Tom reminisced, I have had many friends among the students, indeed many have come to my house especially my tutees but I have never thought about helping them to get more marks than they warranted.

What about Vicky? he asked himself smiling at the recollection of her warm body and exuberant sex. Oh, he had to admit he had acted against the spirit of the student lecturer code those times when they had made love but the feeling had been mutual and there had never been any hint of their intimacy having any effect on his professional judgement. That's easy, he told himself. Vicky was a first class student and did not need any dishonesty to achieve her grades. Would he have helped her in any other circumstances? Well no, he assured himself but was left with a nagging doubt. As for all the others, he had managed to be friendly without any overstepping of the line between friendship and deeper relationships. Perhaps Vicky had been good for him in that sense because even though a few female students had shown quite clearly that they would be open to any advances he might make, none of them came up to his ideal of Vicky. The closest had been Jo Wayne who had kissed him hurriedly one day as she left his office but he had ignored her and the threat had gone away.

All he could do was to wait until after the exam board and see what comments were made by the external examiner.

The exam board met in the Department a few days later. All the lecturers involved sat round the table with the Head of Department flanked by the External examiner at top of the table. There were two occasions in the life of the department which caused Tom endless amusement, the Departmental Meeting and the Exam Boards. This was the time when academics manoeuvred for position, tried to score points off each other without causing too much resentment and attempted to enhance their standing in the hierarchy. Most times any ill feeling was contained but sometimes it boiled over into a blazing row. Tom loved goading his colleagues into disagreements though now he had to be careful because he had two colleagues who might start manipulating for his position.

The exam board that morning was no exception. As the grades were read out, academics nodded them through unless they were near a grade boundary. Then the manoeuvring started. One academic would champion one student but try to do down another. That student would then be championed. The Senate Representative would valiantly try to uphold the rules of the University by applying these to particular cases. The External examiner would give his opinion. After much argument, consensus would be established and they would move on to another student group. It may not be scientific, Tom often mused, but it produced the right results most of the time and could be seen to be fair. The only quarrel he had was that the board appeared to spend a long time discussing those students who would not enhance the reputation of the university by dint of their dreadful marks. Those students plainly gaining first class or upper second marks caused hardly any discussion. The one issue which did get an airing was Moira Oliver's Transport Policy mark and how this stood out from all the others.

Pauline Watts, asked to comment, had merely said that Moira appeared to be enthusiastic on the module and had worked hard. The External had remarked that this should be watched and other lecturers might be able to get Moira working hard on their modules.

" Not on your life," Tom had muttered to Craig Hind sitting on his left hand side. " In her case there is no chance that she will ever get more than adequate marks in Transport Management. I have even tried talking to her about what she has to do to get higher marks for her course work but that has had no effect. Still, if everybody is happy, we will have to let it pass."

" I have no idea what she is like because she doesn't take any of my modules." Craig remarked in reply. " If the external is satisfied, lets get this over with and off down the pub."

After the exam board, they adjourned to the pub for a drink while the official marks were posted by the Council. It was always pleasant to have a drink with his friends after the board knowing that he could then concentrate on his research for the rest of the summer. Jane and he had booked a holiday in a cottage near Tenby and he prayed that the weather would be dry and sunny. There was a dread he always had that when they had planned a beach holiday, it would rain.

A few days after the exam board, Tom was summoned to Professor Marriott's office once more.

He found the Professor sitting in an armchair with coffee pot on the coffee table and some papers on his lap.

" Take a seat Tom and pour yourself a coffee," Professor Marriott indicated an armchair near the coffee table.

Once Tom was sitting in his chair with his cup of coffee, Professor Marriott spoke. " Call me over suspicious but I have been looking through all the written work submitted by Moira Oliver. It is a curious fact that all her Transport Policy work has been completed in what I see as a different style to her other work. It is much more lucid and logical. Here you are. You have a look through her work."

Professor Marriott handed a file of papers to Tom. With widening understanding, Tom read through the coursework and exam papers. It did not take much studying of the written work, of styles of writing and of turns of phrase to deduce that the Transport Policy submissions were in subtle ways different.

Tom looked up and sighed. " Lets not jump to conclusions too quickly," he said, stalling for time while he thought about the consequences of any action they might take. " It might be that she picked up the language and the flow from all the references she read and absorbed."

Professor Marriott reached down and picked up a paper from the floor by the side of his chair. " Read this. Then tell me I am being hasty."

Tom took the paper and read. In tone and style there was much in common with Moira Oliver's work. Turning the paper over he was confronted with what he had been trying to avoid thinking about. The paper was written by Pauline Watts.

" Well?" Professor Marriott's word dropped like an echo of doom into the silence of the room. Tom's thoughts turned to a vision of Pauline being hauled before the Vice Chancellor and stripped of her lectureship. It was something all lecturers dreaded but it did not happen very often. The rules referred to gross misconduct and this was usually interpreted to mean having an affair with a student with the suspicion of bias, bringing the university into disrepute by some outside activity and helping a student to gain an unfair advantage. Because cases were so rare, each incident had to be judged on its merits without much precedent.

" What can we do now?" Tom stared at Professor Marriott his mind churning. " The exam board met and approved the marks. After that the Senate signed off the results. The lists have been published and posted on the official notice board as laid down in the university statutes. As far as the students are concerned everything is above board. It would be an admission of failure on our part, on the external examiners part and for the university if we were to reconvene the exam board. Christ, the newspapers would have a field day."

" I hear what you are saying, Tom, but we cannot ignore it. As I see things, we have some evidence that one of your lecturers has helped a student get higher grades than she would have done if left to her own devises. One of the staff will have to take her aside and warn her that this will not be tolerated in the future." Professor Marriott smiled benignly at Tom.

" Oh no not me," Tom shook his head vigorously, a look of horror on his face. " This is a job for the Head of Department. You have bags of experience and the authority to make decisions."

" I think I should be left in reserve, Tom," Professor Marriott smiled and looked smug. " Besides, she is one of your Transport group. As such she is your responsibility. Call her into your office as soon as possible and have it out with her. Hopefully that will be the end of the affair."

" Thanks!" Tom said as he left the Professor's office.

There is no way in which I can go through with this, Tom thought as he walked through the building back to his office. How can I to start? Do I confront her? Do I apply diplomacy? What possible motive could she have for helping a student like this? What happens if she denies the whole thing? But Tom gripped the file in his hand. Proof, if she demanded it, would not be to hard to establish. I hope she doesn't demand I prove my suspicions. Lets hope she agrees and gives me an explanation.

Pauline Watts came to his office the next day as he had requested. She was as usual dressed in a trouser suit, functional shoes and her hair was cut short. Her face was devoid of makeup.

"You wanted to see me?" she asked after taking a seat.

"Yes," Tom replied tentatively. "Professor Marriott asked me to have a word. Look, there is no way I can say this other than being blunt. There are some question marks over the marking of one of your exam papers."

Tom could not be sure but he thought he detected a slight narrowing of Pauline's eyes. It was as though she was quickly hiding her apprehension.

"Which one was that?" she asked just as bluntly.

"Moira Oliver and the Transport Policy paper," Tom shuffled the papers on his desk.

"She worked hard and deserved her marks," Pauline shot back but she did not look at Tom.

"That's the problem," Tom said calmly. "She might have worked hard but all her other marks are way out of line with her Transport Policy marks. Now how do you account for that?"

"As I said at the exam board, she obviously like the subject," Pauline replied.

"That could be true but it is highly unlikely," Tom shot back. "If you look at all the other students in her year, there is no such discrepancy between one module's marks and another module's marks. There might be what could be termed the scatter gun result where all the marks are all over the place but not one module almost getting first class marks while all the others are third class. I know I am not as experienced as some of the more senior people in the Department but I have seen enough sets of exam results to notice that this seems out of the ordinary. What happened?"

" She must have liked the subject," Pauline insisted.

Tom picked up the papers in front of him and pushed them across the desk to Pauline.

" Look at these," he instructed her. " Is this a paper written for the Chartered Institute of Transport by you?"

" Yes," Pauline answered her forehead creased in a worried frown.

" Look at these," Tom pushed some more papers across the desk. " Is this one of the coursework essays which Moira handed in to you? They must be because it has your comments written in the margins."

" Yes that was the second essay she wrote for me," Pauline shrugged.

" The styles are very similar," Tom said. " Indeed I would go so far as to say they were written by the same person."

"Are you accusing me of helping her?" Pauline' voice rose sharply and her body bristled with indignation. With her mouth a thin line, she gripped the table edge and half rose from her seat thrusting her face towards Tom. " If you are, you had better be careful what you say. If the other lecturers get to hear this, I could sue you and the Professor for defamation."

"There is no need to threaten me," Tom shook his head and waved her back to her seat. " The exam results have been approved by the exam board and the Senate. They have been posted on the notice board and all the students have accepted their grades. Come on Pauline. You know it would cause a lot of hassle to get the subject of your marking opened up again. No. What the professor and I are trying to do is help you avoid any unpleasantness in the future. If there is any hint of this happening again next year, the external examiner is going to query your results. We will not be able to contain things in house and then it will come to the attention of the Vice Chancellor. If that happens it will be out of our hands. All I want to know is how and why you did it. Then we can agree that it will not happen again."

Pauline sat belligerently staring at him for a long time and then slumped back in her chair. Tears wet her eyes and she blew her nose in a white handkerchief.

" OK," she began obviously reluctantly, wiping her eyes. To Tom she looked very vulnerable and, without any makeup, much younger than her twenty eight years. " It is hard for somebody like me to explain to somebody like you. Girls attract me and I want to hug them and kiss them. I can see from the expression on your face that you don't understand. There are not many people outside my circle of friends who really understand. Things are improving now, though, because we are becoming more open about our feelings. To put things bluntly, I like other women in the same fashion as you do. To me Moira Oliver is very attractive. In her first term, as you know, I was her tutor. She was very lonely and homesick. Things were not going well for her. She came to my office most weeks for somebody to talk to. Then before she went home for the Christmas holidays, she came and was very agitated. At first all I could get out of her was that she would most likely not come back after Christmas. She could not cope with the work, her marks were bad and she had no friends. You must have had students like that."

" I have had a few," Tom admitted. " Both boys and girls have sat in that chair and used my tissues to dry their eyes from the big box I keep for that purpose. I try to calm them down and then talk through their problems."

" Have you never been tempted to let things go further?" Pauline asked bluntly.

" No. I have always tried to keep a proper tutor student relationship," Tom stated but his mind immediately thought of Vicky. Ah, he told himself that was different. She was the one who pushed our relationship, he silently justified to himself his times with Vicky. I have never taken advantage of a vulnerable student, he congratulated himself. " I know it is hard at times but we have to maintain or integrity."

" You didn't really answer my question I notice," Pauline laughed. " I hear that there were rumours of your relationship with a girl student a few years ago."

" You must mean Vicky," it was Tom's turn to laugh. " She was my tutee and one of the best students we have ever had. She came to see me every week, which I was trying to get all my tutees to do. Why when they have the chance to get help and advice do they never come? Still that is another matter. What happened between you and Moira?"

Pauline hesitated looking at Tom as though she was gauging what to say. It was obvious she came to some conclusion.

" What do you know about homosexual relationships?" she burst out abruptly.

" Nothing," Tom said equally bluntly. " Don't get me wrong. I am aware of women being attracted by other women and men attracted by other men. I have had friends and some students who I suspected were attracted by the same sex but I have never been curious enough to look into it. It's like most things. If it affects your own life, you get to find out about it. If not, it just passes you by."

" Thanks for not looking shocked and kicking me out," Pauline replied with a sigh of relief. " I have never thought about having to explain my feelings to somebody like you."

Tom looked genuinely puzzled. " Why should I ever think of condemning you like that?"

" Oh there are a great many people in this world who think that people like me should be pushed off the face of the earth," Pauline replied bitterly. " I am a lesbian in that I am attracted to other women. Like you I suppose. I am not a man so I cannot compare the feelings. Moira Oliver was so vulnerable when she came to my office that I had to put my arm round her shoulder to comfort her. One thing led to another and we became lovers. Then she was having problems with her exams and course work. I could not bear the thought that she would fail and not be here anymore. So I helped her get enough marks in the exam to make sure she passed. What do I do now?"

" Do what I do," Tom grinned. " Try to help the students without getting involved. Never try to favour one student over another. Try not to let your attraction for a particular student spill over into a more intimate relationship. If you cannot avoid that, make sure you do nothing to compromise yourself. Remember, relationships do not always last and getting involved with a student runs the risk of subtle forms of pressure."

" Thank you Tom," Pauline looked serious. " I will try to make sure that I am discreet about my feelings in the future."

Those words of advice were destined to come back and haunt Tom quicker than he had thought. Vicky, he realised, had been a special case in that she was a brilliant student and there was no grounds for her to try to put pressure on him in their university dealings. In other circumstances it could have been different he now realised after speaking to Pauline.

All the lecturers in the department had to become industrial training tutors for students going into industry for twelve months after their second year. While away from the university, the students were supposed to learn about the company, how it was organised and what the working environment was like. For many students, it was the first taste of management work and of having to take responsibility for their actions. The usual practice in the department was for a lecturer to tutor one of that lecturer's personnel tutees while they were out in industry.

On this occasion Tom had been asked to take on the tutee of one of the other lecturers, Brian Roberts, because, at the time, Tom did not have any of his tutees going out into industry. This will balance the load, Tom had been told. He did suspect that he had been given one of the more difficult students to handle but did not complain because it was what he could have done if he had been asked to pass one of his tutees to another lecturer.

Her name was Lucy Meredith. Tom had hardly spoken to her in the two years she had been in the university. He remembered her as rather a plump girl with brown hair. She wore glasses and was always dressed in jeans. In fact, Tom had never seen her dressed in anything else other than sweater and jeans. To Tom she was quiet but not studious.

She had been given a post with a merchant bank in the City. Her first report showed no problems. Tom informed her that he would visit her at the beginning of the term giving her time to settle into her job.

Out of the blue one morning before the end of the summer break, he had an unexpected phone call. Lucy was almost hysterical. She told Tom emphatically that she would not stay in the job. Even when asked bluntly what was wrong, she would not answer. Understandable, Tom reasoned if she is phoning from work. There was nothing Tom could do other than but drop his research and go to London the next day.

He met Lucy at a cafe to talk about what she thought had happened. Tom reasoned it was best to get her side of the story before he met up with her employers. It came as a surprise when he joined her for coffee to find her dressed in a tailored suit, tights and high heels. Her hair was shorter than he remembered and had obviously been groomed by a hair dresser.

After they were seated with their coffee, Tom asked, " Well?"

Lucy looked nervous and twisted a handkerchief in her hands under the table. Her voice was quiet and withdrawn " Things were all right when I first started. I had a woman for my boss and the work was interesting. They were following the plan agreed between Brian and Mr. Tunneycliffe. I was to spend a couple of months in various sections of the bank. Well, you know all that because you have seen the papers."

Tom smiled faintly. " Yes, I read all the papers when Brian handed supervision of your placement over to me."

" It was when I joined a section run by a Mike Noland that things started to go wrong. It was not the work. I found the work interesting. However, Mike Noland started to make suggestions to me about seeing him after work and at weekends. Now I knew he was married so I refused to go out with him other than when the rest of the people working in that section went out in a group. For some reason this angered him. Soon, he started to warn me that things could go bad for me if I didn't come out with him. Then he started to criticise my work. At times he told me off in front of all the others. I complained to higher management but they took no notice seeming to believe Mike rather than me. Tom I can't stay with that man!"

Tom reached over the table and squeezed her hand. " Calm down Lucy. I have arranged a meeting with the Personnel Manager for later this morning. You can explain all of this and we can then see how to keep you working here. Drink up your coffee and we will go along to the bank."

At the meeting were her section manager, David Jackson and the personnel manager, Pamela Wilkinson. David Jackson was plump, clean shaven and dressed in a neatly cut dark suit with a cream shirt and matching tie. He was obviously subordinate to Pamela Wilkinson. She was a tall good looking woman but her good looks were spoilt by the severe expression she wore like a cloak. Her hair was cut short, her suit dark, and she wore no make up.

It was an informal meeting where they discussed Lucy's progress to date and what the management felt about her work. The meeting went smoothly in Tom's opinion with everybody staying calm and focused. Only when Lucy had to give her side of the story did things start to go down hill.

Lucy outlined her objections to Mike Noland as her immediate boss. She told about her fear of what would happen if she turned down his advances and her shock at his suggestions. The personnel manager immediately became aggressive making it sound as though it was all Lucy's fault.

Tom was appalled. In a voice verging on the angry, he said so. " This is not a trial of Lucy or Mike Noland. It is an attempt to get to the bottom of her fears. It is not your job to condemn my student out of hand. That, if I might say so, smacks of the company people protecting each other."

The Pamela Wilkinson bristled and replied harshly. " We gave her a chance to work with us during her industrial training period. I admit that her work is reasonable and on that score we have no complaints. She is making unsubstantiated accusations against one of my loyal workers. We have never received any complaints about his behaviour before. I think she is exaggerating what happened."

It was Tom's turn to get angry but he replied in a tight calm voice full of menace. " It was not out of the kindness of your heart or indeed you who offered her a placement. You get a great deal of assistance and work out of placements for very little outlay Ms Wilkinson. So don't you be so fast in condemning my student."

David Jackson hurriedly intervened, trying desperately to head off a blazing row. " May I make a suggestion?"

Pamela frowned, did not speak but nodded.

David continued. " Lucy is undergoing training. Might the best solution be to move her away from Mike Noland and into another job?"

Pamela Wilkinson smiled slightly making her hard expression lighten for a moment. " Agreed. Lucy if you have no objections you will move into Mary Lawrence's section next week. You can take the rest of the week off. Is that satisfactory?"

Lucy agreed readily. David Jackson then took them to lunch. After lunch, Tom went back to St. Pancras Station with Lucy giving him an opportunity to speak to her on her own. She sounded quite happy and in agreement with the deal they had negotiated. Just before she got on her train to Nottingham, she assured him that all would be fine and kissed him in the way of thanks.

Tom travelled home thinking that all was well with Lucy Meredith. With luck he would not have to visit her in her place of work until after Christmas. He could concentrate on the new students and his research until then.

Things did not turn out the way Tom imagined as he left London for home after seeing Lucy off on the Nottingham train. Three weeks after seeing Lucy onto the train, assured that she would be back at work the next Monday, Tom received a phone call from her mother.

She demanded in a voice which was both confused, concerned and almost angry, " Why is Lucy at home and not at work?"

Tom was just as confused. He had assumed that everything was functioning well for Lucy and that she was working in the bank in London.

Her mother went on to tell him, " She returned home one night unexpectedly with all her things and has not budged from the house since. My husband and me have tried to find out what was happening but Lucy will not answer any of our questions. If we push too hard, she goes to her room and only appears at meal times. All she will say to us on the subject of her work is that she wants to see you," Mrs. Meredith concluded.

" When can she come to the University then?" Tom asked, reaching for his diary.

" She says she wants you to come down here and see her," Mrs. Meredith sounded desperate. " I have no experience of this. Can you please come to see her? I know she is not a high flier but I do worry about her."

" Mrs Meredith we treat all students the same," Tom tried to stay calm but his mind was racing. " I'll speak to the head of department about coming to Skegness. He won't be happy but I expect I can persuade him. When can I come?"

" As soon as possible please Dr Houseman. My husband and I are starting to get desperate."

So it was that three days later Tom found himself waking in a strange hotel near Skegness ready to face Lucy and her family. He had hoped to be rescued by Professor Marriot but, to his surprise, the Professor had agreed that it was vital that Tom visit Lucy at her home.

" We have to be seen to be looking after our students," the Professor had said with a smile. " You go on up there and see what needs to be done to help Miss Meredith."

Tom cursed Brian Roberts. He silently wondered whether Brian had known that Lucy was going to be a problem student when he had asked Tom to supervise her industrial placement.

He drove out along the coast road consulting a map until he turned off to the right onto a road lined with bungalows. Peering out of his window he spotted the names on the walls or gateposts until he came to one called Volvatello. This was Lucy's home.

He parked the car and walked up the garden path. The lawn was cut short and edged by plants and shrubs. The front door had an opaque glass window at head height. There was no bell so he used the knocker.

After a short time a short plump middle aged woman wearing a blouse, skirt and cardigan opened the door. She smiled nervously in enquiry and he was immediately sure that this was Lucy's mother.

" Yes?" she asked bluntly.

" Mrs. Meredith?" Tom asked in return. " I am Tom Houseman and you asked me to come and speak to your daughter."

" Come on in Dr. Houseman," she opened the door wide.

Tom followed her down a corridor and through a lounge at the back of the house. Another door led out into a conservatory over looking the garden. As he took the offered chair, Tom noticed that the back garden was just as neat and tidy as the front.

" Lucy is not here," Mrs. Meredith said waving her hand to stop Tom protesting. " She has gone down to our beach hut to sit and look at the sea and keep out of my way. I was told to tell you to meet her there. I know it is autumn and none too hot but there is a paraffin heater in the hut. I go there sometimes in the winter to get away from things. It is quiet on the beach now and can be quite snug in the hut. I have to go into Skegness and help my husband in the shop so it would be best if you went down there and talked to her. I find her very hard work when she is in this kind of mood."

Tom got up from his chair. " Which way to the beach?"

" Carry on to the end of the lane and then there are some steps leading over the sea defences. They will lead to the promenade in front of the huts. Well it isn't much of a promenade, just a concrete path really," Mrs Meredith smiled nervously. " We like to call it a promenade."

"I'll go and see her now," Tom took her hand. "I'll see what I can do to help her."

For the first time since he had arrived at her house, Mrs Meredith became quite animated. The words came out in a rush. "You must get her back to her work. If she packs up now this will stay on her records forever. She said she wanted to go into the bank and I cannot for the life of me understand why she is unwilling to go back. You have to get her to return to her placement."

"I can only try," was Tom's parting shot as he left the house.

He walked passed a couple of bungalows until he reached the end of the lane. A bank rose high above his head and he still could not see the sea. Concrete steps led up and over the bank and he climbed these. There was that peculiar smell and sound which always heralded the closeness of the sea. At the top of the embankment there was the sight of the North Sea stretching away to the horizon. A cold wind was whipping up the waves and blowing sand in Tom's face. He pulled his collar higher round his neck and descended the steps to the concrete promenade at the bottom. To his left was a line of green and grey painted sheds or beach huts as Lucy's mother had called them. To his right the beach curved round the bay.

At first glance all the huts appeared to be shut up for the winter. Each door having at least two padlocks. One however was open. Sitting on a folding chair bundled in a warm coat, woolly hat and boots sat a figure. Its hands were thrust in pockets and it sat gazing out to sea.

As Tom neared she looked up. What he could see of her expression was hostile.

" Hello," Tom greeted Lucy cheerfully. " You asked me to come and see you."

" Not me but my Mum," Lucy snapped not smiling in return. " She wants me to return to that bank. Says I am being selfish by giving up the job you found for me. Oh don't stand there looking down on me, take a seat. There is another chair in there."

Tom fetched another folding chair and sat next to her. To Tom's surprise, as soon as he was seated, Lucy got to her feet.

" Want a cup of coffee, Tom? I'll make you one."

While she was busying herself with the coffee, Tom sat and thought through what he was going to have to say. Until confronted by Lucy, he had only considered how he could persuade her to go back to the bank. That was still his intention but, from her attitude and mood, he realised that he might have to discuss other options with her.

When he had his coffee on the ground next to his chair, and she was sitting back by his side, Tom took her hand in his. " Look Lucy, I am not here to make you do anything. I came because I got a cry for help."

" Not from me you didn't." Lucy barked back, her expression hostile and her muscles tense. " My mother asked you to come like the interfering busybody she usually is."

" Your mother was trying to help you by calling me," Tom picked his words with care. " I know you don't think the same way but just try and imagine what it must have been like when you turned up at home and stayed for longer than your parents thought you were going to. Don't be too harsh on them. They are attempting to get you to do what they think is best for you."

" How the bloody hell do they know what is best for me?" Lucy exploded bitterly. " What they are thinking about is their freedom and their reputation. They think that if I give up this industrial training, it will be a stain on my record and reflect badly on them."

" When I left you in London a few weeks ago, I thought we had solved your problems." Tom realised he was still holding her hand. " What changed?"

" It was Mike Nolan," she said with a shudder and he noticed tears wetting her eyes. " He kept coming into the section I had been placed in and there was nothing I could do to stop him. He did not say much, only to ask me for a date. No matter what I said, he kept leering at me. I could see he thought he had gotten away with harassing me and was out to get me to see him after work. I couldn't stand it. I complained to Mary Lawrence but she thought I was imagining things. Tom, I was not being paranoid about him. He really gave me the creeps and scared me. Don't make me go back there again."

Lucy was openly crying now and Tom instinctively put his arm around her shoulders. She turned and buried her head in his coat against his chest. Her arms came round his neck. To comfort her, he could think of nothing other than to stroke her head through the woolly hat until the sobs subsided.

Lucy looked up when she had some control over herself and kissed him full on the lips. Tom was at a loss as to what to do. He pushed her away so that he could look into her eyes. She did not take her arms from around his neck.

" Let us go inside," she said getting to her feet but holding tight to his hand so as to pull him up. " There is a fire in there and we will be more comfortable."

It was warmer inside the hut with the electric fire turned on. Abstractly Tom noticed there was bunk bed built into a corner. Well it was not only a bunk bed but a set of drawers. By the fire was an old armchair. Lucy sat him in the armchair and made some more coffee. When this was completed, she sat down on the arm of the chair, her legs draped across his body. She had discarded the woolly hat and her outer coat.

" What now?" she asked ambiguously her head on his shoulder.

" Well," Tom hesitated. " If you cannot go back to the bank, we will have to find some way to explain your year out without an industrial training transcript and certificate. The only way I can see out of this dilemma is for you to apply for leave of absence from the university. That way it will be up to you how you explain to potential employers why you had a year away from your studies."

" Can you do that for me?" Lucy asked him. " My Mum won't be too pleased but she will accept that if it means I will not have too big a strain on my reputation."

She kissed him again and started to undo his coat buttons.

Tom tried to ignore what she was doing and said. " I will have to convince the Head of Department when I get back but I think I can do that."

" Thank you Tom," she said kissing him before getting up and closing the doors. When she returned she took his hand and led him over to the bed.

" This is my way of thanking you," she whispered pulling him down onto the bed.

They made love slowly and when they had finished, Lucy was more relaxed and thinking about what she could do with the time away from the university. In his thoughts about what had happened, Tom dismissed his conscience and his remembering of what he had advised Pauline. He justified his actions on the grounds that he was helping Lucy get over her fear of returning to her job. By making love to her on her terms, he felt he was showing her that not all men were ogres but some were willing to help.

All thoughts of Lucy vanished when he arrived home. He knew that something was up as soon as he walked into the sitting room on arriving home that evening. Jane looked up from the television and got up from her chair. This was unusual because normally she would wave and indicate the kitchen when he was late home and she was absorbed in a programme.

" I have some bad news," she said in her straight forward way. " I had a phone call from your mother. I hate to have to tell you but she told me that your Dad has been diagnosed with cancer. I have been waiting all afternoon for you to come home. I was dreading having to tell you. Sorry I was so blunt."

She put her arms round his shoulders and led him to a chair. " Can I get you a gin and tonic?"

Tom blinked as though seeing her for the first time trying to stay outwardly calm. " Ah? Oh yes that would be great. Tell me the whole story."

Jane poured the gin over the ice and lemon slice, twirling it round to cool it down. Then she added just the right amount of tonic. Handing this to Tom, she waited while he drank deeply.

" There is not much more to tell you. You know your Dad has been complaining about pains in his bladder and difficulties with passing water. Well he went to the doctor some time ago and the doctor sent him to the hospital. X-rays and tests show that he has Pancreatic cancer."

" How long?"

" They could not say. Your mother was very uptight so I expect she thinks not too long."

" Why didn't he tell me all about this before?"

" Oh Tom," Jane kissed his forehead. " I expect he thought it was nothing and that you had enough on your plate what with your children and work to worry about him."

" Have you told the children?" Tom asked looking towards the stairs.

" Not yet. I thought we would wait until we knew more."

Paul sitting beside that hospital bed listened as his father breathing became more agitated. His heart missed a beat for a while as he imagined signs of consciousness. The ping of the machines seemed to speed up such that he was on the point of fetching his mother. Then they settled back into the measured sounds they had made since he came into the room. I must have been imagining it, he thought.

It was a long and hard fifteen months, Tom remembered. He tried to be cheerful and hopeful all the time especially when he was with his father. All the family tried to put on a brave face. Tom went through life mechanically during that year. He made sure that he accompanied his father to all the home football matches. Spent time with his parents and made sure that his children visited frequently.

He became divorced from politics. Although he received notification of Labour Party meetings, he did not go. It was as though he only cared for his father and wanted to devote his time to helping his mother.

Though their relationship had got off to a bad start all those years ago when his father had come back from the war, over the years they had found an accommodation. They were never close in the same way as Edward and his father but they came to respect and like each other. Tom realised when he graduated and saw his father at the ceremony, how his father was so proud of his sons. The picture of him in his board and gown with his parents had, alongside Edward's, been displayed in a prominent place. Besides, his father fell in love with Jane from the first time they were introduced. He would go out of his way to help her. She appeared to be the only person with whom he could have a long conversation. Jane reciprocated that affection and would not hear a word said against Tom's Dad.

It was amazing. As though the Gods were on their side, for the first time for a number of seasons, Porthampton Town played well. They topped the league for a large part of the season but more importantly had a long run in the Cup. During the run they knocked out several first division sides and got to the semi-final at Villa Park. Porthampton Town versus Manchester United.

Tom and Edward queued for hours to get tickets. They joined in the banter, searched for food and drink, moaned about the wait and then emerged triumphant with the precious tickets.

By the time of the match, Tom's father was being more and more affected by the cancer. He had lost weight and had that far away look in his eyes every so often of those facing death. All three took the special train to Birmingham and then a bus to the ground. It was a wonderfully colourful occasion. Cheering crowds, rattles making the noise louder and a sea of red and white scarves. The match was close for almost two thirds and then United stepped up the pace and scored twice. Even then there was a twist in the tail as Porthampton scored five minutes from the end and pounded away to no avail. Walking back to the bus, the three men were exhausted, a bit sad but immensely proud.

Seeing a young boy with his father on the train, Tom felt tears coming to his eyes. It was only then that he realised that this might be the last time he went to the football with his Dad. Of more importance was the feeling that his son Paul would never go to the football with his Granddad. Though Tom had been unfriendly to his father until he was about twelve, his father had taken him to the football from the time he had reached six years old. Paul was six that year and Tom had had this vision of introducing him to the pleasures of football in the company of his Grandfather and his uncle. Now there would be no outing together.

It was shortly after the semi-final when Tom received a phone call from his brother.

" Tom? We must meet somewhere as soon as possible," Edward sounded strange as though he had lost something.

" Is everything all right with your family?" Tom countered.

" It is too much to talk about on the phone. Can we meet at the Jolly Sailor this evening? We can have a proper talk then."

Tom made sure that Jane was agreeable and then drove to the Jolly Sailor near the river. The place was pretty full but Tom spotted Edward in a corner and joined him after buying a pint.

" Well?" Tom asked as he took his seat.

" Have you heard of Militant?"

" That far left group? We talked about them when I was your agent. That Mike Pearce brought the paper and spouted nonsense from it all the time."

" Yes, that about sums it up. We both thought they were such a small number there was no danger from them. If we laughed at them enough they would go away. We were wrong. They have taken over my constituency and deselected me as a candidate."

Tom laughed. " But that's silly. They can't have that much support in your constituency."

" No they haven't. The trouble is they as a group go to all the meetings. You know how most members are. When was the last time you went to a meeting?"

" Last autumn, I suppose," Tom shrugged. " What with Dad being ill and Mum needing support, I have let that slide I suppose. We have a good committee there, loyal to the party and to the MP."

"That's not what I hear," Edward said with certainty. "Anyway, the militants as I say go to all the meetings. They keep the meetings going until a many other members give up and leave. Then they pass motions in the name of the ward. When there are any elections to officers they make sure they have the meetings packed with their supporters. It is not too far fetched to go from there to the domination of all aspects of the business being controlled by them."

Edward shook his head. "You know Caroline Hobbs and George Nesbitt? They were the only remaining committee members from the time you were election agent. A couple of months ago, despite protests from some of the members, they were voted off the committee and replaced with militant supporters. That Basil Weston, the school teacher you remember from many of our meetings? He has become the ring leader and the committee chairman. At meetings, he makes sure that only militant voices are heard and that anybody who disagrees with his ideas, is ridiculed and silenced. He firmly believes that capitalism is a treadmill for the workers. All the benefits go to the bosses. When challenged by some of us, he has to admit that there are some gains for the workers in terms of better standards of living. These, he claims are only short term with only short periods of uneasy solace for the workers. When any economic upswing falters and a boom gives way to recession, employers will try to unload the burden onto the shoulders of the workers. He claims that Capitalism can only offer, in the long run, war or slump, annihilation or penury, to the people of Britain and all other countries. Where he gets these phrases from is straight out of the pages of the Militant newspaper and Marx."

" You sound just like Mike Pearce," Tom remarked. " When I was your election agent, you remember, I asked him to help with the strategy. He used to spout things like that until he was certain I was not going to take any notice."

" I would look out for that Mike Pearce if I was you," Edward was serious. " He is the leading light in your constituency. From what I gather, he has been voted onto the committee and is scathing about anybody who does not hold his views. To go back to what I was saying about Militant."

" Aren't they in danger of being a party within a party which except for affiliated organisations, is against the constitution?" Tom asked seriously

"Ha! You see that is what is so subtle about Militant," Edward shook his head sadly. " They claim that it is only a newspaper reporting what is happening and letting people use its pages to put forward their opinions. It does not organise anything. Therefore it is not a party within a party. From what I have been able to find out, we have all been sleeping for the last ten years since the paper was first published."

" They cannot be that strong or I would have noticed, surely," Tom was clearly puzzled.

" Not really," Edward laughed bitterly. " They have a policy of quietly infiltrating the inner workings of the Labour Party over a long time. Now they are coming out of the woodwork because the Labour Party is in trouble. As all Marxist splinter groups associated with the Labour Party have for as long as the Labour Party has been in existence, they want detailed plans for production industries every five years. This can only be achieved on the basis of state ownership of all industry employing more than twenty workers. They tell all workers that shop stewards, technicians and even small shopkeepers are the next to be axed by the capitalist monopolies."

" I have heard all that crap many times especially while I was at university. Even now some of my students talk like that but I make them substantiate their claims." Tom grimaced. " In engineering departments in universities there might be quite a few conservatives but among the students there are a great many Marxists. They argue that way all the time. The trouble is in theory it is a compelling argument. There is an imbalance in wealth between those at the bottom and those at the top. In addition, it does always seem that those at the bottom always take a disproportionate share of any bad times."

" But Tom," Edward sighed. " Even you have to admit that in order to make things better for everybody we first have to generate the wealth. My view is that we have to get rich by letting people invest, like us, but then redistribute that wealth to everybody through taxation, support and help. Let us not make the generation of wealth a criminal offence."

" You know we think much the same on this, though I am loath to admit it," Tom grinned. " I still cannot see how these militants can be such a threat to the Labour government."

" Because they think that their plan to go more left wing is the only 'practical' plan which could guarantee victory for Labour at the polls. We have to ensure a change in society and make a return to Tory reaction impossible, they say. Labour may well win elections without such a programme, but it will surely go down to bitter defeat, crushed by big business, they write. Tom we have to fight it. There is no way the electorate is going to take on board that sort of nonsense. You have to go to the next meeting and try to stop this in its tracks. If you want to find out more, phone Caroline and she will tell you. I am certain she will be pleased to talk to you."

Edward then smiled. " On a lighter note. Our investment fund has reached three hundred thousand pounds. I expect to double that when a couple of opportunities come our way by the autumn. I have invested some more in our income bonds so that we now have one hundred thousand each. That will give us an income of about six thousand a year. So we are doing well on that front."

" I still get cold feet about what you are doing with our money but Jane tells me not to worry," Tom admitted. " How long before our fund goes over the million pound mark?"

" With a bit of nifty foot work, this time next year, I expect. You see, Tom, once we are running the fund expands compound. I will keep adding to our safe income portfolios as we get richer. That way we will reap the benefits of our investments by being able to spend some of the money. Well I am off to fight the militants in my constituency. Give my love to Jane."

Tom was thoughtful over the next few weeks. Like a good academic, he went to the library and read every article he could find on the rise of Militant. To advance his education, he obtained copies of the newspaper and studied this. It was soon obvious that starting with a simple idea that the poor and the working class were getting a raw deal, Militant had, like all Marxists, jumped to a startling conclusion. It was far better to tear down the whole edifice and rebuild it rather than try to tinker with the structure as it was. Better to destroy and then build anew. He also soon learnt that they viewed the world in very stark terms. Those who are not in complete agreement with our philosophy, are our enemies, they wrote. What this meant was that anybody thought of as a supporter had to agree to everything without question or they would be outlawed.

The next time there was a Labour Party meeting in his area, Tom went along. A few people who he knew greeted him like a lost brother but others were much more hostile. He did not recognise many of the people in the room though he did know Mike Pearce among those on the platform.

The business dragged on and Tom was aware that he had been warned about this by his brother. People started to drift away, some to go home, others to the bar. Stubbornly Tom stayed.

" Next item on the agenda." The chairman Dave Dowling stated. " The nomination of two delegates to the Labour Party conference."

" I propose Dave Dowling and Mike Pearce," a thin face woman said from the floor.

" Thank you," Dave Dowling said. " I will have to step aside while a vote is taken if there are any other nominations. Well?"

He glowered round the room.

" I nominate Tom Houseman," a quiet voice spoke from the middle of the room.

Mr. Reynolds, thought Tom, looking round. Stan Reynolds sat with his wife Betty defiantly looking at the committee. He was dressed in a suit and tie, grey hair slicked back. His lined face showed his concern and determination. His wife was dressed in a cardigan and skirt. They must have been well passed retirement age. They had been coming to these meetings for a long time so Tom had gathered when he had talked to them after joining from the other constituency. They were the sort of old fashioned Labour people who believed in equality of opportunity, redistribution of wealth and society. For them the health service was the best thing that had ever been devised. Their children had gone, like Tom to grammar school and then into professions, one a teacher, the other doctor. They were proud of their children and grandchildren but they never lost sight of their roots and the need to give people a chance in life. They supported the monarchy and the countries institutions. As Tom's mother would have described them, the salt of the earth. Ordinary people leading ordinary lives.

Dave Dowling scowled. " Seconder?"

May Reynolds raised her hand. " I second Tom Houseman. He will make a very good delegate to the Conference,"

" Is that constitutional? You are his wife." Dave Dowling grunted.

" But we are individual members of the Party. Therefore we have the right to nominate and second who we like."

" Do you agree to this nomination, Tom?" Mike Pearce asked bluntly.

" Yes," Tom smiled sweetly. " It looks like you will not get the shoe in you expected."

" Those nominated will have to leave the room," Dave Dowling stated glowering at Tom. " Brian will take the chair for the vote."

All three trooped out. A waste of time, thought Tom looking round the room. There are only a couple of people like Mr. and Mrs. Reynolds left. All the rest are the supporters of Dave Dowling. Tom was proved right. Dave Dowling and Mike Pearce were easily elected.

After the vote Mr. Reynolds moved a point of order. " Are we quorate? There don't seem to be many people here."

" Of course we are quorate," Dave Dowling now back in the chair snapped. " I would not have taken a vote if we were not quorate."

" Another thing," Stan persisted. " Why was such an important item placed towards the end of the agenda? A lot of brothers and sisters left before we got to that business."

" They knew what was on the agenda so it is their fault they were not here for the vote."

" Who draws up the agenda?" Stan asked not giving up.

" The committee, you ass hole!" Dave Dowling snapped.

" There is no need to call me that. I was asking perfectly valid questions," Stan stood his ground.

" No it wasn't a valid question. The committee draws up the agenda from all the business that needs to be discussed. That is the trouble with the party. We have to keep faith with members like you and your wife. You are from the past. You want to be civil with all sides. You believe in decency and equal opportunities. Redistribution of wealth but not getting rid of those who exploit the working class. Christ, you should not be in the party. We need to turn back to a Marxist agenda. Nationalise all the means of production, finance and business. The best thing you two could do is to leave the party to the likes of me and Mike."

" That is not right. My wife and I have been working for the party for years and years. We have supported it through the good times and the bad."

"Look old man. Go home and leave the proper politics to those who know what they are doing. You are not wanted. You are part of the problem."

Tom could see they were almost in tears and reacted angrily. "There is no need to insult these good people, Dave Dowling. You might think that your education and ideas are superior to theirs but they are only ideas. Leave them alone."

Dave Dowling smiled cruelly. "What do you know of working people, Tom Houseman? You are the product of an elitist system. You went to grammar school and then to university. You work in a university now. What do you know of struggle?"

"Coming from you that is rich," Tom laughed. "My father is at least a working man. Yours was a school teacher just as you are a school teacher. My convictions come from a deep rooted source. I believe in equality of opportunity and redistribution of wealth. But there has to be the creation of wealth in the first place. People have to earn money before they can pay taxes."

"But as is shown in Russia, there can be wealth without exploitation."

" Rubbish! Which is the richest country on earth?" Tom asked. " The United States."

" But they exploit the poor unlike in Russia."

" Rubbish again. In Russia they put people in Gulags who disagree with the government. In the United States you are free to criticise the government. You can vote out those in office."

" To help the working class we have to have a left wing agenda."

" To carry out your agenda you have to get elected."

" With a left wing agenda and ideas, there are more working class than the rest, so we will get elected. The trouble with this government is that it is not radical enough."

" Now you are either being silly or you have your head in the clouds. With a programme like Mike is always advocating there is not a cat in hells chance of this party getting elected. Hopefully the Tories have shot themselves in the foot by electing a woman as leader. If Jim Callaghan goes to the polls this autumn, we have a chance but not with a manifesto like you are going to advocate at the party conference. Now you leave these good people alone in future. They have a perfect right to be here and a perfect right to ask questions. If you are so unsure of your position that you have to insult life long Labour members, there is something wrong with your arguments. Come on Mr. And Mrs. Reynolds. I will give you a lift home."

" Don't you dare call me a coward, Tom Houseman!" Mike exploded.

" Mike grow up and start acting like an adult. You are going to put this party in a right mess if you are not careful." Tom grinned. " The next thing you will do is start to advocate locking up anybody who disagrees with you. All you have to do is look at dictatorships down the ages to se where hat leads. Even better, go and buy a copy of animal farm and read that if you can read and understand what it is saying. It will save you a great deal l of heart ache in the future."

Tom ushered them out of the building and into his car.

" Thank you for standing up for us," Mr. Reynolds said as they arrived at his house. " I don't know what the Party is coming to when people treat other people like that."

" We have to make a stand against the bullies of the left," Tom smiled in reassurance. " Lets make sure we are there next time."

Tom tried to hold on to the images, tried to keep his dreams going but they slipped away. A grey mist overcame him and he slipped once more well below the surface.

Chapter 7

Paul stretched and rose from his chair beside the bed. He was wishing that his brother and sister would take over so that he could get a cup of coffee and walk around. Just as he was thinking this his mother came in accompanied by Luke.

" You go and get a cup of coffee. We will sit with him for a while. Mary is waiting in the waiting room. When Luke has been here for a while, Mary will come and take his place."

Paul reluctantly left the room.

Luke took his father's hand. " Hi Dad it's me, Luke. I came as quickly as I could. We are all here now. I phoned Uncle Edward and spoke to Aunty Sarah. They said they will be over as soon as they can to see you. Freddy and Alexandria send their love. They say to tell you their Mum and Dad will keep them informed of what is happening. I shot an eighty last weekend. The lessons you gave me for Christmas must be paying off. We got beat in the league for the first time last week. Four nil but by the top team. Now you get better soon or we are going to miss the local derby when we all plan to go. Well all except Mum. She wouldn't go to a football match even if forced."

Turning to his mother, he asked, " Has there been any sign that he is coming round, Mum?"

Jane looked hard at her son. " There are small signs I think but they are hard to detect. I might be kidding myself. Even so, I will not countenance any thoughts that he will not wake up."

Luke looked sad and a little hurt. " I was not suggesting that he would not recover. I was hinting at some reason to hope, that is all."

Jane smiled slightly but her face was drawn and lined. " I have to hope, Luke. What would I do if he was no longer there? We have been so close all these years with never a hint of either of us going off the rails. I would be lost and so lonely. He has to get better."

Luke squeezed his mother's shoulders. " Lets continue talking to him like the doctor told us to."

She resumed her seat and her monologue. " I always wondered why you fell out with your brother Edward so violently all those years ago when Mrs. Thatcher surprised everybody by winning the election in seventy nine. Before that, you and Edward were always so close. You both went with your father to the football every other week. You helped him in the seventy election when he was a candidate for Eastfield. He never stood a chance there though. Even I knew that and I was not passionately interested in politics."

The mist swirled and Tom was back near the surface again. Then he wished he could sink back into the soft certainty of the darkness.

It was Christmas nineteen seventy eight. They were all there at Edward and Sarah's house. Betty and Phil, their two son's, their wives and five grandchildren making up the whole family. It was a struggle, trying to be cheerful and exude the Christmas spirit. His father was nearing the end of his life, that had been obvious for some time. The pain killers kept him subdued. He was painfully thin such that all his clothes hung on his body as though on hangers in the wardrobe. Tom suspected that his father was hanging on in the hope of seeing them all together one last time.

Among other things they talked of politics as they always did when the three of them were together. Phil was upset about the state of the Labour Party which he had supported all his life.

" Why did it all go wrong?" Phil asked. " We got back in seventy four and had the power to do something for working people. Now nobody seems to like us."

" They didn't have much of a chance," Tom pointed out. " When they came to power in nineteen seventy four, they did not have a majority. Only after the snap election in October were they able to command a majority and that was small. They also had to face high unemployment and high inflation. It was difficult then. They never really recovered."

" They did manage to re-negotiate the EEC terms and have them endorsed in that referendum," Edward was searching for something good to offer.

" You think that was good do you?" Jane who was passing with some drinks butted in. " Worst thing the government ever did."

" We all know your views on the Common Market, Jane," Edward grinned. " I profoundly disagree though Dad is in agreement with you."

" I think we will all come to regret that vote but we have to live with it now," Phil frowned. " I thought that Callaghan would do a great deal of good when he took over. After all he was a union man unlike Harold Wilson who is an academic.

Besides, he had held all the great offices of state before becoming Prime Minister."

" He had the same troubles as Harold Wilson, Dad," Tom remarked. " His position became difficult when he lost his majority due to defections and bye election defeats."

" That's exactly what is happening now," Edward sounded bitter. " It was the left wing then forming the Scottish Socialists and now it is Militant. The only difference is that Militant does not want to leave the party but to take it over internally."

Phil shook his head. " I see what you mean. He did a job by surviving without a majority I suppose. How the hell he could enter into a pact with the Liberal party is beyond me. I started to give up on politics and the Labour Party then. Most of my friends were opposed and were glad when it collapsed in seventy eight."

" We should have had the election in the autumn. The economy was on the up after Roy Jenkins' budgets and the government had increased its poll rating." Edward again shook his head. " Talk about shooting yourself in the foot. Standing up at the TUC and singing ' Waiting at the Church'. He was the laughing stock of the country. I suppose he thought that a pay policy would hold back wage inflation but he is a fool. We all see what happened. With inflation high, there was bound to be a backlash. Now we have industrial unrest, strikes and silly wage claims all over the place. Mark my words. All he has done is hand a chance to Margaret Thatcher."

" I don't think it is that cut and dried." Phil stated emphatically banging the table with his finger. " Surely most people will not believe that her version of monetarism will make them richer."

" Dad. Tell people that you are going to cut taxes and they will fall for it," Edward laughed helplessly. " She has it about right. What has to happen is for the party to attract enough voters to get elected. She is going to have the upper classes on her side just as Labour will have the real left wing. There is no where else for those people to go. They only have a stark choice. Whether to vote for their party or not at all. Therefore Mrs Thatcher can ignore the hard core labour supporter. Now what she has to do is give enough incentives to those lower down the income scale for them to believe that they will be better off. If she can convince enough of those, hey presto she will be Prime Minister. When you have a majority, you can then do as you like until the time to gather in the votes at the next election."

" That is what I was telling Mike Pearce early in the autumn. As a party it is all very well sticking to hard principles but in order to put in place your vision of how society is ordered, you first have to have power." Tom shrugged. " The trouble with the left at the moment is that they are not interested in first gaining power but only in sticking to their hard and fast principles."

Edward laughed. " I can't agree with that. They or many of them, believe that by putting forward a left wing agenda, they will get elected. Caroline Hobbs was only arguing like you the other week in Eastland Labour Club but they howled her down. She is a brave lady that one. They have been trying to force her out of the meetings for ages but she attends each one. She tries to stick up for those ordinary people who do not believe in these way out theories. I try to help her but it is a losing battle in Eastland."

After the holidays, Tom sat at his desk in work and tried to put his thoughts in order. His father was dying. They had given him only a few more weeks to live. The situation in the country was getting worse with inflation taking off and wage demands spiralling. The local government workers had threatened strike action.

Phil Houseman died at home in the middle of January. All the family gathered shortly afterwards to discuss what to do. There was no possibility for a funeral for the foreseeable future because the cemetery workers were on strike. They would have to wait for the funeral. Edward raged about the insensitivity of the workers for going on strike. Betty Houseman was numb and just calmly waited. Tom tried desperately to keep the peace with his brother.

He did see Mike Pearce in town one day. It was all he could do to stop himself hitting him right there in the High Street. They did not speak much, only to pass the time of day. As a parting shot Tom could not resist the comment that he hoped Mike was proud of his advocating strike action among his fellow trade unionists.

" What do you mean by that?" Mike belligerently, demanded his accent very pronounced.

" My Dad died last week and we cannot have the funeral," Tom remarked in a hard voice with no attempt to keep the contempt for Mike and his cronies out of his talk. " It is not the upper classes or the bosses you are hurting but ordinary people at a vulnerable time in their lives. I just hope you can live with your conscience after this."

With that parting remark and not waiting for a reply, Tom turned on his heel and walked away. What was happening hurt and puzzled Tom. He was sympathetic to the demands of the workers realising they had had a raw deal in the past. That was all very well but they had chosen one of the most traumatic times in peoples lives to make their point.

To try to help, Tom agreed to go to church with his Mother and Jane on a Sunday a couple of weeks after his father had died. He told Sarah and to his surprise Sarah agreed to come as well.

And so it was much to the half delight and half bewilderment of Pound Street Church congregation, that Betty, her sons, their wives and her five grandchildren turned up for the morning service. Tom never remembered much about the service. He remembered from his childhood that smell of dust and polish which always hung like a blanket over the chapel.

After the service, he was surprised that over a cup of coffee in the hall quite a few people came up to greet him like a long lost friend. His mother was soon surrounded by other people and Edward was talking to some old friends. Sarah looked the part of a caring daughter in law by her mother in laws side. It had never been like this when I was a teenager, he mused. Many of the congregation were actively hostile to Edward and me. Time is a great healer. As people came to say hello, he struggled to remember their names, many having grown old in the years since he was last at the church. Of course he told himself, it is Jane they remember not me. Her mother and father are long standing members of this church.

After a little while, Belinda came over to meet him. He had forgotten that she was a member of the church and still came whenever she felt the need.

" Well well well, what have we here?" Belinda asked smiling. " Seriously though I think it is wonderful that you have all turned out to support your mother."

" It was the least we could do." Tom smiled. " I thought you had given up coming to church. Tony was always sceptical and as far as I know hasn't been since you got married."

" Oh he doesn't encourage me, preferring that we lie in on a Sunday," Belinda shrugged. " Every so often I feel the need to come and worship. It helps calm me down somehow. Besides, my mother likes to see me here. It's a small price to pay to keep her happy. You know what she can be like."

"No I don't," Tom muttered more to himself than Belinda. " She always made plain that I was not included in your circle whenever she was involved in organising things for the young people as she was want to call us. Look over there. She is frowning in my direction even now. If she had the courage, even at our age, she would be across here telling you not to speak to a reprobate like me."

" She is most likely trying to work out who you are," Belinda snapped back.

" Don't give me that," Tom snapped back equally fiercely. " Your mother knows exactly who I am."

" Actually Tom," Belinda smirked. " Now you have a respectable job and are married to Jane Brookes, you are accepted. Christ, excuse my French, that was twenty years ago or had you forgotten. I must go and speak with Mrs. Brown. See you Tom."

Tom watched her walk away and start talking to a rather formidable woman in her sixties who he remembered ran the Boys Brigade when he belonged to Pound Street Church's company. Idly he wondered what had happened to all those boys he had know then. One such heaved into view.

" Tom Houseman!" a rather fat man taller than Tom greeted him.

" Hello Victor," Tom thought back to the days when they played football together. Victor was a tall heavily built youth, the stalwart of the defence. Nobody got passed him unless they were too quick. Now he was over weight and looking at heart trouble unless he started to exercise.

" It is a long time since we met. I was sorry to hear about your father. How is your mother coping? We see her every Sunday but your father never came to the services. He did come to some of the outings and activities. I hardly knew him. " Even the effort of standing talking to Tom seemed to make Victor out of breath. The boy who could keep going all afternoon and then come back for more, thought Tom. Where has our youth gone.

For some reason, Tom and Jane continued to attend Pound Street Congregational Church every Sunday after that. The rhythm of the services brought comfort to Tom and he was surprised at how quickly he was accepted into the congregation.

The strike came to an end as all strikes do and so they were able to have a funeral for Tom's father. It was held at the local crematorium, both Tom and his mother thinking that a service in their church would be inappropriate. Edward read from the bible, Tom talked of his father's life.

When they emerged from the chapel, Tom was surprised to find he knew many of the people who had attended. There were some of his father's work mates and a representative from the union as was to be expected. Edward and his mother shook the hands of some of his mother's friends. What touched Tom more than anything was to see Derek and Marlene with Ray Downing and Joe Fox and their wives. He had not seen Ray and Joe for years. Ray played in a band and Joe was now manager of a football team. It helped to keep Tom's mind off the sadness which threatened to engulf him now he had delivered his reminiscence of his dad. Finding out what had happened to his friends, took his mind off the present tightness in his mind.

A month after his father's funeral, Derek telephoned and asked Tom to meet him in the Jack of Diamonds that night. It was the first time that Derek had wanted to see Tom for a drink outside the meetings of the board since the setting up of the company. That was not surprising because they met on a regular basis for drinks after the board meetings.

The bouncer of the Jack of Diamonds nodded to Tom when he walked through the entrance and his colleague held open the door. At the reception desk sat a man instead of the half dressed girl who usually checked the membership and took the coats. The man looked at Tom with hard eyes but waved him through without comment. Inside the club was quiet with hardly anybody drinking but there were several hard men in places strategically round the room. The barman spied Tom and indicated for him to go up to the office. Tom climbed the stairs wondering what was going on.

Derek shouted for him to enter after he knocked on the door to the office over looking the dance floor. Several men filed out past him as Tom opened the door. Derek was sitting behind a desk writing notes in a book.

He looked up and smiled wearily at his friend. " Come in Tom. Take a seat over there. I will call for a drink."

Once the drinks had been served, Derek joined Tom in a comfortable chair and took a large gulp of his whisky.

" Sorry to call you like that out of the blue but I have a need to talk to an old friend," he said after placing the glass on the table. " As you might have noticed on the way in, times are tense. I know you are only involved in the legitimate business as a non executive director but what has happened will effect you as well."

" Your not making much sense my friend," Tom smiled remembering the times he had given Derek advice in the past. " What's the matter? Its not like you to be less than blunt."

" Sorry, Tom," Derek grinned. " To get to the point. Mr. Hunt had a heart attack and is in hospital. The last I heard was that he did not have much chance of surviving the night. The doctors are doing all they can and his family are at the hospital. I have spent the day trying to keep his organisation together. I haven't any authority but I am trying. There are a great many people out there who would like to get a part of the action. I am trying to make sure that does not happen. Hence all the hard men around this place and across the road in the office."

Tom shrugged. " What can I do? To be blunt, it is your problem what happens to that aspect of Mr. Hunt's activities. I have never had anything to do with what goes on there. From the start I made clear I would only deal with the legal aspects of Hunt Enterprises."

Derek looked at Tom and smiled faintly. " Tom, you are my oldest friend. In a way it was you who got me into this. You remember down by the allotments? I am not asking you to become part of the shady world I inhabit most of the time. All I want is somebody to talk to who I can trust. You have always been that person."

It was Tom's turn to smile. " Ok Derek. What is the problem?'

Derek shrugged. " If Mr. Hunt dies there is going to be a vacuum in Porthampton. His field of operations will come under attack from all sides. Usually in these circumstances it is the family who defend the position of the organisation. His son's, as you know, do not want anything to do with his business. They both went to university and work in finance. John is in Hong Kong, Brian in New York. What I would like to know is if it is worth spending a lot of effort keeping the activities of the organisation together?"

" How did Mr. Hunt keep it under control?"

Derek scratched his head. " He could be ruthless when required and very harsh on those he thought had betrayed him. In the main though he got a great deal of loyalty from the ordinary men because he looked after anybody who worked for him no matter how lowly. If somebody got caught and sent to prison, he looked after the family. When they came out, he was there to make sure they got started again. Well not him. He set up systems and people to do this for him."

" After listening to what you say, that is what you have to do. Call in the loyalty cards from all those who owe Mr. Hunt and you favours. Make sure everybody is aware that you are going to carry on in the same way as Mr. Hunt managed the organisation. In other words, make sure everybody believes it will be business as usual. The other thing you have to do is make sure the people who made sure Mr. Hunt stayed out of the clutches of the authorities are on your side. I imagine that will be Rob Wilson and Malcolm Warne. As soon as is possible you have to call a meeting with them and your trusty subordinates."

" You should join the organisation," Derek laughed. " You would be better at this than all the rest of us put together. I will do as you advise.

Changing the subject, he said, " How is Jane and your family?"

They sat together companionably talking of their families and their concerns. Two old friends passing the time of day.

Derek did not mention his problems with his work again. It was late when Tom made his way through the now crowded club and out into the night air.

All his family were in bed when he got home and he made himself a coffee and sat in the sitting room staring at the blank television. Was he kidding himself? he asked himself. He had always justified his involvement with Mr. Hunt in terms of the legitimacy of the company for which he was a non executive director. What Derek had made plain as they sat talking was that the two sides of the business where intimately linked in many ways. He had not said so explicitly but the hint was there. The operation of the legitimate businesses were a way of getting some of the money from criminal activities into the real world. That was why he was paid such good remuneration. How it was done so that the authorities did not suspect was not his worry. Tom supposed that Malcolm Warne had looked after the accounting systems. On the other hand Hunt Enterprises Limited did employ a lot of people in their legitimate businesses. They were efficiently run and made profits despite the murky finances of Mr. Hunt.

Now that it is out in the open between Derek, and me Tom told himself, I should resign and leave the business to others. My conscience tells me this. But I like what I do and Mr. Hunt has never been arrested or questioned by the police. In the eyes of the community he is a rich and successful businessman who gives a great deal of time and money to local organisations and charities. Who am I to question whether he is legitimate or not?

Anyway, he told himself as he cleared up his coffee cup and headed for bed, I will not have to make a decision until after Mr. Hunt dies.

Mr Hunt died a couple of days later. Ten days after that Tom went with Jane to the Crematorium for the funeral. The service was conventional but it was the people there who fascinated Tom. Jane and he arrived early and took a seat at the back. From there they were able to observe the other mourners as they arrived.

Civic dignitaries rubbed shoulders with some of the low life of Porthampton. A few people Tom knew, others he recognised from pictures in the paper. The ones in dark suits and dark glasses he took to be rival gangsters. When Mrs. Hunt, her two sons and her daughter followed the coffin into the chapel, large men in dark suits spread out around the walls. Derek, Tom noticed discretely waved these men into position. Rob Wilson and Mark Warne followed the family and took seats in the row behind. The service was conventional but the sons did say a little about their relationship with their father. Afterwards everybody was invited back to Mrs. Hunt's home.

There were reports in the local press of fighting between rival gangs and there were some arrests. None of the main players in Mr. Hunt's organisation were mentioned however. Tom scanned the local paper every evening searching for any sign that his friend Derek had been hurt or arrested. It appeared on the surface that, like Mr. Hunt, Derek Jones was managing to stay above the sordid business of the gang warfare.

A week after the funeral a meeting of the board of Hunt Enterprises was called for the main offices in Tudor Square. Tom made sure he could reschedule his lectures before driving to the meeting.

It was a bit like one of those movies where the gangsters are having a war as he approached the square after parking his car in a nearby car park. Hard looking men were placed strategically round the square, watching closely anybody who approached the offices. Tom was frisked when he entered the building despite his protests. Nervous times, he thought.

The whole board was in the meeting room waiting for him when he arrived. They all looked at him as he took his seat and he noticed that Mr. Hunt's chair at the head of the table had deliberately been left empty. Mrs Hunt sat between Rob and Mark. Rob was as usual immaculately turned out while Mark even though in a well cut expensive suit looked as though he had been wearing it for a month. Mrs. Hunt smiled across the table at Tom.

Rob Wilson took the lead with what to Tom was a veiled criticism. " Now you are here Tom we can begin."

Tom replied starchily. " I am here before the designated time, Rob. I could not get away before."

Rob nodded. " I am not accusing you of being late, Tom. We are all on edge and most of us have been here all day. Now to business. We have to decide what to do with the businesses now that Mr. Hunt has passed away. Mrs. Hunt, Mark and I have had extensive talks on this matter. She is now the largest share holder and along with here sons controls the company. They have told her that she must make the decisions because they do not want to play an active part in the business. This is what we have decided to put before the board and the share holders. Are there any questions or comments?"

There were none forthcoming from those round the table.

Rob continued. " We will ask Derek Jones to take on the role of Chairman with all that implies. He will have to appoint a security director to replace himself. I will take on the role of managing director of the holding company. My able assistant, Joe Short will become the company secretary in my place. Mark will retain his position as finance director."

He then went through the other posts before saying, " Tom will retain the post of non executive director along with Allan. That seems to cover everything."

Mrs. Hunt spoke then. " Thank you all for being so supportive after my husbands death. Like my sons I do not want to play an active part in the businesses. All I can say is that I hope we will be able to retain our control over the progress of the enterprise, as Mr. Hunt always called it."

Rob signalled for Derek to take the chair.

" I will not keep you all much longer. Thank you all for your support. I am sorry if anybody was annoyed at being frisked when they arrived but we live in dangerous times at the moment. There are a great many people out there who would love to get a slice of our action. I have moved to counter that threat. So far my actions have met with success. I will endeavour to put into practice the lessons that Mr. Hunt taught me. I call this meeting closed. There are drinks and snacks at the back of the meeting room."

Tom was balancing a beer and a plate of food while talking to Allan when Mrs. Hunt came up.

" Can I have a word with you before you leave? I will be in my husband's old office." She frowned and then sighed. " Derek's now I suppose."

Tom smiled. " Of course. Just let me finish my food and I will be with you."

Vivienne Hunt was sitting behind the desk with the three different coloured telephones when Tom came into the office. She gazed steadily and gravely at Tom with wide apart blue eyes. He was struck once more how, even with sadness clouding her eyes, she was still a strikingly good looking woman. All right, her face was slightly lined and her hair showed grey streaks. Her plain dark dress showed off her full figure and she waved slightly with a well manicured hand towards a chair.

"Sit down Tom," she ordered in a flat voice.

As Tom lowered himself into the chair he was suddenly struck by how strange it was that Mr. Hunt was not sitting opposite. He also noticed that the gauze curtains were now drawn back letting the full light of the day stream into the room.

" I hope you don't mind my asking you to see me this afternoon," she began slowly. " As you know, I have not had much to do with George's business interests. I suppose you could say that I have been content to sit back and reap the rewards of what my husband did. That is not strictly true. By marrying me, he was able to enter society and rub shoulders with some of the wealthy and aristocratic. My parents did not like it at first but once the money started to accumulate, they changed their tune. Its funny how wealth can overcome the most deep seated of prejudices. I never came to terms with their change of heart and had as little contact as possible after we were married. Did you have this trouble, Tom?"

" Not really, Mrs. Hunt." He did smile at the memory of Belinda's parents. He did not want to say too much because he was wondering where this conversation was leading. " By the time I asked Jane to marry me and we went to see here parents, I had a job at Porthampton University and my Ph. D."

" Call me Vivienne, Tom. George could never understand why you always called him Mr. Hunt." Mrs. Hunt frowned.

" My father always told my brother and I that we should look up to the older generation and call them by their titles and surnames. " Tom shrugged.

" What do your students call you?" Mrs. Hunt smiled.

" Tom but that is different."

" Why? You are the next generation to them."

" Education is not about one generation dictating to the next at least not in university. It is about a mutual learning experience. All right, the tutor has to guide the student, lay down the outline of what must be studied but by discussion and argument, each bounces ideas off the other. That way we push forward the boundaries of knowledge. As my tutor told me when I was at university. ' I provide a shoulder to climb on so that you can see over higher walls than me.' You can only do that if everybody is on the same level."

" Any way, enough of that," Mrs. Hunt smiled. " What I wanted to say was that I am going to retire to our villa in

Spain. You and your lovely wife must come out and visit sometime. There is plenty of room. I think the business is in good hands when it comes to Derek. He will have all the experience of Rob and Mark. The other thing is that he respects and trusts you like my husband used to. As I gather things, he is a life long friend of yours."

" We grew up and went to junior school together."

" He will need somebody he can talk to and that somebody is you. Try to help him if he needs you."

" Mrs Hunt I told your husband a long time ago that I would only get involved with his incorporated businesses. What happened in the other parts of his activities was not of my concern. That still applies."

" I don't mean for you to get involved. Just be a friend, that's all."

" OK Mrs Hunt I will be there if he needs me."

She got up from her chair and came round the desk. Tom clasped her hand and kissed her on the cheek.

" Good bye for now. Don't worry. The business is in good hands."

As things turned out, Tom and Derek did not meet socially for a while after the funeral of Mr. Hunt. They met at meetings of the board of Hunt Enterprises but these were business meetings with little time for social chit chat. It appeared to Tom at the time that Derek was tied up with defending Mr Hunt's other interests as Tom always thought of them. At the board meetings this was never overtly referred to but to Tom, who had over the years been able to gauge Derek's moods, he was other wise engaged.

On the other hand, Tom thought, it might have been that Derek stuck rigidly to their agreement that Tom would not get involved in his other activities. Tom would be left to salve his conscience by telling himself that what he did was not criminal. It was a legitimate business enterprise for with he was a non executive director. Even then he did tell himself that his large bonuses every quarter were from the efficient running of the company.

Sitting reading the local paper one evening, his conscience was pricked. It was reported that some known criminals had started turning up dead in various parts of the city. When one of the men who had guarded Mr. Hunt in the reception of the office was charged with one of the killings, his suspicions were fully aroused. The newspaper did not deepen his worry because they hinted that as long as ordinary people were not harmed, letting a few criminals kill each other was no bad thing. This helped Tom turn a blind eye to these activities. They are of no concern of mine, he told himself. Jane did not help. She appeared oblivious to what was going on with Derek, secure in the freedom that the wealth brought her and her family.

Edward was more suspicious but even he could not find fault Tom's explanation. Besides, Tom thought after a particular questioning by Edward concerning Hunt Enterprises, Edward is pleased to take my money and build up our investment fund. He had to admit that his brother was very good at his job. Their fund had grown from small beginnings to over a million pounds since they started it ten years before. Now they each had one hundred thousand pounds in income related investments which doubled Tom's salary from the university. It never entered Tom's mind to question his brother's methods. Because his brother worked in the city, Tom accepted that everything was above board. That the result of his brother's investments might be that ordinary people lost their jobs and, in some cases their fortune, never bothered Tom. If he had thought about it he might have realised that he should have had more of a conscience about the effect of his brother's decisions rather than the strong arm tactics of his friend Derek.

From snatches of overheard conversation at the board meetings, he gathered that there was a turf war going on over the legacy of Mr Hunt. Who was winning, he never asked. Months later, Derek appeared to relax and Tom knew then that his friend had prevailed. It made him think back to that meeting in the wasteland the other side of the allotments from the council estate. He had advised, without any clear knowledge of what he was proposing, that Derek attach himself to Mister Big. Now it seemed Derek himself was Mister Big in Porthampton.

They did have time for a game of golf and a friendly drink at the Bishopstead Golf and Country Club. The conversation was general about their families and the golf.

One thing Derek did say stood out in Tom's mind. " We have come a long way you and me, Tom. We are both wealthy and held in high esteem in our fields. Who would have thought it all those years ago? I often wonder what became of Mavis and Pat. I suppose in my position, I could easily get them traced. Enough of that though it is connected. I am in the process of buying a villa in Spain. If you fancy a holiday there, let me know."

In the event Tom did not take Derek up on his offer for a long time. All thoughts of a holiday went out of the window when politics intervened in everyday life. There was big argument during one of the constituency party meeting he attended. It concerned the question of whether it would have been better to have gone to the polls in the autumn rather than leave it all until the last minute. Tom argued that the economy had been picking up and the Labour Government standing in the opinion polls was improving. He blamed the timidity of James Callaghan for the state of the party now. Dave Dowling was adamant that the delay gave the Labour Party time to organise a left wing agenda.

" We can put forward policies which would benefit the working class," he had remarked. " With socially correct policies we will wipe the board with the Tories and that woman."

Tom tried to argued against this but was howled down by the majority of the people in the hall. He was grateful that, despite the derision his remarks had encountered, once more he had the support of Mr and Mrs Reynolds.

He had to admire their courage and their tenacity. Supporting each other, they doggedly came to the meetings whenever the meetings were held. This despite the fact that they knew they would be subjected to unwarranted abuse from Dave Dowling, Mike Pierce and their supporters. Between them, they tried to ameliorate the worst excesses perpetrated by Dave Dowling and his supporters. During the meetings, they seldom won a vote but they kept coming time after time. Tom kept telling himself that he must come to all the meetings if only to give the Reynolds some moral support. The trouble was that home life, work and other leisure activities like the theatre and opera prevented him from attending all the meetings. A little voice nagged at his mind whenever he thought about what was happening to the party and how he was not serious enough to fight the leftists. If you are serious about saving the party from destruction, you should get more involved. I did my bit when I acted as agent for my brother, he justified his participation or lack of it, to himself.

Tom had been with his brother when the news had shown Jim Callaghan coming back from an international meeting in Guadeloupe denying that there was a crisis.

"Why is it that politicians always hold international meetings in such glamorous places?" Edward had asked him. He had gone on to grumbled good naturedly, " Not Porthampton but always some tropical paradise."

Tom had tried not to laugh. " You sound just like one of my colleagues. She is always claiming that I get to go to conferences in tropical paradises while she has to put up with Birmingham."

Now, they sat in the golf club just after his last constituency meeting talking about what was happening and when the election would take place. Both were under no illusions that if he had his way, Callaghan would try to last out right up to the last possible opportunity. Edward made clear that he was worried about whether the left wing would place the party in an unelectable position if they got their way.

" It is as though we have a death wish," was his disillusioned remark. He sounded depressed when he continued. " There might be a great many working people, as the left wingers in my constituency say. The trouble is that most working people don't all want a far left agenda. All they want is to get on with their lives in their own way. Most want a quiet life with their friends and family. All they are interested in is getting a feeling that they are having a fair share of what's going."

Even worse, to Tom, was that the government lost two by-elections to the Tories at the beginning of March. As he told Edward this boded ill for any election which had to be held that year. He was not really interested in the devolution debate. For years he had been telling anybody who wanted to argue with him that if the Scots wanted independence then it would be good for England if they left the Union. He did agree with the argument of how devolution would affect England. How would it be possible for Scottish Members of Parliament to vote on English legislation when English Members could not vote on certain aspects of Scottish policy? The West Lothian question as it was called. Tom could not understand why the Scots were not allowed devolution after they voted for it in a referendum. Something about a forty percent rule meaning that at least forty percent of the electorate had to vote for devolution. How this tied in with historical British forms of democracy where one vote majority was enough proved beyond Tom.

He watched in dismay as the Labour Party split over this issue. It appeared that some Labour Members of Parliament would rather have a Tory Government after an election than grant devolution to Scotland and Wales. What are they doing? he asked himself as he watched the news on television one night. His worst fears were realised when the Government lost a vote of no confidence on this issue. The Scottish Nation Party withdrew support for the Scotland Act and the Conservatives posted a motion of no confidence. It was carried by one vote. The Prime Minister announced that Parliament was dissolved and called a general election for May the third.

Tom was depressed after the election was called. Not clinically depressed but I suppose his father would have called it brassed off. On any measure of life's satisfaction he shouldn't of been. He had a very satisfying family life. He loved Jane and she reciprocated. His children gave him endless pleasure though he was approaching the question of where to send Paul to school once he was eleven. At work he was successful in both his lecturing and his research. He had a growing reputation world wide for his expertise. There were hints that in a few years he would be offered a personal chair. With a grin he acknowledged that this was a ploy by the university to keep him in post. That he did not need the money what with the successful investments by his brother did not come into the equation. It was the prestige of a chair which mattered most. Professor Houseman, it sounded good.

No it was not his life in general that caused him to feel depressed. When the election had been called he had immediately offered his services to the local Labour Party to help with the election. Dave Dowling had made it quite plain that he was not welcome. Shortly afterwards he had had a phone call from the Reynolds pleading with him to help them gain some recognition from the party. All they wanted to do was be a part of the election campaign even if all they were required to do was to stuff envelopes. With sadness Tom had to tell them that he had been told that his help was not required. We can attend the meetings as we are paid up members, he had lamely finished. So he was depressed. It got even worse when he had a phone call from Edward telling him it was much the same in the Eastfield constituency. It was obvious that Edward was angry. They had told him that he was not a part of their election team. To Edward this was madness. The last two elections he had been the candidate. Now, even though he had been voted down as the candidate, he was willing to help in any way he could. They had refused his offer.

Tom had then phoned Caroline

" Hello." Her voice was tired and full of stress.

" Hello, Caroline, Tom. I was just phoning for a chat but if it is the wrong time, I'll call back later."

" No Tom," she said hastily. " I always find time to speak to you. Its just that things are stressful at the moment. My husband was given his redundancy notice the other day. Then the Eastfield party told me I was not required on the election committee. They graciously said I could help with the envelops but not the campaign. Tom, they haven't got enough people to do all the things they want done. How can they refuse my help?"

" You are not the only one," Tom tried not to show his depression. " My constituency have told me that I am not welcome at election meetings. They have alienated some of the most loyal of our members. What can they hope to accomplish by what they are doing?"

" Oh they genuinely believe that the working class will rise up and support them in droves if only they put forward a left wing manifesto. Tom, they also hate people like you more than they hate the Tories. I was talking to Fred King, the chairman, the other night and he was putting forward the view that we did not have to worry about Mrs. Thatcher. The British people will never elect a woman, he told us. What we have to make sure is that the Labour Party puts forward a socialist agenda. We have to promise to soak the rich and redistribute the money to the poor. Now I am all for a redistribution of wealth towards the poor but not such that we drive the rich away from this country. Can we meet and have a chat sometime? I miss seeing you."

" Do you have time off work during the day?" Tom thought he was on fairly solid ground with this suggestion. Last time he had spoken to her, she was working full time. He thought what he suggested would be refused but it would give her the impression that he was still friendly.

" I have Wednesdays off now because they want me to work on Sunday," Caroline surprised him. " I could meet you then."

" The best thing would be for you to come to the university and we can go and have a coffee and sit in my office and talk. How does that sound?"

" I'll come next Wednesday morning about eleven," she replied.

Caroline arrived at the department reception dead on eleven o'clock. Tom took her to the coffee shop for a coffee and then backs to his office. He still found her attractive though she had put on some weight and there were lines radiating out from the corners of her eyes. They talked of their families and their lives at first. Then they got round to the subject of the party. It was as though the flood gates had opened. Caroline spoke from the heart about how she was disillusioned and upset. After all the work she had done for Eastfield constituency party, they had excluded her this time. All Tom could do was place his arm around her shoulder and agree with her. He took her out to lunch at a country pub and even though she made it quite plain that she wanted to make love, he kissed her good bye after lunch and returned to work.

It was a strange feeling to act as a spectator for that election in nineteen seventy nine. For the last few elections, Tom had been involved with the party. Now like quite a few of the old guard he continued with his ordinary life and did not go to the Labour Club. The Reynolds telephoned to ask him if he was going to the club on election night but he said he was staying at home. There was no doubt in his mind that he should have gone along with them but all the enthusiasm he usually had at election time had vanished. He knew that he should be there fighting for his type of party but he did not have the energy to fight anymore.

So he sat at home watching from afar through the evening news as the election campaign unfolded. He wondered where the left wing policies were but then reasoned that the left wing may have grabbed control at some local levels but the party was still controlled by experienced people. The theme of the Labour Party was in line with Tom's philosophy by pledging support for the national health service, full employment and lower income tax. He did think that Callaghan had put out a sop to his left wing by hammering away at the theme that the Conservatives would pull everything up by the roots and start again. It was obvious to Tom that though that was what the Conservatives were advocating, a lot of ordinary people were looking for that type of change. The basic Conservative theme was according to Callaghan to free up the market and let firms go to the wall even though that would mean high unemployment. Was it too big a gamble with the ordinary peoples welfare, Tom asked himself time and time again.

Mrs Thatcher banged on about controlling inflation. More significantly to Tom she promised to reduce the power of the trades unions. This struck a cord with the ordinary voters especially after the winter of discontent. She is very shrewd, Tom thought one night early in the campaign. It was the first time he had a suspicion that the Labour Party was going to lose. The Conservatives had employed the advertising agency who announced they would try to attract labour voters who had never voted Conservative before and first time voters. Much to Tom's dismay she wooed the owner of the Sun newspaper. All this appealed to ordinary citizens especially when she stated that Labour was now extreme. Sitting watching the election unfold night after night, Tom began to understand why people were won over by Mrs Thatcher.

On election night he sat by himself, Jane having gone on to bed and watched with mounting frustration as seat after seat fell to the Conservatives. Though Tom soon realised it was a southern victory with lower swings in the north and Scotland, never the less by the time he went to bed, Mrs Thatcher looked as though she would be the next Prime Minister.

The next morning when he awoke the radio told him that Britain had the first woman Prime Minister in the western world. Many famous people had lost their seats and skilled and unskilled workers had voted in large numbers for the Conservatives. It was like turkeys voting for Christmas, Tom thought.

Over the next few weeks Tom learnt to live with a woman Prime Minister. He was nauseated when she vowed to bring unity to the country. How the hell can somebody with her philosophy bring unity to the country? It was like expecting the Queen to start mixing with ordinary people.

Then the Labour Party really turned in on itself. He had been away at a conference and while he was driving home he heard the news. He could not wait to telephone his brother when he arrived home.

" Edward. Have you heard the news?" Tom's voice was shrill.

Edward sounded as though he had lost something he had cherished. " Yes. It is madness. How the hell do they think we are ever going to get elected again? Michael Foot! I ask you. We have thrown away years of experience and knowledge. We always elect somebody who is seen in the eyes of the public as acceptable. I do not understand them."

" From what I heard on the radio it was close between him and Dennis Healey. Only ten votes." Tom almost shouted down the telephone. " Don't they understand what they have done? I suppose many people in the party like Mike Pierce and Dave Dowling will be over the moon. Even Michael Foot sounded surprised. The right wing of the party will have to do some serious thinking."

" Healey is trying to help by saying that it is the will of the party and he will work loyally with Foot towards securing a Labour victory at the next election," Edward remarked. " This could really split the party you know. What will you do?"

" I have to help those in the party who oppose this madness." was Tom's prompt reply. " Some members will see this as a way to unite the party. Dennis Healey is mighty unpopular you know."

" But did you hear what he had to say at his press conference later?"

" Go on tell me."

" He intends to lead a demonstration against the government's policies on the economy and unemployment in Liverpool. Liverpool! That is where the seat of our problems lies. There are so many radical left wing people there that it is like a little soviet all on its own. The papers will have a field day. Even if his aims are laudable, he has to start seeing himself as a future Prime Minister."

" Not only that but he has to look like a Prime Minister against Thatcher."

" He was very forceful in his press conference on the need to dismantle all British nuclear weapons and make the issue of nuclear disarmament one of the foremost international considerations. All this is laudable but it is madness in today's climate. He did modify this in saying he was in favour of staying in NATO. Big deal."

" You know there has always been a fundamental difference of view between us on nuclear armaments. You think they are needed to keep the peace in Europe by countering the Soviet threat. I have always had reservations about us having these weapons. Even so I think he was wrong to put things in such blunt terms."

" I think it will be a disaster but only time will tell."

Time did tell as Tom was about to find out. Michael Foot had been elected so Tom and his brother understood, as a uniting candidate in a party that was tearing itself apart. Tom had witnessed this at local level with the treatment of the Reynolds and those loyal members like them. Now the hard left was growing in strength in the wider party. There were mutterings at meetings of a revolt by the right of the party to force the party to be more in tune with the wider populous. At a special conference drew up an electoral college where forty percent of the votes were given to the trades unions via the block vote, thirty percent to the members of parliament and thirty percent from Orlangy members. Tom argued long into a meeting of the local party that this meant two things. Some members had more than one vote and the left wing through the local associations, members of parliament and the unions would end up controlling the party. He was howled down. Nobody else seemed to care that the left wing was making the party unelectable.

To Tom as he walked out of that meeting, all those middle-of-the-road, respectable members of the party appeared to have given up the fight. It was as though they were ready to take a back seat until this lunacy passed and they could look at ways to get elected again.

Tom stopped going to meetings and plunged into family life and his work.

He had a phone call at work in late January. It was his brother Edward who sounded all excited.

" Tom have you heard? They have finally done it. David Owen, Shirley Williams, Bill Rodgers and Roy Jenkins have put out a declaration. They are trying to rally all the members of the party and those who might be ready to join a new movement,' committed to the values, principles and policies of social democracy. They say that this is the time for a realignment of British Politics. David Owen says he is no longer prepared to support a party increasingly dominated by left wing ideas and policies. There is no place in the modern world for hostility to British membership of the Common Market. We must not unilaterally disarm. Tom this is it. What we have been waiting for. I have called a meeting of some of my friends at my house next week. I hope you will be there."

Tom was not certain but he agreed to attend.

When he arrived at Edward's house, several other people were already there. Some of the people he knew by sight but others he had never met before. Spotting Christine Hobbs, he found a seat by her side.

After they all had a drink, Edward began. " Thank you all for coming. I know it is a very fraught time for supporters of the Labour party. All those who believe ion Social Democracy must be upset with the turn of events lately. For me the last straw was the election of Michael Foot as the leader of the party. It was bad enough that the trades unions made sure with their antics over the winter that the Labour Government would be defeated."

A man who Tom did not know butted in. " You can't blame it all on the trades unions. Jim Callaghan did not exactly help when he hinted that there was no crisis and delayed the timing of the election. We might have won in the autumn and avoided the unpleasantness of the winter."

" Josh. We lost and the left took over." Edward shook his head.

Tom joined in. " I think we are being rather naive thinking about the election. The problem has been brewing for a while. It was started slowly and stealthily but it was successful. In my constituency the left took over a little at a time. They managed to get a few people onto the committee by the backing of the trades unions. I must admit many of these were hard working. I first came across it a long time before the strikes. It really came home to me when they had a go at Mr. and Mrs Reynolds. They had been coming to Labour Party meetings for a long time but they were howled down and made to look insignificant at every meeting. God you have to admire the courage of those two people. Even in the face of hostility and down right contempt, they kept coming. We have to do something for those people."

Christine joined in. " Tom. I admire your loyalty but we have been doing this for a number of years with no effect. I am fed up with going to meetings at my ward and being called all sorts of ugly names by the hard left. The other night I was called a Fascist whore by some jumped up kid with spots. A number of people at the meeting actually cheered. There comes a time when we have to think seriously as to whether we can save the party."

Edward held up his hand for attention. " That is a good point Christine. We all know that David Owen and the others have put out a declaration and are calling for the formation of a new party. Like Christine, I have had enough of these left wing Marxists taking over the party. Its not just their philosophy, which I have never agreed with, but their methods. I have always believed that the party is a broad church as the saying goes. There have always been a wide range of views but we all agreed to respect others views while disagreeing."

Joan Biggs, a large woman with well groomed hair and well cut clothes, who Tom had met at one of Edward's parties, said. " I think it is time to think very seriously about the state of the party. I joined the party when I was at university. It was not my natural party. I joined because I wanted to see an end to poverty. The way to do this has always been to redistribute wealth through the tax system while giving all children the help to reach their potential. Those idiots in charge now want to pull everything down and build what they see as utopia in its place. It will not work. On the one hand there are not enough people out there who will vote for their programme. On the other, they have to encourage wealth creation before they can redistribute the money. I am intrigued by Roy Jenkins and Shirley Williams. From what I have heard they are saying the right things."

" I agree with Joan," Edward remarked. " The only hope for those of us who believe in social democracy as opposed to Marxist socialism is to break away from the damaged Labour Party and start anew. It is not the intention of this meeting to decode anything. All I wanted was to gather together those who were worried about what is happening in the party."

Tom was suddenly very angry. " What the hell are you saying? That we should abandon all the struggles we have had to get a voice for working people? Just because a few people disagree with our way of thinking? I think you are wrong."

Edward bristled. " I am not advocating leaving behind all of our traditions and loyalties. It is the people who are in control of the party now who have abandoned us. They will not listen to any counter argument."

" He's right Tom," Christine added.

" I know he is bloody well right!" Tom said harshly. " At times in my ward and at the constituency level I have been a lone voice crying in the wilderness of the left's intransigence. Well not exactly a lone voice. There are still a few who think it is important to fight. The trouble is they have been getting smaller and smaller in number. These people live ordinary lives but believe in the power of politics to change things for the better. They do not believe in revolution but gradual change. Do you think we should abandon these very people?"

" We are not abandoning anybody," Edward stated. " A new party would embrace the principles for which they have long fought."

" Rubbish!" Tom's knuckles were white as he tried to control his anger and frustration. " Any new party will be a move away from the principles on which our life has rested. I don't care what Shirley Williams might say."

" What do you think we should so then?" Christine was trying to avert the approaching argument between her friends.

" Stay in the party and fight for what we have always believed," Tom stated firmly. " What would Dad say if he heard you now? I know Mum might be pleased if she was outspoken enough to think you have moved away from the left."

" You leave Mum and Dad out of this." Edward's face was starting to go red.

From then on it became a personal argument between the brothers. It was as though they were in the room all on their own. They others sat and listened. There was not any shouting. Edward would put his point and try to convince Tom of the rightfulness of the need to change. Tom countered always with the tradition and the position of strength of collective will. He accused Edward of following his City instincts and leaving the working class behind.

In the end, Edward was adamant. " We have to start all over again. I will join the new party."

Tom shook his head and climbed to his feet. " If that is how you feel, count me out. I think you are abandoning all you ever believed. Dad will be watching in disbelief. I'll let myself out."

When he arrived home, he told Jane all that had happened. " I will not join the new party. Though I might not go to many meetings, I will stay Labour. Hopefully the party will come to its senses and I will be able to take part again."

Then the mist descended and with relief he allowed the waves to close over his head.

Chapter 8

Luke left the room to get a coffee when Mary arrived. With a sad smile, he emphasised that they were going to talk to their father for long as there was hope. It is what the doctors have told us to do, he added as he walked off.

When she was alone, Mary sat by the bed holding her father's hand. Her face was white and she was trying to hold back the tears. She looked at he father's face, pink with the grey hair emphasised even against the white pillowcases. His face was so drawn and lined, she thought to herself. She longed to pull the tubes out of his nose and to stop the pinging of the machines. It had not always been like this where she felt so helpless and in many ways alone even tough he was there in the bed.

To Mary, Tom had been the centre of her life for as long as she was aware. No matter what had happened, he was always there to talk to her. At first face to face but lately over the telephone or via email. Since she was very young, they had laughed a lot together, kept little, unimportant secrets and played sport in the back garden. She remembered the shock of their first argument when she had wanted to go out with makeup on her face. Even though she felt grown up at fourteen, her Dad had objected. In a fit of anger, she had not spoken to him for a week. Then something had happened and they were laughing together again. She could not remember what had caused their mirth but it meant that they were friends again.

How could she forget the look of apprehension mixed with pride as he drove away from her hall at Nottingham University? leaving her standing watching from the gate. She had been glad that he had not warned her of the dangers of university life only asked her to keep in touch. This meant emails every week but even then they had contrived to say funny things. Now he lay with wires attached and he needed her but she did not know what to do to help.

Looking at his face, she almost panicked and rushed out of the room. What could she say now to get a response? she asked herself. Like the rest of her family, she was at a loss for words. It had only been a few days since she last spoken to him. They had exchanged all the news they could manage in a short telephone call. What was she going to say?

More to break the silence than with any purpose, she started to talk. Putting into words the first thoughts that came into her head. One thing she had never satisfactorily found out was why he had sent her to private school in nineteen eighty seven. Not that she did not enjoy her time at the school. It had been the best school in the district but knowing her father's convictions on education, she had always been surprised that she had finished up at a private school.

She had no idea why the subject of her private education led her onto one of her father's students but it must have been the same time as her going to the High School which triggered the memory.

" What happened to that Chinese girl who used to baby sit for us?" she suddenly asked. " She was not much help really, you know. When she came to our house, she used to sit in the study and do her course work. Paul always made her tea rather than the other way round. He was twelve, I suppose. She used to eat all the chocolate biscuits you put out for her. One thing. She seemed really grateful that you let her come to the house like that. Isabel Chueng, that was her name. I must go back home and look at your email address book. There must be people out there other than those at the university that would like to know what is happening. I will try to compose an email to them all when we go back."

It was a different voice. Somebody he should remember. He reached towards the voice but the mist still swirled around his head. He tried but he could not break through the fog. The fog lightened and he drifted away from the voice and was back in the university.

Tom was sitting in his office surrounded by bookshelves stacked with brightly coloured volumes on as many subjects as you could imagine. He recalled giving a lecture once on the paperless office where all communication would be electronic. All the students would have portable computers downloading the notes from his machine. Lectures would be about the subject with less emphasis on handouts. All this before the advent of the laptop. In his dream he looked around his office at the books, files and paper.

Tom was in love again. He knew he was in love because he had had this feeling before. It was entirely different from being attracted to somebody sexually. Vicky had aroused him and their sex was wonderful. When thinking about it, he knew he was not in love with Vicky. She might have been in love with him but he doubted it. Of all the women he had slept with over the years, only one had generated these feeling in him before. That was Jane and he still loved her.

How could he tell? Well when they were apart, he missed Jane. Even when they were in the same room at a gathering of their friends or at church, his eyes were always making sure he knew where she was. There is nothing like that feeling of anticipation when they had been apart for a while and they waited for the other to come. Amusing incidents took on the form of a folk story and they laughed at similar things. Unlike the sexual charged atmosphere between two people whose sole purpose was to make love and then leave, Jane and Tom could sit for long periods not saying anything but happy in their companionship. They did not have to explicitly tell each other to come to bed to make love. A glance, a word or a sixth sense and they would go to bed holding hands.

Now he had these feelings again. He waited impatiently for her to arrive, missed her terribly when they were apart and made excuses to see her. When they were in the same room, they kept glancing at each other as though to reassure the other that they still felt the same way.

This situation brought new thoughts to Tom. Something he had never had to think about in the past. Can one person love more than one person at the same time? Obviously they could in the sense of a father's love for his daughter or a grandmother for her grandchildren. But physical love between adults? He loved Jane. His love permeated all of his life. It influenced what he did and how he fulfilled his ambitions. Could he at the same time love another person in the same way? He knew there had been instances in history when on the surface this had been the case but was that real love or was it a wish fulfilment the result of lust? It was very hard to answer these questions.

He could tell you however the precise day on which he fell in love. Just as he could tell you the precise day and almost hour when he fell in love with Jane. That as he reminded himself was at the party held at the flat of Belinda and Tony's. Sitting at his desk thinking about what was happening to him, he recalled the way Jane had looked standing at the patio windows looking out into the night. He had been drawn to her then even though he had been with Amanda and she with another Eric.

The department had received a request from a student studying transport at another university to transfer courses. She would complete her first year and then transfer to Porthampton. It was not an unknown request. For a number of reasons students would find that though they might still like the subject they had started to study, they did not like the place where they had chosen to study. Then they looked round for a new university with a similar course.

Tom collected her from reception and took her back to his office. She turned out to be a young Chinese girl.

Tom smiled. " Isabel Chueng? I am Tom Houseman."

Isabel smiled shyly, the corners of her lips just about turning up. When she stood, Tom found she was only about five feet tall.

" Hello Dr. Houseman. Thank you for agreeing to see me," she said with a slight bow.

" Come back to my office and we can talk about your request." Without another word, Tom led the way along the corridor.

Isabel sat demurely on a chair, her small hands in her lap. Her round rather flat face was framed by a mass of deep black hair. Her eyes were almond shaped, her nose perfectly shaped for her features and her mouth just short of generous. With a clearness not usual, Tom noticed a rather square body with round breasts showing through the jumper which was revealed when she had taken off her coat. She had on a plain knee length skirt and high boots. From his limited view from behind his desk, her legs were sturdy. When she hung her coat on the hook behind the door, Tom noticed her shapely bottom. For a brief instant he had an overwhelming desire to reach out and caress that bottom.

" Well? How can I help?" Tom asked seriously.

" I am at Aston University at the moment studying transport," she replied, her facial expression serious and guarded. " I have almost completed the first year. I would like a transfer to your course."

Tom could not help smiling. " Just like that?"

Isabel blushed. " Sorry, I did not mean to sound presumptuous but there is not another way I can put it."

" A bit blunt don't you think," Tom smiled again. " Of course there are procedures to go through before any decision can be made. In these circumstances, first I have to be sure that you know what you are doing. Have you found out about our course?"

" Yes," she replied. " The admissions office sent me the details. I also have the department and the course brochure. I have read these in detail. The more I read, the greater my wish to transfer."

" It is not that easy." Tom looked at her. " I have to ask you some questions. The obvious one is why do you want to leave Aston?"

She sat with her eyes on her hands resting in her lap twisting a handkerchief for a long time. When she did look up, her eyes were moist.

" It is hard for me to put it into words." she said drying her eyes. " I am not happy there. I do not get on with many of the lecturers or with most of the students."

" Why."

" It is hard to explain to you," she replied frowning. " I am the only girl in my year and they treat me different from the other students. The year students don't have much to do with me. I am lonely."

She is hiding something, Tom thought but said, " How will it be different here?"

" There are more girls in this department because it is Management as opposed to Civil Engineering," she smiled. " I have read your papers and books and would like to work with you."

Tom laughed. " Flattery will get you a long way. All right, we will see what we can do. Obviously if you are not happy with the place, it is better if you change. You have to make a formal request to my department for a transfer. I will then have to compare your course modules with our course modules. If there is a match we can put forward a case for you to join our second year subject to you satisfactorily passing the first year at Aston. If there is little correlation between what you have been studying at Aston and here, you may have to start the first year again."

" I can get you the Aston modules and send them to you," Isabel stated. " I have looked at what I have done and what comes in your first year and cannot see too much of a match. Some of the stuff is done in your second year. However, Dr. Houseman, I am prepared to start all over again."

" What will be the financial situation if you do have to repeat the first year?" Tom was trying to think of the right questions.

Isabel smiled. " I am being funded by my father and he will give me the money. You don't have to worry about that."

" I am thinking of the implications of any decision you make," Tom grimaced. " I would not like to encourage you and then find out that you were short of funds. If you were being funded by your home country, Hong Kong, they would have to agree to the switch. All these things have to be sorted out before any of us comes to a decision. I will get you a form to fill in. Will you do that here or do you want to take it away?"

She sat at his desk and filled in the application to transfer form. Tom sat the other side of the desk trying to look through some papers but could not stop himself from looking at her face very serious as she concentrated on her writing. Out of her bag she picked a file and used this to fill in the details. She did ask him one or two questions and he had to bend over by her side to see what she was pointing at. On one of these occasions her breasts brushed his hand as she leaned forward and he felt a stirring of his desire. They were very close and she did not pull away.

When the form was completed, she left. Tom showed her out of the building and pointed her in the direction of the bus stop. He stood on the steps watching her walk away. She looked back, waved and smiled a misty smile. For some reason Tom could not get the image of that smile from out of his mind.

It was some time later when he had a phone call from the reception to say that a Miss Chueng was asking to see him. Indeed, he had given up the thought of her coming to Porthampton reasoning that she had had second thoughts. That in itself was strange. With all other applicants, whether just out of school or a special request, he would have forgotten they existed until their next communication. Times were too busy for Tom to keep all these in his head. On a weekly basis he would go through the file of outstanding applicants and dismiss those he thought were not going to materialise. It always amazed him that some prospective students went through the applications process and even took time to come to the university for a discussion, Tom never thought of them as interviews, and then just drop the whole matter without any further contact.

With a sense of growing excitement, he went to meet her. Why he felt like this he wasn't certain at the time. There had been something about Isabel Chueng that had affected him in a way he was not too sure of. It was amazing that he had thought of her almost everyday and at the most odd of moments.

She was sitting in a chair in the reception area patiently waiting. Her black hair reaching passed her shoulders shone in the light coming through the windows. Something passed between them when she looked up and saw him come through the door. It was subtle, almost unnoticed but it was there non the less. It left Tom rather confused. Isabel smiled that misty smile and gracefully climbed to her feet.

" Hello, Isabel," Tom greeted her with a smile of his own.

" Hello Dr. Houseman," she said in a voice that Tom thought was full of enigmatic promise. " I was going to post the form to you but I have been given a car by my father so I thought I would drive down and deliver it myself. I hope I am not disturbing your work? If you had not been available I would have left it to be handed to you."

" Bring it to my office," he replied taking her arm and pointing her in the right direction.

They sat side by side as he examined the documents and when they were finished, Tom went back round the desk once he was sure everything was in order. As he sat down, he caught a slight smile on Isabel's lips. Once more he understood he had moved away because he was almost overwhelmed with the desire to kiss Isabel.

He forgot about Isabel for a while once every thing was in order. The admissions department took over after it was plain that the department would accept her if she reached the university requirements. What made him forget or at least push Isabel to the back of his mind was a summons to the Vice Chancellor's office shortly after Isabel had visited his office.

When he arrived at the Vice Chancellor's office, he found Professor Marriott there already. They had some news for Tom. In a rather pompous way the Vice Chancellor offered Tom a personal Chair. It appeared that Professor Marriott and the Vice Chancellor had had this in mind for a number of months. Now they needed to get Tom's agreement before putting the proposition on the agenda of the appointments board. Without hesitation Tom agreed. He would have to give up his role as admissions tutor .In return he was promised one new appointment to his lecturing staff meaning there would be other people to take on this task. The appointment was to be from September. They would find a suitably sized office for him and a secretary for his group. Tom wondered why had to move as he was quite comfortable where he was.

It surprised Tom how much stuff he had accumulated over the years. The move gave him a chance to throw away a great deal of his stuff but he was reluctant to let anything go. In a way he wished Jane was there. Whenever they had a clear out at home she was ruthless. Anything that had not been used or looked at for more than two years was thrown out.

There was then the question of tutees. He insisted that he kept those who he had tutored through their first and second years. The other lecturers did not want him to have many tutees. They argued that as the Professor in charge of their group, he should be free of students so that he could concentrate on looking after their welfare. In the end they compromised and he was allocated three. As he had had dealings with Isabel and she was a special case, he asked if he could have her on his list. It was agreed.

It was a strange experience for Tom when the A level results were released. For a number of years he had been the one who correlated the results with the offers made to prospective students and answered the telephone questions of those who did not quite make the results. Some times there were tearful mothers on the end of the phone who begged that their child was given a place, other times it was angry fathers. Tom had learnt how to deal with all of these situations and had come to enjoy the time in a strange way. It was a vital time in the life of the university and was non stop effort for a few days. During the time the adrenaline pumped. At the end everybody involved was exhausted. Now it was one of the other staff who took responsibility for this task and all Tom could do was wait until the statistics were produced. Once the numbers were known, the individuals could be assigned tutors.

On the day the fresh students arrived, Tom sat in his new larger office reading a research paper and feeling left out of the induction. It was now Pauline Watt's job to introduce the students to their course and Professor Marriott as head of department. She would then introduce the students to their allocated tutors. That was the only contact Tom would have until he started to lecture.

When he arrived at the lecture room, Professor Marriott was just finishing his talk on the university, its history and its structure. As Tom found a seat at the back of the room, Isabel Chueng looked round and smiled. He smiled back.

Pauline went through the objectives of the tutor scheme and introduced the other lecturers from the course. Then she allocated tutees to their tutors.

Tom collected his three tutees and took them back to his office, Brian, Morgan and Isabel. With only three it did not take long for the introductions to take place and to answer any questions. He advised them that they should try to make a point of seeing him every week. It was a policy he had tried to encourage through out his working life but it was usually only a few students who took advantage of his offer. He blocked out a couple of hours during the week when the students did not have any lectures and he was free for this purpose.

Isabel proved to be one of the students who came every week. At ten o'clock on a Thursday she would knock on his office door. They would sit and talk about her work, the course and anything she wanted to for as long as they were allowed. Some times, much to Tom's annoyance, they would be interrupted by some other student arriving. By the look of disappointment on Isabel's face when she had to leave early, the feeling of disappointment was mutual.

Nothing happened between them which in any sense could be construed as improper. They just seemed to be relaxed when together and were able to talk with out pause. Their hands did meet sometimes when they were handing each other work to check or information. Her breasts rubbed against his arm when they sat side by side looking at some article or piece of information she needed for her assignments. It might have been his imagination but she appeared to hold that position against him for longer than was really necessary. All of these things happened and the look they gave each other when they smiled was special. None of this could however be constitute as crossing the invisible line between the relationship of a student to a tutor and attraction between a man and woman.

Tom arrived home one day to find Jane in a right state. It appeared that their baby sitter had phoned to say that she could not sit that Friday. Jane had tried all the others they usually used but to no avail.

" We will have to cancel the dinner," she sighed.

" Not so quick, Jane," Tom gave her a hug. " What if I ask one of my students to help us out? The children are not babies now. All they need is somebody with them."

" Do you think there is somebody you could ask?"

Tom thought of Isabel and then nodded. " There are a few who I think would be willing to help. We will have to put on a supper though I will make it quite plain that we do not pay for baby sitting. If one of the students does do it, they can sit in the study and do their course work. I'll see what I can do. It is the annual bankers dinner and you would not want to miss that. Maybe if it works out, we can have another baby sitter on our list."

While he sat waiting for Isabel to appear the next day, Tom thought deeply about how he was going to ask her. He knew from their conversations that she had a number of younger sisters but with her wealth he expected she had had maids and nannies to look after them when they were younger. Maybe, the doubts started to surface, she would look in horror at the very idea of her baby sitting.

When she came with her misty smile, he could not help but to be blunt. " I have a problem. Jane and I are due to go to the banker's dinner and dance tomorrow but we have been let down by our baby sitters. If you are not doing anything else, would you be prepared to sit for us?"

Isabel chuckled. " Of course I would do that for you. In fact I would do anything you ask. What does it entail? I have no experience of baby sitting."

Tom shrugged. " Well actually they are not babies. Paul is eleven, Mark is nine and Mary is seven. They all know what to do and when to go to bed. Your job will be to make sure they are in bed at the right time. Jane will give you a list of their bed times. It will be up to you but you could go and tuck them in if you wanted to. While you are there, you can use my study to do your course work."

" It sounds like fun."

" Can I pick you up at six thirty then? I know you had to give up your car because first year students are not given parking places on campus."

" I'll be ready."

It all went smoothly. Isabel was ready when Tom arrived at her hall. The children were asking Isabel all about Hong Kong and her family when they left the house. The dinner and dance was enjoyable. They met a number of friends including Tony and Belinda who had been invited because Tony was undertaking some legal work for one of the banks. When they arrived home all the children were in bed and Isabel was working away in the study.

After a coffee, Tom drove Isabel back to her hall. In the car she was quiet and Tom was content to let the silence last. When he arrived at her hall, he stopped the car by the main entrance.

" Thank you Isabel. You were a great help."

" Oh it was a pleasure. Your children are no problem. Paul even made me a cup of tea and brought my supper to the study. If you need me to sit for you again, all you have to do is ask. Besides it gives me the chance to see you other than in lectures of your office."

" There will be some social occasions before Christmas so if you come, we will see each other then. Then in the spring there is the student organised dinner. If we organise ourselves, we can make sure we sit on the same table. Lastly, in a few weeks I will be sending out an invitation for my tutees to come for a drink one evening at my house. I usually invite them once a term. Jane likes to meet everybody. So you see there will be plenty of opportunities to see me outside the lecture room or my office."

" I must go," she said. " I will look forward to those occasions."

She lent across the car, put her arms round his neck and kissed him passionately. Tom tried to hide his surprise but he held her shoulders and kissed her in return. Reluctantly he let go and watched as she climbed out of the car. After she had shut the door, she waved and walked into the building.

On Monday morning between lectures she called at his office.

" Hi Tom," she greeted him. " How are you this morning?"

" Hello Isabel," Tom smiled. " What can I do for you?"

" Oh I was passing so I thought I would say hello." She came into the office, shut the door and kissed him. " I'll see you at the student social evening on Thursday."

" I'll be there though I might be later than you lot. I expect Don Bright and that lot will be there at seven o'clock and go on to the Wizard afterwards. I can't keep up these days."

" As it is in the Lord Nelson just off the campus, you will be able to walk me home or give me a lift afterwards. My hall is on the way back to your house. I must be off. See you on Wednesday morning at the usual time."

The students taking the transport course traditionally held a social evening each term to try to integrate the new students into the group. There had been a feeling in the early days that with so many lectures in different subjects where the transport students mixed with students from other courses, there was a lack of identity as a class. Now that there was a degree course in transport studies, there was a group identity but the social evenings were still held each term. It was argued, if there was any need for justification, that this was a good opportunity for all three years to mix socially. It was also a chance for the students to invite the lecturers and meet them outside the constraints of the academic environment.

The Lord Nelson pub was a large establishment within walking distance of the university and Tom home. So that he could drink that night, he walked across the park to the pub.

The social evening in the upstairs function room was in full swing when he arrived. Students sitting in groups, the duke box playing at full volume and pint glasses on every table. As soon as he walked through the door Don Bright, a large lad who played rugby for the university and the chairman of the organising committee, grabbed Tom and propelled him towards the bar.

" A pint for my tutor," he called above the noise. As though by magic a pint appeared. Other students came over and soon he was pulled into their world. He had to admit to himself that though he mixed with these young people all the time, as he got older he found it more and more difficult to stay on their wavelength. His children were growing up so he had a smattering of the latest pop gossip but half of the songs being blasted out from the duke box were alien to him. It was obvious when he went to take part in quiz nights at the Labour Club, the church or a pub that when it came to the latest pop music and artists, he was lost. It was just the same if there was a round on soap operas. He had to hope that somebody in his team would at least be able to bring up the right answers. He smiled at the thought and brought a drink for some of his tutees.

Somebody waved to him from one corner and he realised it was Isabel Chueng sitting with a group of first years. Excusing himself from the students he was talking to, he pushed his way through the crowd to her table. They moved slightly and there was a space on the bench between Isabel and Doreen Marshall, a big breasted girl with long brown hair. As he squeezed between Isabel and Doreen, Isabel ordered one of the students nearer the bar to get him a drink.

It was a thoroughly enjoyable evening if somewhat confusing. Students kept coming up to the place where he sat and offering to buy him a drink. In turn Tom brought rounds of drinks for his tutees. They talked about the course, their boyfriends and girlfriends, where they lived and the latest news. Some of the students mocked good naturedly his support of Porthampton Town and he countered by mocking their team. The other members of staff and researchers mingled such that everybody mixed. Don Bright made sure that the finalists talked to the first and second years. He is a natural at this, Tom thought.

Just before the pub shut, the students started to drift away calling their farewells to Tom who was the last of the staff to leave.

" How are you getting home?" Isabel asked squeezing his hand which she had managed to hold under the table whenever she had a chance.

" I walked here so that I could have a drink, so I will walk home. It will take me about twenty minutes."

" We'll walk with you," Doreen remarked. " Our Halls are in the same direction. There will a number of students going that way."

He walked along the road towards his home, Doreen with her arm through his on one side and Isabel on the other. Don Bright led the way and rather noisily as a group they made their way back to the university. With cries of goodnight Prof, students left to find their way back until there was only Don, Doreen and Isabel. They arrived at the gate to their hall and waved goodbye as Tom walked on down the road. He had just reached the park when he heard footsteps running in his direction.

Turning ready to fend off whoever was chasing him he discovered Isabel hurrying towards him.

" I wanted to kiss you goodnight," she said through her heavy breathing from her running. " I could not when the others were there."

In a dream, Tom took her hand and pulled her into the park away from the light from a lamppost. He kissed her directly and she responded. His hands stroked her bottom and she clung to him. He felt her heart beating through her coat as his hand caressed her breasts. There was a murmuring in her throat when his fingers slid under her blouse and stroked her nipples. With a great effort, he took his hand away from her body, kissed her one more time.

" Good night," he said his voice hoarse with emotion. " Hurry back to your room before I cannot stop myself pulling you into the bushes."

Isabel's eyes were big and shiny in the faint light but she kissed him and turned away.

" See you in your office next week," she said as she walked away.

At the same time in his life Tom had been asked by the church elders to become the church's representative on the Council of Churches and the Free Church Federal Council. At first he was reluctant to accept the nomination. It was not that he was worried about sitting on committees. He had done enough of that in his life. Even now he was on the regional committee of the Institute. No it was more to do with whether his faith was solid enough for him to take on this responsibility. He imagines the Councils being full of the most fervent Christians who wore their religion on their sleeves. Though, he told himself while he wrestled with the offer, that is what it tells you to do in the Bible. In many ways Tom was content to go to church on Sunday, listen to the sermon and make his own mind up about what was preached. He did not want to get too involved.

Jane was more involved being on the catering committee and running coffee mornings. She pushed the Christian Aid envelopes through the letter boxes of as many streets as she could get her family to help her with. Tom did help her to collect the full envelopes though he found this more daunting than canvassing on behalf of his brother. The abuse directed at him and Jane by some of the people was nasty. Why, he asked himself over and over again are people so frightened of Christianity?

In the end with the encouragement of Jane, he accepted. It meant that he had to attend Church meetings where the policy of the church was decided by a vote of all the members. At these meetings he had to present his report of what had happened at the Council meeting he had attended. One problem he did have was that the committees wanted to pass resolutions and act on them at each meeting. Tom was forever telling them that he could not agree to any resolution which committed his church to any action before it had the agreement of his church meeting. The Anglican and Roman Catholic priests shook their heads at the convoluted nature of the United Reformed church. Tom remembered with amusement their anger at his jibe about only certain people being important in their churches.

It was at the free church federal council meetings that he met Joshua Darling. He was the pastor of a Pentecostal church with a majority of black members. The church was on the way from Tom's home and the meeting place at the Methodist Central Hall. Shortly after meeting Joshua, Tom had offered to give him a lift whenever there was a meeting. It will save us both taking our cars, he had said. Those drives to and from the meetings were illuminating for Tom. Joshua and he talked about their differing views on religion and what it was like to be black in Britain at the time. Tom cringed when he heard what people did and said to make sure that Joshua and his people never forgot they were black. Joshua told Tom that they prayed for the strength to forgive these people.

With unemployment rising and people desperate to survive, the Council of Churches organised a redundant factory to retrain people. The idea was that by retraining and equipping these workers with skills needed in the market place, they would be able to find employment.

Just before the Christmas holiday and the students leaving to go back home, Tom arranged for his tutees to come to his house for a social evening. Jane cooked cottage pie and cheese cakes, Tom got in a load of beer and wine. Most of the students walked from the university so that they could fill up, as they put it, on Tom's beer. As usual, Tom had give those living off campus a lift because the busses were few and far between in the evening. It meant he could not drink much but he did not mind. It was good to have his tutees in his house

It turned out to be a wonderful evening. All the students eat and drank as though they had not had a full meal for ages. Isabel showed another side to her character which Tom had never noticed. From the time she arrived she insisted on helping as much as possible. She also went upstairs to say hello to the children. There was a great deal of laughter emanating from their rooms for a while.

At the end of the evening approaching midnight, Tom rounded up those he was giving driving back to their halls and took them back to their digs. They all thanked him profusely. When he arrived back home, all the students had gone except Isabel.

Jane smiled and shrugged when Tom raised an eyebrow at the sight of Isabel finishing the wiping up. " She insisted on staying behind after the others had gone to help me clear up. It was nice of her. She says she will walk home but I am a little concerned at her walking though the park on her own at this time of night. I insisted that you gave here a lift home after we have finished."

Tom grimaced outwardly though his heart started beating too fast at the prospect of being alone with Isabel if only for a short while. " I was hoping to get a drink before we went to bed. Still, it would be best not to insist on her walking back alone. Lets have a coffee before I drive her home."

He drove Isabel the short distance back to her hall. It was late and the roads were almost devoid of cars. There were hardly any people on the streets either which made Tom glad he had agreed to drive her back. Isabel sat by his side dreamily smiling. Once out of sight of the house, she moved so that her hand was on his thigh and her head on his shoulder. When they stopped at a set of traffic lights, she lent over and kissed him. Outside her hall, he parked in the shadows and pulled her close. Kissing her passionately he could not stop his hand caressing her body. She sighed and did not resist kissing him passionately in return.

Pushing him away, her eyes were misty. " Are you coming in for a drink?"

Tom smiled and shook his head. " I had better not. Jane will wonder where I have got to if I come in with you and are gone too long. Besides it is not very good policy for a Professor or any other staff to be seen in a hall of residence late at night. We will have to wait patiently to be alone together when there is no pressure of time. I'll see you next week."

With that comment he pushed her away and she reluctantly opened the door. After a pleading look, she turned away and shut the car door. Tom watched her disappear into the accommodation and then drove home.

She came to see him in his office shortly after, to say good bye. She was going to London for a few days and then flying out to Hong Kong to be with her family for the Christmas holidays.

Tom sat behind his desk and watched her go. I am being silly, he thought as the door to his office closed. A forty two year old man getting upset when a twenty year old student leaves for a few weeks. I will miss her coming to my office every week, he told himself. Still. Most of the time I will be with my family and not at work. It has to be remembered that she will be back after the holidays. Will I manage to get her into bed to make love? It happened with Vicky though only when we went to the conference together. Even though I miss her in the same way that I miss Jane when she is away, there is no way I will compromise my marriage for the sake of fulfilling my love for Isabel. Does that mean that I do not really love Isabel then? Not in reality. Jane was there a long time before Isabel came along and she is the mother of my children. This has to make a difference. If Isabel came back and told me to get lost would I fell sadness or relief? I suppose I would be depressed but then life would have to continue. He still believed that it was possible to love two people at the same time.

Isabel returned with all the other students in the New Year. Life continued in the same way. Isabel came to his office every week and they kissed and caressed each other but there was no opportunity for them to make love. Tom was involved with the council of churches project to help the unemployed but only as a helper. He was very open with the committee that he did not want an active leadership role but would help all he could. He attended a couple of conferences, one in Australia, the other in Vienna. His colleagues joked again that he got all the good places while they had to put up with Manchester or Birmingham.

In the spring, two things happened which at the time did not appear significant but later proved to be important. There was the annual dinner and dance organised by the students in the department and a picnic in the park organised by the council of churches.

Isabel came into his office one day unannounced and not at her appointed time.

After kissing him, she burst out, " There is this student dinner in a couple of weeks. Do I have to come? If I do what will I wear?"

Tom shook his head. " It is purely voluntary. Most of the students make the effort to be there. Besides I will have a table with some of the first year students. I was going to make sure that you were on my table but if you are not coming, I will have to change my plans."

Isabel frowned. " I have never been to one of these before. What do the female students wear?"

Tom laughed. " My wife would tell you not to get me to think about fashion.

She says if it wasn't for her I would look like a tramp all the time."

" Would Jane mind if I phoned and ask her for advice?"

" I expect she would be only too happy to help. She will be home after four this afternoon so phone her then."

Isabel threw her arms round his neck and kissed him. " Thank you Tom. I will take your advice."

Jane and Isabel met to go shopping that weekend. Tom and his sons and daughter went to watch Porthampton Town. When they arrived home, Isabel and Jane were preparing a meal.

" Successful day?" Tom asked as he opened a bottle of wine ready for dinner.

" I think so," Jane laughed. " Isabel seemed happy enough with what she purchased. She made me promise not to tell you what it looks like. I said you would give her a lift home after dinner."

The picnic in the park was an annual event organised by Christian Aid and involved all the churches of the town. When Tom arrived with his family many people were already there. They had set up their groups with circles of canvass chairs and rugs spread on the grass. Some children were playing rounders. A group was playing songs on guitars and singing. Tom did quickly notice that there was not much mixing of the various churches, each church forming a separate group. There were some people determined to mix mainly those who took part in inter church activities.

Seeing Joshua sitting with his family and some of his church people, Tom led his family across the grass to join them.

" Hello Joshua. Can we join you?"

Joshua smiled and got to his feet. " It would be a pleasure, Tom. This is Pat my wife. Abraham, Benjamin and Ruth are my children. Please sit down."

" Jane this is Joshua who I give a lift to the Council of Churches meetings." Jane smiled and kissed his cheek. " Paul, Mark and Mary my children."

Jane spread the rugs while Tom erected the chairs. Soon they were all speaking at once. Paul was looking at Ruth as she was about the same age. Tom had noticed that Paul at twelve was just starting to notice girls. In the end Paul said something to Ruth and they went to join in the rounders. The other children followed and soon they were integrated into the crowd of children being organised by some volunteers. Jane was deep in conversation with Pat and the other ladies from Joshua's church.

"It is good to see them playing together," Joshua remarked looking at his children laughing and shouting with the rest. " I was reluctant to come you know. Pat convinced me we should. It is not that I do not trust other Christians but we meet such prejudice in the country that we try to keep our heads down."

" But you come to the Council meetings," Tom answered.

" Once more it was only because my church asked me to go. Some of my congregation wanted to ignore the opportunity to meet other churches through the Council. I must admit to you that I was sceptical at first but I have met some nice people." He stopped to wave to somebody who was passing. " It is not like this all the time. My people are shouted at, called insulting names and even told to leave some places. It is not every body who are like that. There are people like you and your family who do not appear to see the colour of my skin. I am afraid Tom, you are few. Ah, they are all coming back so it must be time for tea."

They spread their tea out on the rug mixing everybody's contribution. A couple of Jane's friends and their families had joined them and so it was a large group. It was a wonderful picnic.

On the way home, Paul remarked that it had been fun. Tom had seen the way he said goodbye to Ruth. It was remarkable because Paul was starting to be reluctant about coming to church every Sunday. If he could find something else to do which his parents approved, he was happy to miss the services.

" What nice people," Jane remarked on the way home. " We must invite them round for a social meal sometime. Make sure you mention it next time you give Joshua a lift."

The student dinner was held in a restaurant on the outskirts of Porthampton overlooking the sea. The students arrived almost unrecognisable in their dresses and suits by coaches. Professor Marriot and the student social committee sat on the top table while the other lecturers were spread around the room each one at a separate table. Tom found the table list once they had drinks set up in the bar. A tap on his shoulder made him look round. Isabel stood behind him having just arrived on the last coach. She was dressed in a cream blouse and blue skirt topped off with a red jacket. The skirt reached just above the knee showing off her legs further accented by high heeled shoes. Her hair was brushed until it shone and curled around her face.

Make up enhanced her oval eyes and emphasised her lips.

" Hello Tom," she said in a voice full of promise. " Hello Jane."

" Hello, Isabel. You look stunning," Jane replied nudging Tom in the side.

" Hello Isabel. You look gorgeous."

It took all of Tom's willpower to sit through that dinner with Isabel on one side and Jane on the other trying to suppress the urge to stroke Isabel's body or to kiss her at the slightest opportunity. Somehow he managed. He was helped when the student Chairman called for speeches. It was customary for the Head of Department to say a few words and one of the students to reply before the dancing. As soon as he stood up it was obvious to everybody that Professor Marriot was drunk. His words were slurred and he leaned heavily to one side. The students on Tom's table were appalled but the finalists wee taking bets on how long before his head hit the table. Everybody was looking in Tom's direction.

" You'll have to do something before this gets in the papers," Jane whispered.

Tom got up in a dream and walked round the edge of the room signalling for Don, one of the other lecturers to help. They caught Professor Marriot and led him out into a back room.

Pauline Watts appeared with Professor Marriott's wife. " You had better get back in there and quell the students. They are getting restless. I will help Don with the Professor."

Tom hurried back into the dining room and took Professor Marriott's place at the head of the table. Holding up his hands for silence, he said. " I am afraid Professor Marriott has been taken ill. He is being attended to outside." He then went on to tell a few jokes and to thank the students for arranging the dinner. At the end he hoped that he had calmed down the atmosphere. While the dining room was being cleared for the dance, he was told that Professor Marriott had been taken home by his wife.

Jane was in her element. Tom sat back and watched her not only dance with many of the students especially his tutees who had visited his house but also chat away to them. Tom danced with as many of the girls as possible. Then he danced with Isabel in a slow tempo. They held each other tight and spent some of the time looking deeply into each other's eyes. At the end of the dance Isabel asked one of the other lecturers to take a photo of them together. Tom was taken aback by the remark that they had better hide the evidence. Do many people suspect what lies between us? he thought. Isabel seemed unconcerned.

One evening before Easter, Jane made an announcement which excited Tom. " I have arranged for a few days off before Good Friday. The children are on holiday and Sarah has suggested that we all go up to London and stay at their flat for a few days. I can take the children to the art galleries and to a show. What do you think?"

Tom shrugged. " It is a great idea. As you know I have a series of meetings that week at the university so could not come. What about Freddy and Alexandria?"

" Alexandra will come with us but Freddy is off camping with his mates. We will have a great time."

When he was tidying the sitting room and the kitchen before going to bed, Tom was at last able to think of the implications of what Jane had arranged. For a few days he would have the house to himself. Dare he mention this to Isabel? On the one hand she might jump at the chance of spending time with him away from the university or the company of other students or Jane. In reality, he did not know how she would react. Oh she had kissed him and let him caress her body but there had never been a chance of them going any further. This would be different. He would be alone. If he asked her to come to his house, would she accept the invitation? What would be her motives for accepting? Would she come out of a feeling of obligation, because he was her tutor or out of a genuine desire to be alone with him? If she refused the chance, would that be the end of their relationship? He realised after the implied promise of their meeting in his house, there could be no continuing in the same way.

Then there was the tutor student relationship and all that entailed. Is there a chance that I might be stepping into the danger of jeopardising my job and my marriage? She could quite easily submit and then use this as a lever to extract concessions from him.

All these thoughts went through his head over the next two days and even when Isabel came to his office, he did not mention the subject. Then it occurred to him that it might be all in vain because it would be the Easter holidays and she would most likely be going home to Hong Kong.

When she came to see him a week before the university term ended, he asked her whether she was going home.

"No," she answered grimacing. " I have coursework to catch up on and if I went home I would go out all the time and not complete my essays. Still, if you are around, I can see you more often when there are not many other students about. Maybe we could go for a lunch time drink."

Tom looked at her weighing up his next words. " Well there is something. Jane and the children are going to London for a few days the week before Easter. I cannot go because I have meetings in the university. I will be at home on my own most nights. If you would like to come round for a drink one evening you would be most welcome."

Isabel lent over the desk and kissed him. " Let me know the dates and I will come to your house. If anybody says anything, I will say that I was asking you about the coursework and you were too busy during the day. I took a chance and called round your house in case you were in. They all know that I baby-sit for you and know where you live. That will cover any wagging tongues."

Tom waved goodbye to his family as they caught the train to London. Sarah was already there and she would be at Waterloo to meet Jane. He drove back to the university for another of his meetings eager to finish and get home. He had no idea when Isabel would come or even if she would. In a way it was good that they had left things up in the air. That way Isabel was in control and could come or not as she saw fit. To Tom this might lead to a frustrating evening but that was a price he was willing to pay on the chance that he would see Isabel while his wife was away.

He made sure he had his evening meal on time and had soon cleared everything away. With his papers spread across the desk of his study, he tried to conclude a report he had to write for the research committee. It was hard to concentrate on his work. At times he found himself looking out of the window at the garden but not seeing the plants or shrubs. At other times he would just stare at the wall his mind blank. Then the phone rang and he spent half an hour completely forgetting Isabel as he talked to his family. He had only just put down the phone when the doorbell rang.

When he opened the front door, Isabel was standing there. She was dressed in a top coat because it was none too warm outside.

" Come on in," Tom waved her into the house. " I didn't know whether you would be able to come tonight."

Isabel slipped out of her coat revealing a blue blouse with frills down the front and a shortish skirt. She handed the coat to Tom. " I finished the course work I was working on. It seemed only natural that I should come to see you."

Tom led the way into the sitting room. " Sit where you like. What can I get you to drink?"

Isabel sat on the settee letting her skirt rise up her thighs. " I'll have a coca cola if you have one."

" Ice and lemon?"

" That would be nice."

When Tom returned with the drinks, she was looking at the newspaper. Tom placed the drink by her side and sat on the settee. She lent over and kissed him. They talked between bouts of kissing but when their drinks were finished, Isabel got to her feet still holding Tom's hand.

" I have wanted this for a long time," she said quietly, her voice catching in her throat. " To be able to make love to you was one thing but all night."

" Are you certain this is what you want?" Tom asked as he got to his feet.

" Certainly." Isabel kissed him again. With her arm round his waist she propelled him towards the stairs.

They made love all night even though Tom soon realised that Isabel was inexperienced. She let him explore her body and then she explored his with her lips and tongue. In the morning they lay in each other's arms totally satisfied. They did this for the next two nights until his family arrived back home. It took all of Tom's strength to make love to Jane the night she returned.

Tom tried to hold onto the feeling of warmth and love but the grey mist swirled round his head and he sank back into limbo.

Chapter 9

As she sat by his bed lost for words gazing at his grey face, Mary thought she detected a movement of her father's eyes. In the dim light, she could not be sure. She stared at his face, trying to ignore the tubes and wires. The eyes did not move. No matter how much she willed those eyes to move, there was no sign of stirring. Mary sighed. Like her mother she wondered how long they could all keep this vigil up. If only there was some response, any response, she told herself. But there is nothing. There is no sign that he even knows we are here with him.

Mary lent over and, being careful not to disturb the wires, kissed her father on the forehead. His skin was moist so she wiped it with a paper towel from the container near the bed.

" Daddy. Why did you send me to a private school? The boys were allowed to stay in the state system but you made me take the entrance exams for the Girls Grammar School. Why? You have always, from what I hear, been an advocate of the state system. You were educated in a state school. Why go against your conscience and send me private?"

Mary sighed again. In reality she already knew the answer or part of the answer. She was old enough now to understand what a struggle inside her father it had been to make the decision to give her a private education. By bringing up the subject Mary was hoping it would light a spark and she would get some response. After all, she told herself, that is what we are trying to do. Find a subject which either excites my father or annoys him. Before his stroke, he would always respond in an outspoken way to anything he was passionate about.

The mist was clearing. The light was getting brighter. Soon he would break through into consciousness. He struggled towards the faint glow in the mist but he could not break through. Then he was once more sitting at his desk in his office at the university waiting for four of his male students to come and see him.

He had been happy for greater part of nineteen eighty four. Most of what he wanted to achieve at the start of the year had taken place. That was about to change. Though he had not known it at the time, he was about to enter a period when many of his basic beliefs were to be challenged.

In the autumn term Isabel had left the hall where she had been staying. There was only enough accommodation on campus for a proportion of the students and the first and final year students had priority. Those students who could not be accommodated on campus had to find alternative accommodation in the town. Many liked the opportunity this gave to live away from the restrictions of hall living. Others found it difficult especially if they had to live in run down flats or shared houses. Isabel had moved into a flat in a tower block overlooking the river. Like Vicky before her, she had asked Tom to go and look the place over before she decided to rent it.

Much to her surprise, Tom had asked Jane if she would help him look at Isabel's flat. Tom justified this to Isabel on the grounds that Jane would know far more about the living spaces and the attraction of the flat than he would. Besides, the flat was much more expensive than most flats or houses rented by the average students. It was in a privately run block with security patrols and entrance codes. The front door could be opened by the flat owner from the flat but only after viewing the person wanting to visit.

After looking over the flat with Isabel, Jane approved. Inside, the flat was small. A bedroom to the left of the front entrance, a sitting room straight ahead, kitchen and bathroom on the right was the layout. There were carpets on the floor and reasonably maintained furniture. Isabel had to start renting from the end of her first year rather than when she came back from Hong Kong in the autumn. The bedroom held a double bed and Isabel discussed with Jane the type of bedclothes she would have to buy.

When she returned in the autumn, Isabel resumed her weekly meetings with Tom. All the time she hinted that he should visit her in her flat to see how she had arranged things since moving. He was vague about when he would come. What worried Tom was that his visits would become a regular event. Instead of meeting in his office once a week for a kiss and a cuddle after the discussion of her work, it would be making love in her flat. The more they did this, the greater attachment he would feel for Isabel and the more danger there would be of somebody specifically finding out. He had long admitted to himself there were rumours about his relationship with Isabel but he was sure nobody could put substance to the rumours. It was quite natural for students to visit his office. He was a tutor after all. That most only came when there was a problem was their decision. When meeting his tutees for the first time he always made clear that he would like to see them once a week but the arrangement was voluntary. A few did so like Isabel but most did not.

The weekly arrangement to meet in his office and Tom's resolve held for half the term. Then a week went by without Isabel coming to see him. He had noted that she was not at his lectures either. On making enquiries with the other lecturers he found that she had not been seen around the department or the campus all week. At the end of the week, he asked the administrator whether she had heard anything but drew a blank. He did not take kindly to the remark that this would give him an opportunity to visit her in her flat but decided to ignore it. Actually the administrator did seriously suggest that somebody from the university ought to visit her flat to find out what was wrong. Professor Marriott recovered now from his ordeal at the student dinner, suggested that as Tom was her tutor it was his concern and he should lead the inquires as to her whereabouts. Tom tried to maintain that he was doing this under protest.

The administrator supplied him with Isabel Chueng's address when he explained what the Professor had asked him to do. He even asked her if she would accompany him but she refused making some remark about it was his responsibility.

That afternoon, Tom found himself sitting in his car in the car park by the block of flats where Isabel lived. For a while he sat and stared up at the mass of balconies rising into the air in front of his car bonnet. Nagging in the back of his mind was the thought that this might not be such a good idea. After not meeting her for over a week, he wanted to see Isabel. To counter the longing to see her was the problem of how she would react to him on her ground without the restraint of his office. Still, he told himself, nobody knows what has happened to her and I have been ordered by the head of department to find out.

With that justification ringing in his head, he got out of the car and walked purposefully across the car park to the entrance to the flats. A row of buttons next to name plates under a loudspeaker greeted him. Finding Isabel Chueng's name, he pressed the button. He waited but nothing happened. This time he pressed again for a longer interval and after a while the loudspeaker crackled.

" Yes who is it?" Isabel's voice sounded weak and strained.

" Its Tom. Can I come in?"

" Tom!" her voice brightened. " Come on up. You know the way."

The door clicked and he walked into the entrance hall. Taking the lift, he arrived outside her flat. The door was ajar making him anxious. He walked into the flat and through the hall to the sitting room. There was no sign of Isabel.

Tom went into the bedroom. Isabel was lying on the bed, her eyes closed. She was dressed in a pair of jeans and a sweater. From the door Tom noticed her hair was a tangled mess. She had no make up and her face was pale and drawn. The flat smelled of unwashed bodies and vomit.

Tom gently shook her by the shoulder. She opened one eye and groaned. Putting the pillows at the head of the bed, Tom helped Isabel to a sitting position. She smiled wanly.

" Tom. What are you doing here?"

" You had not been seen in the university or by any of your fellow students for over a week so I came to see what was wrong."

" I felt so ill. I could not keep any food or drink down. I just lay here and felt sorry for myself."

" Didn't you get in touch with anybody?"

" No. I thought it would go away."

" Would you like me to get you a drink?"

" Yes please. There is English tea in the kitchen and coffee for you. There is some powdered milk as well. I expect the milk in the fridge will have gone bad by now. Thank you for coming."

Tom searched the kitchen and found the tea, coffee, powdered milk and some chocolate bars. Once this was ready, he took it through to the bedroom. Sitting on the bed by her side, he poured the tea. Silently Isabel drank the tea and attempted to eat a chocolate bar. Tom sat watching her as he drank his coffee.

" Would you like a shower?" he asked her.

" I haven't the strength," she replied in a faint voice sinking down the bed. " I know I need a shower. I feel dirty and horrid. At the moment I could not stand in the shower for very long."

" What if I helped you? Would you be willing to try?"

She smiled faintly. " With your help I might be able to try but it will be hard."

" Come on. We will give it a try. Sit on the edge of the bed and I will help you to undress."

She swung her legs off the bed and sat with her feet on the floor. Her face was pale and, even with that little effort, she was breathing heavily. Sweat moistened her forehead. Tom reach down and pulled her sweater over her head. She was not wearing a bra. Undoing her jeans, Tom made her put her arms round his shoulders while he lifted her and slid them over her legs. Pulling down her panties, he threw these onto the pile of her other dirty clothes. He then undressed himself. Isabel smiled and reached for him but he pushed aside her hands.

Helping her to her feet, he took her into the shower room. She had to hold onto him while he washed her understanding now why he had undressed. With difficulty he washed her hair and then dried her body all the time resisting the urge to make love to her. Once she was dry, he laid her on the bed while he searched for her pyjamas. He had to laugh when he attempted to dry her hair but in the end all was well. Isabel looked a lot better when he had finished. She was starting to fall asleep again when he kissed her before leaving.

When he got back to the university, he called the student welfare people and explained what had taken place. He was upset that they were suspicious of his motives at first but in the end at the mention of Professor Marriot, they agreed to send somebody to assess Isabel's needs.

She returned to the department the next week looking and feeling a lot better.

" Thank you Tom for looking in on me," she said with a beaming smile when she came to his office. " I was feeling dreadful. Was it you who sent the doctor to see me?"

" Not exactly. I informed the student welfare people and they arranged everything from there. I am glad to see you are feeling a lot better. Are you going to make up the work that you missed?"

Isabel grimaced. " I will have to somehow. I can borrow the notes of somebody to copy and ask the lecturers if I have any questions. I don't know how I will cope with the work load."

" You will manage though you should put in an impaired performance form as soon as you can. That will help if there is any effect on your performance this term. There is no way in which your illness can be raised at an exam board unless you hand in that form. Even I will not be able to use that as a means of discussing your work."

Isabel smiled and came round his desk. " That is all the formal business. Now give me a kiss and a cuddle. It is a shame that you have all your clothes on now. I wish I had been feeling better when you stripped off in my flat. When can you visit me again?"

That day, Tom stepped over an invisible, psychological line and started on a journey which he had always in the past sheered away from. It was not that before he had stopped at all chance of sex with a student but this time he was making a conscious effort to arrange meeting times. Previously he had just let the opportunity come along and then taken advantage. Now he was planning how he could visit Isabel without it having an effect on his marriage or his work. It was not easy but there were times of the week especially Wednesday afternoons when the rest of the university indulged in its passion for sport.

Isabel did not do sport as she put it. Oh I play an occasional game of tennis for leisure but not serious sport. It was all she could do to try to understand how Tom could put aside every other Saturday and some evenings in the week so that he could go and watch a football game. With patience Tom tried to explain his attachment to Porthampton Town but it passed Isabel by.

This university attachment to Wednesdays being sport afternoon meant that they could meet in her flat for a couple of hours most weeks. Tom had insisted in making plain to Isabel that there was no future in their relationship, that as soon as she graduated and left the university, that would be the end of their time together.

It was a Wednesday evening after a particularly satisfying bout of love making with Isabel, when Jane got very angry. Not angry with Tom but angry with the education system. At the beginning of the school term Jane had been asked to become a volunteer parent. Whenever she was available, she agreed to help the teachers supervise pupils when they left the school for out of school activities.

That afternoon she had helped Paul's teacher take his class to the local church where the pupils were trying to trace the local history. This was now the subject of her wrath.

" Mary is not going to that school!" It was the first time for ages that Tom had heard her so emphatic about something. " There is nothing we can do about Mark but Mary is definitely not going to that school!"

Taken aback by her anger, Tom asked mildly, " What happened this afternoon to bring this on?"

" Tom you would not believe it," Jane almost spluttered. " All the boys joined in with various degrees of enthusiasm. I know there are always keen ones who want to learn and others who follow along for a quiet life. But many of the girls sat at the back discussing boys, make up and going out. They had no intention of learning anything. When I asked them what they hoped to achieve by sitting there they gave me such a mouthful. They want nothing more than to get through school and then get a job. Tom it was dreadful."

" It cannot have been that bad surely. What about all the teachers?"

" Tom, the teachers were only interested in two things. Those pupils who showed some interest and look as though they want to learn get all the attention. The teachers will go out of their way to help them. All the other pupils they just want to keep quiet. If those pupils sink beneath the academic waves, too bad."

" But Jane surely Mary will be one of the ones who will want to learn? Paul is doing OK and according to his teachers will do well when it comes to his A Levels.

Mark is even more intelligent and will be OK. Why are you so worried about Mary?"

" Paul and Mark are not only academic but are reasonably good at sports. They will both fit in no matter what the peer pressure. Mary will find it very difficult to resist the peer pressure if she goes to that school. Believe me. I was there today."

" What are you suggesting?"

" There is only one answer as far as I am concerned. That is to send Mary to the Girls Grammar."

" But that is a private school and we both believe in State education. You must know how I feel about the question of paying for education."

Jane put her arm round his shoulders. " Tom, I know how you feel about private education. You must know that I have never been quite so closed to the idea of paying for education as you have. Lets face it. We have the money. A great many of our friends have made great sacrifices to send their children to private schools since the abolition of the Grammar Schools. It would not be a such a sacrifice for us."

Tom frowned. Angrily he retorted. " What you are asking is for me to compromise all the principles and living philosophy I have believed for most of my life. I never thought I would hear you advocating that we send one of our children to a private school."

" Tom, please don't get angry with me. I have thought of nothing else but what we can do about Mary since coming home. It is not as though I do not know how you feel. I know what your principles are. You were not there."

" If you know how I feel, why do you ask me to think about this?"

" If it was only a matter of principle, I would not ask. It is all very well you standing on your high horse and arguing for state education when it is theoretical. This is not theory, Tom. This is not some academic discussion like those you have in the staff common room at lunch time. This is your daughter's education and subsequently her chances in life. Do you want her to slip below the standards we expect because of the girls she has to mix with?"

" That is a very arrogant remark. All girls going to Paul's school are not working class without ambition. They do send some girls to university surely?"

" I must admit there are some but not as many as the boys."

Tom looked lost and beaten. " What do we have to do?"

Jane smiled. " I phoned Sarah when I got home and she filled me in with the drill. Mary would have to take the entrance examination in two years time. Sarah reckons we should find a private tutor who helps children get through the entrance exams. It is so competitive that most children who do not have a tutor fail."

" This is something I have never thought about. How do we find a good tutor?"

" I will ask at work though most of the people I work with have children at university or babies.'

" I'll do the same."

Tom lay in bed that night unable to sleep. He could feel Jane by his side breathing evenly, her body warm. It brought no comfort. Tom lay there far from sleep confronting the chance that he would have to overturn his principles. It had always been a pillar of his beliefs that education should be provided by the state and all children should be treated equally. Many a time at university he had argued long into the night with some privileged public school educated friend that their parents buying of privilege was wrong both morally and socially. Morally because in some cases it deprived the country of very intelligent and resourceful citizens because their education was lacking. Not only did private schools give education to the rich but they employed many of the best teachers. This was a handicap to those aspiring pupils from disadvantaged backgrounds. Oh, he had to admit that there was still a great deal of prejudice among the working class about education. He remembered Pat from all those years ago down in the recreation ground telling him that she had passed her eleven plus only for her dad to tell her that she was not going to grammar school. She was to leave school as soon as possible and get a job to bring money into the house. But surely, he told himself, things have changed for the better. It is the nineteen eighties and women are far more prominent in society. Even though he could not stand her or for the privilege she stood for, he had to admit that Mrs. Thatcher was a good example for women everywhere.

On the other hand, he knew from the experience of talking to people that this attitude still applied in many working peoples' households. He had been occupied all his life to make the chance of a good education open to all. In this he was a big supporter of the comprehensive system. If we can only get every child in this country to reach their potential through education and training, he had often told people, this would be such a vibrant country. It had been hard work and there was still a great deal of nepotism from the so called upper classes.

Now all his beliefs were being questioned on the altar of convenience. He smiled to himself. Since that time in the Jack of Diamonds when you met Mr. Hunt, your life has been a compromise, he had to admit. If you can ignore the implications of what you are doing as a non executive director for Hunt Enterprises, surely you can compromise your principles for the sake of your wife and daughter? And then there is the other part of your life which you do not question. Edward is very good at his job, you say, never questioning the methods by which he produced such good returns on your investments. No, all of that is legitimate and does not involve my principles. On the other hand, sending my daughter to a private school goes against everything I have ever argued for.

The next day Tom asked as many of his colleagues as was possible about the entrance examinations for the Girls Grammar School and what this entailed. Though a great many were liberal like him, quite a number had been through the same exercise as he was pondering. They advised him in the same way as Sarah had told Jane that it would be far easier if he got a tutor to coach Mary in exam technique and the type of questions asked. By the end of the week he had a list of likely tutors.

That weekend, Jane and Tom exchanged their lists and decided on a short list of likely candidates. Their first criteria was locality. The three chosen all lived within an easy drive, indeed at a push, Mary would be able to walk. It was strange Tom found going round with Mary and talking to the tutors in their own homes. It was difficult to decide who was interviewing whom. There was little difference in the cost. Tom found himself watching Mary's reaction and the way she spoke to the teachers.

When they had seen all the prospective tutors, Jane and Tom talked at length about what was right. Even at this stage, Tom felt very uneasy. It was as though he was getting rid of something that had been a part of him for a long time. At last they with input from Mary agreed on a Mrs. Black. Mary was to start in September of the next year meaning she would have two years of extra tuition before the examinations.

While all this was going on, Tom was asked at a meeting of parents at Paul's school if he would be prepared to sit on the parent teacher committee of the school. He agreed to think about the idea and was dully elected when he let his name be put forward. The school was delighted to have a Professor from the University as one of their parents and Tom was pleased to have an input into the workings of the school.

What surprised him and was going to come back later to affect his loyalty to the school, was the way the school compromised on the equality of treatment arguments. It was written into the terms of reference for the school that there would be no streaming. All teaching would be in mixed ability classes. Though there were misgivings about this philosophy among some of the parents mainly in the realm of disruption by some pupils stopping their children learning, most parents accepted the general case for this principle. The head master proclaimed loftily when ever the subject came up that every pupil must be given the opportunity to reach their true potential. That would not be achieved by streaming pupils and making out that some were more worthy than the others. We must not make the pupils feel that they were inferior to other pupils.

Tom worked out after his first committee meeting at the school that the principle of mixed ability classes so trumpeted by the school to the wider world was fudged. The school took its pupils from the six junior schools in its catchments area. One of the classes in every year was taken from the top academic children from two of those schools. The one that Paul had attended was one and the other was equally down the road from the university. The majority of these pupils had academics as their parents. All the other pupils were spread in a random fashion through the other classes. It was from Paul's class that all the pupils took the A level examination plus those from the other classes who managed to fight their way through the system. The best teachers were concentrated on these pupils as well. Tom was surprised but did not want to rock the boat by saying too much. Besides, his son Paul was in that group and doing well. Any animosity would not be directed at Tom but at his son Paul.

A few weeks later Tom was confronted with a further situation which tore at another of his core beliefs. It was Sunday. He had just finished his breakfast and was getting ready to go to church when the phone rang.

" Yes," he spoke into the receiver.

" This is Joshua. Sorry to bother you at this time on the Lord's Day but we have just opened our church and it has been vandalised."

" What have they done?"

Joshua sounded near to tears. " They have broken the table, ripped some of the choir robes and smashed the cross. On top of that they piled the bibles in the centre of the church and set fire to them. Tom, we don't know what to do. It must have been targeted deliberately because they have sprayed paint all over the walls. There are things written there which I would not expose my wife and children to."

" Things like what?"

" The least offensive is Nigger go home."

" OK Joshua, I will be over in a little while and we can assess what is needed and what help you could do with. Then I can work out how to help you. See you in a little while."

Tom found Jane in the bedroom sorting out some washing. On seeing his face, she asked anxiously. " Who was that on the phone?"

" It was Joshua from his church," Tom replied. " The building has been vandalised. I will go and see if there is anything I can do to help if that is all right by you."

Jane smiled. " You go while I take the children to church. I will load the car with cleaning stuff. When you have seen what needs doing, come and collect the children and me from church. Before you arrive, I will see if there is anybody else who will help."

Tom kissed her. " You are a jewel you know. I'll tell you what. You talk to some of the other members and I will make an announcement when I get there. I will ask as many as possible to come with me to help. How's that?"

Jane looked doubtful. " I will do what you ask but I am sceptical about their response."

Tom drove across town to the Pentecostal Chapel. Parking the car as near as possible, he walked the short distance to the Chapel thinking about how he would be greeted.

The door was open and he let himself in. What greeted him was gut wrenching. The Chapel was a mess. It was as though an angry child had been let loose. Many chairs had been upended and slashed. The communion table was broken and the cloth brown and singed from a fire. Bibles and other books were thrown around the building with the pages torn and crumpled. A pile in one corner had been torched.

What was worse was the paint. It had been splashed on the walls from open tins. Then brushes had been used to paint slogans on the walls. " Nigger go home.". " Blacks not wanted here.". " Black bastards will die." were some of the hurtful things written.

Joshua looked round at the door when Tom entered. He was sitting crying with some of his congregation.

" Tom," was all he could say.

" Who did this?" Tom asked more to say something than to get an answer.

" We have no idea."

One of the women tears running down her face asked, " How could they do this? We have never hurt anybody."

" What are you going to do?" Tom was blunt.

" We have no idea. With people like this what are we supposed to do?"

" Joshua! You are a follower of our Lord Jesus. He told us it would not be easy."

" But our building is ruined."

" I have had this argument many times, my friend. Can I ask you a question?"

" Of course."

" What is a church?"

Joshua waved his harms round the building. " This is my church."

Tom shook his head. " Joshua. This is a building. Buildings can be replaced or cleaned. What is a church? Look around you. Your congregation are starting to clean up the mess. They are the church. They are the ones who pray, praise the Lord and sing their songs. They are the ones who go out into the world and do God's work. They are the ones who will stand in the rain and pray and praise the Lord. Joshua. A church is the people not the building."

Joshua smiled crookedly. " My friend, you shame me."

Looking round, he called all the people together. Picking up a battered bible he thumbed through the pages.

" Right everybody. I will read this passage from the bible. We will then pray and after that we will start to clean up our church."

And he read. " Come unto me all ye that labour and are heavy laden and I will give you rest. Take my yoke upon you and learn of me; for I am meek and lowly in heart; and ye shall find rest unto your souls. For my yoke is easy and my burden is light."

" Now let us say the Lords prayer." And amidst the wreckage, they prayed for strength to carry on.

When they had finished, Tom said to Joshua. " I am going back to my church to see if I can recruit some of the members to come and help you. We will arrive with as much cleaning stuff as we can carry. Do not give in to helplessness. We will prevail."

Jane was waiting for Tom in the porch of the church. " What happened?"

Tom shrugged. " It is worse than I thought. I have to get people in our congregation to help."

Jane gripped his arm. " You be careful Tom and be ready to be disappointed. They are a conservative lot this congregation. I should know having grown up here."

" I can only try."

It took some fast talking but the minister agreed to allow Tom to address the congregation when the opening sentences had been read.

Facing the stern faces of the members, Tom felt his heart sink. He addressed them never the less. " Thank you for giving me this opportunity to address you before the service. Something has come to my attention which I think concerns you all. This morning I had a phone call from Joshua Darling the Pastor of the Church of Christ our Lord, a mainly black church. I met him at the Council of Churches meetings. He told me that his church had been vandalised last night. There is paint all over the walls with the most offensive slogans. The hymn books and bibles have been torn up and thrown on the floor. In one place they have piled up books, table cloths and choir vestments and set fire to them. Our Christian brothers and sisters need our help. I ask those of you who are willing to help to go straight away with as much needed cleaning material as possible."

There was a stony silence from the congregation. " Is nobody willing to help?"

Again there was silence. Tom looked at Jane and she shook her head. " I am going now with my family. Anybody can join me who is willing to help."

Jane with Paul, Mark and Mary watched from the door as Tom walked down the aisle between the pews of immovable people. She could see all the signs and prayed that he would not explode.

Tom was confused and angry. He could not understand how people who called themselves Christians would not give up their service and come and help fellow Christians in need of support. It was what the Christian message is all about. Even though it was only recently on the death of his father that he had come back to the church, it disillusioned him to think that these people did not live out the Christian message of love.

Once out of the church, he heard somebody calling his name. Turning he found a young couple called Vera and John hurrying towards him.

" Mr. Houseman. We will come to help. Tell us where to go."

Tom gave them instructions. Lisa the leader of the Guides came out as well with two of her older guides. Tom smiled.

" Were is this church?" Lisa asked in her best Guide Leader voice. " We will go and collect some more of our pack and then join you."

Once again Tom gave instructions, climbed into his car and drove to the Pentecostal church. Joshua greeted them at the door.

" Thank you for coming, there are a few here all ready."

Tom grasped Joshua's hand. " My family have come with me. Some of our guide pack are coming and another couple. I am sorry it is so few."

Joshua greeted Jane. " How are you Mrs. Houseman? I will show to my wife. She is organising the women."

They worked away for the rest of the morning. There were a few people from other churches and they started to have an impact. The men were organised into grouped of three, each group taking a patch of wall and scrubbing away at the paint. The people who had come to clean the church had supplied all sorts of different cleaning fluid and implements. Surprisingly, Tom found the whole experience companionable.

At lunch time Joshua called a halt. Some of his flock came into the church with steaming bowls of West Indian food. They sat in a circle and Joshua said grace. Even though the work was far from over, they all had a sense of achievement. Tom did notice that his children sat with Joshua's for their meal. The children sat under the watchful eye of a large lady eating and talking. If anybody ever tells me that black people are different, I will hold this picture in my head and argue back, Tom thought. He did notice during the rest of the afternoon that his son Paul and Joshua's daughter Ruth appeared to be side by side most of the time. They looked happy.

It was getting dark when Joshua called a halt. A great deal of the paint had been cleaned with only small traces remaining. Most of the offensive slogans had disappeared. A group of women had repaired the clothes, cleaned the floor and found another table cloth for the communion table. Others had repaired the choir robes.

Spontaneously, they gathered chairs and sat facing the stage and the table. Joshua came to the front and smiled.

He held up his arms and said. " Thank you all for coming to help. The church now looks much better. I think we will hold a small service to thank the Lord for our companionship."

A woman got up and read from the bible and Joshua led prayers. The choir got them all singing. They all left with a sense of accomplishment.

Two weeks later the Pound Street Church held its monthly church meeting. Before Tom left home, Jane warned him to be careful of what she was not too sure. Ever since the asking for help for Joshua's church she had sensed a certain hostility in her friends at the church.

At first the meeting passed off peacefully. Mostly it was routine business about the buildings, the finances and mission into the community. There were some very polite arguments and disagreements but these were soon resolved. There was always an item on the agenda concerning relations with other churches and Tom spoke to this about the Council of Churches and its work.

Martin Dobson, one of the Elders, raised a point of order. Not many people understood what he was on about until he spoke.

" Can our delegate to the Council of Churches please tell us why he endeavoured to halt our Sunday morning service the other week for no good reason?"

Tom could feel the frisson of support ripple around the room. Beside him he sensed Jane tense. Looking round the room Tom was aware that all the eyes were on him. He knew from experience that most of the members present were the keen traditional members of the church. I will have to be careful, he thought.

As mildly as he could, he said. " I received a phone call from one of the members of the Council of Churches committee. Joshua Darling the pastor of the Church of Christ our Lord was in tears. Vandals had broken into his church and trashed it. I agreed to help and promised to see if any of our members would help."

" Then you came here and asked us to abandon our service?"

" No. I asked anybody who would like to help to come and join me. Not many did."

" Does that surprise you?" Molly Meager put in. " Sunday is the day of the Lord, the Sabbath. It should be spent in worship not trailing half way across the town to help a church we have never had any dealings with. I think you were out of order trying to get us to abandon our service."

" If that is what you think then our ideas of following our Lord are different. There are many references in the New Testament about giving help. The Good Samaritan to name one."

" But this is an alien church filled with immigrants."

Tom tried to stop his anger building but failed. " Oh is that what has upset you Molly Meager. If it had been a white church down the road, you might have considered helping. But it was black church across town and you do not want to know. Shame on you. Where is your compassion? Where is your love? These Christians were in trouble and needed our help."

Tom paused to look around. Jane placed a restraining hand on his arm but he was too irate to stop. " I do not recognise your brand of Christianity. You have lost the idea of love, of everybody being equal in the eyes of God."

Turning to Mike Thompson the minister who was chairing the meeting, he snapped. " You had better find somebody else to sit on the Council of Churches and the Free Church Federal Council. From this moment I resign."

Martin Dobson rose to his feet. " I think it goes further than resignation from representing this church on these committees. I think it calls into question the membership of this church of Tom Houseman."

Molly Meager harshly agreed. " I second that. I propose it be put to a vote."

There was stunned silence round the table.

Mike Thompson looked very uncomfortable but he had to agree. " By the constitution of the church and the rules of the church meeting we have to put this to the vote."

Another member, Audrey, who Tom did not know well spoke. " This is monstrous. We have always prided ourselves on being a church which encompasses all views as long as it does not fundamentally digress from our faith. I cannot see how Tom has violated that sense. Don't you all think this is a trivial matter which should be dropped. Tom has always represented our church on these bodies according to the wishes of this church meeting. That Sunday he was only appealing for help for another set of Christians. Why are Martin and Molly so eager to censure him?"

Mike Thompson held up his hand. " Enough. I think we should go straight to the vote. Tom will you leave the room."

Tom squeezed Jane's hand and left the room. He sat in the main hall dangling his legs over the stage wondering whether it mattered if he won the vote or not. Following the death of his father and in support of his mother, he had come back to the church. Later out of loyalty to Jane he had continued to attend. As his political convictions led him, so he had been carried along by the message of love and compassion for the poor and helpless.

The words spoken by Joshua in the wreck of his church came unbidden to his mind, sounding as clearly as though Joshua was sitting by his side. " Come unto me all ye that labour and are heavy laden and I will give you rest. Take my yoke upon you and learn of me; for I am meek and lowly in heart; and ye shall find rest unto your souls. For my yoke is easy and my burden is light."

He prayed then for God to give him the strength to face whatever the result of the vote. Sitting back staring into the gloom of the dimly lit hall where he had first become aware of girls, he felt calm and ready to face his critics. He had spent a great deal of his formative teenage years in this hall. Now he wondered would he ever be back.

Audrey came out of the meeting room and smiled at Tom. " They are ready for you back in there."

When Tom resumed his seat, Mike spoke. " The vote was an overwhelming majority against the proposition of Martin and Molly. Are you sure you would not reconsider your decision to resign as our representative on those committees?"

" I have made up my mind, Mike. You will have to find somebody else."

On the way home, Jane filled him in as to what had taken place when he was out of the room. It appears that the vast majority of people in the room had rounded on Martin and told him not to be so stupid. They argued that you only wanted to help another church and if Martin did not want to help he was quite at liberty to refuse. She got a promise out of Tom that he would not give up the church even after what happened that night. Tom gave her a promise though he did not promise to stay quiet if he disagreed with what was being done in the church's name.

It got worse a few months later. Porthampton through the Council of Churches had a pulpit exchange between the various denominations. As part of that process Pound Street had a visit from a young, earnest Anglican Priest. His sermon was on the subject of subjugating our inner desires to the work of Christ. A worthy topic. It was when he got onto the subject of homosexuality being a sin and had no place in the church that Tom got upset.

After listening politely but feeling the embarrassment of many in the congregation, Tom had had enough. Douglas, one of their members, they all knew was a homosexual living with a partner. A better Christian you could not find anywhere. He was kind and considerate and very gentle. On occasions like Christmas and Easter, Johnie his partner came to church as well.

Jumping to his feet, Tom confronted the young priest. " Do we have to sit here and listen to this diatribe against the evils of homosexuality? There are only obscure references to it on the bible. Where is the love for thy neighbour as Jesus told us to practice?"

" It states quite clearly in Deuteronomy that no man might lie with another man."

" Look your understanding of theology must be more knowledgeable than mine. However it has been established that homosexuals cannot be blamed for their leanings or their feelings. Therefore we have to be tolerant of their sexuality and not condemn them out of hand."

" That is not what I have been taught."

" Maybe it is because you are concerned about your own sexuality which makes you persecute those who are different. If that is all you have to preach to us, I will not stay and listen." With that Tom stalked out of the church.

His whole belief system was being further undermined. It was as though he was having to confront all his demons at the same time. Before this he had been able to suppress them when they attacked, to push them back into the dark recesses of the mind where these things always lurked. It had never taken too much mental effort for Tom to justify whatever he had been doing. Now he was having to dig deep for those justifications and he was not liking the answers he was arriving at.

When they arrived home from church, Tom had to listen to Jane's anger once more.

" Tom Houseman, don't you ever do that again," She raged. The children disappeared into their bedrooms. " I did not know which way to look. There was a wave of disapproval when you left. The minister was left speechless."

" I am sorry Jane but I could not sit and listen to such hatred in a church. It is against all the teachings I have been brought up to believe. If the church members disapprove, they will have to vote again to exclude me."

Jane stormed off into the kitchen. That night, though, she did hint that it was not Tom's views she disagreed with but the rude way in which he had expressed them.

Tom was still thinking of this while he sat behind his desk waiting for the students he had asked to come to his office to arrive. He had no idea how he was going to open the discussion but felt for the sake of Isabel that he had to do something. One problem was that one of the students was the most focused, intelligent and hard working he had known since starting lecturing. Ryan was even better than Vicky in Tom's estimation and that was praise indeed.

There was a knock at the door and Tom asked them to enter. They sat down on the chairs in a circle the other side of Tom's desk. As though trying to judge what this was all about, they all looked at him suspiciously.

" Thank you all for coming," Tom started while clearing his thoughts and watching their reaction. " I have a request to ask of you all. I have heard that you all make suggestive remarks to Isabel Chueng all the time. Is this right?"

Ryan spoke. " Not really. We do engage in banter and horse play from time to time. All of the group join in."

Tom waved his hand for Ryan to stop. " Was it banter to upset Ray Reynolds so much that he transferred to another course?"

Ryan smiled a superior smile which upset Tom. " He was a loner and at times pathetic. Nobody could say anything to him without him crying."

" What you mean is that he was not one of your set and did not treat life like you do. You can be most cruel to those who are not as gifted as you but will not submit to your leadership."

Ryan frowned. " I am not cruel. He could not stand the heat of normal student life."

Tom looked stern. " We are not here to talk about Ray Reynolds. We are here to talk about Isabel Chueng. You have all upset her and she wants you to stop."

Ryan laughed. " As I say it is only horse play between fellow students. I can't think how we will stop that."

Tom was now angry but he kept calm. " Is squeezing her breasts and patting or pinching her bottom general horse play?"

Ryan got to his feet and lent over the desk." Has she made a formal complaint? I have never touched her, just had a joke and a laugh. If she is accusing me, I will complain to the Head of Department."

" I see that you are now taking on all the attributes of the bully which I never thought you were. You don't like it when the boot is on the other foot. The answer to your question is that she has not made a formal complaint against you or anybody. She wanted to avoid that. She came to me so that I could have a quiet word with you all and get you to stop. It might not have been you but one of your gang fondled her breasts when they were working on a project together."

Greg owned up. " It was me. I said I was sorry at the time. It was an accident. Patting her bottom and making lewd remarks is part of being a student."

" Thank you Greg. Now I want this to stop before it goes any further. No do not protest. One of the problems with Transport Studies is the lack of girl students. They cannot bandy together for protection. You lot have a moral obligation to help any student in my group. That includes Isabel Chueng. Now let us not have any more of this so called banter. Agreed."

Ryan looked at all the others and they all nodded. They all trooped out of the office.

Tom sat back in his chair staring at the door. Deep down he knew that he had not achieved much in his talk with the students. Lets face it, he told himself, they had all the aces. I was acting on very little information and no legal authority. If there had been an official complaint, there would have been an inquiry but Isabel did not want the questioning. All I can say is that I tried.

That he had tried but not succeeded came home to him a few weeks later. He was sitting quietly with Jane watching the news on television after the children had gone off to bed, when the front door bell rang. They exchanged looks but Tom got up and answered the door bell.

Two policemen were standing on the front door step. Young enough to be my sons he thought inconsequentially.

Tom raised his eyebrow. " Yes?"

One of the policemen smiled. " Professor Houseman?"

" Yes."

" Can we come inside?" He held up his warrant card for Tom to see.

Tom hesitated but stepped aside to let them into the hall. He closed the front door and led the way into the sitting room. When the policemen followed Tom into the sitting room, Jane looked up with a worried frown. The young policemen sat on the settee obviously ill at ease looking at their note books. Both Tom and Jane remained silent waiting for one of the policeman to speak.

" You are the tutor of Isabel Chueng at the university?" he asked finally to break the silence.

" Yes," Tom answered shortly wondering where this was leading. His heart missed a beat when the thought occurred that she was in trouble. He tried to hide his feeling behind a blank expression.

" I can think of no other way of putting this to you but bluntly. Isabel

Chueng has climbed out onto the roof of the block of flats where she lives and is sitting on the edge threatening to throw herself off. She won't listen or talk to anybody but asks for us to get you to speak to her. It took us a while to find out where you lived but here we are. Would you be willing t speak to her?" The young policeman looked and sounded as though he was pleading with Tom.

Tom looked at Jane and she nodded. " All right officer, I will come with you. Just bear in mind that I suffer from a fear of heights sometimes. What I will need is a packet of cigarettes, a packet of Hamlet and a lighter."

Tom got to his feet and went to collect his coat, scarf and gloves. Jane helped him on with the coat looking very worried.

" You be careful, Tom," she pleaded. " No heroics. Officer you make sure the police keep my husband safe."

The young constable looked rather sheepish. " We will do our best."

The car drove through the dark evening but Tom did not see the lights or the passing buildings. He was wondering what he was going to say to Isabel if he ever bucked up the courage to join her on the edge of the roof. It was something he had never had to deal with before and for once he was at a loss to think of what he would do. What was he trying to accomplish? he asked himself. Obviously to get her to come down from the roof and not try to kill herself. Was it his job to find out why she felt so desperate that she wanted to kill herself? Actually he partly knew. That was when he came to the realisation that he had failed in his attempts to get his students to desist from bullying Isabel. He hardly noticed when the car drew up outside a shop and one of the policemen went inside to buy the cigarettes.

They stopped outside the block of flats where Isabel lived. There were fire engines, police cars and an ambulance in the car park. The firemen where hastily blowing up a large cushion which Tom reckoned must be to break Isabel's fall when she jumped from the roof. God I hope it does not come to that or that I have to jump with her, he thought looking at all the activity.

A policeman in a peaked cap met Tom as he got out of the car.

" Professor Houseman?"

Tom nodded.

The policeman pointed upwards. " Miss Chueng is up there outlined in the spotlights. One of the firemen will take you up."

Tom looked up through the blinding light. " Superintendent. Could you either turn off the spotlights or at least tone them down? It must be blinding up there."

" I'll see what I can do but we must have some light."

" Shine the bloody light on the mattress or the side of the building but not on me when I get on that roof," Tom replied angrily. " There will be quite enough light from all the reflections without you shining it in my eyes. I have to see what is going on."

" All right we will turn down the lights."

" Thank you," Tom nodded as he made his way to the entrance.

A fireman in full gear including a helmet met him by the open lift door and followed Tom into the lift. It would have been funny if the time was not so serious but there as an advertisement for the Samaritans attached to the lift mirror.

The doors opened on the top floor. The fire man led the way out into the corridor. He pushed open a safety door, holding this for Tom. They entered a dark stairway which the fireman illuminated with his torch. He pushed open a door at the top of the stairs and they emerged onto the roof of the flats. Two men, one a policeman, the other who to Tom looked like a social worker were standing by the door.

" Professor Houseman," the fireman stated. One of the policemen pointed and led Tom round the side of the structure which Tom took to be the lift mechanism.

" The Chinese lady is over there sitting with her legs over the edge. We daren't get any closer because any move on our part and she starts to slide off the roof. Can we rig you in a safety harness?"

Tom smiled crookedly. " I would appreciate that especially as I hate heights. But it would give the wrong indication to Isabel. She must be out of her mind to be sitting there and if I wore a safety harness she would suspect that I am going to try to grab her."

" Please yourself but I think it would be safer for you." The policeman grinned and shrugged.

" What are you going to do?" the social worker asked politely.

Tom grinned. " Tell her I am here and then go and sit with her. Hopefully after talking and smoking for a while, I can get her to leave the edge and put herself in your hands. Wish me luck."

The roof sloped slightly down towards where Isabel was sitting. Tom walked carefully out into the open and stopped about ten feet from where she sat. He was aware of the drop where her legs disappeared over the wall on which she was sitting. Looking up he could see the lights of the tower blocks beside the river and the arching bridge further down stream. The other way was the golf course and the football pitches of the sports centre. Deep down he wondered whether he was able to go any further but he bit his lip and waited,

" Hello Isabel. It is Tom," he said in as calm a voice as he could manage. " You asked me to come."

She looked around, her hand resting lightly on the parapet. Tom was shocked at the sight of her face. It was tear stained and white. Her usually well combed hair was a tangled mess. She did not say a word. Her almond shaped eyes looked at Tom pleading with him for what he could not fathom.

" Can I come and sit with you?" he asked gently.

At first he thought she had not heard because there was no response but then she said in a very quiet voice, patting the parapet by her side. " If you promise not to grab me, come and sit here."

Isabel looked forlorn and lost. " Thank you for coming. Don't try to pull me back or I will jump."

" All I want is to come and talk," Tom told her as he walked slowly forward towards the edge of the roof. His slowness was not only caused by his desire not to scare Isabel but also from his fighting down the feeling of vertigo which was trying to engulf him. He knew it was silly but there was nothing he could do about the blind panic that often overtook him whenever he was confronted by an abyss at his feet.

Behind his back, he could feel the tension in the men watching him from their place by the lift housing. It was as though they were willing him to make it to the edge without disturbing Isabel too much.

Tom almost stopped dead when he could see over the edge. His head started to spin, sweat broke out on his forehead and the void seemed to beckon him over into oblivion. He took deep breaths and tried not to look down. His hands were shaking and his palms wet.

The lights along the river spread out in the distance as he swung his legs over the parapet. Soon he was sitting a yard away from Isabel with his limbs dangling in thin air. He tried desperately not to think of what a mess he would make if he fell.

The breeze ruffled his hair and felt cold against his skin. He noticed with a glance down that the blow up mattress was half inflated. To take his mind off the drop, he tried to light a cigarette with shaking hands. When it was alight, he handed it to Isabel. His hands had almost stopped shaking when he lit his cigar. Making sure he kept a space between him and Isabel, he sat back and drew deeply on his cigar.

They sat like that for some time, lost in their own thoughts. In any other circumstances it would have been companionable but where they were it was filled with anxiety.

Tom was the first to break the silence. " Are you warm enough? I brought a flask of coffee with me. Would you like a cup?"

Isabel nodded. Tom poured coffee into the beaker from the top of the flask and pushed this in her direction. Isabel picked it up and drank gratefully.

" There is nothing left for me to live for," Isabel suddenly said.

" Don't be stupid," Tom snapped. " You are young and beautiful with all your life in front of you."

" Don't you speak to me like that, Tom. You do not understand."

Tom smiled to himself. He had extracted a response from her." Why do you say there is nothing left to live for?"

Isabel looked at him, tears running down her face. " My grandmother died and I could not get back for her funeral. She will never forgive me. I have not even been able to send an offering for her through a temple. Then I have been given poor marks for my last three essays. I know this is because I could not concentrate but it is bad. My father is paying for me to go to university and he will lose face if I fail."

Tom waved his hand. " Wait a minute. Why did you not come and tell me about your grandmother?"

" You have been so busy the last few weeks we have hardly seen each other. I came to your office last week but you were away at that conference in Liverpool. I missed you so much but you were not there."

" I am sorry Isabel but I have to work for a living."

" Tom don't blame yourself. I know you have to live your life without too much thought about me. You have been wonderful to me and I did understand from the start that there was no future in our relationship. You told me we would have to live each moment together as though it was our last and I have stuck to that ideal. Besides, what would you have been able to do for me if you had been there?"

" Officially not too much but I would have been able to comfort you. As for your essays, I have told you before when you have been given poor marks even by me, you have to forget those marks and make sure that you get better marks in the future. I am certain you will not fail your second year. Nothing is as bad as it appears in the mind."

" Then there is the attention I am getting all the time from Ryan and his group. I know you had a word with them but they did not stop. Greg backed me into a corner the other day and put his hand up my skirt. There is only one person I would allow to do that and that is you. I hit him and they all laughed at me. They said that if I complained nobody would believe my word against theirs. I can't fight it any more Tom. There is no point in me carrying on."

" Don't be such a fool my Isabel. There is a great deal to live for. I promise I will deal with Greg and Ryan. They will not touch you again. Now it is up to you. Have another cigarette and think about it."

Tom lit another cigarette and cigar, handing the cigarette to Isabel. He sat back and poured another cup of coffee. Without looking at Isabel, he drank the coffee and deliberately replaced the cup on the top of the flask. He could hear voices from down below drifting up on the breeze. At his back he could feel the men inching across the roof in their attempt to hear what he was saying. It seemed as though he had been on that roof with his feet dangling over the edge for hours. His mental clock told him that it was most likely less than an hour.

They sat side by side waiting for something to happen, blowing smoke into the air. Then Isabel broke the silence.

" What should I do, Tom?" she almost wailed.

" You have to make a choice," he told her bluntly. " You can either jump or move over here and let me cuddle you. If you choose the latter, when you are ready we will step back onto the roof. I am afraid I will have no control over things then. The police and the other authorities will take over and it will be taken out of my hands. While you are making up your mind, remember that I love you in my way. I know things have not worked out how you might have imagined but I am married with three children. You accepted this at the start."

Isabel smiled for the first time since he had climbed onto the parapet by her side. " Stop blaming yourself Tom. It is not your responsibility. Several things came up at the same time and I could not see my way through them. I have been happy with our relationship since I came here. When we make love, I am satisfied for the rest of the week. I know there should be more to our relationship than once a week sex but I understood that was the way things were from the start. No it is all those other things that have happened. I know I am not making much sense but I love you."

She moved then and got to her feet. For a minute Tom thought she was going to jump. He heard the intake of breath from behind and felt the anxiety coming up in waves from the ground. All Isabel did was move to sit beside him and lay her head on his shoulder. Tom placed his arms around her shoulder and hugged her.

" Come on Isabel. It is all over now. You will be all right. Trust these people. They will be trying to do the best they can for you. Let us go and meet them."

They both swung their legs over the parapet and stood on the roof. Four figures emerged from shelter of the lift housing and walked towards them. A policewoman took Isabel's arm.

" Its all right Professor Houseman. We will take over now. Come on Miss Chueng. We will take you to the police station for questioning and examination."

Tom let go reluctantly and demanded. " Treat her gently, please."

To Isabel he said, " I will get one of my friends who is a solicitor to come and look after you in the police station. Don't say too much until he gets there. I will come and see how they are treating you in the morning."

Tom watched Isabel being led away between two policewomen. She looked despairingly over her shoulder and all Tom could do was to wave. He stood there feeling confused. Logically, he told himself he had saved her life. That was not the real point though. He stood there and watched her go, abandoning her to her fate. Whatever happened to her was now out of his hands. Mentally he shrugged realising that there was not much more he could have done.

A policeman approached and saluted. " Thank you Professor. You have helped resolve a tricky problem with out any mishap. Come with me. The Super is waiting outside the flats. We will get the lift down."

Tom nodded, unsure that he would be able to reply in a civil manner. He silently followed the policeman down the ladder to the landing and the lift door. It was a while before the lift returned and they did not speak. There was nothing to say, Tom thought. All I want is to get home and go to bed. Jane will be waiting and wondering what had happened.

When the lift door opened on the ground floor, the Superintendent was waiting.

" Thank you Professor Houseman. I don't think we could have managed so well without your help." The Superintendent smiled. " Before we go out to the car, you had better prepare yourself. The press are waiting for you out there. I couldn't think of any way we cold smuggle you out of here so you will have to answer their questions."

Tom's heart fell. All he wanted was to get into the car and get back to Jane. Shaking his head, he pulled his shoulders back and grinned at the Superintendent.

" Lead on Superintendent. I have had to face the press on more than one occasion in the past so I will answer their questions as best I can."

In reality, it was straight forward. The questions were mainly about how he got involved and what his feelings were while sitting with his legs dangling in space. With practised ease he was able to fend off most of the questions and it was not too long before he was in the car on the way back to his house.

Then the white mist came up and he was slipping below the surface again. There was nothing there.

Chapter 10

Jane came into the room just as Mary thought she had seen a flicker in her father's eyelids. In the dim light of the ward, she could not be sure whether it had happened or whether it was a figment of her imagination. Mary smiled slightly but did not say anything to her mother. She reasoned that it was not fair to raise her mother's hopes. Not that her hopes were very high at the moment. Nothing appeared to be happening with her father. He lay there breathing heavily, not giving any signs that he could hear what they were saying. It was the non response which was wearing Mary down.

" Go and get a cup of coffee, Mary," Jane said as she resumed her seat by the bed. " I will sit with him for a while. It is a comfort to me to know that you are all here supporting me. Paul and Mark will go to the café with you. There is not much else for you to do but wait."

Mary hesitated and then burst out. " Will he get better, Mummy?"

Jane looked out of the window at the darkness and saw nothing of the street lights. She faltered in answering, trying to be sincere with her daughter.

" To be honest Mary, I don't know," she said with a sigh, tears not far below the surface of her eyes. " At times I think he is hearing what I am saying, while at other times I am certain he is beyond our help. We can only pray that he can hear us."

Mary fought back her own tears, kissed her mother and left Jane to her lonely vigil once more.

" I wonder what happened to that Tavvy you went round Kenya with while working for the United Nations?" she asked gearing herself up once more to continue talking into the empty air. " He came to visit us a few times and then you lost touch. Kenya was all right but I was scared when you went to Nigeria."

The mist swirled and became brighter. Tom felt he was almost out, in the clear. The buzzing noise was definitely a voice. Whose voice? He strained to make out the words but could not catch what was being said. Then the mist cleared.

He was on an aeroplane and the hostess was serving him coffee. Out of the window he could see an almost cloudless sky and looking down, the brown hills of the Sahara. Glancing at his watch, he realised they would arrive in Nairobi in about two hours. He was on his way to undertake a survey for the United Nations of the transport facilities for the land locked countries. The majority of their exports had to pass through either Kenya or Tanzania with all the problems of distance, customs and politics that entailed. His brief was to look at the rail ferries sailing on Lake Victoria and road and rail connections to those ferries.

As the desert passed below, Tom's thoughts turned to what had happened the last two years and to a certain extent why he was flying out to Kenya. Up until now his consultancy had been confined to what he undertook for the Hunt Enterprises. His other interests were in research, the results of which were propagated in papers and at conferences. The research was used to enhance his reputation both at the university and in the wider world. Over time he had had many offers of employment at other universities around the world but he had been quite content to remain at Porthampton. Besides, he realised that Jane and his children were settled into a life with which they were happy. With his involvement with Hunt Enterprises, his investment trust with his brother and his family life, he was reasonably happy.

Of course he had to admit that things were good back then. Not only did he have his family life but Isabel as well. He could even now see the look she gave him as the policewomen took her away from that roof. When he arrived home, Jane was still up waiting for him. After telling her what had taken place, they agreed that there was little he could do to help Isabel now. Never the less, early the next morning he telephoned Tony and asked if he could go and represent Isabel. Tony agreed and Tom offered to pay the fee.

In reality, it was the end of his close relationship with Isabel. Tony got her sentence suspended and made sure she was not deported. The university authorities insisted that she return to a place in one of the halls of residence so that her progress, both academic and social, could be monitored. Even though Tom was still her departmental tutor, he had little input into her progress other than concerning her academic work. Her life was taken over by the student welfare people and a psychiatrist. She did come to see him once a week as was usual but their time together was distant and to the point. Tom respected her attitude and kept his distance.

Whenever she was in his office, it took all of his willpower to keep her the other side of his desk but he managed.

He did however have a heated discussion with Ryan. His student would not at first accept that he had had anything to do with what had happened to Isabel. For the first time Tom had lost his temper with one of his students.

" Ryan you will bloody well listen to me and drop that I am superior to everybody else attitude you adopt when anybody stands up to you." Tom's voice was measured and tight which should have warned Ryan. " I know you are the most intelligent student I have ever tutored but you will stay silent and listen to what I am going to say. The other day, I spent the best part of a night sitting on the edge of a seventy foot drop. I was there because Isabel Chueng threatened to throw herself off the roof of her block of flats."

" What has that got to do with me? The view up there must have been spectacular." Ryan remarked with a smirk in his superior way.

At that point Tom saw red. " You bloody fool! You have bullied that girl ever since she has been in this university. Don't look like that as though it was nothing to do with you. You collected a group of male students around you so that they could sycophantically follow you everywhere. As the one they all looked up to and admired, you egged them on and devised ways for them to torment any student who did not conform to your ideals. You might be intelligent but you are the worst type of bully I have ever come across. To put it bluntly, you almost had blood on your hands. Do you like the sound of you as a killer? No, do not say anything. I will have my say first. You were lucky. Neither Isabel or I told the police or the university authorities the whole truth about why she wanted to end her life. All she would say was that things got on top of her. If she had accused you of sexual harassment, even if you had denied the charges and convinced everybody else that you were innocent, some of the mud would have stuck. As it is if any company wants a reference you had better go and ask another of the lecturers because I will refuse to give you one."

Ryan smiled suddenly. " Do you know, I have never seen you so angry before. You usually manage to remain calm in front of the students. When you put things that way, I have to admit I never realised I was causing so much anguish. For that I am sorry. I will promise to make sure that all the other students leave her alone when she comes back. Now I have an idea for my final year dissertation and I think you are the ideal supervisor."

" Before we get onto your dissertation, just one more thing," Tom was still angry. " You can smile and make promises without any intention of keeping them. At the end of the year I will hold you to account for your actions just as any manager would one of his subordinates. I have quite a bit of influence in the university so it would not be wise to try for you to fight me through the committees."

It was a surprise though Tom should not have been to astonished. Ryan was as good as his word and he made sure that everybody else did the same. It was as though he regretted what had happened and that the episode on the rooftop finally brought home to him the effect his words and actions could have on other people. Tom noticed that Ryan pulled Isabel into his circle and became her protector.

At the end of the summer term after the exam boards had met and the results posted, Isabel came to see Tom. She was going home to Hong Kong for the summer holidays and wanted to say goodbye. Again Tom was struck but the coldness of her mien but he ignored this. She did kiss him briefly on the cheek but that was all.

That summer was not good. They had booked to go to Lake Guarda for the holidays and including the Opera in Verona. All should have been well because it was the sort of holiday they all enjoyed. For some reason Tom could never fathom, he and Jane had a row. Well angry words were exchanged. Looking back from his seat on the plane, Tom could not precisely remember what the row was about. In reality it had been an accumulation of, to Tom, small things but the result was the same. Jane stopped all affection and would only talk about practical things. They tried to keep the children out of their argument but they must have realised that all was not right. On holiday it was easy to maintain their distance. They shared a room with Mary so there was no possibility of making love. Actually, the holiday was successful and they did enjoy themselves. When they got home, Jane reverted to being distant once more.

Before the beginning of term, Isabel returned. Just as Tom had anticipated, she went back into hall under the guidance of the welfare people. She came to see Tom in his office but made it plain she wanted to maintain the distance that had grown between them. There was a discussion of the likely topic of her dissertation but Tom realised that he could not justify, even by stretching he intellectual boundaries, making himself as her dissertation tutor. He had to arrange for her to be guided by one of the other staff in her search efforts.

To Tom's disappointment, this meant that even her visits to him as her tutor became less frequent. During these infrequent meetings, Tom did notice that Isabel appeared more stable and happy than before she went home for the holidays. It was difficult for Tom because he had to sit on his side of the desk and appear calm and in control. In reality he was full of desire under the facade he maintained. It was not long before he realised that Isabel still attracted him but there was little he could do about the situation. Through out her visits he maintained his professional poise but it took a great deal of will power. He did think at one time to ask that she be transferred to one of his colleagues but he dismissed the idea as fanciful. Such a move would invite questions about the reason and Tom did not know whether he would be able to come up with a convincing argument. He could cite he supposed the incident on the roof and how he might bring back dark memories for her. It did sound rather weak and any discerning academic would suspect there was more to the proposal than was being admitted. Of course, there was the question of whether he wanted to stop these visits. When he thought about the answer to this question, it became obvious to him. Even with their cold relationship and his dread of her coming to his office, he still wanted to see her alone. Tom did nothing and the pain continued.

It might have been more bearable if his relationship with Jane was better. They had not made love for six months and he missed their passion. They did have their companionship but that seemed a poor substitute to Tom. He would meet Isabel in his office during the day with all the gulf between them and then return to Jane without any relief. At lucid times he understood that he was being selfish but there appeared little he could do to put things right. All he could do was to hide deep within himself the hurt he felt and carry on as though things were the same as normal. How long he could keep this up was an issue he tried to avoid thinking deeply about.

Then to add to his woes, he had problems at work. It was the usual practice in Porthampton University for the Professors in a Department to take it in turns to be the Head of Department. To some it was an honour, to others a chance to take a larger part in the politics of the university, while to most it was a chore that had to be undertaken. To many it detracted from their main interest which was research.

When the Head of the Department announced that he would be retiring at the end of the academic year, the search was on for a replacement. Tom was the next in line and it was duly offered to him. He thought about the offer for a while. There were certain positive attributes to being Head of Department. It would look good on his CV and a successful period as leader would lead to other possibilities for advancement further up the hierarchy of many universities. From these angles it was attractive.

Tom, however, had seen the results of the job in many of his fiends and acquaintances both at Porthampton and other universities. They had become weighed down with the work load and the stress of making sure all the staff fulfilled their obligations. There was also the question of the responsibility to make sure the students were given the promised standard of education as promised by the university.

After considering all the factors involve, Tom informed the Vice Chancellor that he would rather not take up the post. Though it was voluntary, the Vice Chancellor tried everything he could to force Tom to agree to fill the position. In ordinary times this was a bad policy when trying to get Tom to undertake anything. At this time with all the stress and heartache that Tom was suffering, it was dynamite. At the suggestion that he must take on the post, Tom exploded. From then on there was nothing but heated words between them. Finally, with bad grace, the Vice Chancellor accepted Tom's refusal. It was obvious as Tom left the Vice Chancellor's office that he had made an enemy. He had won the argument but was uncertain about the outcome of any conflict in the future. One of the younger, more ambitious professors took up the position.

Back in the Department, both his staff and his researcher made it quite plain that they did not understand why he had turned down the chance to be Head. Even when he explained the complex motives that had driven him to the decision, they did not appear to understand.

Jane was livid when he told her of his decision. She did not understand why anybody would give up the chance for promotion.

" You have always grasped the opportunities when ever they came your way," she stormed. " Why are you turning this chance down?"

Tom looked sad. " Jane I am weary of being at the beck and call of everybody. I do not want to be held responsible for every little set back in the department. We do not need the money. I do not need the kudos. Therefore I want to carry on as I have been."

Jane sneered. " You want to lead an ordinary life. Oh I grant that we do not need the money. By taking this chance you would be in line for a Vice Chancellor's job at one of the universities. This is about academic standing. I will never understand why you turned this down."

For the first time in their married life there was little chance of them working out a mutual solution to any disagreement? With the way they had been treating each other, there was not a great chance that hey could find a compromise to gulf their entrenched positions.

Tom tried desperately to explain, to convince Jane that his decision was logical but to no avail. From then on things did not get any easier for Tom at home.

It was a strange for Tom when he realised that he did not look forward to going to work. When there he did not look forward to going home. Oh he still got a buzz out of helping his students and his research. His colleagues made it quite plain that they did not approve. All around him was mild hostility. Even when he returned home at night there was no relief.

The students organised a social just before the break up for Christmas in a pub just off the university campus. All the lecturers were invited by the students. Because of the locality, Tom was able to walk.

When he arrived, the social was in full swing. The students had occupied a large area in one corner and several of the lecturers and researchers were spread among the company. Tom ordered a pint and found a seat among some of the first year students. The talk was of getting used to university life, of course work and drunken nights out. One of the girls was an athlete and they talked about her chances the following summer. Tom was amazed when she outlined her training schedule. He thought how difficult it would be to fit this in with her work.

After buying a round of drinks, he went to the toilet. When he came out, he bumped into Isabel. Actually the bumping was literal. She was dressed in a red jacket, white blouse, tight skirt and high healed shoes. Her lips were red with lipstick and her eyes were made to look even more almond shaped than normal. To Tom she looked wonderful and very attractive.

He stepped back to let her pass but she stood her ground.

" Hello Tom, " she greeted him her lips bowed as if ready to receive a kiss. " Are you enjoying the evening?"

" It is great to come out socially with the students," Tom answered warily while stopping himself leaning forward and kissing those lips. " How are you this evening? You look like a million dollars tonight."

She smiled a secretive smile which made him even more nervous. " I saw you over the other side of the room but could not get across to say hello. You did not appear to notice me."

If that was an admonition, he ignored it. " The room is so crowded, I missed you. I thought then that you were not here. If I had seen you I would have waved but sat somewhere else."

" Tom oh Tom," she said squeezing his hand. " You have no idea how the last nine months have been for me. Can I see you latter?"

Tom looked bewildered. " We can always walk part of the way back to your hall together. It is the same direction as my house."

" That will be nice. I will see you when things start to break up." She smiled and turned away.

Tom stood and watched her resume her seat. She looked across at him and smiled expansively.

Tom resumed his seat among the students feeling puzzled. He was trying to figure out what had changed since his last meeting with Isabel a couple of weeks before. Then in his office she had been cool as it had been for the last nine months since he had talked her down from the roof of her flat. Wracking his brain for some clue did not help. As far as he could understand, she had changed in that short time. This change made Tom wary, to question whether it was genuine. He started to query her motives in a way which would not have occurred to him when they had been closer. Indeed some people said it was one of his faults this taking as the truth a lot of things he was told. Tom put this to the back of his mind.

For the rest of the evening Tom played the group leader to perfection. He circulated amongst the tables engaging as many of his students in conversation as possible. Of course he had to sit at the table where Isabel was with her group but he managed to squeeze into a space next to Ryan on the other side of the table to that where Isabel was sitting.

The social started to break up later in the evening with many of the students and most of the lecturers drifting away. The hardened drinkers amongst them were gathering in one corner ready to stay for as long as possible. Tom said goodbye to those left and noticed Isabel leaving with a group of final year students. As he watched her leaving, he felt a tinge of disappointment but consoled himself with the thought that at least she had smiled at him and greeted him warmly which was in direct contrast to how it had been. Maybe the worst was over and they could start being pleasant to each other again. Then he thought of Jane and wished that he could do something to change her opinion of him.

When he came out of the pub into the chill of a December evening, Isabel was waiting for him. He paused on the steps to light a cigar and give himself time to get a grip on his feelings. In that one moment he had almost lost control. He had an almost overwhelming desire to grab her there on the steps in full view of some of the students looking on.

She smiled from under her woolly hat but Tom could not see her eyes or read her expression in the gloom. " Hello Tom. Will you walk back to the hall with me?"

Tom realised she said this in case there were any students near enough to over hear her but he smiled in return. " Of course."

Isabel tucked her arm through Tom's as they walked away from the pub. Through the thickness of her coat Tom could feel the round firmness of her breasts as she snuggled close. Their thighs were touching and caressing as they walked. It brought back visions of her lying on the bed in her flat naked waiting for him and he felt a desire to get her like that again. To see her spread out against the flowered background of her duvet was what he longed for at that moment. To feel the anticipation as he undressed in front of her and the fulfilment when they had made love. This is what had been missing for all these months especially because at the same time Jane had been cold and distant.

Then a thought struck him and he alternately mentally shrank away from it and was amused. What, he asked himself, is a forty six year old man doing having those thoughts about a twenty one year old woman? To many people, most of his friends in fact, the idea of a middle aged man lusting after a twenty year old would be abhorrent. They would not understand. Obviously the consideration of what he was doing to his marriage would cloud their judgement but leaving that aspect to one side, they would never understand. In fact, he thought, in many ways I don't understand. Why would Isabel fall in love with me when there is so much of a gap between us? She had explained that Chinese girls did not see love in the same light as western girls but this was not logical. She had been in this country for a while and must have picked up some of the thoughts of British people. For Tom it once more came back to the question of whether anybody could love more than one person at the same time.

Isabel was talking to him. " I am sorry Tom, I treated you like I did. I was so confused and lacked the will to live that night. You returned my will to live but I was without any motivation. My every move was controlled by the welfare people and the medical staff. For that period it was as though they were spying on me all the time."

Tom squeezed her arm. " They were only trying to help."

Isabel shook her head. " I had to tell them at every session what I had been up to since I last saw them. It was numbing. Then the hall warden checked to make sure I was back every night. Not that I went out much. When I came to see you it was as though I had to keep my distance or I would have broken down. It was hard sitting there in your office with you close to me. That is why I left quickly each time. On some occasions I wanted to stop coming but my feelings for you always won."

Tom could not stop himself putting his thoughts into words. " Tell me why you feel that way about an old man like me."

He felt her stiffen through his coat. " You are not old, Tom."

Tom sighed. " Compared to you I am. No don't say anything now. Most girls your age would not look at a man like me. I sometimes wonder why you feel the way you do. Maybe that was partly the cause of your problems and I should have held my feelings to myself. If we had maintained the usual student tutor relationship, you might not have ended up on that roof."

Isabel looked up into his face. " Tom, oh Tom. It is not a question of age. I have never understood why a woman is attracted to one man and not another. It is a mystery to most people. Why I am attracted to you is hard to explain, especially to you. There was something which passed between us that day when I came to talk about changing courses. It was not about the academic work or why I needed to get away from the other university but personal to you and me. I knew then somehow that I liked you and wanted to see more of you. There is nothing wrong with what we have done. Is giving somebody pleasure and happiness wrong? You have filled me with joy at times and it feels right. In some ways you have been harder on me than other students when it comes to my work. That might have been my fault because in my eagerness to be with you I always come to discuss why I have ended up with the level of marks given. I know all the other students have that opportunity but they do not all grasp the chance. Don't blame yourself for what happened to me."

Tom did not look at her but stared off down the road. " A great many people including most of my friends would be disgusted with what we are doing. They would blame me for what happened. I can hear them now behind my back. He should have had more control, they would say. At his age what was he thinking of taking advantage of a young woman. She must have had some other motive to let him get away with it like she did. What can she see in him? The trouble is, I have felt this frisson of excitement whenever I know we are going to meet. After I leave you I am happy. The last few months have been agony for me. I came to the conclusion that you no longer liked me and did not want me near you any more. In my more depressed moments, I even wondered whether you regretted getting involved with me."

They came to a side turning and could see the lights of her hall blazing into the night. Isabel was reluctant to let go but Tom kissed her and moved away.

" I will see you next week and we can talk about this some more," he smiled. It sounded so formal but Tom was still confused at the way things had changed.

Isabel lent forward and kissed him. " Don't look confused, Tom. Things will work out all right. I will see you next week and explain."

She turned and walked toward the hall gates. Tom watched for a moment and then walked off in the direction of his home.

On the Tuesday of the last week of term, Tom sat in his office after returning from his lecture. With only half attention, he opened his mail but there was nothing important that had to be dealt with. Through the window he watched students entering the electronics labs across the road. With an acute ear, he listened for footsteps approaching his office along the corridor outside the door. All the people passed without stopping. Through the walls he could hear the murmur of voices but could not make out words or the sense of the conversation. He was waiting,

How much time in my life have I spent waiting for things to happen? he asked himself. It is not only me but everybody spends a great deal of time waiting. He had to admit that lately he had not waited with a growing sense of excitement for Isabel to come to his office. He had not sat thinking about the warmth of her flesh or her kisses on his lips. It had been with a mounting sense of obligation. If Isabel had been delayed, he had calmly got on with his work and he had not had that feeling of panic that she would not come. Now she was late. Maybe, he mused she has regretted what happened last Friday and has decided to stay away until after Christmas.

Footsteps approached and stopped outside the door. The handle turned and Isabel was coming into the room. She carefully closed the door behind her and walked round the desk. Smiling broadly, she kissed Tom fiercely and threw her arms around his neck.

Standing back and looking into his eyes, she said, " Good morning Tom. It is good to see you."

Tom kissed her back and indicated for her to sit in the chair the other side of the desk. " Hello Isabel. It is great to see you happy again."

They sat and talked about her academic work and how it was progressing. Their conversation was without the tension that had been there only days before. They even joked about some of the things that had happened. At one time they were interrupted by Tom's secretary bringing in some papers that she had copied.

When she had left, Isabel said. " I must be going. I have a lecture straight after lunch. One thing I find exciting is that they have, what did they call it? Signed me off. If I start feeling depressed, they have given me a contact number. I asked if I could leave the hall and get a flat of my own."

Tom was clearly puzzled. " Why do you want to leave the hall? You are well set there and moving will disrupt your work."

Isabel frowned. " I have found the hall very restrictive after having a flat of my own even if that was for only a short time. When I move out, I will be able to suit myself as to who visits me and what I eat and when I eat. There is a flat for rent in a block just round the corner from the hall where I am now. I made inquires and they have reserved it for me from next week. I will have all the Christmas holidays to settle in. Over the Christmas break I am going to visit some friends of the family in Paris for a few days."

Tom tried to hide his concern. " If that is what you want, it must be for the best."

Isabel laughed as she left him " Don't worry about me Tom. When I have settled you will have to come and see me."

Tom wondered whether it would be right for him to resume his weekly visits to her flat. He could use the Christmas break on the back of his not making love to her for nine months as a way of breaking away from her. When he thought about it, he came to realise that the decision to break with Isabel would be very difficult. He only had to think about her and a warm glow filled his body. There was the longing to be with her. To leave that behind would take a great deal of will power on his behalf and he wondered whether he would be able to summon that level of commitment when it was needed. The question that had to be answered was whether he had the will power to over come his attraction for her. Deep down he knew he would not be able to resist the temptation if it was presented to him. The only calming factor was that he would have to wait until after Christmas to find out what her intentions were.

Later that day, he received a phone call from the Director General of the Institute. It transpired that the United Nations had asked the Institute to recommend a transport expert to join a group looking at improving the organisation and transport of imports and exports from the land locked countries of East Africa. It would entail six weeks in Kenya and East Africa over the summer. Tom thought that this would be an opportunity to get away from his troubles for a while. He said that he was interested but would have to talk it over with his wife before giving a definitive answer.

Surprisingly when he told her, Jane agreed. There was very little discussion or objection. It was as though she wanted a chance to be separated from Tom for a while. He informed the Institute and a meeting with the project leader was arranged for early in the new year at the Institute.

After Christmas, Tom took the train to London. Surprisingly, given the circumstances, the festive season had been a very pleasant time. His brother had invited all his family, Sarah's family and Jane's family to their house for Boxing Day. Unlike the image of family get togethers at Christmas portrayed by comedians, this one had passed in a cloud of bonhomie and good cheer.

Edward announced that after the landslide for Thatcher at the last election the Liberal Democrat candidate for Eastfield constituency had resigned. The party had asked Edward if he would become their prospective candidate and he had accepted. He joked that he would not make Tom compromise his principles any more and would not ask him to be his agent this time. To Tom's surprise, Sarah appeared on the surface to accept this development. With her daughters now well into their teens, she was more calm with life.

Edward pulled Tom aside during the evening into his study.

" Our investment fund has reached the total of one hundred million pounds," Edward announced proudly. " Last year we had a profit of ten per cent which was low. It is anticipated that this year with the opportunities that are out there in the market that we will make a profit of nearer twenty percent. Now what should we do?"

Tom shrugged. " I have left that to you and trusted you so I will defer to your experience. What have we now in our income bonds?"

Edward took out a piece of paper from a file. " At the last transfer it comes to five million pounds. That will give you at the worst estimate of where interest rates are going an income of twenty thousand a month. We have come a long way from that close by the council estate you and me."

" Thanks Edward. At least we are back speaking to each other once again. In some ways you were right about the Labour Party but I think they are going to get things right now."

" I would not be too sure if I was you. Unless they get rid of that Neil

Kinnock they have no chance. Still come on and lets get another beer."

Tom looked out of the window at the passing countryside lost in thought as the train sped towards London early in January. The amount of money he was making from his income bonds was causing him to question whether it was right. It was against his sense of social responsibility. All right, he told himself, I do fulfil my obligations to society in many ways. I pay my taxes without any question or like many rich people without getting some accountant other than my wife to fiddle ways in which to pay as little tax as possible. When he looked back at his father and mother's life, he realised just how far his bother and he had ridden the waves of the upward mobility that circumstances had presented. They both had used their education to move into social levels most of their first friends had never even envisaged. To Tom, they had accomplished this legitimately.

Unlike Derek who had climbed up the social ladder by circumventing the law in many ways with the help of Mister Hunt. Derek had managed like Mister Hunt to keep the two sides of his business apart and to surround himself with people who would keep him out of the papers. Somehow he had learnt to act the part of a businessman, to dress soberly and to use only the best restaurants. With his lawyers being paid substantial sums and his men well rewarded for their part, any trail of any criminal activities stopped well short of his door. He had inherited the legitimate business from Mister Hunt and with the social standing of his non executive directors kept these companies above suspicion of laundering money, he appeared to most of the world as a successful businessman.

With his mind in a whirl from the coldness of Jane and the promise implied by Isabel, Tom for the first time acknowledged that he had been on the periphery of crime for a great deal of his life. Well, he told himself, not me actually but some of my associates. I have maintained a distance from the activities of Derek in all my dealings with his companies. Thus justified, he faced the prospect of a trip to Kenya.

He met the leader of the United Nations Development Project in the Institute building in central London. Tom had been surprised that the meeting had been more a mutual discussion than an interview. After an hour they had agreed what was required, the amount of fee and expenses and the timetable. Tom had insisted that the contract be drawn up in conjunction with the university consultancy office even though this would entail giving them twenty per cent in overheads. All was agreed and he looked forward to meeting all the other members of the group in Nairobi in July.

When he returned home from London with all the information, Jane was eager to become aquatinted with what he would be doing while he was in Africa. Her interest did not change the way in which she treated him. All was to be the same as the last few months. When he realised this was going to be the way things were, Tom shrugged and decided to continue his life. Apart from the lack of true affection, family life with his children and Jane was relatively good.

One aspect of his life did change. Soon after he had returned from London and started work after the Christmas holiday, Isabel walked into his office. He was caught by surprise because he did not expect to see her until the term started the following week.

She was smiling when she walked through the door and she deliberately shut this with her foot. Once she was sure they would not be disturbed, she flung her arms round his neck and kissed him fiercely.

Tom did not try too hard but he found it almost impossible to stop her.

" What brought that on?" he asked as he half heartedly tried to push her away.

" Oh Tom," she said like a heroine out of a James Bond film. " I love you. No don't protest. I know there is no future for us but I have to admit the truth. When we were sitting on that roof, I knew then that I could not kill myself because I loved you. All I wanted to do was get down and take you to my bed. But those in charge took me away and took over my life. There was no way then that I could be alone with you off campus. Then it all cleared up and they signed me off. All I wanted was to rush to you but you were so cold. Then at the pub and on the walk home I made quite plain that I wanted you again. You were still a bit cold towards me."

" Isabel," Tom sighed. " I did not know how to treat you after they took you away. As I told you just before Christmas, I had this idea that I might be part of the problem."

" All through Christmas holidays I waited to see you again. I have had almost nine months of having to keep my emotions under control. Now all that has changed. The term starts on Monday and Dave has told me that my project is heading for a two one. In fact all my marks from last term are relatively high. You have told me that if I keep this up I am heading for a two one over all."

Tom pushed her away and into a chair. Like a stern tutor he took his place in the chair behind his desk. This is where I play the tutor and not the lover he thought. This is what I am here for and should not forget that. She needs reassurance like all students preparing for the last push towards their final degree classification. I must divorce myself from my feelings for her as a woman and concentrate on her as a tutee. Looking across the desk at her figure and then into those almond shaped eyes, he fought down his desire to get up and kiss her again. She sat there legs crossed, breasts pushed hard against her sweater and lips pouting provocatively.

Tom closed his eyes momentarily and then said. " It is great to see you happy again and talking about the future. I take it that you have had no problems with the other students lately?"

Isabel smiled. " They have treated me like a lady."

Tom lent back in his chair. " I have looked at your interim marks and you are looking at a two one if your project is up to the mark. Dave assures me that it is progressing fine. Have you thought any more about what you are going to do once you graduate?"

Isabel shrugged. " I saw an advert for a graduate in the transport investment arm of a Hong Kong bank. My father arranged for an interview when I go home at Easter. It sounds like an interesting job."

Tom tried to keep his face expressionless as the clouds of lost hopes swept over him. In the preceding years that Isabel had been coming to his office and he had visited her flat, Isabel had expressed an interest in taking a Masters degree if that was possible. They had joked about having at least another year together if she did this. Behind the curtain of his subconscious mind he had entertained the idea that she would then get work in the United Kingdom. This would have given them an opportunity to continue their love making beyond her graduation. Her brief statement had made his dreams waver and fade like the morning mist. They wee being blown away on the winds of harsh reality. In the bright stark light of a new dawn he would have to accept that the coming end of the summer term and her graduation would lead to an end of their affair. He had known that this was the likely out come but had buried his head in the sands of his delusions of what the future would hold.

He heard his voice saying calmly while his heart was heavy in his chest. " That sounds wonderful. I hope you are successful. If you need a reference, let me know."

Isabel looked at her watch. " I have to be going. The removal van is due at my flat and I must be there to meet it. By next Wednesday I will have sorted everything and will look forward to showing you round my new flat then. Obviously, before then I will see you for our weekly meeting here on Tuesday."

He watched her leave blowing him a kiss from the doorway. The transformation was obvious but Tom wondered whether it was in his best interests to go to her flat. His desire got the better of him and he smiled in anticipation of what was to befall him next Wednesday.

Tom walked across the campus in bright winter sunlight on Wednesday afternoon. The wind was raw from the northeast, biting through his coat and making him shiver. The sunshine however enhanced his feelings of joy, of everything in the world being right and the anticipation of what was to come. He had to admit to himself even as those feelings of happiness swept him away that the last few days had been fraught with conscience. While with his family over the weekend, he had fought the rising tide of doubt which was trying to engulf him. All the time a small voice in the back of his mind warned him that he was getting into a dangerous situation but he ignored it. Once again he had had to struggle with the question of how it was possible for somebody to love two people at the same time. There were differences in his relationship to Isabel when looked at in the light of his love for Jane. With Jane there was a deep affection which in many ways transcended love. Even when Jane had been so cold towards him, he had gone to bed each night believing that things would be different. It had been with a deep feeling of let down when he had turned away and led a lonely night only a few inches from his wife. During that time things had not changed his feelings for Jane. When they were out together in a crowd, he would find his eyes searching the room until he found out where she was. She would always answer with a smile. They might be separated by a distance but they were always together.

With Isabel it was otherwise. Before the incident on the roof, he had set out to meet here full of excitement and anticipation. His heart had raced and he had let his imagination run riot.

That day as he pulled the collar of his coat higher around his neck, and nodded to the staff and students he knew, the excitement was back. For some reason the day appeared brighter and the dark clouds of his depression had lifted. He strode passed the concrete sixties creations of buildings, the patches of green lawn and empty flower beds almost humming to himself.

Outside her the building which housed her flat, he studied the names on a plate by the door. Selecting her name, he rang the bell. A loudspeaker crackled with her distorted voice and he announced himself. The front door lock clicked and he stepped over that invisible line between honesty and prevarication to justify ones acts.

Isabel was waiting for him at the door to her flat. Her eyes sparkled in the light from the window at the end of the corridor and she wore a broad smile on her lips. She closed the door with her foot once he was inside and flung her arms round his neck. They kissed as though they were young teenagers and with a passion which acknowledged the passage of time since they had been alone like this. Then, without any preamble she was pulling him into her bedroom. He did not have a chance to look around the flat. They made love roughly and with an urgency which seemed to say they might not get another chance.

When they at last laid back and felt satisfied, Isabel brewed some coffee. They sat on the rumpled bed sheets very close as they drank and then made love again. The pattern of most Wednesdays was set whenever Tom had a chance to meet her. On the occasions when there were meetings in the university or he met Jane, they both felt deprived.

In many ways it was all part of a long. goodbye. Though they hid this from themselves like somebody ignoring approaching danger, they knew deep down that their love making was going to come to an end. Like an approaching fog bank across a shimmering sea, it was there in the background to all they said and did. For as long as possible they avoided making this fact concrete, ducked the issue of what would happen when Isabel left to go back to Hong Kong. In their bliss on those Wednesday afternoons, they would lie and vow undying love even though they knew that Tom would not ever leave Jane. This had been made explicit and accepted from the beginning but they floated on the warm waters of their satisfaction for as long as they could.

Deep in her heart, Isabel, like all of the other women who had given their bodies to a married man, nurtured the hope that circumstances would change, that something would happen in Tom's family life which would make him available to her. It was a hope which she acknowledged deep in her unconscious would never happen.

Never the less, when he had left to go back to Jane, she would lie in the wreckage of her bed clothes still smelling his scent. She would close her eyes and drift away to a place where they would be together always. In this other reality, he would come through the front door every night and she like a dutiful Chinese wife, would have a gin and tonic ready for him to drink. She would then serve the meal she had prepared and they would eat this by candle light. Following the meal they would sit with their arms around each other watching the television until it was time to go to bed. Floating on a stream of goodwill they would make love slowly, satisfying over and over again their need for each other, until the sun rose to shine through the window across their bed.

To Isabel, it was wonderful to fantasise but it was only a dream, something to hold close at times of stress and dejection. Quietly she would come back to reality, have a shower and make her bed. She would as far as was possible, clear away all traces of Tom and get back into a student mode again. Deep within the most inner sanctuary of her being she knew she had to accept the reality of her life and live with only the fleeting times with her lover. It might be hard to accept at times but it was the essence of her choice of life style. It was always possible she thought to tell Tom that she did not want to see him again but her whole body and soul bulked at the thought of him not coming through her door on Wednesdays.

The day did dawn of course which they had both secretly feared and which they had both tried to avoid thinking about and never mentioned. The final exams came and went with Tom inundated with marking. Even so he still managed to see Isabel at the appointed times. Then there was the exam boards to get through. The result was pleasing to both Tom and Isabel. After all her tribulations and worry along the way, Isabel gained her two one. Tom was the first to congratulate her when the results were posted and she came to his office along with all Tom's other tutees. Then there was that pause between the results and graduation. Before the ceremony Isabel went to visit some family friends in London and Tom slowly came to terms with her absence and what it would be like when she finally left in a few weeks. He used the time to prepare for his trip to Kenya.

When Isabel returned, she invited him to her flat though without the enthusiasm as was usual. Over the telephone she gave the impression that she was dreading what was to come.

After putting down the telephone receiver, Tom steeled himself to face the truth. With all his other loves except Jane it had been a passing phase and he had taken each single meeting as though it was a one off chance for pleasure. There had rarely been any thought on his part or the woman of when or if they would meet again. They had always left this to chance. With Isabel this had been different. They had known that they would meet, that this was an on going relationship. Now it was coming to an end and Tom was not sure how this would affect him.

She was waiting in her hall, facing the open door when he arrived. For once she did not fling her arms round his neck but held his hands and looked deeply into his eyes. Like a drowning woman she clung to his hands and fought against the tears welling up in the deep pools of her eyes. As he sank deep into those eyes, his heart was breaking and he desperately attempted to smile. In turn he fought the hurt he was feeling but his attempt failed miserably. Both of them stood there, forlorn with tears streaming down their faces in waterfalls of regret.

Arm in arm, lost in the cocoon of their mutual sadness, they walked into her sitting room. Isabel reluctantly let him go and sit on the settee while she went to make coffee. He sat in a daze, looking round that familiar room, at the furniture and the peace bells hanging against one wall. The picture of the wave was so real to him, he thought it would crash out of the frame and engulf his regret.

When she returned and was seated beside him on the settee. Isabel cradled her coffee in her hands as though to draw some confidence from the warmth. For what seemed like an age, she looked into his eyes.

So softly that he had to strain his ears to hear the words, Isabel started to speak. " Tom oh my Tom. The time that I have been dreading but knowing I would have to face is here. It is as though it has rushed up and hit me squarely in the face. It is as though in another way it has crept upon me in the night. Today will have to be the last time we are together like this in this flat. If you say too much it will break my heart."

Tom clung to the life buoy of his hope, floating on the surface of his wishes ready to grasp any chance of a rescue. He kept his voice as steady as possible. " It need not be the last time, Isabel. There are times when I get invites to conferences in Hong Kong or you might be sent back to the UK. Surely there will be opportunities for us to meet in the future?"

Isabel smiled wanly. " There might be opportunities as you say when we have a chance to meet somewhere in the world. They will never be the same as we have had for the last few years. There will always be other people around and they will be unplanned."

Tom hardened his heart against his growing desire to tell her that it need not be this way. He could easily tell her that he would leave Jane, Paul, Mark and Mary to live with her. When it came to that line, he was reluctant to cross over. It was easy to sit and contemplate what it would be like but more difficult to make the final decision. He knew that he would not give up his family for Isabel no matter what the temptation. Like an Old Testament prophet, he turned away from enticement of her body and faced the actuality of the world he inhabited.

He sighed deeply. " I am sorry Isabel but we both knew this time would come. I have in the past talked to you about the problems of somebody loving two people at the same time. Now we to accept that certain events are finite and must surely come to an end. It has been wonderful, our time together. I will even look back on our time on your roof with nostalgia. However, we have to accept that all things pass like the seasons."

Isabel smiled and kissed him. " I have accepted that this time would come for a long period. That acceptance does not make saying goodbye any easier to endure when it is happening. When I go back to Hong Kong next week, I will remember our love making. Oh Tom, thank you for all you have done for me. Now let us go and make love."

They walked hand in hand for the last time into her bedroom in much the same way as Aida had gone into the tomb. As though their bodies were attuned to their parting, their love making was slow and measured designed to give maximum pleasure. When they were satisfied, Isabel clung to Tom.

She remarked sadly. " I know it is time for you to go. In two days my mother and father will arrive for the graduation ceremony. They have asked me to invite you and Jane to dinner. I will book up the restaurant and let you know."

He bent over and kissed her. " We will be there. It will be nice to meet your parents."

Abruptly he got out of bed and dressed quickly. Isabel watched him, feasting her eyes on his body. She remained silent. When he was ready, he lent over the bed, kissed her and walked out of the room without a backward glance.

It was a surreal meal with Isabel's parents and Jane. Like a seasoned political prefabricator facing a difficult situation, Isabel adopted the role of a grateful tutee thanking her tutor and giving her parents a chance to meet him. Jane chatted away making it plain that it was very kind of them to offer dinner in thanks for Tom's support of their daughter. Somehow Tom acted the part of an academic and Isabel's tutor as though that was his only role in her life. The evening passed off reasonably well in a cloud of good humour.

After the graduation ceremony, it was customary for the graduates, their parents and the lecturers to gather in the department for strawberries and cream and champagne. Isabel came with her parents. It was easier for Tom to submerge his desires to get Isabel on her own with all the other students mingling around them. She vowed in a moment they had alone that she would write often and that they would see each other soon. Tom in his turn promised to write as often as possible

As the party broke up and all the graduates and their families started to leave, they came and shook Tom's hand to say goodbye. He shook Isabel's parents hands and Isabel kissed him for the last time, more a peck on the cheek than a full blown passionate kiss. As she walked away with her parents, Tom watched her disappear round a corner of the building, that trim solid figure he had caressed and loved.

" Goodbye, my love," he thought. " I will miss you."

His thoughts stretched back over those last few months as he watched the red glow of the clouds pass under the aeroplane. Just as he had wished, he had managed to get away, to leave those feelings of loss and inadequacy behind.

Now he was looking forward with something approaching excitement to the coming weeks. As the plane approached Nairobi airport, he started to think about what he was going to accomplish in East Africa.

The United Nations team assembled in a hotel in Nairobi the day after he had landed. They were there to discuss their separate roles in the project and how they were going to co-ordinate their report. Tom learnt the full extent of their efforts. One group were off to Burundi and Rwanda to study the custom's procedure which might be hindering the flow of goods across the borders. Another group was to look at logistics storage and transport organisation. Yet another was to look at the political dimensions of the movement of imports and exports to those land locked countries. Tom was joined by a Kenyan called Tulley to examine the transport infrastructure especially the train ferries plying Lake Victoria. They set out on a flight to Mombassa the next day. Tom's idea was to try to trace a single container from Mombassa to Kampala by train and ferry. He thought they could then look at the delays caused by faults in the infrastructure as opposed to the customs procedures or the politics of logistics. Tulley was sceptical that they would be able to do this in the time but Tom insisted that they try.

It turned out to be both fascinating and frustrating. From the start two things became obvious to Tom and commenced to stretch his patience. Firstly the whole Logistics and transport system was inefficient. They tried to set up interviews with the heads of department both in the government and the railways and it took them days to get to the right office to arrange an interview. Even then the information at best was patchy, at worst was so vague it was meaningless. That led to the second conclusion. The whole system was hierarchical and beaurocratic. The rigid structure and the sense of seniority and importance meant that they found it impossible to arrange to meet those who might supply the answers they required. Their requests were simply blocked. Those at the top would not countenance their subordinates talking to the United Nations. Somehow through contacts Tom had built up during his University programmes, they did manage to identify a container and get the information of how long it took this to pass through the port. To Tom's regret, they could not follow this to Kisumu on the Lake because they had to fly to Dar es Salem to see the Tanzanian Minister of Transport.

On arrival at Dar es Salem airport, the inevitable happened. Tom stood like a fool watching all the cases go round and round the carousal only for his not to emerge. After a frustrating time at the lost luggage desk, the girl in the office made enquiries for him. She triumphantly informed him that the baggage handlers at the airport had left two cages of luggage on the plane and it was on its way back to Nairobi.

With a smile, she assured Tom," We will have your bags back here in two days time."

It was a lovely smile but it did not mollify Tom. " I have to see the Minister of Transport later today and fly out to Mwanza in the morning."

" Buy what you need and charge the airline," she shrugged. " When it arrives, I will send it on to Mwanza if you give me the address of your hotel."

Tom threw up his hands in horror." Oh no you won't. Losing it once is enough. When it arrives here you will personally look after it. I will come and collect it from this office on the way back."

She smiled and lent forward to write something on a pad showing her pointed breasts. " I will personally deliver it to your hotel if you like."

" I will pick it up here," Tom remarked tamely trying not to offend her, knowing that there was an overt invitation in her comment. Actually he realised, looking at her for the first time, she is rather attractive.

They flew out to Mwanza without their luggage. At Mwanza Tom had his first sight of Lake Victoria with its water stretching away to the horizon as though it was the sea. Fishing boats plied their trade and small coastal ferries overloaded with passengers docked near the train ferry terminal. Birds he could not identify sat on sand banks or swooped over the water, soaring skywards with a flash of silver in their beaks.

On the way into Mwanza town from the airport, Tom was struck by the smoothness of the road. They came upon a gang laying a new surface amid the pot holes. It was a surprise because during his stay in East Africa the one enduring nightmare he had encountered was the state of the roads. Cars carrying him and Tulley between appointments or to the airport had to weave a path between large craters often endangering life as they defied large, little maintained lorries doing the same thing.

Later he was to learn that the Pope was paying a visit to the Lake in the near future. You couldn't have the Pope's body put under the strain of pot holes, Tom thought. It just about sums up the priorities of the Governments in this part of the world. Let trade suffer, kill people every day but the Pope must be protected from such dangers. He realised he had to be careful what he said because Tulley was a catholic and had invited him to dinner at his home when they returned to Mombassa.

At the ferry terminal the next day, Tom felt for the first time that he was getting down to some serious work. There were seven ferries in all, three Tanzanian, two Kenyan and two Ugandan. They were much bigger than Tom had imagined, each able to carry thirty five railway wagons at a time. Even at first glance, it became obvious to Tom that the first problem was the lack of co-ordination between the ferry operators. Each national fleet had their own timetable and their own operating systems. Another problem which appeared obvious to Tom was that they were train ferries and there was no attempt to carry lorries. As an increasing proportion of traffic was now being carried each month by lorry because of the inefficiency of the railways and despite the state of the roads, this severely hampered the transport of exports and imports to and from the land locked countries.

As part of their fact finding mission they visited the ferry maintenance depot. To Tom's surprise he found that this was supplied and managed by the development arm of the Danish Government. That evening Tom had dinner with the Danes running their depot while Tulley went off to meet some of his friends. After a number of beers and a few gins, the Danes made sure they were not over heard and confessed that if they left it would not be long before the whole system went haywire.

" They just have no sense of time and administration," they told Tom sadly. " Making do is what they are good at but not running complex organisations. They are good at fixing things if they go wrong but the concept of planned maintenance is beyond them."

At least after his visit, Tom could now appreciate the distances involved and the speed of the ferries gave him an idea of how long each trip would take. He also had a concept of the size of the Lake, where the main ports were located and the likely schedule. All he needed from somebody was the volumes of traffic and he could work out a valid schedule.

On the way back to Dar es Salem, Tom did not know whether to laugh, cry or be very scared as to his future travel in East Africa. Tulley and he arrived at the terminal building in Mwanza for their flight. Well it was more of a corrugated iron shack than a terminal building. There was no food or drink, hence the water bottles Tulley had purchased in town before they left. Obviously because of the shortage of electricity, there was no air-conditioning and the terminal was hot and smelly.

A girl made way for Tom to sit on a wooden bench. She and her mother who sat ineffectually waving a fan by her side, proved to be from New Zealand doing a tour of East Africa under their own steam. When Tom got talking to them, they introduced themselves as Rachel and her mother Dorothy.

When the time for the flight got close, Rachel said with a grin. " Give me one of your bags and I will grab the best seats on the plane for us."

Tom looked puzzled but the girl grinned. " When the plane lands, it will taxi close to get rid of the passengers coming to Mwanza. After a quick clean, they will fling open the doors and it is everybody for themselves. I will sprint across the tarmac and up the steps of the plane. When I have pushed everybody else out of the way, I will place the bags on the best seats near the front. You can follow with my mum at a more sedate pace which suits you and her. Beside I have known the last few passengers on board to be refused seats because the plane has been over booked."

Tom looked at her mother and she smiled and eloquently shrugged her shoulders. " You go along with her. We have been doing this for the past few weeks and she is very good at getting us seats. Trust her."

Tom handed his hand baggage to the Rachel.

Tom sat back in amazement. When the door to the airside opened, there was a kind of frenzied scrum. People pushed and jostled other people in their rush to get through the door first. Sweaty black faces usually smiling with flashing white teeth were transformed into snarling masks. Rachel ducked and dived and was off across the tarmac ahead of everybody. Tom had a glimpse of her disappearing up the steps of the aircraft.

Tulley shrugged. " This is the way it is here, I am afraid. Every man for himself and forget any of the usual civilities of living. Sometimes I worry that my people will never learn civilised behaviour."

Tom smiled and shook his head as they walked out to the plane with the Dorothy. " Don't you castigate yourself my friend. My country is supposed to be civilised but the same thing can happen there. My experience of your country has thrown up many examples of people who care for others and are very helpful. What about the safety through the ICAO?"

" Technically the regulations apply and are adhered to. If they weren't the airline would be grounded by the ICAO inspectorate. It is everyday operations where they fall down. You saw what a shambles it was coming out to Mwanza and that was from a modern international airport. This is out in the bush. Even Air Kenya which is thought to be one of the better airlines lost your bags." Tulley shook his head.

When the climbed the steps to the aircraft, Tom spotted Rachel saving some seats for them. She insisted on Tom sitting beside her on the journey so that she could talk to somebody else other than her mother. She remarked that she got on well with her mother but an extended period in her company could be wearing on her nerves.

At Kilimanjaro Airport it was even worse. Some passengers got off and some more got on. The aeroplane taxied towards the take off runway with passengers standing in the aisle. Tom could not believe his eyes. He had been on some ropy airlines in his time but nothing like this had ever happened. The stewardess went around the plane and proceeded to collect all the children. These she strapped two to a seat until there were enough seats for everybody. During the flight, Tom metaphorically held his head in his hands.

From Dar es Salem, they flew back to Nairobi. There they changed planes for Kisumu, the Kenyan port on the lake. On a visit to the repair and maintenance yard Tom found that most of the machinery was dated before the nineteen twenties. Looking around, Tom could only admire the engineers who managed despite all the drawbacks to keep the ships sailing. Over a beer that night at his hotel, the chief engineer confided in Tom that the higher management was a shambles and that most of the investment money sent under aid schemes never seemed to reach his works. He did not say it explicitly but implied that it disappeared into the pockets of politicians. From what he also inferred, Tom got the distinct impression that he thought the colonial days were at least better managed and less corrupt.

Once more with trepidation, Tom and Tulley boarded a plane to fly from Kisumu to Nairobi and on to Kampala. They were booked into a hotel on the outskirts near the golf course. When they went to interview the minister, they drove through streets where all the buildings still bore the bullet holes from the civil war. Inflation had taken hold but no new denomination notes had been printed. This meant that everybody had to carry vast amounts of cash with them to pay for anything.

Watching the television in his hotel one night, he was intrigued to see an advert during a football match. It said, " If you want to see the next world cup, wear a condom." It brought home to Tom for the first time the depth of the worry about aids. On the flight back to Nairobi, Tulley pointed out through the plane window how the bush had started to grow back round villages as there were less people to till the fields.

From Nairobi, he returned to Dar es Salem to meet the coffee growers association on his own. Tulley made an excuse of having to meet people in Kenya but later Tom found out it was not about their project but to do with a wedding Tulley was organising. Once more he was presented with an example of the African's disregard for the way things should be undertaken. Back then to Mombassa to trace the container they had picked and its progress through the system. At last his travelling was over and he was booked into a hotel on the beach to write an interim report with Tulley. Secretly he was delighted that he would not have to travel on some of the airlines he had been made to patronise.

He was invited to Tulley's house for a meal one evening soon after they arrived to meet Tully's wife, Kulu, his son George and the rest of his extended family. Living in the same house were his mother and Kulu's sister, Mary. Mary was a nun and was visiting from the convent. There were other friends there and it proved to be quite a party. Kulu was very attractive with a round face, large black eyes and a relatively slim body for an African woman. She moved with a fluid grace that only African women can truly show. At the dinner, Mary made a remark that all most made Tom laugh out loud but he restrained himself.

" Tom you know one of the major problems with this country?" she asked with a smile.

Tom blinked. The conversation up to then had been about England and his work. " No."

" There are too many children," she answered emphatically.

Tom mumbled something while thinking about her beliefs. To himself he thought that if there was more emphasis on family planning, there might not be so many children but he did not say this to Mary. He was after all, he told himself, a guest in their house and he did not want to upset them.

The next day was a holiday and Tom invited Tulley, Kulu and George to spend the day with him round the pool at the hotel. Tulley had business elsewhere but Kulu accepted on behalf of her son. There was to be a barbecue in the garden of the hotel that night and Tom said he would arrange for Tulley and Kulu to join him as his guests. They agreed because Tulley would be back by evening.

It was a very pleasant day mostly spent round the pool. George was in his element swimming and eating the ice creams Tom bought for him. In the evening without George, Tulley and Kulu joined him for the barbecue under the stars. There was a disco and Tom danced with Kulu while Tulley sat and drank. He said he was away again the next day but would get his findings to Tom so that Tom could incorporate them into the report.

The next day Tom was on the balcony outside his room watching the waves break on the beach while trying to concentrate on his writing. There was a knock at the door and he anticipated a courier with Tulley's contribution. Tom was pleased because when he received that he would be able to finish his work here and have a few days relaxation before getting the plane back to London.

When he opened the door, Kulu stood there. She smiled and he stood aside to let her into the room.

" Hello Tom," she said with something that sounded like anticipation in her voice. " It is my day off and George is at school. Tulley had to go away to see some of his relations up country and he wanted these notes delivered. He said that if you got them today maybe you could spend a little time as a tourist before going home."

Tom took the file and placed it on the bed. " I am glad you are here. It will give me an excuse to break for the rest of the morning. Come on lets go down the pool bar and have a coffee."

It was relaxing and congenial sitting with Kulu looking out over the beach to the sea and talking about families, Kenya and Kulu. Tom invited her for lunch and afterwards took her back to his room to collect some things for Tulley. It felt only natural after she kissed him that they should make love. It was a slow leisurely love making with none of the tension that thoughts of the future can often bring. Afterwards Tom sat on the bed and gazed in wonder at the shiny ebony of her skin contrasting with the white of the sheets.

She smiled and pulled his head down to kiss him. " Tulley has not been honest with you. He has not been away collecting data about your project. He has been arranging a wedding for a friend, as is the custom here. I think you would call him the chairman of the wedding committee. The wedding is the day after tomorrow at the Cathedral. He asked me to invite you to come along. Will you come with me?"

" I would be delighted," Tom answered kissing her back.

" A car will come to pick you up at eleven o'clock and then pick me, George and Mary up from our house. I will look forward to escorting you and introducing you to all our friends."

The wedding was held in the Catholic Cathedral, and though undoubtedly Christian was an African occasion. The women all assembled as the bride left the church and danced round her making that peculiar warbling sound that African women employ when happy. At the reception afterwards at the bride's father's estate a whole ox was roasting and the drink flowed like water served by servants in white coats. Kulu made sure Tom was introduced to everybody of importance, explaining why he was there. Many of the guests buttonholed him over the course of the evening to put in their opinion as to why there were so many problems with transport in Kenya. Kulu and her friends took it in turn to dance with him. Later that night, Tom fell into his bed drunk and happy.

As he flew back from Nairobi to London, Tom mused about the contrasting circumstances of his visit. He found it hard to accept in a supposedly developing country which lived on international aid that there was such a gulf between the very rich and the abject poor. It had been made plain to Tom when he had seen the wealth of the bride's father and nearby the grinding poverty of the slums and shantytowns. What made it even harder for

Tom to accept was that the rich living in the bubble of their homes and servants, did not appear to notice the poor. They did not pay any taxes or, other than provide ill paid employment for their servants, help in any way. With his contacts with all sorts of people in all walks of life, he had found the sense of fun and cheerfulness of the people up lifting. Overarching the whole business of living in these countries was the corruption. From the lowest official holding out for a few shilling to process some document to the very top where millions of pounds disappeared into the politicians pockets.

Those at the top were so prickly about their colonial past. They blamed in some cases implicitly, in others by suggestion, their state to the way in which the colonial powers had left them when they had gained their freedom. That was a long time ago Tom thought many times but he did not voice his thoughts for fear of upsetting his hosts. Not that his introspection on that subject helped. When he had suggested to the Minister of Transport for Uganda that the best way to schedule the ferries on the Lake was to disregard nationality and treat them all as one fleet, he thought he was going to cause a diplomatic incident. The Minister burst out that he was trying to impose colonial values on the Africans again by re introducing the East African Federation. Even when he had pointed out many examples of different countries sharing their fleets in the way he was suggesting and keeping separate nationalities and fleets, fierce national pride had raised a barrier to any rational thinking. Even so he had concluded, he would have to include the concept of joint operations in his report.

When he arrived at the station, he was met by Mary and Mark. Paul was away with the scouts, while Jane told them to tell him that unfortunately she could not get the time off work. Tom's heart fell when he realised Jane was not there to meet him after six weeks away and that she would not be at home. All the way home on the aircraft at thirty thousands feet, he had prayed that thing would be different between himself and Jane. When the plane had landed and he had had a chance to telephone there had not been any hint that she would not be at the station to drive him home. Now he felt a little lost and abandoned. Mary and Mark had travelled on the bus so they were thrilled to get back home in a taxi. They chatted all the way back, excitedly asking questions until Tom was caught up in their mood and started to laugh.

When Jane arrived home from work, she threw her arms around his neck and kissed him.

" Oh Tom, I am sorry," she said. " There was an emergency came up and I had to stay at work. Did Mary and Mark explain?"

" They said you could not get away from work," Tom replied smiling.

That night they made love for the first time for a long time. It was strange at first but soon their natural rhythms generated by years of mutual pleasure took over.

Afterwards they lay in the warm glow of their satisfaction. Jane murmured. " I am sorry Tom. I do not know what happened. It was as though I did not want you to touch me but I still needed you around. It was so stupid as well because after a while I had no idea what it was that triggered the whole episode. When I had to come to bed alone I suddenly realised how much I loved you."

Tom smiled in the dark. " There is no need to say sorry. We were both at fault. All we have to think about is the future."

The next day his whole family sat around the table and talked over a meal. It was wonderful to Tom after so much tension in his home and his relationships. Though there was a large disagreement between Jane and himself about the reason why the countries of Africa are in such a mess, it was undertaken in the spirit of discussion rather than antagonism. Jane's argument was that the ex-colonies had had enough time to grow up and they had to start living their own lives rather than blaming the British for all their problems.

" They are like teenage children," she had remarked. " They want to live their own lives but they blame their parents for everything that goes wrong. We should leave them to sort out their own troubles in their own way."

Tom was about to reply when the mist rose up and his family had disappeared. He was angry. Like somebody who had been forced to act in a way they did not want to, Tom tried to bring his family back into his mind. He failed. This made him angry.

Chapter 11

Mark looked closely at his father and then urgently called to his mother who was speaking to a doctor.

" Mum! Mum! Come quickly."

Jane was by his side in no time. " What is it son?"

Mark pointed. " Dad is moving around. At first it was his eyes but now he is moving one of his arms as well as his head. It is as though he was angry."

They both looked and they both saw his head move slightly. His breathing was no longer loud and measured but coming in short sharp gasps. The doctor joined them and looked at the monitors.

" Well?" Jane demanded.

The doctor shook his head. " I am not certain whether this is a good sign or a bad. What ever is happening in his mind, he appears to be coming to some climax."

Mark lent over the bed and spoke to his father directly. " Dad calm down. Mum and I are here to help you. Belinda and Tony are outside waiting to come in and see you."

Tom was angry with himself for letting his images of his family go. Vaguely he could hear voices. Yes they were voices but he found it hard to grasp what they were saying. He got more angry as he tried to hear what was being said but failed. Then he realised it was the voice of Mark and then it was gone.

He was standing in the headmaster's study at Mark's school. His conscience still troubled him about what had happened to Mary. Oh he had proudly dropped Mary off at her new school on the first day in her brand new Girls Grammar School uniform. That night when she came home she had talked excitedly about her new friends and the school. He knew then that maybe his suppressing of his feelings about private education had been in Mary's best interests. From the way she had talked and smiled, he knew she was going to be happy.

Not so Mark. For the first time since transferring to senior school, Mark sounded upset about something that had happened at school. At first he clammed up and there was nothing Tom could do but wait until the time was right for Mark tell his father what was troubling him. It hurt Tom to think that his son could not trust his father with whatever it was that was concerning him. Tom kept dropping hints and at last Mark explained what it was that had upset him.

" Mrs. Denvers, my maths teacher and head of year, accused me of being the reason why Mary has been sent to a private school," he reluctantly told his father while not meeting Tom's eye. " I tried to defend myself but she would not listen."

Tom attempted to hold back the tide of anger which swept through him like a red tide. " Its all right Mark. Don't you let this make you feel guilty and upset. What was decided about Mary had nothing to do with you or how you behave at school. I will sort things out."

Tom was angry, so angry that he was short with his students and harsh with Jane that evening. His fury was such that he telephoned the headmaster, insisting on an interview with Mrs. Denvers. The headmaster agreed and a meeting was arranged for a couple of days later.

Jane admonished Tom as he left home that morning. " Try to stay calm Tom. Find out what actually happened before you start accusing anybody of anything. Remember, Mark has to live with the outcome of your discussions."

Tom was angry but he assured Jane. " I will stay calm, Jane. All I want to find out is why Mrs. Denvers accused my son of such bad behaviour that it was his fault that Mary has gone to a private school."

When Tom arrived at the school, he was escorted by the secretary into the head master's office. The headmaster insisted on being present throughout the interview and that it took place in his office. Mrs. Denvers was plump with her grey hair pulled back in a severe bun. She looked vastly experienced which made Tom wonder why she had allowed herself such an outburst.

" Professor Houseman," Mr. Poulson the head master greeted him, shaking his hand. " You asked for an appointment to see Mark's form teacher Mrs. Denvers as quickly as possible. It is my policy to be present at these times to represent the school. Do you object?"

Tom shrugged. " Mr. Poulson you are the headmaster of the school and are within your rights to be here. Besides, anything I wish to say to Mrs, Denvers concerns the whole school. You are more than welcome to stay."

Mr Poulson smiled but did not take his eyes from Tom. " What is it you wanted to see Mrs. Denvers about?"

" It is a question of good practice and looking after the pupils properly," Tom began slowly and calmly. " My son Mark has been upset about something that has been happening in school for the last month. It took me a while to find out what had happened. He is a very loyal pupil of this school and did not want to upset anybody here. When he reluctantly told me a couple of days ago, I was very angry. It took my wife to stop me coming straight to the school and confronting his teacher."

" What did he tell you?" Mr Poulson had a sceptical tone to his voice. Tom had to fight to keep unruffled. It was obvious that Mr. Poulson was going to try to defend the school by making out that Mark was stretching the truth.

" Mark told me that Mrs. Denvers accused him of being the reason why my daughter has gone to the Girls Grammar School rather than follow her brothers here."

Mr Poulson frowned and turned to Mrs Denvers. " Is this right?"

" Well not exactly," she replied tentatively while not looking at either the headmaster or Tom. " I did ask him why his sister had been sent to the Girls Grammar School and not here. He did not answer my question."

Tom got to his feet and shook his head. " No Mrs Denvers that is not good enough. I believe my son. He would never prevaricate about something as serious as this. You accused him of being the reason why my daughter has gone to the Girls Grammar School and not here. It must have been his behaviour and the way he acted at home which alerted me that there was a problem. He was upset because he could not think of a single thing he had done which could have led you to believe what you were accusing him of was true. Both of those things are untrue."

" Why else would you send your daughter to a private school?" Mrs Denvers asked with all the contempt teachers in the state system have for private education. " Both Paul and Mark are bright and in the top ten in their years. They are mostly well behaved and do all the work asked of them. Something they did or said must have been the catalyst for you to stop your daughter coming here."

Tom shook his head angrily. " The reason Mary is at the Girls Grammar has nothing to do with Mark or Paul. It is to do with the wider ethos of the school and the teachers. Whenever she can, my wife acts as a volunteer on school trips. It was obvious to her that most of the girls were not interested in any academic study. The majority of them sat at the back of the group and talked about boys, make up and other things. The teachers were only too pleased to let them get on with it as long as they did not cause too much trouble. Jane thought that this was not the atmosphere in which my daughter would thrive academically. She might have been able to hold her own but peer pressure would have been hard to resist. Thus we found a different solution."

" What do you want us to do?" Mr Poulson asked.

" Mrs Denvers will have to apologise to my son as a start," Tom stated bluntly looking at Mrs Denvers.

She looked down. " I don't see why I should apologise to one of the students."

Tom exploded. " Because the reputation of the school and you are dependent on this. I could write to the papers and as a respected Professor what ever I say will be printed. I could take my boys out of the school and send them to another school. They would not like that because they like it here."

Mr Poulson hurriedly intervened. " We will agree to that."

" Good," Tom smiled. " If you have a desire to have a go at my children in the future about anything that does not concern their work, you will ask me first. I am angry that you used this as an opportunity to get at me through my children. I have been a loyal parent while they have been here but feel I will have to resign from the parent teacher association from now."

Mr. Poulson shook his head. " There is no need for that."

Tom laughed. " It would be better for everybody if I did resign. It will avoid the danger of the teachers feeling I am against them. Oh don't look like that Mrs. Denvers. They will all rally round and defend you if I am there."

Tom got to his feet and said goodbye.

That New years Eve, Jane and Tom were invited to Derek's house for a party. During the evening, Derek invited him to have a chat in his study. Tom took gin and tonic through and sat by the fire. He was curious as to why it was he and not one of the others who Derek wanted to see.

" We have come a long way me and you," Derek remarked looking at the whisky swirling round his glass. " Who would have thought this was possible when we went to Model Farm Junior School up the road from where we lived. Times were tough then. I still remember that day after I had the fight with my Dad when you advised me to attach myself to a Mister Big. Through all my life you have been the one constant thing. We might not have met socially all the time but you have been there whenever I wanted advise."

Derek paused as though he was thinking of how to phrase his next words. Tom sipped his gin and watched his friend closely. He had seen this mood only rarely with Derek and knew that his fiend was about to tell him something significant. He remembered that evening when he had advised Derek off the top of his head even though he had no idea whether his suggestion was practical or not. I wonder what happened to that girl Pam? he thought.

Derek looked directly at Tom and grinned. " It is a bit like old times. I have something I want to, how do they put it in the States? Run by you for your reaction. I seem to have been doing that all my life."

Tom finished his drink and Derek went to fetch some more. It was peaceful in the study but the sound of music and excited voices could be heard through the door.

When Derek returned, he said. " To come straight to the point. As you must know, we have bought a villa in Spain and are hoping to spend more time over there. Because of that I am thinking more and more about shedding some of the responsibilities I have and handing things over to the younger generation."

Tom smiled. " Aren't you a trifle young yourself to be thinking in this way. We are only forty seven after all."

Derek sighed. " It is not about age Tom and you know it. It is to do with the length of time I have been doing this. I have been the head of this organisation for over fifteen years. It becomes harder and harder to keep the whole thing together. There are rumblings among the ranks about the way we do things. The young always want to change things. Then there is the increasing pressure from the authorities to try to dig some dirt on me."

Tom shook his head. " Don't take this in the wrong way Derek but I have tried to avoid getting involved with the other side of what we shall call your enterprises. I have helped the legitimate side flourish. I thought you paid your lawyer and accountant vast sums of money to keep the authorities off your back. They are supposed to make sure that nothing can be traced to you."

Derek sighed again. " There is more and more regulation out there now and the police have more powers to look into anything they see as suspicious. Toby and Mervin do an excellent job and we haven't had any trouble yet. I have an instinct for these things and can sense that the authorities are getting close to my back. There fore, I think it is time to ease myself out of the front line."

Tom drank deeply trying to think of an argument against what Derek was trying to say. He understood that they were getting close to something he had avoided thinking about over the years since he had first agreed to work with Mister Hunt. He was close to having to admit to himself that much of his wealth had come from illegal sources. Well not all but the base amount that had been used to build up the businesses. He had known that Mr Hunt was a dubious character from the very start of their relationship but the way they had come to an unspoken agreement had allowed Tom to ignore the implications of what he had agreed to do for Mr. Hunt. He had hidden behind the obvious fiction that what he was doing was legitimate and had no connection with Mr. Hunt's other activities. In a strictly legal sense he supposed that was true.

" I have been doing the same thing for almost as long as you. Even thinking of that does not make me want to retire."

" That is where you are wrong Tom," Derek grinned at his friend making him look, thought Tom, like the boy from the council estate he used to be. " Though you might not realise it, you change what you are doing on a regular basis. You concentrated on research, then the conference round, being a professor and now you have started to get jobs around the world for various organisations. Actually it was because of what I have seen you do over the years which has made me look at change in what I am doing."

" What plans have you for easing yourself out of the front line?"

" Again it is partly following your instructions." Derek laughed at the expression on Tom's face. " I am not suggesting that you have written about running gangs or illegal activities. What I do is like a business anyway. I read one of your books about restructuring an organisation. Don't look so surprised. Even though I come from that council estate and left school at fifteen, I can read you know. Using this as a guide I worked out what the component parts of my organisation are. These I have structured into divisions. On paper the structure is already in place. After that, I am looking at the people in my organisation. I have a good idea of who is reliable and intelligent enough to run one of the divisions. Once the structure is in place,

I will put those in charge. Two things will then result. I will be able to give up all the day to day responsibilities to these people. All I will be responsible for is the strategic thinking. The second thing is there will be a pointer to my successor when I finally retire out right. If it all works out over the next few years I will be able to spend a longer time at my villa in Spain."

Before Tom could reply, Derek's wife called them back into the sitting room to see in the new year. Tom did not have a chance to talk to Derek again on the subject for a while.

Shortly after the new year celebrations, Tom was contacted by Mr. Delouse who had been in charge of the work in East Africa. It confirmed what Derek had been saying about Tom changing careers frequently though still staying in the same place. Tom was invited to join a group reviewing the East Africa Land Locked Countries Study and the report they had submitted. The place chosen for the meeting was Hong Kong. To Tom who had attended conferences there on a number of occasions, Hong Kong was one of the most exciting places he had ever visited. It was vibrant and had that go, go, go feeling. Everybody appeared busy all the time. He suggested to Jane that she accompany him but there proved too many problems to overcome so she declined. He wrote a letter to Isabel using the last address he had but did not receive a reply.

Just before Easter, Tom booked into the Peninsular Hotel in Kowloon. Mr. Delouse greeted him like a long lost friend but informed him that the United Nations committee member who was to oversee the meeting would be delayed by at least a day. Those who had arrived on time would meet briefly in the morning and then have a free afternoon. The main business would start the next day. Tom did think of trying to find Isabel's telephone number but thought it was best to leave it as she had not replied. He did feel the frustration of being so close but not being able to see her. On the other hand, he thought, my life has become less complicated since she left and it might be best if we did not meet.

The meeting the next morning in the oak panelled board room with the paintings of historic Hong Kong was concerned with setting the agenda for the week on the advice of Mr. Delouse. During the session as coffee was being served, Tom was called away to the telephone much to the surprise of the other committee members. It was Isabel.

" Tom? I am sorry I did not reply to your letter but I have been away accompanying the investment director to Australia." The familiar voice sounded in his ear and he felt a thrill at the sound. " I had no idea whether I would return in time to see you because our schedule was flexible. As it happened, we arrived back three days ago but there was no time to write. I thought the best idea was to contact you once you had arrived. You had told me in the letter where you would be staying. What is happening with your business this week? Will there be a chance for us to meet? I have kept every night free in my diary for this week."

" Slow down Isabel," Tom sounded amused. " It is great to hear your voice again. When you did not reply I thought I had either got the wrong address or you did not want to see me."

" Oh Tom, of course I wanted to see you." she giggled and then asked bluntly as though any more waiting was going to be too much for her to stand. " When can we meet?"

" We have this meeting this morning and then lunch together," Tom replied trying to keep his voice calm and serious like a professor to one of his students. "

After that I am free especially this evening."

Isabel laughed excitedly, her voice like the sun coming out from behind a cloud after a gloomy day. " I'll meet you by the ferry terminal on Hong Kong at two o'clock and we can explore Hong Kong together. Is that OK with you?"

Tom could not keep the excitement and anticipation out of his voice. " I will be there looking out for you. Though please don't get into hot water at work because of me. I can wait until you finish this evening."

Isabel's voice sparkled. " They owe me some time at work because of being away for the last few weeks. It was suggested this morning that I take the afternoon off. When I told them that my tutor from my old university was here, they ordered me to leave at lunch time. See you at two o'clock."

The rest of the morning passed in a blur for Tom. He found difficulty in concentrating on what the other people in the group were discussing and his contributions must have been bizarre. Though thinking back nobody looked as at him as though he had lost his head so maybe even in automatic pilot, his mind could still function adequately and what came out of his mouth sounded logical. Tom could not test his theory because he could not recall what he had said. He was given some notes to read by the next morning and he tucked these into his brief case in a manner that said to everybody that he thought this was serious.

It is always the same, he told himself as many of the people present wanted to talk to him after the meeting, when I want to depart quickly, there are always those wanting to delay me. He chaffed at the delay and answered questions as quickly as possible. All he wanted to do was to get back to his room and change ready to meet Isabel that afternoon. Change now so that he could leave the hotel as soon as he had finished lunch and get down to the ferry landing stage. In some unfathomable way he wanted to be on the other side to greet Isabel when she arrived.

After lunch, Tom set out to walk the short distance from the hotel to the ferry landing stage. He was excited, like a schoolboy being promised a treat. As he sat on the ferry watching the harbour unfold as they crossed the brown water dodging the sampans and other ships, he thought about his relationship with Isabel. It was a question he had never really considered or tried to answer when they were back in England. Indeed it was like much of his life. As the time passed he tended not to question his motives but to assume that what he did was for the best in the circumstances in which he had found himself. This needed a great deal of circumspection on his part. He justified his actions by telling himself that he was not hurting anybody. Once more he was being made to think rather deeply about what he had done in his life. Was everything he had undertaken legitimate? Derek had hinted that he, Tom, had made his fortune on the back of the illegal actions of his mate and the dubious practices of his brother.

Could this be true of his relationship with Isabel? He had always thought that his motives were crystal clear. He had never pretended that he would leave Jane to live with Isabel. Though he had to admit that in a way he passionately loved Isabel, on a much more profound level he realised he loved Jane so deeply that there was never any question of him leaving her.

If that is the case, he asked himself, why is a forty seven year old man getting so excited about meeting a twenty four year old woman? What the hell can she see in me that she is so anxious to meet me again? In a fashion, even though she had never hinted at such motives, he could have suspected that she was letting him make love to her so that she could gain an advantage over the other students. He had kidded himself that he had maintained that strict professional conduct when it came to her academic work.

All these thoughts vanished when he spotted her walking down the ramp towards him just after he had disembarked from the ferry. The short girl with black hair shining in the sun and being blown slightly across her round face by the breeze. She was dressed in a white blouse and tight grey skirt which showed off her small round breasts and her curved bottom. Her rather chunky though shapely legs showed enticingly below her skirt. His affection for her and his desire rose to great heights as she approached.

She stood in front of him smiling up into his face. Tom's eyes feasted on her features. The almond shaped sparkling brown eyes, the round nose and the smiling kissable lips. Isabel took one of his hands in hers and reached up to kiss him full on the mouth. For a moment Tom forgot the people swirling round them and kissed her back. Tucking her arm under his, she pulled him away from the landing stage and towards a bus.

They spent what was to Tom one of the most pleasant afternoons of his life exploring the Peak and the windy roads leading back into town. Isabel talked excitedly all the time, whether pointing out the sights of Hong Kong or assuring Tom that she had lived for this day. All Tom had to do was follow her lead and answer her questions. He squeezed her arm at times and kissed her briefly when he thought nobody was looking. For afternoon tea she took him to a Chinese cafe where nobody spoke English and the exotic food on display confused Tom. Laughing gaily, Isabel explained what everything was and ordered what she thought was something that Tom would appreciate. The sun shone though it was not too hot and the humidity was low compared to the last time Tom had been in Hong Kong. With reluctance, they parted back at the ferry arranging to meet in the hotel later after changing for dinner. Isabel wanted to take Tom to her favourite restaurant near the beech outside Kowloon.

Isabel was waiting in the hotel foyer when Tom came out of the lift. The lights shining from the high ceiling highlighted her figure as though she was isolated among the hustle and bustle of people meeting, talking and moving in and out of the hotel. To Tom, it looked s though she was standing on a stage amid all the action waiting quietly for her big scene. One of the lights appeared to pick her out as though a spotlight was shining on her. In another way she was like the beautiful heroine from Suzy Wong. The way her welcoming smile lit up her face and the surrounding people, appeared to pull Tom toward her as a moth is attracted to a light on a dark night. Her red dress was tight with a hint of old Chinese style showing off the curves of her body. She looked taller than she was because of the height of her stiletto heels. Once more Tom was pulled into her aura and could not help smiling broadly in answer to her obvious invitation.

She kissed him oblivious of the other people in the lobby and took his arm.

" We have to get a taxi for where we are going," she smiled broadly up into his face.

In a daze of desire and pride at having such a pretty woman on his arm, Tom was propelled through the lobby. All Isabel did was look in the direction of the concierge and a taxi appeared instantly. The concierge bowed as he opened the door and thanked Tom for his tip.

" Good night Miss Chueng," as he closed the car door. Tom blinked at Isabel but did not question her.

They sat in the back of the car close together. As he breathed in her perfume, Opium he thought, he could feel the warm of her thighs pressing his and the firmness of her body. All thoughts of whether this was right or wrong had long since vanished. He was lost in the depths of her eyes and the promise held out by the slight trembling of her body close to his. All awareness of Jane and his family had vanished into the moment, washed away in the flood of desire her presence was raising in him. Smiling with her, Tom let himself sink deep into the pools of her attractiveness. At least relax and enjoy things he told himself. It will only be for one night.

The restaurant proved to be rather exclusive over looking the sea surrounded by its own grounds. They were served cocktails on the terrace while looking at the menu surrounded by very well dressed expatriate British and wealthy Chinese businessmen. The stars were clear in the sky and the air was still and balmy. Tom was enjoying every minute of his evening. Several people came up spoke to Isabel and she introduced Tom as Professor Houseman.

Isabel chose the meal and later full of goodwill and pleasure, they got a taxi back to her flat.

When inside, Tom found that he was high above the Happy Valley race course. A sitting room led off the hall but opposite the door was a kind of raised area with settees in front of the large picture window. Anybody sitting there as Tom discovered was able to look out over the lights of Hong Kong shining in the waters of the harbour. A maid suddenly appeared and served them coffee.

Later without rushing, after sitting with their arms about each other looking over the town, they went into the bedroom and made love on the biggest bed Tom had ever seen.

In the light of an early dawn, Tom made his way through the awakening town back to his hotel. That day was full of good cheer and nothing was going to ruffle the feelings Tom felt. He even enjoyed the discussions on the report and the likely advice they were going to give the governments. He had to have dinner with the other delegates and impatiently waited until it was diplomatic to get away.

Isabel was waiting for him in her flat and she pulled him into the bedroom before he hardly had a chance to get inside the door. They made love repeatedly in that enormous bed. To Tom it proved to be one of the happiest times of his life. It was with great reluctance he had to say goodbye to Isabel on the penultimate morning of his stay. That night, his last in Hong Kong all the delegates were being taken out to dinner and after to a nightclub.

When Tom staggered back to his room in the early hours of the morning, he found Isabel sitting in his bed waiting for him with out any clothes. He was instantly sober but her smile reassured him that nothing was wrong.

" How did you get in here?" he demanded his voice made more harsh by his surprise and the amount he had had to drink.

Isabel grimaced. " Is that all you can say? Not what a lovely surprise and a kiss."

Tom walked over to the bed and kissed her. " It is wonderful. I thought we had said good bye this morning and I would not see you again. It was a surprise to find you in my bed. Don't get me wrong. It is a lovely sight and something I could only dream about. Make me a cup of coffee while I go to the bathroom."

When Tom returned ready for bed, Isabel was sitting in a chair by the table with two cups of coffee. She was naked.

After sitting down and sipping his coffee, Tom said, " Thank you. By the way how did you get into my room?"

Isabel smiled broadly. "The hotel owner was a friend of my father and we often came here for meals. The staff just assumed that you had given me permission to go to your room as they had seen me meeting you before. Anyway it is not important. We can now say goodbye properly."

They made love slowly that night, over and over again as though they both acknowledged that this was likely to be the last time. It was a surprise, snatched from the very jaws of the dragon of their parting and they made the best they could of this time. Later as the dawn lightened the room, Isabel out of character, clung to Tom.

" I will have to go soon," she said her voice choking with emotion, her body pressed close to his. " It has been wonderful Tom, something I did not expect. It has taught me never to give up hope though when we will meet again only God can tell. Make love to me one more time and then I will have to leave."

They made love fiercely. Tom lay back and watched as Isabel got off of the bed and disappeared into the bathroom. He could smell her scent on the bed clothes and feel the still clinging warmth of her body. She came out of the bathroom and he had not moved. Trying not to reach out to her, he watched in silence as she dressed and made ready to leave. At last she was ready. Quite the business woman, Tom thought.

" Goodbye Tom," was all she said leaning over the bed to kiss him.

Tom lay back staring at the door for a long time after she had left. In many ways he was fulfilled and satisfied. One corner of his mind was already starting to get excited about seeing his family the next day. It had been phenomenal meeting Isabel but even he realised it could only be fleeting moments in the wider plains of his life. What was meaningful to him was his relationship to Jane and their future together. He had to admit to himself that though he might dream about running off with Isabel, it could only be a dream. Reality would soon kick in. A twenty five year old woman would not have the same tastes or desires from life as a forty seven year old man. He smiled as a vision of her body lying on the bed next to him only an hour ago came unbidden to his mind as though some gremlin was tempting him to deny what he had been thinking. I have to decide that it is over, he told himself as he showered and made ready to catch the midday plane.

Tom did not know it as the plane winged its way from Hong Kong to London but he was entering a period in his life that would prove to be stable, calm and mostly happy. What Derek had hinted largely came true. More and more, Tom accepted assignments overseas from various organisations.

He helped set up a transport college in Malaysia. This was not without controversy because many in Porthampton University suggested that he was cutting off a steady stream of overseas students who came to the transport group to study transport and in some cases to undertake research. Tom countered with the argument that this venture would increase the number of qualified prospective students and therefore it was a good idea. He was proved right over the years after it was up and running.

His family grew until Paul gained a place at Oxford. It was strange for a while not having him around the house but there were still the other two. More and more they both became independent which gave Tom pause for thought. He no longer had the boost to his ego of helping them especially when they all passed their driving tests and Jane and he brought them cars. It was in many ways a time when Jane and Tom discovered each other again. They had spent so many years looking out for their children as a first priority that it was a joy to suddenly discover that they could look to each other once more. Tom even managed to arrange for Jane to accompany him on a few of his overseas assignments.

At the university things did at times get a little tense. There was no occasion for the academic committees to criticise his work. His research record stood comparison with everybody else in the university. His teaching record was good and his students still swore by his support. There was a large amount of what could only be described as bitchy jealousy among some of his colleagues. This stemmed from his earnings which some hinted could not be sustained while giving his all to the university. The rumours were spread that he did not really care about his post there but used his position to further his own ends. Tom tried to ignore these persistent and irksome mutterings. Nobody came out and accused him to his face or instituted committee discussions against him. Though he tried to separate his university work and his other work, the mutterings did start to affect his relationship with some of the university hierarchy. Tom concluded that there was nothing he could do to stop things and let it pass.

He did get involved with a company in Nigeria. that was something that he had not experienced in all his overseas work. The first time he went there, he was shocked to find the depth of the corruption and violence prevalent in that society. He and his colleague were met at Lagos airport by the company representatives and escorted to the hotel by a police convoy. Then out of the hotel the next morning in a police convoy to the airport. A small plane down to Port Harcourt and into another hotel. They were informed that they were not under any circumstances to leave the hotel unless in the official car with a driver and gun toting guard. They spent their time on a very strict timetable. From the hotel in the morning to the training compound, at the end of the afternoon session to the living compound for drinks and an evening meal and then back to the hotel. This for two weeks.

The third time he had been there, something happened which was to change the way he viewed his work. He and Brian met for breakfast the first Friday morning. The restaurant was like a monastery where all the monks had taken a vow of silence.

Usually there was noise of voices, laughter, angry words and background chatter. This morning there was silence. The waiter took their order without saying anything and brought their food.

" What the hell has happened?" Brian asked looking round the dining room nervously. " They are usually so voluble. I often want to tell them to tone it down in the mornings."

Tom looked round the room and shrugged. " I hope it is not true but I did hear a rumour from some of the students that Ken Sara Wiwa was to be executed today."

" Who is Ken Sara Wiwa?" Brian asked looking uncomfortable. " What did he do?"

Tom shook his head, " If you spent more time finding out about the places you visit rather than looking for cheap beer and women you might have known what was happening. Ken Sara Wiwa is a community leader of the Ogoni people of eastern Nigeria who founded the Movement for the Survival of the Ogoni People. Among other things, he published articles about the environmental impact of the oil industry on his people. He also wrote letters to the Times detailing the abuse of both political and business power down here. Obviously the authorities did not like what he was doing. Hence his arrest, show trial and sentence. The Movement adopted an Ogoni Bill of Rights demanding political autonomy and accused the Shell Oil Company of participating in the genocide of the Ogoni people. A few years ago just before I started coming to Nigeria, a peaceful protest took place outside Shells Umuechem facility here in Port Harcourt. From what I have been told, the police brutally put down the protest and killed 80 unarmed demonstrators. They then on Government orders, destroyed 495 homes of the protesters and their supporters. The demonstration was organised by the Umuachem youth who called for electricity, water, roads and other compensation due to oil pollution of crops and water supplies. A couple of years ago, Ogoni farmers protested in front of earth moving equipment used to lay pipelines for Shell across Ogoni farm land. The Nigerian military was summoned to the demonstration. One demonstrator was killed and another injured."

Tom looked out of the window. " The same year in fact while I was here, a pipeline leak at a Shell flow station resulted in crude oil being spilled over Ogoni farm land into water sources in Korokoro.

The leak continued for forty days without any response from Shell. Throughout this time Ken Sara Wiwa and other Ogoni leaders were detained several times. The Nigerian Government also set up a special task force to deal with the Ogoni crisis. Last year four Ogoni leaders were murdered by a group of youths who accused them of being government collaborators. Ken Sara Wiwa and other Ogoni leaders were arrested in connection with the murders, despite lack of evidence. The arrests and Government violence led to major protests by the Ogoni people. While in prison Ken Sara Wiwa received the Right Livelihood Award, the alternative Nobel Peace Prize. If today is the day when the sentence is carried out the people in Port Harcourt will be upset. He was one of their champions against the government in the north. From what the few people willing to talk to me have said, the charges are without foundation."

" There must have been some substance to the charges or he would not have been arrested surely," Brian looked around.

Tom laughed. " Brian, you are new to this. The government here can do what it likes. It is supported by foreign companies who have to give their backing or they will not be allowed to do business. Come on. From my experience, this is going to be a tense day."

That night they were taken as usual to the compound for dinner. They were just finishing off their meal when the managing Director came and ordered them to stay in the compound over the weekend. It was a tense time because they were locked away with no real knowledge of what was happening in town. The telephones to the outside world were cut. Tom could not contact Jane to tell her what was happening. All he could do was sit out the storm in the compound.

Lying in bed at the guest house, Tom could not get to sleep. Partly it was because he was worried about Jane and what she must be thinking about what was happening to him. He was certain that the trouble in Port Harcourt must have made the news back home but he had no way of contacting her about the situation. In all their married life this had not happened. When either of them had been away, they had telephoned to let the other know they were safe and well. All right, he had to admit to himself, he was not like many people who were in contact everyday. He had often joked that these people must be unsure of their relationship to their partner and had a need to check up on what they were doing. It is not as though they lead such exciting lives that anything might have taken place. Now he could not speak to Jane for reasons he had no control over, he worried that she might start to imagine all sorts of troubles for him. There was nothing he could do about it but sleep still alluded him.

That was the trouble. He had what even he could only call a bit of a conscience. Here he was earning money from a company associated with the government which had executed as far as he could make out an innocent man. Should he have put his belief in justice and the rule of law before his professional work. It was not as though he needed the money. He was in a position to do this work for the love of the work without pay but that would not be politically right. Brian did the work so that he could earn extra money and ease the financial burden on his family from doing an under remunerated job which he enjoyed. No, people could accuse him of giving support to an oppressive regime. Of course, he told himself, I am not doing this to support the company but to help the students better themselves. From all the reports of previous courses this has happened. Deep down a little voice told him he was fooling himself but he chose to ignore this.

On the Monday morning it was deemed by the senior management that it was safe enough for them to return to the hotel to collect their notes and then go to the training centre. When they arrived, the atmosphere was rather uneasy with the students split between support for the government and sympathy with Ken Sara Wiwa. By the end of the day all appeared, as far as their course was concerned, back to normal.

Back at the hotel that evening over a beer before going to bed, Brian remarked. " At least this could not happen in the UK, Tom. There would have to be suspicions and some evidence before anybody was arrested. Then the trail would have to be in public with proper evidence."

Tom smiled. " I am not so sure that the police are above trying to get at people they do not like in ways other than arrest and trial. Look, if they arrest somebody but do not charge them they can influence the life of that person substantially. They can even spread rumours through their friends in the press or drop hints about people they suspect or do not like without even arresting them. You know how difficult it is to shake off a bad reputation even when any rumours are proved unfounded. Still what happened here could not happen in the UK, I give you that."

Tom was called into the office of the training manager the next day when he was relieved for a lecture by Brian. It was unusual because the training manager left them to run the course and only did a review after the course dinner on the Friday.

When he was seated in the office with a beer in his hand, Rupert Dawson, the training manager said rather pompously as though he was nervous about Tom's reaction to what he was about to say. " The company is pleased with the way you have run these courses since you started. They seem to be having an effect with the transport operations looking more efficient and the students looking as though they understand the principles involved in transport operations. I have to tell you this though. We have been contacted by head office and from July all courses in Nigeria are to be taken over by the Nigerians. This means they will pay you out of their budget including your per diem and expenses. What do you say?"

Tom drank deeply of his beer and looked out of the window. On the almost bare football pitch a match was in progress but he hardly noticed. He was trying to think through the implications of what was being proposed.

" I will have to think about this," Tom smiled warily. " From my limited experience of Nigeria and their ways of doing business, I don't have much confidence in their ability to pay me on time and all the money I am owed. There are serious questions to be answered before I make up my mind. How much will I have to give to those in charge? Will I get paid straight into my bank in pounds or in local currency? Instinctively I should say no but I will give it a night's thought."

The manager smiled in turn. " You know Mrs Johnson who will be in charge. She will be here tomorrow and we can all talk it over then at coffee time."

" I will inform Brian and see what he thinks. He might want to organise the courses even if I decline."

Once more that evening they sat in the bar trying to have a quiet beer away from the attentions of all the young women trying to pick up a man for the night.

Tom grimaced and told Brian what had transpired in the training managers office that morning. " The company have decided that they want to change the way training is organised in Nigeria. In many ways I suppose we have been our own worst enemies. They feel that the responsibility for training based on the courses which others and we have run should now be handed over to the Nigerians. This is difficult. I have nothing against Nigerians as such. All right I can hear you thinking that I am being racially abusive in what I am going to say next."

Brian grinned. " I will take your remarks in the spirit in which you obviously intend them to be made."

Tom grinned back. " What worries me is the way in which business is carried on here. First there is the corruption. Everybody you have to deal with wants a kick back. I wonder how much of the money we are promised will actually get into our bank accounts. Then there is the pay. I have known through the Institute when I was on their education committee that the Nigerians owed so much money, the Institute in the end refused to send them any more educational materials or to set and mark exam papers. Will we ever be paid? Third there is the security. At the moment we are looked after by the company and they provide a driver and escort to take us around. Will the Nigerians give us the same protection? This is a dangerous place in which to travel around. What is your opinion?'

Brian waved to one of the girls. A pretty girl in a West African way and not too fat. She had a blouse open down the front and just covering her breasts. Brian waved to the barman and he served her with a beer. She smiled broadly at Brian and sat down with her friends at a table just outside of the residence bar. She was obviously going to wait for Brian.

Brian looked at Tom over his beer. " It is OK for you to have these thoughts. It is well known that money is no problem for you. As you know I have just been promoted to lecturer after doing research for a few years. On top of that we have just had a baby. I was so pleased when you invited me to join you and thought how the money would help. Since being here I have taken to the work and was looking forward to coming back for another course. Things cannot be as bad as all that can they?"

Tom shook his head while glancing over at the girl making eyes at Brian. " Look Brian. I don't think I will take up the offer of more courses. I have been doing this for a number of years now and would like a break. I would not enjoy working for the Nigerians so I will tell this Mrs Johnson tomorrow that I will not be continuing.

What I will do is recommend you to take over from me. Think of another lecturer you can ask and I expect Mrs Johnson will want to arrange things with you in the morning after I have finished with her. How does that sound?"

Brian smiled broadly. " That would be fantastic. Thank you Tom. I'll see you in the morning."

Tom watched as Brian went to the bar and got two more beers. He walked over to the girl and she dutifully followed him to another table away from the lobby. The last Tom saw of them was with arms round each other as he climbed the stairs to his suite.

The next day at the training centre, Tom informed Mrs. Johnson that he had decided to make this the last course he would organise and supervise. She was a thin lady which in a land of very big, wide women was uncommon. Unlike most African women whose full round faces usually smiled, her's was pinched and drawn as though she had the troubles of the world on her shoulders. In most of his dealings with her over the time he had supervised these training courses, Tom had never seen her smile. Despite what they perceived as the oppression and robbery of the bad government people from the north of the country, the people of the Delta were on the whole very cheerful. His driver and guard had always treated Tom with to a wide smile every morning or more accurately broad grins. Because of the change from European control to Nigerian organisation and payment which was sensitive to the Nigerians, Tom set out to convey the impression to Mrs Johnson that it was a decision he had made due to circumstances controlling his future time and commitments. He assured her that he would make sure that Brian had all the information needed to organise successful courses in the future. Mrs. Johnson and he parted on what was on the surface amiable terms. Tom suspected that she disapproved of his decision. It did not take much intuition to work out that she doubted his true motives for resigning.

When he thought about his decision that night after the course dinner, he found that he had an overwhelming sense of relief. It was not the students who caused this feeling to sweep over him. They in the main had been wonderful, keen to learn and become his friends by the end of each course. As is the nature of these things, there were some problems. Tom treated them all as students and it took some getting used to when the students wanted him to be especially polite to one of their number. Usually this was because the man was a chief of some kind. It was not in Tom's nature to bow down to anybody and he treated all the students the same. Once he had established that what ever happened outside the class room, inside he was the tutor and they were the tutees, every student even the chiefs accepted his authority.

In part the feeling of being let off an onerous task was due to the restrictions which were imposed on any foreign traveller in Nigeria. This curtailing of his natural habits had irked Tom from the first time he had arrived in Port Harcourt.

When he was abroad in hot countries, it had been a habit of Tom's to go for a walk after dinner around the area in which the hotel was situated. Usually this as the coolest part of the day and it would afford him a chance to experience the ambience of the country in which he was working. He would sample the smells of the cooking, the flora and sense the atmosphere of the people. On many occasions he would stop and look at a market stall. In Port Harcourt he had never been allowed to leave the hotel except in the allocated car with an armed escort. The only places he could visit were the compound and the training centre. At the accommodation compound almost all of the people worked for the company and were predominately expatriates. Their talk was of the company and very little about the country and what the local people were thinking. In many ways Tom had always thought, there was a lack of knowledge among most of the company managers of what the culture of the country they were working in was really like.

The other part of his decision which made him relieved that he was not coming back again was the corruption endemic in the country. Tom could never work out whether this was a result of poor wages or something inherent in the character of the people. Every official he had met made it obvious that they expected some personal reward for helping him, over and above the wages they were paid, if his progress was to be smoothed. He hated the whole social structure. It was not only the corruption of officials employed by the government but of everybody. Take one example which was close to his expertise. The roads in and around Port Harcourt were a disgrace. It was not as though money was not allocated for road improvements. At every step in the process of getting to the stage of either building a new road or repairing an existing road, money was siphoned off into people's bank accounts. Individuals made a great deal of money out of the system without putting anything into the schemes. There was not a great deal poor people could do to get their hands on services or government help because they lacked both power and influence.

The prevailing situation in Nigeria was a good illustration to Tom of the old axiom that wealth breeds power. Without wealth a person could not hope to have any say in how the country or the local region was governed. Wealth brought influence especially among the poor. Resources managed a person to buy the muscle to make sure that nobody took away your money. Obviously in any country with such contrasts between the rich and the poor, but especially in Nigeria where there was an abundance of potential prosperity for all, poverty bred resentment. In Port Harcourt there was a perception that they generated the wealth through the oil industry but it was spent in the north which was a place with little natural resources. Not many people, Tom came to the conclusion after talking to many of his students, resented the spreading around of the wealth if they felt that they were getting their fair share. In the end, Tom mused as he sat waiting for his flight to be called, that kind of indignity can lead to direct action and protests which in the end can lead to violence against those who are seen to cause the poverty.

Tom arrived home full of delight at seeing his family after the traumas of Nigeria. Jane was at the station to meet him but after her initial enthusiasm at seeing him, Tom became worried that she appeared to be subdued as though something was worrying her. All he could assume that either it was a hangover from her work or relief that he had arrived home safely. He was proved wrong after he had put his case in the bedroom and was sitting drinking a coffee in the kitchen.

Jane broached the subject tentatively. " Marlene phoned me just before I came to the station to meet you. I knew there was something wrong because I have never heard her sound so frightened. She told me that the police had come to the house this morning and arrested Derek. She couldn't tell me any details only to say that they had left a team there to go through their papers. Other than that she could not give me a reason."

For quite a while Tom stared at Jane. His mind had gone completely blank. Then he asked, " Has Marlene got in touch with Bernie Frost the company lawyer?"

" She tried but then found he had been taken to the police station as well or so his wife told Marlene. It appears that..."

Jane never finished what she was about to say because the front door bell sounded. Looking at Tom, she said, " I'll go and see who it is."

A few moments later Jane appeared back in the kitchen followed by two men. Her face was white and drawn. Tom frowned because he felt he recognised one of the men but could not place him. It was the square body that nudged Tom's memory and the face though this was more fleshy than he remembered.

" Professor Houseman?" the man asked looking Tom up and down." I am Detective Inspector Henderson. Will you accompany me to the station voluntarily?"

Tom shrugged. " Why?"

" We want to question you about your relationship with Derek Jones." he stated grim faced.

" What if I refuse?"

" I will have to arrest you but I would not like to do that. It would be easier for all concerned if you came with me."

" Of course," Tom smiled shrugging his shoulders into his jacket.

To Jane he said. " Phone Tony and ask him if he will come to the main police station to help me. Tell him what has happened. Get Belinda if you can to come and keep you company. Then phone Edward and inform him of what has happened."

Tom put his arm round her shoulder. " Don't worry. We will soon clear this up and I will be back with you."

Henderson said to Jane. " We will send some men to search his papers. They will have a search warrant."

Tom followed the policeman out of his house. Jane stood in the doorway watching as he got into a car, waving slightly in reply to Tom's reassuring smile.

The car ride to the station was undertaken in silence. Tom hardly noticed the passing houses and streets or the park by his old school. Deep in thought, he was rehearsing in his mind the likely path of the interrogation. Glancing at his companion, he remembered back to his school days. Phil Henderson had been a classmate but not a friend. In those days he had been something of a loner and had always made plain his envy of Tom's apparent friendship with most of the other pupils. When they had both left school, Tom had gone to university, Henderson into the police. They had played football together for the school team, Henderson a bull of a centre forward,

Tom a fast winger. Even then Henderson had not fraternised with the rest of the team. Tom wondered what effect their earlier relationship would have on the interview. Since leaving school they had met on a number of occasions mainly at civic functions but had hardly acknowledged each other.

The car arrived at the police station and Tom was ushered quickly into the building, down echoing corridors to be placed in a sparse room with a formica topped table, a number of plastic chairs and a standing cupboard with some electronic equipment on top.

" I have to leave you for a moment," Henderson informed him. " I will order some coffee. Constable Barnes will be by the door."

Henderson left and a few moments later another policeman came in with the coffee. Tom sat and stared at the wall well aware that Henderson was playing games, trying to make him nervous about what was going to happen. As he had managed to do in similar circumstances like waiting to address and take questions from other experts at international conferences, Tom sank into himself. He waited, not showing the observing policeman that he was concerned.

About thirty minutes after he had been left on his own, the door opened to bring Tom back from calmness. Henderson entered followed by another man dressed in a rather crumpled suit with his tie lose at his neck.

Henderson pulled up a chair to the table indicating for the other man to do likewise. He placed a green cardboard folder on the table and nodded for the tape machine to be switched on.

" Time 1550 at Porthampton Central Police Station. This is an interview with Professor Tom Houseman concerning his relationship with Derek Jones. Present Professor Houseman, Detective Inspector Henderson and Detective Connolly. Will you confirm you presence?"

Tom smiled. " Professor Tom Houseman."

Henderson sat back and surveyed Tom. " We will start with some background information. When did you first become aquatinted with Derek Jones?"

Tom ignored the disparaging tone of the question, rubbed his chin and shrugged. " That is difficult to say. We grew up together which means that I have no real idea of the precise time when we became friends. Anyway, we went to infants and junior schools together."

" There is no need to be evasive," Henderson snapped.

Tom grinned broadly. " I was not being evasive. I was merely trying to answer the question you put to me."

Henderson bristled. " I will be the judge of your answers. When you went to Grammar School and Jones to the secondary modern, why did you keep in touch? You started to move in different circles then."

" I don't expect you to understand. We lived close and continued to see each other. We played football for the same youth team and just remained friends." Tom shrugged again much to the annoyance of Henderson.

" When were you first aware that he had a criminal record?" Henderson snapped.

" As far as I recall, though it is a long time ago, it was round the time when he beat up his dad."

" When did you become aquatinted with Mr. Hunt of Hunt Enterprises?" Henderson looked at his file. " Were you introduced by Jones?"

Tom sat back and made a steeple out of his fingers. " In a manner of speaking, he did. I was with my wife having a meal at

Mr. Hunt's club and Derek was there with Mr. Hunt. He introduced me to him."

There was a knock at the door and a constable came in and whispered in Henderson's ear. Henderson looked surprised but nodded. The constable went out and Tony came into the room. He nodded to Henderson and sat next to Tom.

" Mr. Jarvis, Professor Houseman's solicitor," he introduced himself.

" I know who you are and why you are here," Henderson barked.

" Please carry on," Tony ordered, placing his brief case on the table. " I will judge what Professor Houseman needs to answer and what not."

Henderson took a deep breath. " Why did Mr. Hunt ask you to work for him?"

Tom looked at Tony who nodded. " I was just completing my P HD and we talked about what was happening in transport. He seemed interested and asked me to write a report on likely investment opportunities. As an academic, I agreed especially as he offered a good rate for the job. Strictly speaking I did not work for him but acted as a consultant."

" That's splitting hairs, surely. If he was paying you, you worked for him."

" Not in the sense that you are hinting at. I was engaged to write a report which I dully delivered at the time specified in my contract. I was then paid for the work. That was all. Apart from that Mr. Hunt had no call on my services."

" When did that change?"

" In a legal sense it never did. Mr Hunt decided to set up a company to administer his investments and invited me to become a non executive director of that company. All the papers were drawn up properly. I was paid a directors fee and still undertook some consultancy."

" Were the university happy with the arrangement?"

" I cleared the whole idea with them and they agreed. It is something that universities encouraged at that time because it meant that lecturers were gaining experience of the world outside the university. The theory being that the experience would feed back into the knowledge imparted to the students."

Henderson consulted his file once more. " You appear to be very well off?"

Tony interrupted. " What has all this got to do with Derek Jones?"

Henderson growled. " When Mr Hunt died, Derek Jones took over his business. I am only trying to establish the connection between Professor Houseman's wealth and Hunt Enterprises."

Tony looked at Tom. "You do not have to answer that question."

Tom nodded but answered anyway. " My wealth as you put it comes from the investment fund I set up with my brother who was working in the city at the time. He was very good at his job and managed to increase the size of the investment year on year. Don't ask me the details. The money put into the fund came from my earnings."

" Is there anything else?" Tony asked bluntly. " My client has answered all your questions concerning his relationship with Mr. Jones. You are now fishing for information. Come on Tom. I think we can leave."

To the tape machine he said. "Seventeen thirty-five and the interview is terminated."

Henderson nodded to the policeman who turned off the tape.

Turning to Tony, Henderson remarked, " I could tell your client as you call him to stay here while we analyse what he has told us."

Tony laughed. " Detective Inspector Henderson don't push your luck. It is obvious from the way your questions were phrased and followed up that you have no evidence with which to charge my client. All you are doing is fishing in the hope that something will turn up. If you arrest my client, which is the only way you can hold him here, I will go to the court and get an order for his release. The judge will ask you for evidence that you need more time to question my client. You have no obvious evidence. Therefore if were you I would let him go without a fuss."

For the first time since asking Tom to accompany him to the station, Henderson smiled faintly. " You win this time, Jarvis. I will be in touch with Professor Houseman if we have any further questions."

Outside of the station as they walked towards Tony's car, he asked Tom, " What is it with this Henderson? It sounded to me that here was more to this than the purely police enquiries."

Tom laughed and breathed deeply of the air. Even though in the centre of any town the air could not be called particularly pleasant to Tom it was manna compared with the room he had just left.

" As you know, Henderson and I went to school together. He was always resentful of the way I appeared to get on with everybody. He had a sense that he had to work hard at anything while everything came to me without any effort. I suppose that has spilled over into this case."

Tony grinned. " I remember now. He was a loner, always on the periphery of things. I never had much to do with him. If I recall, the masters always put you into his group or the other way round whenever there was group activities. He was in your house as well. Now I can see what the under currents were."

Tony gave Tom a lift back. When they got to Tom's house they found Belinda and Jane waiting for them. It took Tom a while to tell them what had happened but eventually they got to bed.

It was two days after his talk with the police that his prophetic words to Brian in Nigeria caught up with him. He was forced to recall what he had told Brian. The police in this country cannot arbitrarily arrest somebody and then charge them. There are checks and balances in the system. The police, however, can, by taking somebody to a police station for questioning, cause all sorts of problems in their life. This is especially true if the police make sure that the local media are feed a biased view of the story before the person they have taken in for questioning has a chance to put their side of the story.

The day after the interview with Henderson when Tom arrived home from a meeting in London, Jane was waiting to show him the local evening paper.

" Have you seen this?" she asked frowning.

" No. I have been too busy working to look at the local paper." He looked at the paper that Jane presented to him.

The large headline on the front page screamed out at him and all the readers.

" PROFESSOR ARRESTED ON SUSPICION OF HELPING LOCAL GANGSTER!"

The article then went on to detail his life and how he became friends with Derek Jones, the alleged Mr Big of Porthampton, who had been arrested and then released the day before. It reported the connection between Hunt Enterprises and Tom in great detail. It hinted that the police believed that Hunt Enterprises were a front for the criminal activities of Derek Jones and his cronies. The article was hedged about with the usual phrases about alleged activity and there being no direct evidence but conveyed the impression that there could be no smoke without fire. It seemed to imply that if the police had wanted to question the Professor, there must be some truth in evidence they were acting on. It contained at the end details of his work at the university and made much of his high reputation in academic circles. Finally, the reporter had to admit that Tom had been released without charge. As a footnote it did also point out that Derek Jones had been released without charge.

" Well?" Jane asked when Tom lowered the paper.

" It is a rather biased report but as far as it goes it is quite accurate," Tom shrugged.

" That is not what I mean," Jane snapped. " How will it affect your job?"

Tom looked puzzled." Why should a biased report in the papers affect my job? It has nothing to do with my work at the university. It is part of my private life."

" Tom you be careful when you go into work in the morning. You haven't been there since this all blew up. For the last two days you have been at the Institute in London. There are members of staff in the university who recent your wealth and position. They will try to make political capital out of this situation. I expect there will be an item on the local television news this evening. You mark my words. That Henderson will still be digging around to try to find something they can pin on you. Why that Henderson dislikes you so much is beyond me. Anyway, as the police found out when they searched the house, all our papers are in order. There is nothing they can investigate here. As I have said you be careful tomorrow and try not to antagonise the Vice Chancellor."

Both his words to Brian and Jane's warning echoed loudly in his head the next morning. His secretary urgently informed him that the Vice Chancellor had left a message on his answer phone ordering Tom to see him as soon as he got back. Tom was even more surprised when the Vice Chancellors secretary gave him an appointment in thirty minutes when he rang. In most times he would have to wait for days.

He was ushered into the Vice Chancellors office as soon as he arrived. The office looked empty when he entered with the large oval table ready to seat a dozen in conference, blank and uncluttered. The glass fronted cabinets lining the walls reflected the sunlight streaming in through the large picture window at the far end of the office from the door. Prominent on one shelf clearly visible to anybody in the room were the books written by Professor Keeley, Porthampton University's Vice Chancellor. In front of the window was the biggest desk Tom had ever seen even when compared to those of some of the pumped up government ministers in places he had visited.

Behind the desk with the light at his back in true Hollywood fashion sat Professor Keeley. A small man with balding head but surprisingly broad shoulders, Professor Keeley was one of the most eminent scientists of his generation.

" Come and sit down Tom," Professor Keeley indicated one of the chairs on Tom's side of the desk. As Tom sat down he took note of the copy of the local paper with the screaming headline lying on the top of the desk.

" You wanted to see me?" Tom asked politely.

" I will come straight to the point," Professor Keeley picked up the paper and held it up for Tom to see. " I suppose you have read this?"

" Yes," Tom replied his eyes narrow but his face expressionless.

" Can you explain what it means?"

" What is reported in the paper," Tom waved at the paper in Professor Keeley hand. " It is supposition about my private life and as such is no concern of yours or the university."

" Let me be the judge of what concerns the university and what does not."

Professor Keeley snapped, throwing the paper onto the desktop. " Any adverse publicity for the university whether involving one of the staff or the whole university has an effect on the reputation of the university in the wider world. Having policemen come to the campus with a search warrant to get into one of my professor's offices came as quite a shock."

" Did they find anything?" Tom demanded.

" I have no idea. It is not something they would have told me."

" So on no evidence of wrong doing, you are going to apply sanctions to me or take me before the council?"

" That is a university procedure. If any member of staff is engaged ion activities which bring the university into ill repute, they have to answer to the Council."

" I have done nothing wrong. The police let me go without any charges being offered. That says I am innocent of any wrong doing."

" You were still taken in for questioning by the police." Professor Keeley was being stubborn.

" So if we take this to its logical conclusion, if you do not like somebody you can get your friends in the police to take them in for questioning and then discipline them even if they have done nothing wrong. That smacks of a police state."

" Don't be silly Tom. You will have your say at the Council. What do you suggest I tell the Council people when they ask?"

" Tell them what you know," Tom shrugged.

Professor Keeley steepled his fingers above his desk. " That is part of the problem. I only have the report in the local paper and the television item to go on. I was hoping you would fill me in with your side of the story."

Tom shook his head. " I still think this is all part of my private life and no business of the university. Everything I have done which might have affected my standing in the university and the university's reputation has been with the agreement of the university committees. It really bugs me this attitude of you and some of the Council. You have been quick to take part of the credit for my research findings especially when it has been successful and gained publicity. I have always made sure that the name of the university is prominent whenever I give a paper at a conference or publish anything. All of my consultancies have been taken under the university procedures and a great deal of money put into the university coffers. What more could I have done?"

" But it is your association with a known criminal that worries me."

Tom got angry then. " Who the hell says that Derek Jones is a known criminal? Where is your proof? If a student included that sort of accusation as a fact in one of my essays I would tell them to back it up with examples before including it. Now where is your proof?"

Professor Keeley sat upright in his chair. " I grant you that there is no proof about Derek Jone's criminal activities but you were shown to be an associate of a man with a very murky life."

" Stop there, Marcus," Tom ordered. " You are in danger of libel. He is the Chairman of a listed company, Hunt Enterprises that owns many sub businesses especially in the transport field. I have known Derek all my life. We lived close to each other and went to the same school as infants and juniors. All right I passed the eleven plus and he went to secondary modern but we stayed friends. He introduced me to Mr. Hunt of Hunt Enterprises and I did some consultancy work. Mr. Hunt turned Hunt Enterprises into a limited company and asked me to be a non executive director. After consulting the university authorities, it was agreed. I have been a non executive director ever since. Derek succeeded Mr. Hunt when he died. That is the story of my friendship with Derek Jones. As even you have to admit there is nothing sinister in our friendship."

" I hear what you are saying but I still have to put your arrest before the Council," Professor Keeley spread his hands. " The next meeting will be in a month. Make sure you are there."

" I must protest," Tom said angrily. " You do not have any grounds for putting me before the Council!"

With that closing remark, he stormed out of the Vice Chancellor's office without saying goodbye.

As soon as the meeting started Tom realised he was not going to win the backing of the majority of the Council. There were too many other professors and academics who, for some reason, appeared to resent his position in the university and the outside world. They were supported by many of the non university members. Why he could not say though that might have been the product of the way Derek and the other board members had built up Hunt Enterprises. No matter how he put forward his arguments and his defence there were many voices raised against him. It was as though they believed the police and wanted there to be truth in the matter. Even many of the people who he regarded as friends remained silent in the face of so much hostility.

After the meeting, Tom now very angry and trying to contain his erupting emotions, barged into the Vice Chancellor's office. The security guard in the foyer tried to stop him but one look at Tom's face and he quickly got out of the way. After all Professor Houseman was one of the senior academics in the university. Professor Keeley's secretary tried to stop him but Tom barged passed.

Professor Keeley was standing by the window talking to one of the other professors Hugh Morely.

" What is the meaning of this?" Professor Keeley demanded putting down his cup and reaching for the bell.

" Hugh would you leave us please?" Tom asked politely.

Hugh put down his cup and left.

" Sit down Professor Keeley," Tom ordered. " I have something to offer you as a way out of our problem."

Professor Keeley sat down behind his desk. " Nothing has been decided yet about how the university is going to deal with you."

Tom laughed. " Professor Keeley you were at the meeting. There were enough staff and outsiders against me for me to realise that if it comes to a vote, I will be asked to resign. In other words I will be sacked. Now I will fight any dismissal right to the top of the profession even appealing to the Privy Council if need be. That would not do the university much good would it?"

" It would cause grave danger to our reputation," Professor Keeley conceded.

" Now this is my proposal," Tom smiled. As he had that day in Nigeria when he had decided on a course of action, he felt at peace with himself. " The university is asking staff who are over fifty to put in for early retirement. They are giving away ten years enhancement to the pension. I will put in for early retirement on those terms. You will then give me a contract for sixteen hours a week, the hourly rate to be determined, to complete my research contracts. Don't say anything until I am finished. There are many universities both in this country and abroad who would jump at the chance of employing me. Now all but one of the research contracts I am fulfilling at the moment are in my name. I would be within my rights to take these with me if I left. Is my proposal acceptable to you? Will it be accepted by the rest of the university?"

Professor Keeley looked as though he had been manoeuvred into a corner and did not like the feeling. He looked around the office as though trying to find a way to refuse but finally he nodded his head.

" You have us in an untenable position, Tom," he said eventually looking at Tom over the top of his glasses. " Some of my colleagues are not going to like this. I will have all the papers drawn up and sent over to you as soon as possible."

" Good," Tom turned to leave but then turned back. " Oh one other thing. If I am to help you out in this way you will have to get any chance of me being censured off the agenda. I will follow the minutes of the next meeting of the Council with interest."

That night Tom over dinner told Jane what had happened.

" I told you that there might be trouble, Tom," Jane smiled ruefully over her coffee cup. " That has always been one of your problems. You think everybody likes you. I know, I know. Through most of your life you have not come up against open antagonism but it has been there. People do get uptight about the way you never seem to try hard but all the rewards fall into your lap. In a way it will be good for us. We have the money and I might start to cut down on my hours at work. I will see my boss tomorrow and sound out the possibility of part time work. We could travel more together then. Go to some of the places we have always wanted but never got round to."

Much to the frustration of Tom the mist came down again and everything went dark.

Chapter 12

It was now late into the night though in the enclosed space of the ward there were no clues as to how much time had passed since Tom had been hurried to the hospital. His breathing still came in short gasps followed by long sighs. To Jane there were no signs of him awaking even though Mary had told her that she had seen his eyes move. Beside her was Belinda and the other side of the bed Tony. They had arrived some time ago. Her children as she still called them though they had all left home, were still in the waiting room.

When Belinda and Tony had arrived they had tried to persuade Jane to go and have a meal but she would not go far from Tom's side. It had been over twenty-four hours since they brought him into the hospital and Jane was trying not to show how she was feeling depressed and stressed at the lack of progress in Tom's condition. She had tried to sleep in a room provided by the hospital that afternoon while Paul and Mark kept vigil but she had soon been back in the waiting room.

"Have there been any signs of movement or Tom regaining consciousness?" Belinda had asked when the children left as she bent over the bed and looked into his eyes.

"Mary reckoned she saw his eyes move this afternoon but I have not seen any signs," Jane replied stroking his forehead.

Tom could hear voices in the background. It was as though he was lying in a hotel bedroom and could hear the murmur of voices through the adjoining wall. Somebody was stroking his brow. Oh that really felt good. He strained to break through the surface, to hear clearly what was being said. There was a great urge to see who was so sexily stroking his forehead. Then a loud phone rang.

He was lying in bed with Jane naked beside him stroking his forehead. They had gone to bed early because they planned to get away the next day for a few days in the Lake District. Nothing was planned or booked but they knew of a scattering of small guest houses where they could stay for a few days. Then the phone rang loudly.

Jane stopped stroking his forehead and looked down at him, her eyebrows raised in question. Tom's stomach always turned to ice whenever the phone rang late at night especially when he was in bed. All he could speculate about was which of his friends or family had fallen into a disaster. This was especially true with Paul working for a bank in London, Mark undertaking research at Oxford and Mary at Nottingham University.

" Aren't you going to pick it up?" Jane asked nudging him with her foot.

" Hello?" Tom said trying to keep his voice calm.

" Tom this is Marlene. Derek has been shot. I am at the hospital." It sounded as though she was close to hysterics.

" Stop Marlene, stop for a minute." Tom tried to calm his thoughts which were screaming alarm in his head. " When did it happen?"

" Tonight. We had been at the club having dinner with some of our friends. When we arrived home. as we got out of the car, a man shot him. He did not have a chance." Marlene sounded a trifle calmer but there was still the hint of hysteria in her voice.

" Which hospital did they take him to?" As he asked, Tom realised he would have to go and support Marlene, at least until her sons arrived.

" The Porthampton General."

" OK, Marlene. Who is there with you?"

" Nobody except Billy our driver. The boys are on their way but it will take time for them to get here. I phoned the people we were at dinner with but they all told me they were going to keep their heads down."

" Who would not come to help you?" Tom was blunt and, he had to admit, rather surprised.

" Lester McAvoy and Barry Roche his accountant and lawyer. They were part of the group we were with. They are part of his other business side, the one you will not talk about."

" That might be why they ran away," Tom laughed. " They must have been watching too many American gangster films. I will be with you as soon as I can. Tell Billy to make sure nobody comes into the room without your permission. See you shortly."

Tom looked at Jane and grimaced. Getting out of bed he started pulling on some clothes. Jane watched him, a worried expression on her face.

" It looks as though our trip to the Lake District will have to be put on hold for a while. That was Marlene as you gathered. Derek has been shot. I don't really know any details. Marlene is at the hospital all alone. Her sons will arrive later.

I think I had better go and keep her company until they arrive to be with her."|

" What happened?" Jane was trying to fight back the tears.

" As I said I do not know the details. Marlene said that when they arrived home this evening somebody was waiting for them and shot Derek. It sounds like a gangland hit to me."

" Is Derek's life in danger?"

" I don't know. Marlene did not say. I will phone when I have any concrete news."

Fully dressed, Tom kissed Jane and walked out of the house. During the drive to the hospital, he had time to think. Even with the limited information which Tom had gathered from Marlene, he had to admit that this looked like a case of one criminal gang targeting another. There you go, he told himself, you are at last acknowledging the grey misty side of Derek's life which you have been trying to avoid all these years. Oh you helped him start on that career but you have hidden from yourself the connection between what you have done and Derek's other life. Deep within his subconscious, Tom accepted that the start of his wealth came ultimately from Derek's and, before him, Mr. Hunt's criminal activities. All right, he assured himself, my wealth comes from the investments my brother made on my behalf not from my work for Hunt Enterprises. He was still denying to himself the connection between the foundation of his wealth and Derek's criminal activities.

Tom arrived at the hospital and found that it was easy to park which showed how late the hour was. It was dim in the car park and he hurried to the main entrance still suspicious of the shadows. Christ, he told himself, I am acting in the same way as all the others. I am seeing assassins lurking behind every tree and gunmen jumping out to attack me at every turn. He could not prevent himself casting glances over his shoulder to ascertain whether anybody was following.

He was relieved to get into the light but even here in the main foyer there were very few people about. A sleepy night porter looked up through the glass of the reception counter. He asked what Tom wanted in a bored voice. After telling him why he was there, the porter did get onto the phone. After a short conversation he directed Tom toward Ward Twenty One. The corridors were largely empty and his footsteps echoed off the dimly lit walls and down side passages. It seemed that it took him a long time to get to the ward but eventually ward twenty-one appeared above his head.

Marlene was sitting in the waiting room all on her own, her head in her hands. She looked up when Tom entered the waiting room, her face tear stained but she did manage a slight smile.

" Thank you for coming Tom," she said kissing his cheek. Tom gave her a hug.

" Tell me what happened?" Tom insisted gently. He realised he had to try and get her to talk so that she could start to come to terms with what had occurred. He had a horror of sitting there in nerve loaded silence. It had happened to him in the passed when he had had to rush to a hospital to sit with a friend while they waited for news of a loved one who was on the verge of death. It had been dreadful and Tom had resolved always to try to get people in those circumstances to talk. He had had some difficulties with Jane over this because she was a great believer in sitting and holding somebody's hand if that was what they wanted.

" We went to dinner at the club with Lester and Barry. When we arrived home, a man stepped out of the shadows and shot Derek. He did not stay around but ran to the gate and jumped on the pillion seat of a motorbike which was waiting. As I told that policeman, he had a helmet on so there was no way I could describe him. Billy gave him as much information as he could manage but even that was not much. He did describe the bike however. It appears he is into bikes. The police have left a constable to sit in the room in case he comes round and can give them more information." Marlene's Porthampton accent which she had tried to modify over the years as Derek became more and more engaged with Porthampton society, was very strong, so strong it made Tom smile. All that effort and when there was a crisis, she reverts back to her natural way of speaking. I suspect we are all like that. Then he remembered a Professor once said on the radio referring to a ship in trouble that everybody panics in their own language.

" Sorry for the questions but what is happening now?" Tom frowned.

" They have taken Derek down for an operation and will let me know when he comes back."

" Can we get a cup of coffee?" Tom asked.

" There is a machine along the corridor but I did not like to leave in case they come back with any news. I could do with a cup of coffee." Marlene looked relieved that somebody was there with her.

Tom went and found the machine. It was with relief that he was spared the need to find change because he had enough in his pocket.

Once back with Marlene, he asked about her boys. " I told them what had happened and they both said they would be here as soon as possible. It is not easy for them living so far away."

" I'll stay as long as you want but at least until your sons arrive. What happened to Lester and Barry?" Tom was puzzled that they had not come running when Marlene needed them.

Marlene looked sad and bewildered. " They both sounded scared on the phone as though they thought this was part of a much larger problem. Barry talked about the need to keep his head down and the hospital was the last place he wanted to be seen. It is understandable I suppose. For years they have hinted that this might happen."

Tom grunted not wishing to open up his feelings about their cowardice to Marlene. " I will have to call a meeting of the board for tomorrow so that they can elect a temporary chairman in Derek's place. I will see Lester and Barry then."

" Will you take on the role of temporary chairman, Tom?" Marlene asked. " Derek would want that. I don't trust the others to do the right thing especially as they appear to be running scared of the unknown."

" I don't know about that," Tom scratched his head. " It has to be a joint decision of the board members. Besides which I don't know whether I want to take up that position."

" If you tell them that I wish it to be and that I speak for Derek, they will listen," Marlene insisted.

Tom laughed. " I have been trying to keep my distance from all the day to day business of the firm ever since I joined the board. Derek and I are the last of the originals. All right I will do the best I can."

" Thank you Tom. You have been a true friend of Derek's all his life." Marlene squeezed his hand.

The door opened and Detective Inspector Henderson walked in. Tom was immediately silent.

Marlene almost snarled. " What do you want?"

Henderson smiled slightly. " I am here investigating the shooting of a man on my patch. It does not matter who that man is or what he has done. The police will investigate any attempted murder."

" Even though you might be the reason why he is here?" Tom asked evenly.

It was obvious that Henderson was far from pleased with Tom's question. " What are you insinuating professor?"

Tom did not hesitate or hold back his feelings." You employed the oldest police course of action in making sure that your questioning of Derek Jones was given the greatest amount of publicity possible. It has been obvious for a long time that the police can influence the way the public thinks by controlling the way in which stories are reported. If those people taken in for questioning do not have the means to counter your slant on the story until they are released, the polices' version of events is entrenched in peoples' minds."

Henderson looked hard at Tom. " You had better be careful what you say Tom Houseman. Are you accusing me of trying to stitch you up?"

Tom grinned. " Not really accusing you of having the intention of getting me sacked from the university but that is the direct result of your arresting me a few months ago. You are not so thick that you had no inkling of what would result from your actions that day."

Henderson looked as though he was going to hit Tom. " I can assure you that was not my intention at all. I am sorry that you lost your job though it will not make much difference to your way of life will it?"

" If you mean financially, no." Tom spread his hands. " There is also the subject of reputation. I remember in Nigeria the morning Ken Sira Wawa was executed telling my companion that that could not happen in England. I did add however that the police could make somebody's life hell by hinting at things. He did not believe me at the time. He does now."

" I will speak to you again later," he said to Marlene, glowered at Tom and turned on his heel to leave the room.

Marlene frowned. " I might not have your education or be all that bright but there was more to that than just him arresting you."

Tom laughed. " We went to school together and he was always jealous of how I got on. He resents the fact that I have accumulated a great deal of wealth. In addition he cannot understand, other than there must be more to it than meets the eye, why I remained friends with Derek. To him when I went to grammar school I should have left all the council estate people behind. Still we will see what happens."

A doctor came into the waiting room and smiled. " Mrs Jones?"

" Yes," Marlene answered quickly.

" We have operated successfully and removed two bullets. You husband was very lucky. They missed his organs but he has lost a great deal of blood. I am afraid he will walk with a limp for the rest of his life. He is in the recovery room at the moment. As soon as he is returned to the ward, you can go into see him."

" Thank you doctor," was all Marlene could answer.

They sat in the waiting room hardly talking their imaginations running wild with speculation. Tom was thinking about what he had to do in the morning or later that morning while trying to ignore the thoughts of what state Derek would be in when they brought him back to the ward. There was not a great deal Tom could do other than to sit and keep Marlene company.

The next time the door burst open it was Jake, one of Marlene's son. They embraced and Marlene explained what had happened.

When they had finished, Tom said. " Hello Jake. If you are going to be here with your mother, I will leave you and go home."

Jake nodded. " Brad will be here in a while. Thank you for rallying round my mother, Professor Houseman. We will let you know how things are when he comes back from the theatre."

Marlene hugged Tom. " Thank you Tom. I will be all right now with my sons here."

Tom hugged here back. " From what the doctor told us just now, he is going to be OK. I will do as you ask and get as many of the board together tomorrow as I can. See you sometime tomorrow even if it is in the evening very briefly."

When Tom got back home in the early hours of the morning, Jane was in bed. She sat up when he came into the bedroom and sleepily asked how things had gone. Tom explained what had happened and answered all of her questions as best he could as he got undressed.

When he was finally in bed, he asked her, " Do you think I should take charge of the board meeting tomorrow? I have never tried to get involved to that extent. I always saw my job as non executive director as keeping a watching brief on the business and making sure that all was legal and above board. This will be to step over that invisible line onto a path which I have avoided treading before. I am not sure where it will lead or whether I want to get involved that much."

Jane kissed him. " Derek is your oldest friend and deserves an effort from you to keep his business going until he can return. It is your moral duty to help."

He slept fitfully that night, his mind a whirl of contrasting emotions. Tossing and turning to such an extent that Jane suggested he get up and have a cup of tea. What he was trying to decide was whether he had the courage to take the lead in making sure Hunt Enterprises did not suffer from the shooting of Derek Jones and the loss of confidence this might entail. He had spent a great part of his life lecturing and advising people how to run businesses successfully. In many ways though he had sat on the outside looking in on what was happening. He had not had to suffer the agony of having to watch as his profits fell or the business struggled. When times are tough, he had always pontificated abstractly, the business must look at its priorities and get back to basics. Even if that meant getting rid of staff. This was great in theory but could he actually face the kind of decisions in practice? Oh he knew that as a chairman he would not have to face the consequences of any sackings because even though the board might have to retrench it was people lower down the hierarchy who would have to carry out the plan.

The next morning after phoning the hospital, Tom went the offices of Hunt Enterprises. Sally, Derek's secretary, rushed out to speak to him.

" Do you know how Mr Jones is?" she asked anxiously.

Tom put his arm round her shoulder. " I phoned the hospital this morning before I came out. They told me he was progressing satisfactorily and is not in danger. He will be in hospital for a few weeks."

" Thank God," she burst out following Tom into the office.

It was strange to be in this office without Derek sitting behind the desk. He remembered how he had thought what a large office, stretching as it did across the whole width of the building. Walking to the widow, he looked over the square. All appeared calm with cars parked at the curb and a few people walking by. The large desk was still in, one corner by the window, the desktop covered in leather now rather scuffed and worn. He thought of how Mr Hunt would not have approved and would have had the top re-covered long ago. The three phones still sat on the desk, one white, one red and one black and Tom had an irrational desire to pick them up to see who was on the other end. He sat down in one of the easy chairs and asked Sally to get him some coffee. It came as a surprise when she bustled out without question. It was as though she had been waiting for somebody to give her instructions.

When she returned with the coffee, Tom said tentatively, " I know I do not have the real authority but somebody has to take the lead. Will you get on to every board member and call a meeting for this afternoon. I need Lester McAvoy and Barry Roche to be here."

" I'll get onto that straight away," she replied.

Tom sat and drank his coffee. He tried to work out what he was going to say at the board meeting but had to admit that he might be over ruled. There were many people there who might not agree to him becoming a temporary chairman. In the end he had to decide to let things develop.

Tom sat in his usual place across the table from the empty seat where Derek habitually sat. Most of the board members were there. At first there was confusion and no clear idea of what was the agenda. Everybody was talking at once, not through the chair but to each other.

In the end, Tom grew impatient and banged the table. Suddenly there was silence and all eyes turned in his direction. " As some of you know and the rest must have heard, last night Derek was shot by an unknown gunman. I went to the hospital as soon as I heard to help his wife and he was in the operating theatre. When one of his sons came, I left the family together. This morning I telephoned the hospital and they told me that he had come through the operation well and was stable. I have no idea how long it will be before he is back among us. Therefore we have to elect a temporary chairman. It might be presumptuous of me but Mrs Jones asked me if I would take over as Chairman while Derek is in hospital. Do you all agree?"

Lester McAvoy butted in sharply. " I do object. As company secretary it is my job to find a chairman."

Several voices were raised in agreement and Tom soon realised that he would find it difficult to sway the board.

" As it appears I do not have the support of the board, I will withdraw my offer of taking up the post of chairman." Tom smiled at everybody round the table.

" No Tom I was not saying that you should not be chairman. All I was claiming was the job of inviting somebody to take up the job." It was Lester's turn to smile. " The chairman has to be somebody without executive power. That does not apply to most of us round this table. The two non executives are you and Robert. I think you are eminently suited for the job but I wanted to get the opinion of the board members before putting you into the chair."

Tom shrugged eloquently. He knew that Lester had been technically right but it was a trifle bumptious of him to make such a stand. I'll have to see what Marlene's reaction is, he thought. In many senses he would have been relieved if Lester had stood his ground and found somebody else to be the chairman of Hunt Enterprises. Deep down he realised what he really cared about was holding the business together until Derek was better. Lets face the reality, he then concluded, the actual running of the company is in the hands of Lloyd Baldwin the managing Director rather then the Chairman. He it was who made the plans to carry out the policy of the board.

Tom did not move to the chairman's preferred place. " If there are any other candidates can they declare now."

There were no dissenting voices.

Tom looked at the agenda and announced the first item. There was the usual discussion but the talk was rather subdued. In fact it did not take long to conclude the meeting and Tom soon found himself winding up.

Before they could leave, Tom said to Lester and Barry. " Can I see you both in Derek's office straight away, please?"

Barry's eyebrows were raised but he did not make a comment. Without waiting for them to reconsider, Tom marched out of the room and into Derek's office. He was once more unsure of his next move but he was determined to make sure that there was some response to his friends shooting from the organisation as he started to think of Derek's other activities. He was not competent to undertake this task but if Barry and Lester refused to help he would have to think of somebody who might help. Before he had time to think more deeply, Lester and Barry joined him.

He asked Sally to bring coffee and waited patiently until they wee all sitting in the armchairs with their drinks.

" Well?" Barry asked letting the import hang in the air between them.

" What are you going to do about Derek and what happened to him?" Tom came straight to the point. He could find no benefit from slowly getting to the subject.

" I fail to understand the question," Lester answered rather pompously.

Tom kept very calm. " Derek was shot last night as you both know. We have no idea who did the shooting but we can be quite certain that it was not anything remotely concerned with his legitimate businesses."

" How can you be so certain of that?" Barry demanded belligerently.

" In a way I suspect you might be right but from my experience legitimate business people try to get an advantage from their rivals by competition and being more efficient that involves making sure you give what the customer requires." Tom got no further.

Barry interrupted. " Don't you get all academic with me. I know what is required from business as well as you do. I concede that what happened must have some connection to his other activities. I thought you have always been scrupulous to keep away from that side of Derek's activities."

" You have to admit that you have shied away all the time from even acknowledging that there is another side to Derek's business activities. Why the concern now?" Lester looked sharply at Tom.

Tom frowned. " In the end all aspects of my life have to come to the surface. Deep down, I have always known what Derek represents. If you must know it was me who introduced him to the concept of working for the Mr Big of Porthampton all those years ago. Now because of what has happened, I have to be honest with myself. That is not to say that I want much to do with his and your criminal activities. Derek has been my friend all my life. I feel I have to do something to protect his activities."

" Surely it is for the police to find out who shot Derek?' Barry put in.

" You have met Henderson, haven't you both?" Tom grimaced. " You have to be aware that he is more concerned with putting Derek behind bars rather than solving the question of who shot him."

" I still think it is best for the police to track down the killer rather than our organisation getting involved." Barry was adamant. " We have no idea who is involved."

" I know and that is the problem we have," Tom remarked. " If it is criminal not personal, it might be a group of our people trying to push to take over from Derek and control the organisation. On the other hand it could be another organisation trying to muscle in on our territory. The two scenarios pose different problems."

" What do you mean?" Lester asked. " I have no idea what you are hinting at. In many ways I cannot comment. All I have ever done is to provide the legal basis to under pin Derek's organisation. I have had nothing to do with the actual day to day activities. My job was to keep the police and the authorities off his back. I would not know where to start in trying to find out what happened and who is loyal or not."

" I am in agreement with Lester." Barry looked determined. " I think we should keep our heads down and leave it to the police. In fact after this meeting I am going home and then not emerging until I feel it is safe."

" I hear what you two are saying even though I do not agree." Tom spread his arms. He was now resigned to having to shoulder the whole of the burden. With no idea of where to start, he had to put any action on hold for a while. " I will do things without by your help then. One thing you will have to do. Barry, you will make as much cash available as I need. You know the form more than me so be prepared for my money demands. Lester, you will put all your legal expertise at my disposal. Both of you must realise that the usual rules will apply. If anybody helping me gets caught, we will give him the best representation that money can buy. If they have to serve a prison term, we will look after their dependants. Is that clear?"

Lester stiffened. " If I refuse?"

Tom smiled grimly. " I am afraid I hold all the cards, gentlemen. I know some of the secrets of this organisation and could make life very difficult for you. I will have the tough resources of the organisation at my disposal as well."

" Are you threatening me?" Barry looked shocked.

" No just reminding you of what your obligations are under these circumstances. Besides, you will have to answer to Derek when he recovers. That will be hard if there is not much of his organisation left when he comes back here. Will you be the one to tell him that you were too afraid to do anything?" Tom lent back in his chair.

Lester stood up. " I will do as you demand. Let me know when I am required."

Barry joined him. " I will have the cash available when you need it. Tom don't do anything silly. Whoever it is shot Derek, they have an agenda. Try to think of somebody who will help you who is dependable and loyal to Derek. See you later. Like Lester, I am off to keep a low profile for the next few weeks."

Tom waved as he left and sat back in his chair. Who the hell was loyal to Derek? He drank another cup of coffee while he went through the people he knew who were part of the organisation. It came to him quickly that because he had always maintained this fiction that the legitimate activities where somehow divorced from the criminal, he did not have a real idea of who was involved. He had answered Derek's call for advice in restructuring his organisation but he had even then maintained the fiction that this was advice and theoretical rather than practical. What this meant was that he had nothing other than a vague idea of who was involved.

One person he knew that Mr Hunt had always trusted was his driver body guard Bernie Brown. Over the years that he had been concerned with the affairs of Mr Hunt, he had come to understand that Bernie was completely loyal to Mr Hunt. It was a long shot because a great deal of time had elapsed since Mr Hunt died. Derek had employed Bernie as a driver but he had retired some time ago.

Tom walked over to the desk and picked up the white phone just as he had often seen Derek do when he was in the office. " Sally, could you find out if we still have the address of Bernie Brown? He used to be Mr Hunt's driver back a few years ago."

" Oh there is no need to find out. He is on my list of those I send a cheque to every month. I have his address in a file. I will bring it in to you as soon as I look it up."

A few minutes later Sally came in with Bernie's address on a piece of paper. " This is what you were looking for. He lives in a flat over towards the river. Can I call him for you?"

Tom smiled. " You are most efficient Sally. Could you arrange for him to come and see me as soon as possible? Do we have a car and a driver available at short notice?"

Sally smiled back. " We always have a car and driver available. Mr Jones insisted. I think it is Rod Fisher waiting in the foyer.'

" If Bernie can come straight away, will you send the car for him?"

" Are you going to do something about Mr Jones, Professor Houseman?"

" Sally that is what I am trying to do. The trouble is I have no idea of what needs doing."

"You'll manage, Professor Houseman. Mr Jones was always telling me how you were there to give him advice all the time."

Tom once more had to sit and wait for other people. He telephoned Jane to tell her what was happening and then sat back to wait. Sally informed him that the car had been despatched to pick up Bernie and Tom tried to remember what Bernie had looked like the last time they had met.

At last late in the evening, there was a knock at his door and Sally came in. " Bernie Brown here to see you, Professor Houseman."

Bernie followed her into the room and looked around the office. He must have been a large very fit man in his prime. Now he walked with the aid of a stick, his hair was almost white and his shoulders hunched. The hands holding the stick were huge to Tom and the grip he employed to shake Tom's hand was still strong.

" Its good of you to come, Mr Brown," Tom greeted him warily.

Bernie grinned broadly. " Call me Bernie, Professor Houseman. It still after all these years appears strange to me to walk in here and not find Mr Hunt sitting behind that desk. What d you want from me?"

" You must have heard by now that Derek Jones was shot last night," Tom looked at him hard.

Bernie stopped grinning and looked serious. " I heard from my son this morning. It is a rum business. Have you any idea who did it?"

Tom shook his head. " I have no idea. Lets face it Bernie I have no concept of what is involved with Derek's activities. All I am professionally is a non executive director of Hunt Enterprises. What is more important is that I am Derek's friend. My father taught me, among many things, that one thing we must not do is run away when one of our friends needs help. Bernie, believe me I want to help but I do not know where to start."

Bernie grinned some more and reached for the beer that Sally handed him. She placed a gin and tonic next to Tom's elbow. He wondered how she knew what he liked but let it ride.

" Have you talked to the police?" Bernie asked. " I would not but I am prejudiced."

Tom laughed. " Always suspicious of the police, Bernie just like Derek. I remember years ago being told by a girl who lived on the same estate as Derek never to trust the police. But it is not any innate suspicion of the police on my part. I have spoken to one of the police in hospital last night while sitting with Mrs Jones waiting for her son to arrive. I have a problem. This policeman, Detective Superintendent Henderson has hated me ever since we were at school together. As far as I can make out he is far more interested in trying to get Derek and me behind bars than in finding out who shot Derek."

" So the police are out," Bernie remarked. " It looks as though we will have to do it our way, then."

" What I need from you is somebody we can trust to find out who is behind this shooting," Tom looked at Bernie. " I have no idea who is reliable or who I can trust."

" Is that why you called me in?" Bernie grinned. " I have been away from the front line so to speak for a while. What can I do for you?"

" Who do you think we should ask to look into this shooting then?" Tom asked forlornly. " The problem we have is that it could have been an inside job."

Bernie frowned. " As far as we know it might have been an inside job as you say. We have to find somebody reliable and trustworthy. Look I have just the person for you or so I think. My son is head of the loan section which Derek set up a few years ago. Now I can vouch for him. He is loyal to the organisation and to Derek Jones. What do you say?"

" In a way I am in your hands on this one. It might work though. How would you like to become the co-ordinator for this operation?"

" That sounds a grand title but what does it mean?"

" As I see things, we have to try to keep Hunt Enterprises separate from this operation. As we have no idea who was behind this shooting, whoever we ask to help us must be kept a secret from all the other people in the organisation. It will not be easy but if it is a group trying to take over the organisation from the inside, we have to try to make sure they do not know what we are planning. Look if you think we can rely on your son, we will do that. I do not have much choice. What I had in mind for you was to act as a go between. Nobody will suspect your son of anything while he is visiting you. We can have you visit me here to report whatever your son wants me to know. You can always tell any curious onlooker that you are sorting out your pension. Look it is getting late now. How about you and your son coming here at ten tomorrow and we can then thrash out the details?"

" A good idea. I will see him tonight and we will be here in the morning."

When Bernie left, Tom sat back in his chair thinking about how he was going to make this work. He was still worried that he was out of his depth and he might be playing into the hands of Derek's enemies. With a sigh he acknowledge that he had to start somewhere and had to start trusting somebody. He wondered what Derek would do but he could not put his ideas to Derek so he had to do it on his own. The office was mainly dark when he left though he did notice that a young tough looking man was sitting at the desk in the foyer. The man nodded to him as he walked through the hallway. So deeply buried in thought as he got into his car, Tom did not notice when another man detached himself from the shadows and got into a car to follow him all the way back to his house.

When he arrived home, Jane was waiting for him. After he was sitting on the settee drinking a coffee, he told her what had happened at the board meeting and how he had been asked to be the acting chairman until Derek returned. For some reason he was reluctant to tell her about

Bernie and his son but in the end he told her everything.

" You be careful, Tom Houseman," she admonished him looking worried. " I know you are only doing this for your friend but you are a bit out of your depth. This is not an academic research exercise over which you have complete control. The men you are dealing with have been criminals all their lives and they know what goes on in their murky world. You might think this an intellectual exercise but it can be dangerous as Derek found out. Somebody shot him the other night and they are still at large."

Tom looked at hard at her. " That is why I am trying to find other people to carry out the investigation. I can co-ordinate and help by sifting the information they bring but it will be up to them to dig into those places I could not go. We will see in the morning. It looks like we will have to put on hold our holiday in the Lake District for a few more days."

Early the next morning Tom said goodbye to Jane and drove back to the office. He noticed a car following him out of his road but did not think too much about it. He was more worried when it pulled into the car park behind him at the office. He recognised the driver and was about to drive off again when the doorman came across and opened the door.

" If you don't mind me saying but you should use the official car," he remarked waving to the men in the car that had followed him. " I hope you don't mind Professor but I detailed Randy and Taffy to follow you home last night and escort you to the office this morning. These are troubled times and we would not like you to end up like Mr Jones, would we?"

Tom looked hard at the door guard. " I am sorry but I don't know your name."

" Harry." he replied grinning.

" Thank you, Harry. I did not think I would be in any danger. Who would you recommend to be my driver then?"

" Randy has been assigned to you with Taffy riding shotgun. I know to you that might sound dramatic but it is better to be overly cautious than to be sorry."

" If I am to have a car and driver, could you get one of them to return my car to my house sometime today?" Tom reluctantly handed Harry the keys to his car." I'll telephone my wife and tell her what is happening."

" I will do that Professor. Will you find out who shot Mr Jones?"

" Harry, we are going to try."

" Thank you."

It was such a heart felt statement that Tom was rather taken aback. He was starting to realise that many of the members of organisation held Derek in high regard. It came to him suddenly that many of these men felt partly responsible for what had happened. This was silly on their part because there was no way they could have prevented it other than to never let Derek get out of the car until they had made sure all was secure. But even Tom realised this would have needed a great deal of manpower to accomplish.

Randy followed him into the building. " The car will be ready for you when you require it, Professor Houseman. Just ask Sally to phone the front desk and it will be by the front door. One of us will return your car home this morning."

" Thank you Randy," Tom smiled faintly. " I am not used to this sort of treatment so bear with me until I do things naturally."

Randy grinned back. " We are all loyal to Derek Jones here and from what Harry says you are the best hope we have of keeping the organisation together until Mr Jones returns. We have to protect you. Besides, if anything happened to you before Mr. Jones returns, I would hate to be the one to have to tell him."

Tom walked up the stairs deep in thought. It came as a complete surprise but was rather worrying that all these people had knowledge of what he was doing. He had wanted to sit in the background and pull the strings but it looked as though that was wishful thanking on his part. All he hoped was that their trust in him was not miss placed.

Sally was not in the office when he arrived. It was not surprising because it was only eight o'clock and she did not start until eight thirty. Tom made himself a coffee and sat down behind his desk to wait for Sally. He knew what he had to do. Lifting the phone he called one of the road haulage depots near the docks.

" Mr Norris? This is Tom Houseman. I am acting as the temporary Chairman until Mr Jones is back behind his desk. At your depot you have a couple of empty offices. I would like to take over those offices. There will be a group of men moving in whose task is to look at security in our road haulage industry."

" Are you saying that my company has a bad record?" Douglas Norris sounded disturbed.

" Douglas that is not what is happening. Your company has a very good security record but the incidence of highjackings and robbings is increasing. All I am asking is that you give my people the use of those offices. You will most likely not notice they are there except when they ask you for help. We have to increase our security and this is the way I plan to do it."

" OK Professor. We will get the offices ready for your men. When can we expect them?"

" In a few days. The details have to be worked out. Thank you for your co-operation."

Tom sat behind the desk in Derek's office and waited for Bernie and his son. They arrived at the appointed hour. Vince was large, over six feet with a head which appeared to go straight into his shoulders without a neck. Whether for effect or fashion, Tom did not know but Vince had a shaved head. He looked like a bouncer from a nightclub.

Bernie smiled. " Professor this is my son Vince. Vince, Professor Houseman."

" Hello Vince. Thank you for coming," Tom shook his hand.

" I came because my Dad reckoned you needed me." Tom realised at that moment that Vince was blunt. It was obvious that Vince spoke his mind without any fear of what other people might think. It was a refreshing in many ways but showed that Vince had no fear. For a moment this worried Tom, made him consider whether Vince was the best person for the job in hand. He dismissed this out of hand.

" Well Vince what I want is to find out who had a hand in shooting Derek Jones." It was not well said but it was the best Tom could do in the circumstances." I have no idea where to start thus I asked your Dad to put me in touch with somebody who might have an idea as to how to go about finding out who and why."

Tom shook his head. " Whoever is behind this could pick up the pieces when the dust settles. It could be a one off with somebody from the organisation or outside having a personal gripe with Derek. What worries me is that it might be another gang trying to break into your territory. What I would like you to do if it is possible and you want the job is to dig around and see what you can find out. What do you say?"

Vince laughed and cracked his knuckles. " It sounds like a great job to me. What are the terms?"

Tom laughed nervously. " Some would say you agreed to that to quickly. Am I being taken for a ride they would ask."

Vince screwed up his face in puzzlement. " Look Professor Houseman, I am loyal to Derek. 'e gave me a chance to rise in the organisation which many people would not have done. 'e told me on many occasions that you advised him all those years ago to get attached to the Mr Big of his day. 'e did that and rose through the ranks. When he took up your suggestion of putting the business into sections with a section heads under Derek as leader, he ask me to be the head of the loans section as he called it. There is a certain amount of tension between the section heads especially when the rumour swept the organisation about the imminent retirement of Derek Jones. I am happy doing what I do and would go out of my way to help Derek Jones if he was in trouble. My Dad knows that and that is why he asked me to meet you."

Tom smiled and shook Vince's hand. " Vince. I had to be certain of your loyalty. As I have already told you, I have no experience of this sort of thing. That is why I need somebody like you. Will you work for me?"

" Of course, Professor." Vince laughed. " What have you in mind?"

" I have secured a couple of offices in the haulage depot near the docks.

Douglas Norris the depot manager thinks you are to be in charge of a group looking into how security can be tightened around the haulage fleet. I'll leave it up to you but you have to give the impression that you are serious about road haulage security. On another subject I will leave up to you who and how many people you want to put into your team. It is best that I didn't not know who these men are. In fact the least I know of what you are doing, the better I will be able to cover any tracks which might lead towards the firm. The best policy is to channel any requests and reports through your father and he will deliver them to me. He can then deliver back any suggestions I might have. That way I will be kept at arms length. Does that make sense?"

" Perfect sense, Professor." Vince nodded to his father. " It is a good ploy to channel things through Dad because there can be no questions asked about why I am visiting him at his home. I see him at least once a week now. If I require any more help or anything clarified I will tell dad to tell you. Every week I will send you a report on our progress."

Tom picked up the phone and spoke to Sally." There is a briefcase in the safe, Sally. Could you bring that in for me please. Barry McAvoy left it this morning."

" Straight away Professor." she answered cheerfully.

Like many of the staff in the offices it was as though a great weight had been lifted off their shoulders once somebody had showed some leadership. Even Barry had appeared more relaxed when he had brought the briefcase to Tom that morning. Deep down Tom wondered if they would be quite so cheerful and confident if they realised how out of his comfort zone he felt

Sally brought the briefcase into Derek's office and placed it on the desk in front of Tom

She smiled. " Can I get you anything else?'

Tom smiled back. " Coffee for me. Bernie and Vince?"

" Coffee will be just fine," they both answered. " It is a bit early for a beer."

Tom turned the briefcase round and opened it for Vince to see what was inside. " There is twenty thousand pounds in used five pound notes. It is up to you how you spend it. I will want a report of how it was spent but do not commit anything to paper. Keep it all in your head. When you need any more, tell your father and I will provide it. Is there anything else?"

Vince cracked his knuckles again. " Not that I can think of. I will move into my offices this afternoon and start recruiting straight away. Mike Marsh will be in charge of my section while I am busy elsewhere. He is a good man and knows the ropes. Every so often I will turn up and check that he is handling things."

Vince stood and enclosed Tom's hand in a vice like grip. " Don't you worry about a thing. Tell Mr. Jones when you see him that everything is under control. I'll keep you informed of progress through my dad. It is best if I avoid this building until this is all over."

" Thank you Vince. I will be away for a few days. I promised my wife that we would have a few days in the Lake District before this all blew up. Now we are set, I think we will leave the day after tomorrow."

Tom watched Vince leave the room and then turned to Bernie. " There is a desk in the small room next to Sally's office. You can use that when you are in here though I don't expect that will be very often. I will give you the grand sounding title of car pool organiser. What I will do tomorrow is get one of the students I used to teach to help you while doing their final year dissertation. That way the whole thing will look legit and we might get a better schedule for our car fleet out of it. I had better ring Norris and tell him who will be in charge of the haulage security unit and using his offices."

Bernie grinned. " You sound just like Mr Hunt in arranging things. He always delegated to other people when he could. I'll be off home then. See you when you get back."

A week later Tom returned refreshed from his holiday. Jane and he had done what they wanted and not rushed at anything. Deep in the countryside they had immersed themselves in walking and visiting all the sightseeing locations. It had helped Tom forget the trouble which was brewing in Porthampton. As arranged, Sally left him in peace which was pleasing because if anything had needed his attention she would have phoned.

When he came back to Derek's office, he never referred to it as his, there was no news or messages. Sally told him that Bernie had been in a few times and that Miles Baker had started to examine the method of allocating pool cars and drivers. He had taken the information away and was working on it. When he needed some more advice, he would be in touch. She smiled when she said this but told Tom that Miles and Bernie had hit it off from the start. She believed there was a great deal of mutual respected between them.

The next few weeks were relatively quiet for Tom. He had the Chairman's tasks to fulfil but found they were not too onerous when compared to his work at the university. He was still going into the department to monitor the research projects that were in his name but this was more of a habit than a vital need. His research students knew what to do and could phone him if they had problems anyway.

There were persistent rumours in the local papers that a war had broken out among Porthampton criminals but there was no concrete evidence. It appeared that there were some men ending up in the accident and emergency department of the Porthampton General Hospital and the police were investigating the deaths of a number of shady characters.

Tom watched and waited. He knew that this was part of Vince's effort to find out what had happened with regard to Derek's shooting but he had given Vince the authority to carry out the investigation in his own way, so he was not expecting a detailed report every week. Whatever methods Vince used to gain the information, the agreement was that Tom would let him decide. Besides Tom had no desire to interfere with Vince's operation even if things appeared on the surface to get out of hand. So Tom acted the part of the Chairman of Hunt Enterprises and waited patiently for Vince to contact him.

Bernie came in one day looking glum.

" What happened?" Tom asked fearing the worst.

" Rusty, Vince's best mate got shot last night. I fear for the enemy. Vince will be even more determined to get even now. I hope he stays calm and collected." Bernie shook his head. " I would not like to be out there on the streets now."

" Tell Vince that we will make sure Rusty and his family are looked after. I will get onto Buster straight away. Lets hope your son and his mates do not go too far."

" As I said, I would not like to be in the shoes of the opposition," Bernie grinned. " Vince knows this town and the people. He will root out the men involved I have no doubt."

Sure enough, the next week was as bad as Bernie had predicted. Men turned up at the hospital beaten senseless and the police had four more bodies to deal with. Many shady characters were in hiding.

One morning as Tom was drinking his coffee, Sally phoned. " They have a policeman called Henderson in the foyer. He demands to see you personally. Shall I get them to send him up? Derek never let policemen into the building without a warrant and would meet them in the club across the road if they wanted to see him."

Tom almost laughed at the thought of Derek sending Henderson across the road and then got serious. " Get the reception to escort him up to my office. Make a pot of coffee when he arrives and show him straight in to me. It will be interesting to find out what he wants."

Henderson heaved his bulk into Tom's office behind Sally. " Detective Superintendent Henderson, Professor Houseman. I will get a pot of coffee."

Tom stood and indicated for Henderson to sit in the comfortable chairs. " Let us relax while you tell me what I can do for you, Phil."

Phil Henderson sat heavily into the chair, frowning all the time. Looking around, he remarked. " Nice office you have here."

" It is not mine as you well know," Tom did not smile. " You made sure that all the rivals to my friend Derek knew about his arrest and made him vulnerable. He was shot because of you or because of what you did. Now somebody has to act as Chairman of Hunt Enterprises until he returns. They have asked me to act in his place hence this office. Put the coffee down here and pour the detective a cup." Tom ordered Sally.

After Sally had left, Tom asked Henderson. " What do you want from me this time then?"

Henderson lent forward in his seat. " Look it is hell out there on the streets. All our contacts have deserted not only us but also everybody. They are terrified. Your men are beating them up and killing a few. Not only can't I get any information, I cannot even find the people."

Tom held up his hand. " Hold on. I have no idea what you are talking about. As you can see, I am the acting chairman of Hunt Enterprises. All of what you are telling me is above my head. I have nothing to do with what is happening on the streets as you put things. They are not my men, as you put things."

Henderson looked really angry. His voice rose and he gripped his mug tight such that his knuckles were white. " Christ Tom you have to help me. If this goes on much longer, one of my men is going to get hurt in the cross fire. Besides, lately most of the men being injured and killed have been black, of West Indian origin. My superiors are getting worried about a race war on our doorstep. I have no idea why the black population is being targeted but it will lead to riots if we are not careful. Call off your men! That is an order."

" Phil, you are not listening properly to me. It is like the old days when we were in school together. Even way back then, you would never listen to other pupils." Tom spread his hands and spoke slowly, emphasising each word. " I have repeatedly told you I am the Chairman of Hunt Enterprises and have nothing to do with the criminals who are killing each other. I would not know where to start in trying to put a stop to this. As to any racial element to this, that is something beyond my understanding."

" Tom you are a friend of Derek Jones. You have to admit that he has a dodgy side to his life." Tom noticed the first name Henderson had called him. For the first time he had to admit that Henderson was no longer playing. He was scared and it showed.

" I would be stupid if I did not notice that Derek had other irons in the fire of life which did not involve me," Tom answered evenly. " Even you must have things you do which you would not want everybody to know about. I know Derek had another side to his life. All I can say is that I am not involved with that side at all."

" Don't you hear things?"

" Ah that is different," Tom frowned and looked thoughtful. It was all a game to him. He was thinking that Henderson was trying to get him to admit that he knew what was going on but Tom was not going to admit any such thing. It did not occur to Tom that Henderson was genuine and not playing a game. Even more outlandish to Tom was the thought that Henderson would not take further anything Tom admitted. It was in the nature of any policeman to use any information that they might come across no matter the circumstances in which the information was acquired.

" The impression on the streets as you call them, as I have overheard some of my drivers talking, is that you, the police have no intention of finding out who shot Derek Jones. All you want is to put him out of business. Therefore certain elements of his circle are going to find out for themselves. That is all I can tell you. In fact it is all I know and then it is only conjecture. The best thing you could do is to let them play this out right through to the end."

Phil Henderson laughed for the first time. " I have my superiors on my back so it is hard to ignore. I tried to tell them that it was only the bad guys getting hurt but they feel we should react to any disturbance on our patch. Thanks for the information."

Phil finished his coffee and shook Tom's hand. " If you hear anything that might help me. Let me know. Like when this is finished."

Tom smiled. " Phil we have had our differences but rest assured that I will let you know if I hear that this is all over. Of course you could always trace the shooter and it would end there. See you again."

Tom sat and watched Phil Henderson leave. He remained in his chair for a long time thinking about what had taken place and wondering how he could have helped Phil more than he had. It was difficult for Tom. His instinct was to come clean with the police but not if that was going to interfere with his revenge for the shooting of Derek. The others must be taught a lesson, shown that they could not muscle in on Derek's territory without a fight. Derek was unable to direct operations so somebody had to do this. Why not his best friend?

The next day Marlene phoned during the morning to tell him that Derek was being discharged from hospital and could Tom meet him at their home that afternoon.

When Tom arrived he found Derek ensconced in an armchair looking out over the garden. The two old friends embraced.

" Derek, it is great to see you home again. I was beginning to think I would have to carry on in your place for a lot longer. How are you my friend?" Tom was smiling as he hugged Derek.

Marlene interrupted. " Tom. You will carry on for a while longer. I am taking Derek to our villa in Spain for a few months for him to recover. No Derek there will be no arguments. Your sons and I have agreed. Tom has done a good job of being chairman and looking after all our interests, he will not mind doing it for another few months."

Derek looked sheepish and winced when he moved. " She is right you know. I still get quite a lot of pain if I move my leg quickly. My chest throbs in the cold weather. You carry on for a while and then we will see."

Tom looked thunderstruck. " I have been filling in for you while you were in hospital. I have retired from lecturing, you know. At the end of this year I will have finished all my obligations at the university and will be truly finished. Jane is looking to finish as well. We are planning to travel all over the world taking our time. I have a yen to try to write some fiction in the future. Derek, it was getting to the stage where I was going to talk to you about packing it in all together."

Derek held up his hand. " Tom don't say any more. I will go to my villa and recuperate. You can give me another few months and then we will discuss what to do about the business."

He looked at Marlene. " Its funny my love. Many of our friends have split up by now and yet we are still together. The same with Tom and Jane. You have been hinting for a while now that I should pack it all in and leave it to the others. Well I expect this shooting has made you even more determined for me to hand over to somebody else. We have enough money to walk away. We will talk about that while I soak up the sun in Spain.'

Turning to Tom, he grinned. " Besides Tom you have unfinished business I hear. Oh don't look so surprised. Billy might be a bit thick but he does take in what is happening around him. You carry on Tom. I am off to Spain in a few days. Let me know the outcome."

Tom grinned back. " Leave it to me. I'll see you when you get back."

Two days later Sally phoned Tom at his home. " Bernie wants to see you as soon as possible in the office. It is to do with the road haulage security group."

" Tell him I will be in the office as soon as possible."

When Tom arrived at the office, Bernie was waiting for him.

" Professor. Vince wants to see you at the depot. He said that it was vital and important for you to see him as soon as possible." Bernie looked serious.

" Tell him that I will be down straight away."

Tom called for a car and was driven the few blocks to the road haulage depot. Douglas Norris was not there so Tom made his way through the depot to the offices of Vince Brown. Vince was waiting for him.

" Thank you for coming so quickly, Professor," Vince ushered Tom into a chair. " How about a beer?"

" That would be most appreciated," Tom answered with a grin. ' What is so important that you needed me to come here to see you?"

" We agreed that I should not come to the head office to see you while this is going on," Vince frowned. " I have used my dad as a go between up to now but I think this is so important it is best if I report directly to you."

The beer arrived in the hand of a really tough looking man.

" Thank you." Tom took his glass. He noticed Vince and his father drank out of the bottle.

" Right Vince. Tell me what has happened."

" I heard from my dad that the police had been to see you about the beatings and killings on the streets. I am sorry about that but we could not avoid what happened. As soon as I got the go ahead from you, I put together a team of four men I knew. They are all tough but more intelligent than most. Working out a strategy, we came to the conclusion that the first thing we had to do was make sure it was not internal to the organisation. Two Fingers and Doc shook down some of the low life from the bottom of the organisation. They found nothing. We could not stir up any antagonism. Sitting down and discussing this, we then decided that we had to get out onto the street and see what we could find out."

Vince shook his head. " It was difficult because we had no real idea of where to start. I engaged a number of thick but tough men and sent them out to shake up some of the villains who do not work for us. The result was a number of men ending up in hospital because they are tough and we had to make sure all the men knew we were serious. There was no hint at first so we knew we were having to look outside of the usual people we knew about. It was dad who suggested that we look at the West Indian connection. We have all been aware for a number of years that they are encroaching on our territory especially with the drugs trade. Derek Jones was willing to live with that as long as they did not affect our operations too much. Lets face it. They do operate in their own areas. We have recruited several black people in the past. Indeed Rusty is black and my assistant. It upset our group when he was shot."

" How did that happen?" Tom asked.
" I thought you would have those eventualities covered. We have made sure that Rusty and his family are being well looked after."

" Professor it is not that easy. You might be able to plan intellectually but there are always circumstances where things go wrong. We have been trying to protect you since Derek was shot but we cannot cover all eventualities."

" You do not realise how scared I was at first when cars started following me everywhere. I thought it might be the enemy. Following me until Billy told me what was happening. I wish they did not have to sit outside all night."

" There is no other way of doing it. We could not ask you to move and had no way of assessing how to put people in the garden. It is too small. Sorry if we scared you."

Vince looked serious. " We worked our way up their hierarchy steadily. Some were more helpful than others, some had to be persuaded and some resisted too much. In the end one name was repeated time and time again. Lionel Morgan. It appears he had been going around boasting that he had ordered Derek Jones shot. He even told his gang that he was sorry the assassination had not been successful. We watched and waited because everybody was running scared. They had problems in fighting back because we had more men and more money than them. We could flood any area with men and fire power, do what we had to do and be gone before the police arrived. One night we had a tip off that this Lionel would be in a certain pub with his cronies. It was too easy. I think he thought that in the Ballard area he was safe surrounded by his people. We surrounded the pub and burst in. You should have seen the way they all dove for cover but there was no escape. We lined them all up and pulled

Lionel out of the back room where he had run. I almost laughed. This Lionel was dressed like a black Hollywood character actor. Suit, loud tie, shiny shoes and hat with dark glasses. He protested that we could not take him away because he was the son of Buster Morgan the Mr Big of the area. We asked some of the others what he meant and they told us that he was the son of the West Indian equivalent of Derek Jones in Porthampton."

" What do you know about this Buster Morgan?" Tom looked anxious.

Vince laughed. " We have come across him before. He tried to negotiate a pact with Derek Jones a couple of years ago. He wanted complete control over Ballard District. Derek told him that he would have to submit to Derek's control. There was no agreement as you might sense. Since then there has been an uneasy truce with Derek allowing Buster to control the drugs in the Ballard area for a fee. There have been a few instances of violence but we have harder men than him so it did not go too far."

Tom stroked his chin. " As I see things this Buster Morgan must have been muttering like Henry the Second about getting rid of a troublesome priest and his son took him serious. Hence the shooting of

Derek. Now we have his son, we have all the cards. We have to hope that he wants his son back. Most fathers would though I can think of a few who would tell us to carry on with what we had in mind because they were well rid of their troublesome sons."

Vince grinned. " You are getting good at this aren't you? That was a very clear analysis. From our ferreting of information Morgan will want his son back. What we have to do is give him the opportunity to get in touch with us."

Tom looked out of the window at a lorry manoeuvring in the yard. All his time lecturing he had always had admiration for lorry drivers and their skill in getting lorries into almost impossible places. He acknowledged frequently to his students that he would have trouble backing a car into some of the places lorry drivers managed to fit their vehicles.

" We will wait for Morgan to contact us," Tom stated as emphatically as he could. " Vince, I know you are the expert but you will have to be guided by me on this. You might not like it but will have to do s I say. I have given you the freedom to make the running on this and you have done a fantastic job.   Doing this my way is not a criticism of your work or what you have done so far. Will you accept my leadership on this?"

Vince looked startled. " It is strange but you are the boss on Derek's orders. Why the change?"

It was Tom's turn to grin. " Thank you, Vince. I expect your father told you that I have had a visit from a policeman about your activities. His name is Henderson and all he wants is to put both Derek and me behind bars. Its a long story but sufficient to say it goes back to when we were at school together."

Tom stopped because Vince laughed. " I thought privileged people like you did not have those problems from the past."

Tom shook his head. "You would be surprised. What goes on in academic circles might not be as physical as your activities but it can be equally vicious. Now back to what we were discussing. When contact is made, we will treat Morgan as any other businessman. You will invite him to meet me in the boardroom at the head office. I will want you and one other will to be there with me. I will leave it up to you to pick who you want to accompany you. Bernie will be there in the background taking notes. Morgan can be accompanied by two others. We will demand that he submits to our authority in Porthampton before we return his son. If we set up the meeting this way, it will look like a normal business meeting to any watching policemen. Henderson is bound to try to have us watched. If we tried to hide the meeting, he would be even more suspicious. How does that sound?"

Vince chuckled. " As I said just now you are getting good at this."

" Thank you, Vince. You let me know when you have contact from Morgan. Come on Bernie. Back to the office."

It was only a few days later when Bernie walked into Tom's office mid morning. Tom was working through a report on the performance of the entertainment division but he put this aside after one look at Bernie's face.

" Buster Morgan has been in touch with Vince and wants to see you," Bernie observed. " Vince has laid down the rules as you dictated and we wait for a response."

" How did they contact Vince?"

" One of their men left the message through one of the pubs he knew some of our men go to. The message was passed on."

" Where is Lionel being held?"

" Oh, I suppose you have no idea of our methods," Bernie laughed. " I forget how new to this you are. We have a lock up in which there are three cages which used to hold circus animals. We have put in toilet facilities and that is where we hold anybody we want to keep off the streets. Do you want to come and have a look?"

" No," Tom answered hurriedly. That would be getting him too involved. How they kept their prisoners was of no concern of his.

Bernie laughed. " Too much for your sensibilities I suppose."

Tom shrugged. " Besides my sensibilities, lets say me going to your prison would put me too close to your criminal activities. We will leave it there and wait for reply from Morgan."

The next day Bernie came into Tom's office with a grin. " You have your wish Professor. Buster Morgan has been in touch with Vince and has agreed to our terms. He will meet us here tomorrow at eleven o'clock."

Tom smiled back. " We will have to get a name out of him before we let Lionel go. How do we make sure he is telling us the truth?"

Bernie shrugged " I have been thinking about that. What we have to do is to put the name to Lionel where he is being held before we let him go. I think our men will be able to tell from his reaction if he is telling the truth. By then he is going to be so scared what with the guns being loaded and the knives honed just the other side of his bars for a week. Leave that to Vince and his men."

" Once again I will have to trust you, Bernie."

Tom was in the boardroom early the next morning making sure all was in order. He made sure that his group would occupy the chairs with their backs to the window. He would sit in the high backed chair with the carved logo of the company, have the gavel by his elbow and the official looking note pad on the table. Near the end of the table he was to place Bernie with a pad and pen to take notes.

Vince and his assistant Nobby arrived before the meeting was due to start.

" I have asked Bobby to stand by the phone so that we can contact my men in the lock up when that is needed. He will make sure that Buster is telling the truth with the name before phoning back. If he is convinced of the truth, I will order them to bring Lionel to the square. What happens then?"

Tom sighed. " After Buster Morgan has signed the agreement drawn up by me and typed out by Sally before he arrives, I will request that Buster Morgan has a car ready and we will transfer Lionel straight into the car outside in the square. Buster can watch from this window. Of course Buster will think that Bernie has been preparing the agreement as we negotiate but in reality there will be no negotiations. He will agree to our proposals or he will not get Lionel back. We have all the cards and will have Buster Morgan and his lieutenants here in our building. Trust me. There is no way that Morgan will be able to get out of our clutches once he is here. And we have his son. You have demonstrated how ruthless you can be. Before we start, we will keep Buster and his men waiting for a few minutes to stew. Are we all ready?"

Vince and Nobby nodded. Tom almost laughed at the look of almost awe on Nobby's face.

Buster Morgan was a big man in every sense of the term, Tom saw when he was shown into the room by Bernie. Not only tall, broad shouldered but he had what could only be described as presence. Tom was wary from the start.

" You must be the one they call the Professor," Buster Morgan greeted him in a voice that was deep and melodious. He held out his hand and shook Tom's with a firm grip.

" Some people call me that," Tom replied. " Welcome to our board room. We thought it was best to meet in this way so that the police will think it is two businessmen talking. If we had tried to meet in secret they would have been suspicious."

When they were all seated, Tom started. " I will be blunt. We are here to negotiate the release of your son, to come to some agreement about your future activities in our area and for you to tell me who shot my friend Derek Jones."

Buster's voice took on an even deeper tone with a hint of menace thrown in. " We are here to ask you why your men have been attacking mine. As to the agreement, that is a non starter. All is fair out on the streets. We will have our share of the action.'

Tom waved Vince to silence and smiled. " I do not think you understood a word I have been saying. This is surprising. I have spent a great many years explaining the intricacies of the transport problem to a great many students of all nationalities. They had no difficulty in understanding what I am saying."

Tom spread his hand out and sat back in his chair. " We will take things one at a time then if that is how you want to play."

Buster started to rise from his chair. One of his men reached under his coat before stopping as Bernie held his hand in a vice like grip.

" I would not do that if I was you." Bernie grinned as though he was enjoying himself. " I might be old but I can still move quietly. We knew you had a weapon under your coat but thought it was polite not to challenge you out there in the foyer in front of our people. The Professor told us we had to trust you lot. Now give me that knife if you want to leave here in one piece."

For a moment the man hesitated, sweat breaking out on his face before drawing forth an ugly looking knife with a serrated edge. Bernie took this and placed it on the table top just out of reach of the man. Buster looked thunderstruck but he waved his other man back into his seat.

Tom shook his head. " Well that was a rather stupid move. I don't know your name. We were not introduced."

" Wayne Trimble," Buster snarled.

" What a silly thing to do, Wayne my friend." Tom sat forward and picked up the knife. He carefully placed it on a table at his back.

" I am not your friend," Wayne growled scowling in Tom's direction.

" Please yourself." Tom laughed. " I must admit it is hard to be friendly with somebody who has tried to pull a knife on one but it is a figure of speech. Now Mister Morgan shall we get down to business?"

" Don't you get on your prejudiced high horse to me. I know we are black and you hate us but we are human just like you."

Before Tom could reply, Vince interrupted. " You are even more stupid than I thought. You are addressing the most non racial person I have ever met and that includes many ethnic people like you. He has taught students from all over the world and invited them back to his house. Besides his son is married to girl whose family came from the West Indies only a generation ago. So I would be careful of accusing him of racial prejudice."

" Let us leave the subject of my philosophy and get down to business." Tom was now very serious. " I was trying to be civilised but it is obvious that you do not wish to discuss this in a civilised manner. This is what is going to happen. Before we give you back your son you will sign an agreement to submit to Vince Brown on dealings in our area."

Vince looked surprised but did not say anything. " Second you will tell me who it was shot my friend. There is no need for you to protest about not knowing because your son has already boasted about getting a killer to kill my friend. Do you agree?"

Buster Morgan did not look pleased. " What if I disagree?"

" I wouldn't do that if I was you." Tom smiled and looked at the three men opposite one at a time " Let me put it plainly. I am rather new to this but it looks quite clear to me. You are surrounded by my men in my building. Oh sit down. The main factor in your dilemma is that we have your son. I do not know whether he is worth having back but your being here does indicate that you have thoughts about that. Now who shot my friend?"

Buster Morgan scowled but then smiled. " You do hold all the cards, I have to admit. The man you are looking for is Randy Roberts. The only problem you have is that he is now back in Jamaica. You will have a problem getting to him there."

" That is our problem not yours," Tom growled. " You will be surprised at how long our arm is across the world."

Turning to Vince, he said," Telephone your men and make sure that they are convinced by Lionel that this is the right name."

Buster looked shocked for the second time. Tom had been convinced that Buster Morgan had been reluctant to give up the name, that he resented the power which Tom could bring to bear and was not used to being ordered to do anything. Tom resolved to make sure that Vince was warned to watch his back once this was all over.

They sat in silence waiting for the phone to ring. Buster Morgan fidgeted in his seat, Vince sat back with his hands behind his head and Tom pretended to read what Bernie had written. With a slight smile he ordered Bernie to take the notes to Sally and have them typed up.

The phone rang and Vince answered. He spoke briefly and then returned to the his seat.

" Lionel confirms the name. I have ordered my men to bring him to the square outside."

" Thank you Vince. We will get Mr Morgan to sign the agreement and then we can hand over Lionel."

Buster Morgan bristled. " I have not agreed to anything."

" Yes you have back then before the assassin was named." The door opened and Sally came in with a piece of paper. Taking this Tom thanked her.

Placing it in front of Buster Morgan, Tom handed him a pen. " Sign this. The details have been left to you and Vince Brown to negotiate. Just remember he has the full backing of our organisation."

As though being strangled, Morgan signed the paper. Throwing down the pen, he got to his feet, signalled to his men and walked out without a backward glance at Tom. Turning to Vince, Tom shrugged. They both went to the window and looked out over the square. To one side by the museum was a large grey car with tinted windows. Waiting in front of the offices was one of the organisations car with two men leaning against the bonnet. Other cars were parked at strategic spaces round the rest of the square and Tom could see scruffy looking men leaning against lamp posts or in the doorways to the buildings. At the gates to the church a rather shiny car was parked with two men in the front. Tom had a clear view of the man in the passenger seat and sighed. Henderson was keeping his eye, as he would put it, on things.

Tom was brought back to reality by Vince speaking. " Why did you tell Morgan to negotiate with me? Surely you are in charge and should negotiate with him."

Tom laughed. " Look out there Vince. I suspect it was you who made sure that all the angles of watching the square were covered. My mind does not work like that. I am an academic, good on theory but bad in practice. No don't protest. I came into this to make sure that the organisation that my friend Derek had developed from Mr Hunt's time was still intact and functioning when he was ready to take over again. Nobody I knew from the organisation was willing to do that. They were all running scared. I had no idea where to start but several people helped me on the way especially your father. Then you took my instructions and carried them out. I would never have got as far as you did. No you are the obvious leader of the organisation. When we have managed to catch up with Derek's assassin, I will clear things with Derek and hand over to you."

Vince gripped his hand. " Thank you Professor. I will not let you or Mr Jones down."

They stood side by side watching as Buster and his men came out of the building. He hesitated on the steps and then walked with an upright carriage to his waiting car. He did not get into the vehicle but stood by the door looking across the square to the car parked outside the office. Even from his vantage point at the board room window Tom could feel the tension. He noticed that the men who had been nonchalantly leaning in doorways were now upright and fully alert. Some were not looking at the Morgan car but down the streets leading to the square. Two stood one on each side of the doors to the church. Henderson was leaning forward in his seat, a camera taking pictures of the activity.

Time was suspended for a short moment as nobody moved. Litter blew across the flagstones in the breeze but that was the only thing stirring. Then the door to the organisations Ford opened and two men stepped out onto the pavement. One dressed in a sober suit looked up to the boardroom window and waved slightly. The other dressed in a rather rumpled striped suite, loud shiny tie and black and white shoes looked across the square at his father waiting by the car. There was sweat clearly visible on his black face. He started out but the other man restrained him with a hand on his elbow. There was a slight struggle which caused everybody to tense but in the end the two men started across the square at a stately pace. When they reached the car, Morgan shoved his son inside, followed him abruptly and the car drove off with burning rubber, Morgan's companions desperately trying to get inside.

Tom watched as his men dispersed and Henderson was driven away from the square.

Resuming his seat, he said to Vince. " I have no idea whether we won or not. It looks as though the gun man has escaped."

" Oh we won all right. We have Morgan where we want him. As for the other, I have an idea," Vince rubbed his chin. " I have heard of a group who for money will have anybody killed. I will ask around and see what I can do. It will cost us but to you it will be worth it. Actually, it will show Morgan that our reach is long. Leave it to me."

A week later, Vince contacted Tom. " I have made tentative feelers to the person we were talking about. He has set a fee, half to start and half on proof of completion. He asks us to supply as much information regarding this person as possible. I have a photo from Lionel and a district in Jamaica from one of our men where he is known to hang out. I will supply these to our man and then agree to hand over the money if you approve and can get it for me. What are your instructions?"

" Go ahead, Vince. I will get the money to you shortly."

A week later Vince phoned again to tell Tom that it was completed to his satisfaction. The second traunch of money has been delivered, he concluded.

Tom was elated. What he had set out to do had been accomplished. Then the mist descended, swirled and brightened. He opened his eyes or to be precise one eye. The other felt as though it was being dragged down in the corner and he could not focus. With his one good eye he saw Mary bending over and then she was shouting. Suddenly there were people all around, the pinging sounds of machines and Jane kissing his forehead. He was awake!

Epilogue

The sun felt hot on his face as he sat in the garden. It had been a long road to get here but he was now home. His face had now taken on a much better look since that first time he had looked in the mirror after he had come round. The left side no longer drooped or his eye half closed. He remembered the fight to try to lift his hand to his face. They had encouraged him to try and he had persisted.

His mind wandered. He had recommended to Derek that Vince take over the running of the organisation. From his home in Spain Derek agreed. Vince set up an office away from Hunt Enterprises office in the square. It was ironic but at last as Mr Hunt had forecast there was a complete separation between the criminal organisation and Hunt Enterprises.

He was proud that all his children were now settled. Paul working in the bank his brother had worked for all those years. Tom wondered whether this was right.

Jane had retired completely and they were off on a round of holidays to all those parts of the world they wanted to visit. As promised, Tom resigned as a non executive director of Hunt Enterprises. He could now concentrate on his writing and his leisure.

It had been a great day when his grand daughter had come to visit him in hospital. Ruth and Paul had married shortly after he had graduated and got the job in the bank. Miriam had come along a few years later and Tom doted on her. She had sat on the end of his bed her eyes large in her dusky face.

" You better, granddad?" she had asked in a very serious voice.

He struggled but answered. " I am improving, Miriam."

She stroked his face. " Your eye still looks funny."

Ruth tutted. " It is better than it was. Are you doing the exercises they have told you to follow every day?"

Tom had tried to smile but it felt more like a grimace. " I am trying to move everything as instructed, Ruth."

Ruth was blunt. " You are like your daughter Mary. She is an academic and does not take well to having to follow other people's instructions. You are too used to getting other people to do what you want them to do."

The sun was hot and he laid his head back on the rest at the back of the padded chair. Slowly he raised his left hand and scratched his nose. Things were getting better. He had managed to walk into the garden unaided and without his stick today.

Mary it had been who had first noticed him open his eyes that day. She had been sitting there with her mother trying to continue talking to him. She had told him later that it was the most exciting thing that had happened to her. To be perfectly honest with him, she confessed that over the two days she had sat with her mother she was beginning to wonder whether he would ever come round. Then out of the blue his eye had opened and he was looking at her. She had screamed for the nurse.

The real work had begun then. He had lost the use of his left side and they had to try to get this back. The physio had been in most days and he had been given a series of exercises to follow. Though they had all assured him that he was making progress, to him nothing seemed to change. His left eye still drooped alarmingly, he could hardly move his left arm and he was pushed around in a wheel chair all the time.

Jane had told him about the day he had had his stroke. He could no linger remember. You started to complain about lack of feeling in your feet and hands, she had related to him. Then your speech became very blurred and you were not making much sense. I phoned for an ambulance then and you started to bump into things. They told me to keep talking to you. God that is one of the binds of the last few weeks. They have kept telling me to speak to you, to try to get a response, any response. All the way to the hospital I talked. I might have been nonsense for all I knew but I kept talking. The paramedic was fussing about giving you injections and monitoring all your functions. All through that seemingly endless ride to the hospital I talked. Once they had god you into bed with all the wires connected, I talked. Paul talked when he arrived. We thought you were a goner though.

" It must have worked," Tom told her. " I could vaguely hear voices in the background and they made me want to come round and find out what they were saying. It was not a waste of time though it must have appeared that way for a while."

He remembered now sitting on his own in his garden what had happened after Derek's assassin had been dealt with. He had found Derek relieved to be able to hand over the organisation to somebody else. It did not take much to convince Derek that

Vince was the right man for the job. It had been agreed that Tom would give up his non executive directorship as well. In many ways it had come as a wrench to leave the Hunt Enterprises building for the last time but he had not looked back.

His brother had sat with him in the rehabilitation annex. Together they had discussed the future and what they were going to do with the investment funds. It was concluded that they were in good hands and to leave things as they were. It had helped Tom think when his brother was there, helped his brain start to function properly again.

His son Mark had been visiting from Nottingham University and his studies that day when with the aid of a stick Tom had walked the length of the corridor. It was as though Porthampton had won the cup. They were both so excited. Afterwards Tom was exhausted but still triumphant. Mark insisted in phoning Jane straight away.

He had been on his own the day he managed to get his left finger above his left eye and rub an itchy patch. They had been patiently measuring how high he could get his hand each day. Then they were not there. It was so irritating that itch and he did not want to call the nurse just to ease the prickle. So with out thinking he had lifted his hand and scratched his forehead. It was done before he realised the significance. When the nurse came with his morning coffee, he demonstrated what he had done and she noted this on his file.

The day arrived when he was to go home. It was strange stepping out of the ward and walking to the front door of the hospital. It took him quite a time but the ambulance driver did not seem to mind. He wanted to hurry, so eager was he to get home. Indeed he had really wanted them to push him in a wheel chair but they had insisted that he walk. The neighbours were all there to greet him. Then his family came and he knew he was truly home.

He heard footsteps behind and then two smallish hands were hiding his eyes.

" Guess who?" a very familiar voice asked.

For a moment Tom could not speak so surprised was he at sounds. On the air he caught a hint of that perfume and his eyes brimmed over with tears.

" Isabel. Is that really you or am I dreaming?" he choked on the words and reached up to hold her hands in his. " How did you find out?'

She dropped her hands and came round to face him. It had been twelve years but she looked to him just the same. Square body with small round breasts. Round face framed in jet black hair. Those deep dark eyes he had tried to avoid gazing into during lectures. It was the Isabel he remembered.

She bent over and kissed his lips, stroked his face and smiled. " You do not look as bad as I thought you might look. Jane told me you had a droopy face and one eye was partly closed."

" Who told you?" Tom smiled back.

" Jane went through all your email contacts and sent a message to those she thought might be interested in your plight." Isabel sat in a chair and held his hand. " I did not know whether I ought to reply at first but then the worry about what was happening to you got the better of me. I have been in touch with Jane ever since."

" How did you get here?" Tom insisted.

" That was pure luck," Isabel laughed. " I was trying to work out how to get to see you when the bank ordered me to visit the UK branch in London. I was so relieved. I phoned Jane as soon as I arrived and she told me that you were now at home. We thought a surprise visit might cheer you up. So here I am."

Tom squeezed her hand and smiled. " It is wonderful. I never thought I would see you again after hat goodbye in Hong Kong."

They sat and talked for a time and then Jane brought out drinks before dinner. It was wonderful to Tom though he came to the realisation that there was no longer any sexual desire for Isabel. He would not want to rush out to see her so that he could get her clothes off and make love. It was much more like a long friendship. By the time she left that evening. they had talked themselves out.

In bed that night, back beside Jane after a long time when they had slept apart, Tom brought out the thought that was troubling him all afternoon and evening.

Looking at Jane, he remarked. " You knew didn't you? All the time you knew I was seeing Isabel."

Jane laughed. " Yes I knew fairly soon after she came that you two were going to be lovers. There is only one other person you have looked at in that certain way which I find hard to describe and that person is I. We are strange creatures us humans. We can ignore something which is obvious to most people around us if subconsciously we do no want to know. It is as though we are protecting ourselves from the consequences of any admission that something is not as we would like. In this case I knew what was happening but made a conscious effort to ignore it and not let it affect my life. We do that in many things. You had until Derek was shot lived in what many others would say was a fantasy world. You knew that Derek and before him Mr Hunt were criminals and that much of their wealth came from those activities. That did not stop you accepting their offers of work while pretending that what you were doing was not part of their criminal activities. We are all guilty of double standards in that way."

Made in the USA
Charleston, SC
01 December 2016